"A REFRESHING AND STRONG NEW VOICE IN HISTORICAL ROMANCE"
Kathe Robin, *Romantic Times*

"The rhythms of nature are all around us," he said, tracing a fingertip down the length of her neck. "In the sliding of your thumb under the peel of that orange, again and again, to free its hidden succulent treasure."

Eleonora cupped the fruit she still held and raised it from her lap. "And what if the treasure, once revealed, is found to be wanting?"

"One cannot tell by mere looking," he said. "The treasure must be tasted, its flavor discovered." He took a section of orange and ran it over her bottom lip. A droplet of juice hovered there and he touched it, then blatantly licked his fingertip with his tongue. "The treasure is not found wanting . . ."

Praise for Patricia Camden's
Surrender in Scarlet:
"Superbly written . . . I loved this book!"
Catherine Hart

"If you like your relationships hot and your action suspense-filled, this one's for you!"
Patricia Rice

SCARLET KISSES

PATRICIA CAMDEN

AVON BOOKS ◆ NEW YORK

SCARLET KISSES is an original publication of Avon Books. This work has never before appeared in book form. This work is a novel. Any similarity to actual persons or events is purely coincidental.

AVON BOOKS
A division of
The Hearst Corporation
1350 Avenue of the Americas
New York, New York 10019

Copyright © 1992 by Patricia Camden
Inside cover author photograph by Michael Marois
Published by arrangement with the author
Library of Congress Catalog Card Number: 92–90333
ISBN: 0-380-76825-9

First Avon Books Printing: December 1992

AVON TRADEMARK REG. U.S. PAT. OFF. AND IN OTHER COUNTRIES, MARCA REGISTRADA, HECHO EN U.S.A.

Printed in the U.S.A.

RA 10 9 8 7 6 5 4 3 2 1

In memoriam
Craig Keith Griffith
1955–1987

Acknowledgments

I am particularly fortunate in having very special people share their lives with me, both personally and professionally.

Close to my heart, I have the inspiration of my parents, who have always shown me that the "happily ever after" parts really can be happy, and I have the unwavering love and support of my husband, who proves again and again that not all heroes live in the pages of books.

Professionally, there are two wonderful writers to whom I shall always be indebted: Diane Dunaway and Paula Detmer Riggs. Over the years, they have been unstinting in the giving of their talent, creativity, and support.

And, of course, I have the sine qua non of a writer's life: a gifted, hardworking agent, Nancy Yost, and a talented and perceptive editor, Ellen Edwards.

Thank you. Fate has indeed been kind.

SCARLET KISSES

Chapter 1

Château du Peyre
Eastern France
Spring 1741

Achille, the comte d'Agenais, sat in the relative solitude of a deep window seat, peeling an apple with a sharp fruit knife. As he watched the blade slice through the deep red skin, a bead of juice formed and began to drip down the rounded fruit. He slowly skimmed the pad of his thumb through the droplet. It left a glistening trail that reminded him of the sheen of passion on a woman's skin.

He was left alone. Though his host and hostess, the marquis and marquise du Peyre, had invited scores of guests to their country estate, and though he sat in a salon that served as a corridor between the front of the château and the living quarters beyond, only the fearless or the desperate broke in on the reverie of the comte d'Agenais.

Feet shuffled nearby, interrupting him. He let his gaze drift to the man's shoes. Diamonds encrusted the buckles, and the red heels—more suitable to the court than to the country—had been polished to a too high gloss. "I am occupied, Vigny," he said.

"Of course, monsieur, your pardon," the vicomte de Vigny answered with an obsequious bow, "but a most amusing incident has just—"

"You're a gossip, Vigny." Achille glanced across the room to a group of courtiers trying not to show how avidly

1

they awaited the vicomte's rejection. Perhaps even gossips could be useful, Achille thought idly, and nodded his unpowdered head ever so slightly. The courtiers looked surprised, then disappointed, and turned away to find other amusements.

The vicomte forced a chuckle as he bowed his gratitude and carefully sat down, powder drifting from his wig onto the gold brocade cushion covering the window seat. "Quite a diverting party, don't you think? Du Peyre seems to have invited half the court." Vigny gave a sly glance toward Achille. "The half that counts, of course," he added fatuously. "Paris must be crushingly dull with everyone here in the country."

Vigny chuckled again, this time with genuine amusement. "*Almost* everyone, that is. Daussard bolted. Ah, monsieur, it was delicious! Drove up as elegant as you please, coach and four pulling up smartly, and he leisurely descending, then sauntering up the front steps as if he hadn't a care in the world." Vigny laughed, dusting the cushion with more powder. "At the top, a footman came up to him and bowed, announcing that you, monsieur, the comte d'Agenais, had requested that Daussard join him. Ha! The man turned whiter than his wig, spun around, and flew—flew!—down the stairs to his coach! Last I heard, his horses were working up a lather near Joinville."

Vigny wiped at his eyes. "Poor Daussard has never recovered from the time when you threatened to challenge him to a duel if he didn't cease alluding to that old gossip surrounding your parentage—"

The blade of the fruit knife was suddenly pressing into the flesh under Vigny's chin. His head tilted back, his eyes wide with fear.

"And what old gossip is that?" Achille asked, his voice deadly calm.

Vigny tried to answer but could not. He tried to shake his head. He sucked in a desperate breath. "Monsieur ... monsieur, please—a slip of the—" A bead of blood dripped slowly down the blade. "No gossip, monsieur! I am aware of no gossip. None. I swear!"

The knife was pulled away.

Achille studied the drop of blood on the blade, then wiped the knife on the man's immaculate and ruinously expensive brocade breeches. He resumed peeling the apple. "Amusing gossip, you said, Vigny." Achille took a bite of apple and concentrated for a moment on the crisp sweetness in his mouth. "I have not yet been amused."

The vicomte dabbed at the tiny wound under his chin. "You're a black-eyed devil, d'Agenais."

"One does try." Achille watched the trembling lace that edged Vigny's silk handkerchief. There was a mixture of defiance and apprehension in the man's gaze, and Achille made a silent wager with himself on whether the fear or the anger at the fear would win out.

"You do more than try, monsieur," Vigny said with an ingratiating laugh.

Fear had won, it seemed. As it usually did. Somewhere inside Achille, where it didn't matter, he felt a tiny stab of regret.

"I've heard the stories," Vigny went on. "Everyone has. You fought on the battlefield like a demon from the farthest depths of hell." Though he kept his gaze riveted on the knife in Achille's hand, some of the apprehension had left his eyes.

"But by God, monsieur, you lived as though you have never left the battlefield!" The gossip's smile had become stiff and shaky. "Perhaps ... that is, you might be more comfortable if you didn't act as if life were a line of troops to be broken or a hill to be overtaken. Watching, watching, like a commander of the field, then *attack*.

"It is said that pleasure and pain are one with you. That you taunt fate, as if wanting the consequences. You once publicly refused the king's mistress. You've spent the last year traveling from one château—including the notorious de Gemeaux—to another, seeking ... seeking what, monsieur? And you haven't returned to Paris since that night when you challenged one of the most powerful families in France and left three men—"

Vigny's apprehension returned in full force, and he snapped his mouth shut.

"Dead, Vigny. I left three men dead." Achille studied the blade of the knife, his grip tight on the porcelain handle. "My father's honor demanded it."

"Of—Of course, monsieur." Vigny twisted his stained handkerchief in nervous fingers. "You are d'Agenais. Hero of the last war, a proud chevalier raised by the king to a comte, fêted, indulged . . . envied."

Achille watched the edge of the knife gleam sharp from recent honing. It always started with envy or spite, yes, but it never stayed so simple. The envy would grow, turn into whispers, the whispers into gossip. But he had dealt with it. The son of the chevalier d'Agenais whose line went back centuries had dealt with the envy and the gossip—with his sword.

The image of his father filled his mind. Golden-haired Constantin, always smiling and laughing and telling tales of Tristan, Parzival, Lohengrin, knights fighting for honor and—occasionally—a lady. His father had died when Achille was nine, but that laughing image would never die, would never leave him.

Still, over the last years, his father's laughter had seemed to dim, until that last night in Paris, and those following days in the château de Gemeaux, had shadowed that laughing image with sadness. Somehow, somewhere, though he had meant to honor his father's strongly held beliefs, he had come to betray them.

Achille threw the knife and the remains of the apple onto the floor. "Envied, indeed," he said.

Vigny swallowed hard in relief as two footmen scurried to clean up the mess. "Monsieur—" the vicomte began.

"You are glib enough in recounting my sins, Vigny," Achille said, "but you offer no avenue of redemption." He certainly had need of it, but he already knew where salvation was to be found.

In war. As it had for his father and all the d'Agenaises who had come before him. He had, in fact, already arranged to rejoin the army. A colonel with the French army in Bavaria was willing to sell his commission, and Achille was at his leisure merely until the courier arrived to deliver it.

"Tell me, gossip," Achille said, watching the other man swallow uneasily. "Tell the devil how he can be redeemed."

The vicomte opened his mouth, but no words came out.

"The magpie has nothing to say." Achille crossed one leg over the other. "Interesting. Do you think me damned for all time, then?"

A group of three women sauntered by, their wide skirts swaying and their eyes flashing promises, but their smiles turned to frowns of disappointment when Achille did not interrupt them.

"Some might say salvation can be found in a woman's arms," Achille mused. "Or should I choose the safer route of going off to war?"

"Whichever you prefer, monsieur," Vigny said in a voice choked with the realization that his conversation had headed into too deep waters.

"*My* choice, is it?" Achille said with mock concern. "What an odd notion. A man in charge of his own salvation." The mocking air left him. "Or of his own damnation."

He was silent for a long moment, then stretched out his open hand. "Within my grasp—salvation or damnation. War or . . ."

Another woman walked by, dropping her fan as she passed him. A courtier rushed to retrieve it, and she made a moue of disappointment at Achille before continuing on with her new gallant.

Vigny relaxed a bit and glanced at the passing woman. "Or a woman's arms, monsieur? Madame de Madelmont has been in love with you for weeks."

Achille shrugged. "Madame de Madelmont thinks I am a cure for her ennui. She, however, is not a cure for mine." He narrowed his eyes in thought. "But war . . ." His blood speeded in anticipation of returning to battle. "War with

Austria will be inevitable once the king's agent signs the alliance with Frederick of Prussia."

Vigny looked taken aback at the ardor in the comte's voice. "But, monsieur, surely you would prefer softer charms? I have heard that Madame du Fachaux and her sister—they are twins, monsieur!—have been asking about you."

"Novelty no longer amuses me, Vigny." Achille lounged back in the window seat, a reminiscent smile tugging at his lips. He could feel the hilt of his sword in his hand. "The French army will no doubt march northeast across Bavaria to meet Frederick at—"

A commotion down the hall interrupted him. The wife of his host, Madame du Peyre, was trying to navigate a young woman still dressed in a traveling cloak through a group of boisterous courtiers who were all noisily offering her their services. The hostess batted them away and continued toward Achille. As they neared, he saw that the young woman's hood had fallen back, revealing unpowdered auburn hair framing an intriguingly exotic, fine-boned face.

Her disinterested green eyes swept over the two men on the window seat, hesitated, then snapped back to Achille. For a long heartbeat, he saw shocked disbelief and hate aimed directly at him, then the green eyes became empty of emotion once again.

Achille felt seared, as if he'd opened the door of a warming stove, and a flame had licked out and burned him. Few had ever looked at him with such hate—or with such lack of fear.

Without a word, and with only the barest nod of acknowledgment, Madame du Peyre and the young woman continued down the hall. Achille abruptly stood.

"Monsieur!" Vigny said in protest. "You were speaking of Frederick—"

"Frederick be damned," Achille said, and walked away.

Eleonora, Countess Batthyány, let her mother's sister lead her through the labyrinth of halls and stairways to the suite of rooms she was to use during her stay. She didn't see the clouds of cherubs frolicking on the ceiling above her, nor did she notice the rich gilding on the elaborate plasterwork of the walls as she walked by. Music drifted from an open doorway, a delicate flute and harpsichord duet, but she heard only the thud of her own heart.

Had she really expected a creature with cloven hooves? A two-headed monster? In truth, he was neither monster nor beast, but an angel—a dark and fallen angel with black eyes as seductive as Lucifer's when he lured Eve to the apple.

Eleonora realized her hostess had asked her a question. "Your pardon, madame," she said, rubbing her temple. "You were saying?"

"You poor dear, I expect you're exhausted from your trip," Madame du Peyre replied with a sympathetic cluck as she nodded to a footman to open a door. "Such a long way you've come from Hungary! You must have flown from Pressburg." With an elegant wave of her hand, she led Eleonora through the door into an opulent sitting room.

Eleonora gave an appropriately delighted spin and exclaimed at the room's beauty, all the while seeing nothing.

Nothing, except dark brown eyes that slanted upward at the corners, filled with the audacity that led him to wear his own black hair and wear it unpowdered. The devil's son would, of course, resemble his sire.

She blinked away the image that hovered in her mind. "Pressburg? No, I . . . I came from Vienna. My late husband and I had—that is, I have a house there."

"Count Batthyány was in the army, wasn't he?"

"Yes, madame," Eleonora answered.

"Call me Tante Geneviève, my dear. It will be easier for both of us." She patted Eleonora's arm comfortingly. "So hard to lose a husband in such a disastrous battle, and against filthy heathen Turks, too."

Eleonora lowered her eyes. "I do not hold Turks in high regard." Her voice hardened to steel. "We Hungarians have fought them for a hundred and fifty years—wars, occupations, kidnappings, rape—but now they are defeated.

Forever. And they deserve whatever may befall them, the whole lot of them—down to a man."

"Y-yes, my dear," Tante Geneviève said doubtfully. "There's always so much grief when one loses a husband so young." The thud of a trunk in the bedroom announced the arrival of Eleonora's baggage, and Geneviève's smile widened with relief. "Your gowns—a sure antidote for such melancholy talk!"

The older woman rushed into the bedroom, and Eleonora slowly followed her. It would do no good to explain to her newly met aunt that she was six and twenty—hardly "so young"—and had been a widow for two years, nor that she no longer had room for grief or guilt—only duty.

"Did you bring the music your mother promised?" Geneviève asked excitedly. She watched the maidservants begin unpacking, hopping back and forth on her toes, making her wide hooped skirts swing like a bell. "I adore music! Did you hear the harpsichord on the way? That was my sister-in-law practicing for our concert next week." A maid pulled out a long rolled piece of parchment tied with a black ribbon. Geneviève clapped her hands.

"Is it a new Bonni? Are the words by Metastasis? Oh, the Austrians have such wonderful music makers!" she exclaimed, reaching for the rolled parchment.

Eleonora plucked it from the maid's hands and held it at her side, half hiding it in her skirts. "No, Tante Geneviève, this is not new music. Look in that valise over there."

With a cry of delight, the older woman pushed past piles of brocades and satins and velvets. Eleonora glanced down at the black-ribboned tube she held. *No, not music,* she thought. *Nothing so civilized as that.*

"Oh!" Geneviève said breathlessly, clutching a few sheets of parchment. "It *is* a Bonni! Oh, you darling girl! I shall be the envy of absolutely everyone! It's a masterpiece! I know it. I can feel it!" She rushed to Eleonora and kissed her on the cheek. "Such a sweet girl. What a delight it's going to be having you here!"

Still clutching the music, she started to leave, then

turned in the doorway. "How remiss of me! There will be a bit of dancing and cards for my guests after supper. You're welcome to join us, if you're not too exhausted." She smiled and added to herself, "Such a sweet girl."

"Tante Geneviève," Eleonora called out, her fingers firm around the parchment.

"Yes, my dear?"

"The man with the dark eyes and unpowdered hair whom we passed sitting in the window seat . . . What is his name?" She had to be sure. Absolutely sure.

Distress flashed across the older woman's face. "Don't you let him bother you! My husband invited him—God knows why—but if he comes near—"

"His name, Tante?"

Geneviève hesitated for a moment, then said, "That black-eyed devil is the comte d'Agenais."

"Thank you," Eleonora murmured as the woman departed. "I just wanted to make sure."

A clock discreetly bonged seven in the evening, and Eleonora lifted her head from studying the notes spread around her on the bed to locate the source. On the mantelpiece sat a fanciful porcelain statue of the goddess Artemis shooting her paramour Orion, an incongruous round clock-face hovering over the surprised fallen hunter. Apt, Eleonora thought with a smile.

A light supper of roast quail waited untouched on a tray at the foot of the bed as Eleonora sat cross-legged in her *robe de chambre* and returned to the papers. The roll of parchment tied with the black ribbon remained unopened.

"Mother, Mother," she said softly, shaking her head as she reread the closely spaced notes her mother had given her a few weeks before. She smiled at the last one, written in large letters and underlined again and again. *Do not bed him! Once you do, you will have lost him.*

Eleonora wrinkled her nose in distaste, remembering her husband Miklos's groaning, panting thrustings, and shuddered. She had inevitably been sore and bruised in the morning, feeling—and looking—as if she'd been bedded by a bear. Which wasn't so far from the truth. She thought of another, one whose kisses had been sweet, but quickly shook the memory away.

Being a widow meant that her body was hers again—and that was one thing she would never give up. *"Don't bed him,"* she read aloud, then threw the paper down and picked up another. "That one won't be hard to follow," she murmured to herself, "but these others ... 'Sidelong glances, an enchanting giggle, a judiciously dropped fan ...' They seem such paltry tricks to ensnare the son of a devil."

She lifted her head, her long, unbound hair whispering over pale green silk, and stared into the cheval mirror that stood to one side of the bed. Green eyes met green eyes in a direct gaze. "But ensnare him I will," she said, her voice as solemn and as binding as if she were swearing an oath before a priest. "And lead him to his just fate."

The sins of the comte d'Agenais's father against her family were great—and now it was time for the son to answer for them. Monsieur le comte might think he'd been fathered by an old Frenchman, but Eleonora knew the truth—a blackhearted Turk known as El Müzir had sired him.

Eleonora had come west to France to see to his punishment. She would lead him to Vienna, where her family awaited to mete out its justice on the devil's son. He would be chained, accused, tried—and then sent to hell for his father's crimes. But not killed. No, not killed. His hell was to be a living one.

She remembered the light of anticipation in her mother's eyes when they'd learned the devil had a son. It had been a shock at first, one that nearly drove her mother mad.

How can this be? her mother had screamed. *How could a just God allow this to happen? The devil has a son!* She went from one surviving son to the next—Endres, the eldest now, then Gabriel, then Christophe. One son, Imri, was dead. Years before Eleonora had come into the world, the devil had killed her mother's firstborn son.

The devil has a son! Her mother's anguished cries had echoed again and again. *Mine is taken from me, but the devil has a son! How could a just God . . .*

Then one day, the anguish was gone. A secret smile curved her mother's lips, and a fevered light shown from her eyes. *Yes, God is just, my sons, my daughter. Has He not given us a gift? Has He not given us the devil's son to pay for Imri's death?*

But he is not to die quickly, my children. A quick death will not suffice. Death at all will not suffice. There are too many lost years that the devil's son must pay for. Her mother's smile had widened then, and Eleonora had shuddered, for all the horrors she'd been told of since childhood seemed to be reflected in that smile. *My children,* her mother had continued, *the devil was a Turk. So it is only right—and just—that the devil's son be returned to the Turks.*

As a slave.

Eleonora focused on her own image in the cheval mirror in the bedroom of the château du Peyre, then looked away. Her mother's hate of that devil had darkened Eleonora's life since childhood. Would she ever be free of it? Would she ever know laughter that was not shadowed, or sleep that was not broken by disturbing dreams?

Selfish thoughts, Eleonora scolded herself, and once again began to sort through the papers spread around her, the rustling sounds loud in the room. The shadows didn't matter, the dreams didn't matter—only her duty to her family mattered. And her duty was to lead the comte d'Agenais to Vienna, and to do that, she must entice the devil's son into her arms.

"But not into my bed," she reminded herself with a rueful smile as she reread the underscored notes. "I think I can manage that, Mother. It should be simple enough."

An hour later, the maid returned to dress Eleonora for the evening, and she quickly gathered up the papers and tucked them into a box, which she locked. She doubted the maid could read, but it would be foolhardy to take chances.

* * *

Two footmen in gold-encrusted livery threw open the doors to the Grand Salon, and a rush of laughter blew over Eleonora. She entered, lifting her lips in a charming smile and hiding the thoughtfulness from her gaze.

Tante Geneviève shouted with glee when she saw her, and began pushing politely through the crowd. Huge belled skirts swayed and swooped around the room as women danced and chattered like ships of rose and azure in an ocean of white and gold. The sight would make Eleonora seasick if she stared at it too long.

"How delightful you look!" Geneviève tugged at her arm. "Deep green is perfect for you." She leaned closer to add in a whisper, "I shall, however, have to talk to your maid about your hair. It is not at all the thing to leave it unpowdered. It makes you so . . . noticeable."

"Indeed?" Eleonora murmured.

Musicians played on a platform set against a far wall. The music halted for an instant, then began again. Geneviève clasped her hands and closed her eyes as she took a long, rapturous breath. "Oh, the music is divine, don't you think?"

"It is beautiful," Eleonora agreed, smiling at her aunt while her eyes searched the room.

"Come, come, my dear," Geneviève said, and began pulling Eleonora through the rose and azure ships. Her own gown of watered silk trimmed with gold lace moved gracefully with the rest.

Her eyes—carefully wide-eyed and guileless—studied the others around her. She felt a twinge of satisfaction at having left her hair unpowdered, her aunt's caution notwithstanding. The dark amongst the light caught men's eyes, and she noticed more than one pair following her with interest. But not the pair she wanted.

She tried one sidelong glance, then another, noting the effect. The sillier of the courtiers beamed with delight, while the less silly merely looked amused. The devil's son, she expected, would not be silly at all. She mentally modified her mother's instructions and clutched her fan more tightly, careful not to drop it.

Geneviève introduced her to several men, and soon Eleonora was dancing, and making sprightly conversation, and being told her accent was enchanting—but watch the telltale phrases! she was warned. One never lets on that one has not been to Paris.

Madame does not drink *champagne,* she was told, madame drinks *vin du champagne.* She lost a thousand francs at faro, and won two thousand at lansquenet.

There was no sign of the comte d'Agenais. She was tempted to ask about him but knew her request would be gossiped about a minute later, so she settled for listening carefully to the conversation around her. After dancing her fifth dance, a vigorous Venetian *forlana,* and after being presented with her third glass of champagne—*vin du champagne*—she overhead two old roués in a corner chuckling with envy that Monsieur d'Agenais preferred more private amusements.

So much for enchanting giggles and sidelong glances, she thought. He wasn't even here. Flushed and overheated, she flicked open her fan to cool herself, thankful that at least she had had the sense to hold on to it. A footman stepped from behind a column and discreetly opened a glass-paned door, which led onto a wide balcony, to admit fresh air. She smiled her thanks, but the protests of the other guests made him reach to close it. She slipped outside and heard the latch click shut behind her.

It was cool and humid outside. The balcony was nearly as large as a room, and she walked to the stone balustrade and leaned over to watch moonlight play with a mist that was rising slowly from the Peyre River and drifting into the garden below.

She closed her eyes, wishing she were back home in Hungary, wishing that the mist were rising from the Rába River instead of the Peyre. She wished the stables were full of her own horses and that when she opened her eyes, she would see the beloved countryside she'd ridden over since childhood.

The faintest of noises came from Eleonora's right, barely heard over the sounds of dancing and laughter that were muffled by the closed glass doors behind her. Her musings stopped, and though she did not open her eyes, all her awareness became focused to her right.

"Let me cool you," a deep voice said.

She remained still, her eyes closed. The voice was melodic, yet tinged with all things masculine that until now she had not realized were missing from most men's voices. There was a hint of amusement, of command, of sensuousness, in the way his voice had caressed the words. It was a voice she would love to hear again and again—if only she didn't have to deal with the devil's son.

The champagne glass rocked faintly in her hand, as if he had touched it, then she felt his fingers drawing wetly across her bosom. She gasped before she could gain control of her reaction. Her eyes snapped open . . . and she found herself staring into the black eyes of the devil's son himself. A droplet of champagne slipped down between her breasts.

The comte d'Agenais leaned negligently against the balustrade. "You appeared heated when you came out." He dipped his fingers into the champagne again and this time traced from her shoulder up her neck and along her jaw. Another droplet slid down her skin.

She felt bolted to the spot, as if she were one of the statues in the garden, and the stone floor her pedestal. Her thoughts skittered. *So soon!* She had wanted this, prepared for this, and yet . . .

Her hold on the glass weakened, and it wobbled, splashing some of the pale golden wine onto his hand. His sensual mouth turned up in a secret smile, and he took the glass from her. He drew his wet fingers across her lips, then continued down her chin and neck, until he reached the delicate hollow at the base of her throat.

"Cooler now?" he asked, his words as caressing as his fingers had been.

Her skin tingled where he had touched her. The dampness evaporated slowly in the humid night air, leaving her warmer than before. She looked into his dark eyes, fathomless in the moonlight, and let her own lips lift in a small smile. "Yes, thank you," she lied. "I had not expected such consideration."

"Any other Frenchman would have done the same, I assure you, madame."

"A Frenchman, of course. But you . . ." Her gaze drifted from his face to the mist-shrouded garden below, as if she'd grown bored of looking at him.

She sensed him stiffening for the briefest moment, and she silently rejoiced that her intimation that he was not French had hit home, but his languidness returned all too quickly.

"Do you think me a Hungarian, like you?" He sounded amused.

"Like *me?*" The question caught her off guard. Distorted images, as if seen through the pinhole of a camera obscura, swept across her mind, images of devils and nightmares and storms rending her family apart. Her eyes flashed with anger at his insult, and she could not keep the bite of it from her voice. "There is nothing *like* about us."

The stem of the champagne flute snapped in his hold, and the glass fell from his fingers to shatter against a statue in the garden below. She gave a start at the violent sound.

In an instant he was behind her, arms encircling her, hands over hers where she held on to the balustrade. His body pressed against her.

"What . . .?" she began.

His mouth was at her ear. "You are wrong, madame countess. There is much *like* about us. I, too, do not take kindly to insults." His fingers curled between hers until he was gripping her hands in his fists. "And you are quite free with insults to a man to whom you have not yet been properly introduced."

Her breaths came rapid and shallow. "In-introduced . . ." she stammered. Shame washed over her. Her first instinct should have been to scream and struggle, but instead she'd felt a stab of fear that had frozen even her heartbeat for an instant. Control, she had to have control. *Think of your duty.* Now was not the time to let tales of horror from her childhood rule her mind.

Muscle by muscle, she forced her body to relax, the way she had learned to do while riding, to keep her apprehension from the horse. She let her head fall back against the comte d'Agenais's shoulder. Drawing on every ounce of her courage, she looked up into his eyes. Even in the dim light, she saw wary surprise in their dark depths.

"Introduced, monsieur?" She gave a sultry laugh. "As you wish. I am Eleonora Sophia Juliana, the countess Batthyány. And I am not only Hungarian, monsieur, but also Magyar."

The steel-like hardness of his body pressing into hers lessened ever so slightly. His hands released hers, and he drew his long fingers up her arms. "And not only Hungarian, monsieur, but also Magyar," he echoed.

"The last of the ancient tribes," he said, his low voice resonating through her. "Fierce. Passionate. Indomitable. And so fearless that not even a hundred and fifty years of battling the Infidel could tame them. And the beautiful countess is such a one. A Magyar. Are you warning me or tempting me, madame?"

Commanding each muscle in her hand to move, she brought her fingers up to brush against his as they held her shoulder. "*Yes,* monsieur."

He drew in a breath, and his hold tightened. "And I, madame, am Achille Anton Auguste, the comte d'Agenais. A House of France which has borne chevaliers to serve kings—and beautiful ladies—since the Valois first came to the throne."

She felt his breath on her neck, and with a strength that came from years of riding, she shrugged out of his hold. "And so, after four hundred years," she mused aloud, "the House of d'Agenais has . . . *descended* to you."

His sensual lips turned up in an appreciative smile at her gibe. Without a trace of awkwardness, his fluid body leaned against the balustrade. "And shall we *descend* further together?" he asked.

She put her fingers to her temples, careful to let the artifice show. "Ah, you put my head in a spin, monsieur. One insult fires you, while another but amuses." She lowered her hand and gazed at him levelly, making it clear that her head was in anything *but* a spin.

"You play the game well, madame."

"Game, monsieur?"

"Moonlight can give such innocence to green eyes." His fingertips traced the sheen of dampness on her breasts that had not quite evaporated. "Game, madame. Where the winnings are not gold, but the glorious sight of passion shimmering on a woman's skin."

" 'Tis a pity, then, that you must be satisfied with the shimmer of wine." She stepped away from his touch and made for the door into the ballroom. "But no doubt it's a familiar enough substitute."

Chapter 2

Achille remained on the balcony. Through the glazing of the doors, he could occasionally glimpse the striking unpowdered head of the Magyar countess as the steps of a dance brought her near.

An unusual beauty, he mused. Such women were rare commodities. She was also an *intriguing* beauty, and that was rarer still. Achille leaned against the balustrade, legs crossed. He wasn't sure he believed in such rarities.

She had all the requirements for success, to be sure. A quick wit for survival in the salons, nimble feet for the inevitable dancing, and he would bet she played her cards close and sure at the gaming table.

Achille watched her partner bring her to stand by the doors at the end of the dance. The fellow bowed elegantly and, to guess by his gesture, offered to get her more vin du champagne. She shook her head to decline, then with an engaging smile and a tap of her fan on his arm, sent him away.

Achille nearly left then. He knew what would happen next. It was as much a part of the sexual dance as any practiced steps set to music. She would scan the crowd for another likely partner. She would study his clothes. Were they expensive enough to denote wealth? Elegant enough to convey position?

She stood alone, behind the laughing, flirting crowd, idly playing with the orange blossoms of a hothouse tree. Achille frowned. Instead of studying the crowd, she was looking down at her hand and, with the lightest touch, caressing the velvet white flower petals. She brought the scented blossom to her face, closed her eyes, and drew in a long breath.

A soft smile lifted her lips. For the briefest instant, her carefully controlled social mask was transformed by her private thoughts. Achille felt his abdomen tighten. Her face became a mirror, reflecting remembered sensation, remembered laughter . . . remembered pleasure?

Then the mask returned. She glanced at the doors with a guilty start. He knew the dazzling brightness of the candlelight kept her from seeing him, yet she dropped the orange blossom and quickly turned her back. She fidgeted with the fan, darted another worried glance at the doors, then began making her polite but determined way through the crowd.

Perhaps it would be amusing to believe in such rarities—at least until his commission arrived.

Achille let his gaze follow the dark-haired countess in the crowd beyond the doors. She *was* beautiful. And intriguing. There was a fleeting specter of hope in him that perhaps, once, he would find depth in a woman's passion. But immediately he brushed the foolish thought away as nothing more than a remnant of his boyhood fantasies.

A servant came to the doors and with careful, precise movements, stepped onto the balcony. He bowed to Achille.

"Your pardon, monsieur," the man said, "but Monsieur du Peyre has requested your presence in the gaming room."

Achille waved a hand in acknowledgment. "To watch him lose badly or win badly?" he asked, then straightened, knowing he would receive no answer. "Tell him you have faithfully delivered his message."

"Monsieur . . . ?" the servant began uncertainly, then cleared his throat and bowed again. "As you wish, monsieur."

Alone once more after the servant had departed, Achille closed his eyes against the glare of the candles glittering through the glass. He was weary. Almost a year had passed since that night in Paris, yet he was still not free of it. He had run to the château de Gemeaux to try and rid himself of the memories, but in that dark place, far from the lights and laughter of château du Peyre, he had only added to his list of sins.

He drew in a deep breath and tensed his right arm. There, near his shoulder . . . the sting of the wound he had received at Gemeaux was muted now, only an echo to match his lingering humiliation. To have been caught like a schoolboy— He broke off the memory. Gemeaux had been a mistake.

Achille thought of the countess. Was it foolish to have noticed her? He shrugged and straightened. No matter. He might find she was able to amuse him, but it was the battlefield that would lift the eternal weariness that threatened to engulf him; it was on the battlefield that he would find his salvation. He'd learned that at a young age.

Achille strode into the ballroom, then made his way to the gaming room. Brilliant red silk lined the walls, casting the glow of a high fever over faces already florid from too much wine. He had planned on making his excuses, but when he stood behind the marquis du Peyre as the older man won another hand from the gossip Vigny, Achille caught sight of a much more interesting game to watch. Through the doorway behind Vigny, Achille could see the countess Batthyány seated in a gilded chair, chatting amiably with his hostess, du Peyre's wife.

Vigny cursed loudly at the turn of an unfortunate card. The countess Batthyány lifted her eyes toward the disturbance. Her gaze met Achille's, and she turned away without acknowledging him. He wondered at such deliberate coolness.

A man went up to her. Achille didn't immediately recognize him, and when she declined a dance with a quick smile and a shake of her auburn curls, Achille didn't bother to search his memory for a name; since she'd refused the offer, the man was irrelevant.

In most respects, she seemed to be in complete control,

yet something in the way she fanned herself made him think that she was not entirely at ease. There was a commotion at one of the doors. Did her fan increase its tempo?

In front of him, du Peyre threw down his cards with a snort. "You are annoying me, Vigny. Your play is as bad as some young pup's from Gascony." Du Peyre scooped up his winnings. "What can be the matter with you?"

Vigny darted a glance at Achille, his eyes quickly returning to his cards. He shrugged nervously. "I am fatigued, monsieur. Nothing more."

"Well, you're being most disobliging," du Peyre said with ill humor.

Achille nodded toward Vigny, and said, "Monsieur le marquis would prefer you to lose with much more skill."

Amid the chuckles, a man sauntered up to stand behind Vigny. The laughter stopped. Achille's sword hand began to ball into a fist of its own accord. This man should have died with the others on that night in Paris.

The man gave a mocking bow to Achille, sliding his body to the side to make it seem as if the bow was intended for du Peyre. "Since Vigny displeases, perhaps the marquis de Peyre would care to see a real game," the man said.

"Rachand," du Peyre said with distaste. "You are here uninvited."

"An oversight, I'm sure."

Du Peyre turned his head to look at Achille, then shifted his gaze back to Rachand. "I want no trouble."

The marquis de Rachand shrugged. "What could happen on such a modest country estate?" His eyes met Achille's. "Now, in Paris—"

"You are not now in Paris," Achille broke in. "You are considerably farther east."

"D'Agenais, a bit more courtesy, if you please," Rachand said with false affability. "The king himself thought it quite right that I journey here to resume our . . . interrupted . . . game. Surely you can not object to that."

"I do not object to that. I object to you."

There was a stunned silence. Vigny looked sick. Du

Peyre nervously fingered his cards. In Rachand's eyes, Achille saw a flare of rage and hate, and he felt a surge of satisfaction.

"It is *I* who should—" Rachand began, then disappointed Achille by breaking it off as wariness and fear crept into the man's eyes. With a shrug and a forced smile, Rachand said, "I would finish our game, d'Agenais."

"It ended nearly a year ago," Achille answered. "Or has monsieur le marquis forgotten?"

"I forget nothing, you—!"

"Messieurs!" du Peyre cried. He put a hand to his forehead and muttered, " 'A simple country party,' my wife said." He motioned to a servant to bring more wine. "Please, please . . ." he said. "Now, Rachand, I'm sure the king meant for you to be at your ease. This has been an eventful year for you—"

"Murder is an event, isn't it, d'Agenais?" Rachand jeered.

Du Peyre let out an exasperated breath. "Monsieur! This is a party meant to amuse. Take your quarrel with Monsieur d'Agenais to the king. Here, have some burgundy."

Rachand snatched the glass of wine from the servant and threw the liquid down his throat. Achille searched the man's red face. He should see some similarity in the fleshy features before him, some cousin-to-cousin resemblance to . . . to a man he had once called friend.

Achille's gaze turned inward. The sting of righteousness had numbed him like a spider's venom, numbed all but one small corner of sadness in the darkness inside him.

A *harrumpf* intruded. Rachand grabbed the ewer of wine from the servant's grasp and poured his glass overfull. "Let's not ruin du Peyre's 'simple country party,' " he said, sneering the last three words. "A game of faro? A thousand louis to start. I'm the bank."

There was a collective gasp at the amount. Rachand was perennially short of funds, his lands mortgaged to the utmost, and Achille considered commenting on his ability to pay. But in the middle distance behind Rachand stood the countess Batthyány. She had risen at the first hint of a confrontation, clutching her fan.

Why was she so agitated? Achille wondered. The other women were whispering to one another, eyes bright with speculation as to the outcome of the encounter of the two enemies, but her eyes conveyed worry.

A servant moved to close the connecting door. "No," Achille said. His gaze met the countess's for a brief moment, and she went still. "I wish the door left open." His expression was carefully bland when he returned his gaze to Rachand. "A hand, then," he said, "since you are so adamant. But at two thousand to start."

Rachand blanched, then nodded and sat down. The first two cards were slipped from the dealing box and dealt. Achille adjusted his chair to keep both the marquis de Rachand and the countess Batthyány in view.

The play went as he expected. Rachand was the worst kind of player—one who had some skill, but thought those skills greater than they were. Achille split his attention between the countess and the cards. It was a trick he'd learned as a child, absorbed in his reading while his ears remained alert for the soft footfalls of his tutor.

Rachand bet badly, then sat back with bravado. He snorted. "I won't let you goad me, you know," he told Achille. He noisily drank more wine, then leaned forward. "I've let too much time pass, d'Agenais. But no longer. The king is a long way off. *Paris* is a long way off." The man's eyes gleamed at Achille. "But justice is not!"

Rachand was grinning when the last card was turned over. His face fell. "What a bitch!" He swept his cards off the table and stood abruptly sending his chair crashing to the floor. "Enjoy your victory, d'Agenais. It's your last bit of luck! Everything's in motion, don't you see? You're already caught, monsieur le comte—" Rachand clenched his fist. "Caught like—"

"You babble, Rachand, and I grow weary of it." Achille stood. The countess Batthyány put her fan to her lips as if in thought, then hurried away. "You may give du Peyre your note," he told Rachand, and turned to leave.

"Another hand!"

"It is finished."

"No!" Rachand shouted. "Not the game. Not *Paris!* Blood will out, d'Agenais. Rachand blood is on your hands. No matter the distance—in leagues or years—*blood will out.*"

The image of the countess Batthyány's thoughtul face stayed in Achille's mind as he made his way to his apartment. Rachand's threatening words meant nothing to him; the man was a blustering coward.

He threw open the door. "Beaulieu!" he called, striding into the two-room suite. Pale blue striped silk lined the walls, accented by the ubiquitous white and gold plasterwork. He'd had a round marquetry table moved next to the tall window, and in the corner on another table, one with pleasingly sensuous curves, were, of course, his books.

His valet rose from a seat by the fire, where he'd been cleaning the gold braid on Achille's uniform. "Monsieur," he said with an unruffled bow. "There is still no word of the courier, though I'm sure—"

Achille dismissed the man's comment with a wave. "I have need of your services. And of your boy's, Jean-Baptiste, as well."

Achille saw Beaulieu's narrow chest swell with pride at the mention of his son's name. The boy had been born to the valet and his wife late in life; "a miracle child awaiting to perform miracles," as Beaulieu said much too often. Now Achille was relieved when Beaulieu held himself in check with a relatively modest "A good lad, monsieur. He'll serve y' well."

"There is a woman here, newly arrived," Achille told him, going to his books. "Eleonora, Countess Batthyány. From Hungary, she says. By way of Vienna. I wish to know if that is so. I wish to know where she has just come from. I wish to know of her family." Achille chose a volume of poems by his favorite troubadour. "And I most particularly want to know if she has any connections in

Paris. Any at all, Beaulieu. The veriest spider's silk of a connection."

"I understand, monsieur."

"And I do *not* wish my interest to become known."

Beaulieu bowed his acknowledgment, then helped his master prepare for bed.

In moments, Achille was alone. Dressed only in a black silk robe, high-necked and fastening on one shoulder, with a hint of Cathay in its lines, he sat in a chair by the tall windows and stretched his long legs out in front of him. He sipped the cognac Beaulieu had poured him, the book on his lap, and stared out the window, at the wild, unknown night just beyond the safety of the glazing.

He smiled at the fancy. One had to travel halfway into Bavaria before one could truly call the night wild. But one did not have to travel far to find the "unknown"; it was just down the hall.

"Janus-faced females are common enough," he said aloud. "One side is always hiding the other." That was a lesson he had learned early. From his faithless mother.

Once, long ago when he'd been a boy and still had a heart, he had believed with a rock-solid faith that a woman could feel passion and love as strong and as true as he could feel them. His father had believed it, and so had he.

But then Constantin had died. Achille had tried to keep alive the beloved stories his father had told him, but his Jesuit tutors had beaten him when they'd discovered his books. Only his passionate rage had kept them at bay long enough for him to hide the books. He had tried to honor what his father had honored, but the world—and his mother—had intruded.

The rumors of his illegitimacy had started when he was fifteen. Usually the insinuations reached him anonymously, but he always tracked down the source and . . .

At fifteen and a half, he'd challenged his first man to a duel for staining his father's honor. The man claimed he'd once been Madame d'Agenais's lover and was merely seeking to resume their relationship, and it wasn't until

Achille's mother had turned the man down that the gossip had begun to spread.

Achille, still in the flush of new manhood, had challenged him—and won. The victory had gone to his head, until his swollen pride had burst when he learned that the dead man and his mother had indeed been lovers.

Coming face-to-face with the baseness inside him should have taught him humility; instead it enraged him that he had been so deceived. His mother, always a cold and distant figure, now proved to have been unfaithful as well. Heady with hate, Achille had searched, questioned, interrogated, everyone about her past, and found instance after instance of her infidelity to her husband.

Such was a woman. In his self-hate, Achille had become obsessed with the names of his mother's lovers—Maraillat, Auriac, Neuvialle—going over and over the list of men who might have been his father. No, it wasn't Maraillat; his liaison with Lece d'Agenais had ended five years before Achille had been born. Not Auriac; that had ended seven years too early. Not Neuvialle; three years too . . .

And then he knew. There was no talk, not even whispers, of any lovers for nearly two years before he'd been born. His mother, the cold, distant Lece d'Agenais, had, for whatever reason, returned to her husband. Constantin was indeed his father.

The face his mother had shown the world since his father's death was that of a pious grieving widow who thought only of her son. But Achille knew the face she did not show.

He leaned forward in the chair, cupping the bulb of the glass to warm the potent liquid. "And what of your faces, Eleonora, Countess Batthyány? What of the faces I saw tonight? What of those I did *not* see?"

He swirled the warmed cognac in the glass and sat back in the chair. A wariness that had slumbered during his stay at the château du Peyre began to reawaken. Was she connected to Rachand? Connected to that night of hell in Paris?

His jaw tightened. Inside him, a familiar shield fell

across his mind, pressing down on his emotions. It was as solid and implacable as it had always been, ever since soon after his father had died. But ever since Paris, one emotion had been able to slip past that shield—remorse. Remorse that could not be covered, could not be hidden. It had been his constant companion for the last year.

He'd tried to blind himself to it, tried to keep the remorse at bay, but his efforts had failed. They had brought him to the terrible things that had happened at Gemeaux ... things that were best forgotten.

He'd gone too far that night—and the remorse had become a black emptiness. It was as if his future had become a void, a nothingness that admitted no plans, provided no course to follow, that offered nothing but a slow sinking into darkness. He had always expected death to take him suddenly: a quick sword thrust in an early morning duel, or a ball of lead through his heart. Not this slow death of his soul.

He knew hell awaited him. That was probably the only thing the Jesuits and the Jansenists would ever agree upon: that the soul of Achille, comte d'Agenais, would one day be Lucifer's own.

Achille took another swallow of cognac and smiled darkly. Of course, there were those who believed his soul already was Lucifer's own, and he had not cared if it was true or not.

But would the Magyar countess care?

It was deep into the night, and outside his window the darkness beckoned. It had always been there, comfortable and familiar, during the many long hours before a dawn battle.

Perhaps that's what he was doing now, waiting for the battle that was to commence at dawn. The blood-quickening battle between a man and a woman. The image of the countess when she'd stroked the orange blossom hovered in his mind, like smoke above an enemy's campfire. He would wager there was much to the foreign countess that could not easily be discerned ... much that was hidden. He had a fortnight, at least, before the call to arms came; plenty of time for *discerning*.

And if she was working for Rachand? She would pay for that, of course. He raised his glass to the absent countess. Either way, he would enjoy her charms before he was called to war. "We who are about to *win* salute you."

The sound of splashing water broke the quiet of the early morning as Eleonora cupped her hands into the basin and brought the cool water up to her face. It dripped down her neck and shoulders and wet the low neckline of her chemise. She squeezed the water out of a square of rough-woven silk and used it to scrub across the tops of her breasts, up her neck, and under her jaw. Her hand moved jerkily as she tried to wipe away every last trace of d'Agenais's touch. She scrubbed harder, till the skin tingled pink and tender, and the front of the chemise was soaked.

The dress she'd worn the night before lay in a discarded tumble at her feet, and she stared at it for the hundredth time since the night before.

" 'Any other Frenchman would have done the same,' " she quoted, then kicked at the dress. She'd overheard the marquis de Rachand's accusations. *Murderer*, he'd called d'Agenais. How many other Frenchmen had *killed*? And yet ... that seemed not to have mattered to the others around her. They had only watched avidly as d'Agenais had sat down to cards with his mortal enemy.

"Saint Stephen, but what kind of man have I come to deal with?" The question went unanswered. She glanced at the rolled and tied parchment leaning against the wardrobe—and remembered that she already knew what kind of man he was. If she had had any qualms about taking revenge on an innocent man, they had gone. There was no innocence in murder. The devil's seed had indeed been passed on.

The long, rosy-tinted shadows dulled the gilding of the furniture and made the white walls glow the color of blood-fouled water. The stories of a devil's killing rages which she'd heard from childhood, seemed all the more real in the eerie light.

Eleonora rubbed her arms against the sudden chill of her damp chemise. Why was it fear lurked so much closer in the early morning than at any other time?

She hated fear. She walked around the bedroom, then the sitting room, trying to banish her agitation. It didn't work. She went to the locked box and drew out the notes and instructions her mother had given her. Sitting at the writing desk, she covered the elaborate marquetry with the papers, and began studying them once again. But this time, she had no smiles for the naïve advice, only irritation at herself for coming to catch a devil's son with weapons designed for a mere man.

The paper in Eleonora's hand shook and the words blurred. Nightmares, always the nightmares, dark, stormy dreams that had been spawned early in her childhood. She had been haunted by them. Every dark corner had had to be lit, every new face searched for the familiar lines of the devil, and even now those dreams tainted every aspect of her life. The tenseness of being in a crowd. The discomforts of being alone. She'd endured them, accepted the hate and distrust that caused them as her family's right, accepted the poison that infected her and her brothers.

Only once had she tried to let someone get close to her, but then he had died . . . and she'd gone on accepting her family legacy.

Until she'd heard her little niece, sweet, innocent Sophia, wake in the night screaming of pursuing devils—and Eleonora knew it had to stop. No matter the cost. The devil was dead, and what he'd done could not be exorcised—but his son could pay for his deeds, and free her family.

Her family had chosen her to lure the son to his fate. Of what other use was a daughter who could not bear children to a husband? An anguish greater than any hate rose inside her, and she put a hand low on her stomach, as if to hide the emptiness there. Her eyes burned with unshed tears. Eleonora clamped down on the familiar pain. She had her

duty. It was all she would ever have, and she would fulfill
it.

At nine of the clock, the maid arrived to wake up "Madame Bath'ny" with a cup of chocolate and a basket of
freshly baked brioche. She was surprised to find that Madame had already risen, and merely *tsk*ed over the fate of
the green watered silk gown, not seeming overly distressed
that a guest should have a champagne-stained gown crumpled on the floor.

The girl did exclaim over the streaks of angry pink on
Eleonora's creamy bosom and valiantly strove to cover
them with powder and lotion, but Eleonora merely let the
maid dress her quickly before dismissing her and returning
to work.

It was nearing ten when a scratch on the door interrupted her once again. Tante Geneviève peeked into the
room.

"Good morning!" Geneviève said, and scampered in.
"I'm so glad you're awake."

Eleonora turned the top paper on the desk upside down
to cover the rest, then rose and greeted the older woman
with a kiss on the cheek. "You're certainly cheerful this
morning, Tante," she said, gesturing to a chair.

Geneviève sat down, preening a little. "I won ten thousand francs at faro last night! Thank the saints! Now I can
redeem some of that jewelry I lost to . . ." She trailed off,
then shook her hands. "But never mind that. I came to
ask— Oh, but I've interrupted you," she said, craning her
neck to see the papers on the desk. "That isn't more new
music, is it?"

"No, Tante," Eleonora said, going back to sit behind the
desk. She lifted a page as if to hand it to the other woman.
"It's a report from my steward recommending that new
drainage be—"

"*Drainage!* My dear, no, no, no," Geneviève exclaimed,
waving away the paper Eleonora held. "You are here to
enjoy yourself," she began, and had all the signs of someone readying to launch into a lengthy diatribe.

To forestall her, Eleonora grabbed the tray the maid had

brought and held it out to the other woman. "Brioche, Tante? They're the best I've ever eaten. You must be very proud of your pastry chef." She tore off a piece as if to prove her point.

Diverted, Geneviève preened again. "Ooo, I am! I stole him from Madame de la Voulte." She giggled, then got a comical look on her face. "Well, actually, Madame threw him out after she discovered him in bed with her husband. But I snapped him up practically at her doorstep! No one else even knew he was available!" She released a forlorn sigh. "Of course, I don't have to worry about him and *my* husband, though I do have my suspicions about the head footman . . ."

The bite of brioche stopped halfway to Eleonora's mouth. She was unable to say anything for a long moment, shock keeping her mute. "Tante . . ." she began, then dropped the brioche on the tray and started again. "You, ah, wanted to ask me something when you came in . . . ?"

Geneviève clapped her hands together. "Oh, dear, yes! Do you remember my mentioning an upcoming concert?" Eleonora nodded. "Well, my sister-in-law was going to play the harpsichord piece by Bonni, but she has elected not to participate." Geneviève harrumphed. "If you ask me, she's playing this role of being enceinte to excess! And at her age—nine and thirty if you please!" She stopped for a moment as if to regain her composure.

Thinking to comfort her, Eleonora smiled and said, "Perhaps her husband wishes her to be careful."

"Her husband? What has *he* to say to anything? She hasn't seen him in three years. No, she just wants to flaunt herself and have everyone make a fuss over her."

Eleonora sat stunned. The whole society was mad! How easily they let themselves be seduced and how willingly they played games of casual virtue. Perhaps the comte d'Agenais had spoken true when he'd said any Frenchman would've done as he had.

"My dear?"

"I'm sorry, what did you say, Tante?"

"I asked if you would play the harpsichord piece in the concert."

"Of course, Tante." Perhaps she could find a refuge from the madness in music.

Geneviève was all smiles as she rose. "Excellent, my dear. I'm sure you'll do superbly," she said as she made her way to the door. "Oh, and—if you don't mind—I'll send round some cosmetics more to your coloring. You have such an unusual pale ivory skin, my dear, it's a shame to paint it so pink." She canted her head to one side. "In fact, I don't know as I've ever seen quite that color . . . No, no, I have, but where . . . ? Oh! Well, yes, but that doesn't matter." She turned away, looking embarrassed.

"Who, Tante Geneviève? Perhaps I could ask her to give me the name of her apothecary."

"No, I don't think that would be wise, my dear." She shuddered and opened the door. "The comte d'Agenais's mother is a woman to stay away from."

An early afternoon breeze playfully rippled Eleonora's long scarf shot with gold as she sauntered along the path to the garden where dinner was to be served alfresco. The path opened up into a large round lawn encircled with statues and topiary that formed a colonnade. Dozens of other guests were entering from avenues of tall hedges behind the statues that all led to the open area like spiraling spokes of a wheel. Chairs had been arranged in groups of five and six, and garlands of ivy led the way toward the pavilions of food set up at the far end.

A worried-looking Geneviève appeared beside Eleonora.

"Oh, my dear, thank God I found you." She put a hand on Eleonora to stop her in the shade of one of the statues. "I've been so distracted. I don't see how I could have been so foolish. Please, don't mention to anyone that I spoke to you about d'Agenais's mother."

"No, of course not, if you wish—"

"*Especially* not to d'Agenais. His rages are like lightning. They strike in an instant, then are gone. But, oh, what havoc they leave in their wake!"

"Rages?" Eleonora asked with a laugh. "Don't worry, Tante. I have a younger brother and am quite accustomed to dealing with masculine tantrums."

"By the saints, child! D'Agenais is a full-blooded man—there's more hot blood in him than in three of most men—and he is certainly no one's younger brother."

Noises of a squabble by the tables laden with food drifted to them, and Geneviève squinted down at it. "Oh, my Lord, they're at it again. I thought this nonsense had been settled or I never would have invited them at the same time. Excuse me, my dear," Geneviève said absently, and hurried off to deal with the fracas.

Eleonora remained by the statue, not wanting to join the quarreling crowd. She'd seen d'Agenais watching her as he'd played cards the night before. Had he guessed at her concern? She'd been a fool to let her agitation show when she'd overheard Rachand's change of murder. That d'Agenais had killed did not surprise her. That Rachánd and the others would sit down to cards with him did.

She twirled her scarf uneasily. Dueling was condoned, even admired, in this oh-so-civilized country, so it was not the charge of murder that made others find him . . . uncomfortable. It was the man himself.

In his dark eyes, she had seen his contempt of fear, and for an instant, Eleonora had known that it matched her own. But concern was not fear, though he might have mistaken it in her. But that did not matter; if she'd lost ground with him, she would fight to regain it.

She glanced up at the statue beside her—and found herself staring at an overly large masculine attribute. It belonged to a grinning satyr who was carrying a struggling nymph. Eleonora flushed hotly and quickly looked away.

"Silenus," d'Agenais's voice said as he came to stand beside her. "A companion of Dionysus. A fellow particularly fond of—"

"I can see what he's fond of. *She,* however, doesn't seem to be of the same opinion."

"Perhaps he's a clumsy fellow."

"Aren't they all?"

The comte d'Agenais gave her a singularly graceful bow. "No, madame, they are not."

Eleonora flushed again, but dipped into an answering curtsy. "Perhaps you are right. I have seen a few less-than-clumsy horsemen. In Hungary."

"But not in France? You have merely not seen the right horseman. A ride, madame?"

Achille saw a flash of anticipation in those enticing green eyes, and a quick agreement hovering on her lips, but she hesitated.

One end of her long scarf fluttered in front of him, and he idly plucked it from the air, then let the breeze draw it slowly through his hand. He felt her give a start, and on instinct, he caught the end before it slipped from his fingers.

"A ride, monsieur? I do not believe I have the time just now." She seemed to dislike the golden link between them. He gave it a tug as if to bring her closer. She stiffened and shot him a quick green-eyed glance, full of annoyance.

"Madame du Peyre has asked me to participate in a concert. I must practice," she said. She took a step forward and pulled the scarf out of his grasp as she would pluck a piece of straw from her skirts. "Excuse me, monsieur, but my aunt seems to have settled the squabble, and I promised to meet others for dinner." She walked away.

Achille sat near the statue of Silenus, his plate in front of him, watching the poised beauty during dinner as she sat amongst a group of du Peyre's more frivolous guests farther down the colonnade. The exotic Hungarian beauty glanced at him, then looked back to her food. She ate like a piece of clockwork he'd seen as a child in Strasbourg, one bite, then another, then a sip of wine, all the while taking no apparent joy in the taste of any of it.

Achille frowned. Perhaps she wasn't worth his trouble. A woman who took no pleasure in her senses would hardly be likely to give pleasure to his. She bent her head over her plate, the scarf shot with gold lying against her skin with a tantalizing promise. He hissed a silent curse. She was such a beauty, but in bed, the countess would likely be as mechanical as she was at dinner. Once that may have satisfied him, but his tastes were more demanding now.

Yesterday, for a fraction of a heartbeat, he'd thought he'd seen such a fire in the countess's eyes that could burn away the deepest weariness. And she had enjoyed the scent of the orange blossom, he reminded himself. He took a bite of truffled partridge and savored it—and the enigma Madame Batthyány presented.

His plump host, the marquis du Peyre, sat down next to Achille with a satisfied sigh. "Excellent partridge, eh? Excellent." He patted his corseted stomach. "Damn fine chef, don't you agree?"

"I would not be here if I did not."

Du Peyre chuckled. "Ah, that's the way of things! Superb wine, superb food, and"—he lowered his voice—"superb females. I see you've been admiring my latest little piece." The man grinned fatuously toward the group where the countess sat.

The taste of the partridge turned to ashes in Achille's mouth. "Indeed?" he said, taking a sip of wine without noticing its vintage. He handed his half-full plate to a passing servant. "I had not heard that importing mistresses was the new fashion."

"Importing? Ha! What a notion. Something more for Louis's intendants to tax! No, don't let her fool you— that pillowy pink morsel is all French." Peyre wiggled his fingers at the group, and a woman Achille had not noticed, a round, definitely pink chevalier's wife, wiggled hers back.

Achille took another sip of wine, and this time noticed the tang of a fine Mantes. The marquis cast an envious glance at Achille, and added, "Of course, to someone who has actually *turned down* Madame de Madelmont, and the charms of Madame du Fachaux and her sister, she may seem a bit ordinary. We can't all be such demanding connoisseurs as you, d'Agenais. No, all in all, my little rosy peach is quite a find."

Achille watched as across the lawn, in the shadow of a demurely covered marble naiad, a bowing servant proffered the countess a tray of oranges from Portugal. She smiled and took one, then rose, curtsied to the group she had eaten with, and walked down one of the paths between the tall hedges. A light breeze caught at her scarf as she stepped out of sight.

Beside him, du Peyre snorted. "My wife's idea."

Achille raised a black brow.

"Had to invite her." Du Peyre pinched his face and in a falsetto voice said, " 'Just think of that poor little dear so close to all those infidels.' " In his regular voice, he added, "As if she broke bread every morning with a pasha. A niece of some sort. From Silesia, Moravia—one of those godforsaken places people are álways fighting over."

He shuddered. "She makes my nerves jump. Too tall by half. Strange-lookin' too—like a cat with those green eyes. Hate cats. Can't trust 'em. Just stare at a man as if to say they know you're dishin' 'em out nonsense." He stood and stretched. "Glad to see my little morsel seems to have taken her up, though. She needs some tutoring in how to go on. A man likes his woman to look at him with adoring, unquestioning devotion in her eyes, eh, d'Agenais?"

Achille raised his wineglass, but said nothing. Du Peyre tottered off, a self-satisfied smile on his plump face.

Tutoring, Achille thought, his gaze intent on the path down which the countess had walked.

Was she just a woman of clockwork? Or did her coolness cover more than cogs and levers? Could it be that she was merely ... untutored? He remembered the faintest pink on her skin, as if she'd been kissed by the sun, but he guessed that the sun had not caused it. He smiled.

He rose and sauntered across the lawn, nodding politely to those he passed, then entered the path between the hedges that the countess had taken. Perhaps he had done

more than cool her skin last night; he had certainly intended to.

And he certainly intended to do more now. Clockwork
or passion—he would discover which was beneath that
Hungarian poise by day's end.

Chapter 3

$\mathbf{E}$leonora sat in a secluded and shaded bower, absently peeling an orange and reveling in the scent of damask roses, whose long, draping stems formed a canopy of pale lavender-pink blooms overhead. The bower was a small niche that had been carefully cultivated in the hedge, its marble bench supported by dancing nymphs, while across the path was a magnificent statue of a landing swan, its proud neck arched and wings outstretched.

Someone stepped in front of the entrance, making the afternoon light dim to a sudden twilight. A section of orange stopped halfway to her mouth. The comte d'Agenais gave her an elegant bow, her gold silk scarf in his hands. She had not realized that she'd dropped it.

"Madame," he said, "I intrude."

She lowered the fruit to her lap with as much self-possession as she could muster. "As you say, monsieur. I was enjoying the solitude."

He entered without asking her permission and sat down next to her on the narrow bench. Most gentlemen would have seated themselves just beyond the half circle of her skirts spread out around her, but he slid closer, making the brocade of intricately embroidered flowers overlap the deep rust velvet of his breeches.

"Your scarf," he stated, holding it in his far hand and making no move to give it to her. He rubbed it between his fingertips. "It was most thoughtful of you to drop it just outside. I would never have found you else."

Eleonora considered how to answer. Everything he said was a sleight-of-word trick. She silently cursed the useless notes in her rooms. Though she knew the truth about him, the comte d'Agenais was still an aristocrat who was considered sophisticated even by those who excelled in the posturings and artifice and sensual indulgences of high French society. There were no neatly listed rules for her to follow; she had only her instincts.

"Thoughtful?" she said with a careful laugh. "You would have me as subtle as a Jesuit, monsieur. I did but stop to admire the statue. It is the only one in the garden that does not make me blush."

D'Agenais studied the swan with a faint smile. "Then you would not want to hear that Leda is just around the next turning."

She flushed, then shook her head with a laugh. "An innocent swan becomes a disguised Jupiter ravishing his mortal lover. The French! Is there nothing in this garden not intent on seduction?"

His eyes met and held hers. "No."

Her gaze lowered to the half-eaten orange she still held in her hand. "You are wrong, monsieur. There is one who does not think of it." She raised her eyes level with his.

"Do you not?" he mused. There was a glint in his eyes, the kind of light a gambler gets as he awaits the outcome of a turn of the card. "Your introduction last night said otherwise."

"Ah, monsieur, you must forgive an unsophisticated Hungarian stumbling about in such sparkling company. I was but dazzled."

"I am not convinced, madame. The words you speak do not match what your eyes are saying."

She struck a pose, hand to breast, eyes wide with guilelessness. "The aristocracy of France are renowned throughout Europe for the ... delicacy of their amusements. Who would not be entranced by it all? And what is in my eyes? Are they shouting the poetry of love?"

"You are not entranced, and there is no love in your eyes. Though there has been, I would guess."

Her pose disintegrated and she looked away. He put a finger under her chin and drew her back to face him. "And poetry is never shouted." He drew his thumb over her mouth. "Your lips are still touched with the juice of the fruit. Were a man to kiss you, he would find you sweet to his tasting. That is poetry."

"It is but fancy! Where is the meter and where the rhyme?" she asked.

"What is meter but the rhythms of nature set to words," he answered. "And the rhythms of nature are all around us. The sway of a woman's flowered skirts as she walks down a path in the garden." He leaned closer, and she could feel his gaze caressing her neck and shoulders. He drew a fingertip down the length of her neck. "The sliding of her thumb under the peel of an orange, again and again, to free its hidden . . . succulent . . . treasure."

She cupped the fruit she still held and raised it from her lap. "And what if the treasure, once revealed, is found to be wanting?"

"One cannot tell by mere looking," he said. "The treasure must be tasted, its flavor discovered." He took a section of the orange and ran the edge of it over her bottom lip, then coaxed her to take a bite.

His gaze was intent on her mouth. "You see? Its juice must be allowed to caress the tongue, its sweetness sliding into the mouth's dark mysteries. And then . . ." He stroked the front of her neck with a light touch. "And then to spill down the throat, and thus appease the appetite."

A droplet of juice hovered on her lip, and he touched it, then blatantly licked his fingertip with his tongue. "The treasure is not found wanting."

Her pulse was beating much too fast for clear thought, but she garnered her wits as best she could. "I fear, monsieur, that it would be found wanting—by those who have tasted better fruits."

He raised an eyebrow in appreciation. "And have you, madame?"

She let a beat of silence pass, then held out her hand,

palm upward. "The scarf, monsieur. Thank you for return-ing it."

His dark eyes looked into hers. "I do what any French-man would do," he murmured. With a quick twist of his hand, he looped the silk around her wrist and held it taut so that her arm was outstretched in front of him.

"Monsieur le comte!" She tried to politely pull her hand away, but he held it firmly.

He drew her wrist upward and kissed it through the silk. "Such a delicate material. Already I can feel the heat of your skin warming it." He kissed her wrist again, a long, tasting kiss. "I can even feel your pulse against my lips."

He stood, releasing his hold on the scarf. "And that, too, is a rhythm of nature." He reached above her and plucked a rose, then strewed the perfumed lavender-pink petals over her lap. "Enjoy your solitude, madame," he said, and walked back down the path.

Eleonora hurried along the tall hedges. What had been a simple pathway seemed to have become a maze. Which way had she come? Was she to turn right at the statue of Ganymede, or was it left? She went left. No, no, she'd passed no fountain of Bacchus on her way to the bower! She came upon the center lawn unexpectedly and had to sidestep a servant clearing away the remains of dinner to keep from colliding with him.

She walked as fast as was acceptable. Her step was un-steady. She felt unhinged with anger at herself for allow-ing her skin to feel the heat of his touch. In her mind, she began chanting a canticle learned years ago to keep her thoughts from drifting into dangerous channels. The sanc-tuary of her bedroom was all she wanted. To be alone.

Eleonora reached the door to her rooms with an audible sigh of relief. The latch lifted easily, and the door opened nearly of its own accord.

"Thanks be," she exhaled, slumping against the back of the door, eyes closed. She sucked in a breath, then let it out slowly.

Memories welled up, of the time just past, and of other

times—mornings and afternoons and nights. "Miklos, Miklos," she whispered, "you cursed me often enough. Would you curse me now—or laugh?"

No answer came into the yawning silence, no sound—except for a tiny *clack* of wood striking wood. Like a lid closing on a wooden box. Eleonora's eyes snapped open.

Tante Geneviève sat on the edge of the high four-poster bed, feet dangling as she guiltily tried to push away the box in which Eleonora had stashed her mother's notes. Her stomach tightened, but a quick glance to the corner between the wardrobe and the wall showed her that the rolled parchment remained undisturbed.

"Oh, dear. Oh, dear," Geneviève said, plucking at the counterpane. "I only just peeked." She glanced at Eleonora, almost wincing from the expected anger. "There's really no excuse for my being here. I'm just a nosy old busybody. Du Peyre is always saying so."

Eleonora thought of her own unhappy married life and forced a friendly smile. "And *I* say how nice it is of you to greet me after that lovely dinner."

She went and sat down on the bed next to Geneviève. "It had been longer than I'd remembered since I'd eaten . . ." *Sweet fruit from a man's fingers* . . . "Since I'd eaten truffled partridge."

Geneviève looked unhappy. "I've failed you, my dear. Here you are, so beautiful and well bred." Eleonora flinched, but said nothing. "I should have known your dear mother was sending you here to find a husband. Why didn't Delphine just come out and tell me? Your family has more land than the king of France, I'd wager, so finding a suitable—"

"No, Tante," Eleonora broke in. She patted the older woman's clasped hands. "No, I'm not here to—"

"Why deny it, my dear? I saw enough of what's in the box to know your mother was trying to coach you in how to get on." She shook her head sadly. "It's just that du Peyre insisted on inviting this raucous bunch of . . . Well, that's not to the point. Suffice it to say that most of the men here are already married—and most are scurrilous enough not to want you to know it."

"Really, Tante, I came here only to get away from constant talk of war. Charles Albert, Maria Theresa, Frederick, Louis ..." Eleonora squeezed her eyes shut, not knowing who had the greater bloodlust: her brothers or her mother. Their enemies were different, but the annihilation they so relished was the same.

"Frederick of Prussia invaded Silesia," Eleonora began, reciting a litany she'd heard much too often. "Maria Theresa wants it back. Charles Albert of Bavaria wants to be elected Holy Roman Emperor—an honor held by Maria Theresa's family for far too long, he says—so he sides with Frederick. And Louis of France wants to be lord of all Europe and sides first with Frederick, then Maria Theresa, and now flirts with Frederick again. But everyone knows where all this royal *wanting* is leading—to war. I was about to go mad from it all."

When she opened her eyes she found Geneviève staring at her in shock. "Talk of war? Oh, you poor dear! Don't you worry now. I know what *really* matters."

Geneviève trailed off, her finger tapping the side of her nose. "There are few eligible men here—but I can invite more, no matter what du Peyre says. Uhmmm. There's St. Trivier ... No, he wouldn't do. He's so poor, he has his coats made out of old family tapestries. There is de Solennel." She giggled and gave Eleonora a sly glance. "No, I don't think so. He and the pastry chef ..." She crossed two fingers and wiggled them.

"Then there is de Claix or St. Juste ... Uhmmm. Possibilities, possibilities. That leaves only d'Agenais, but of course, *he's* out of the picture."

Eleonora's heart thumped heavily in her chest. "Because he's married?" she asked.

Geneviève shuddered. "What a notion! Mark my words—he'll end up in the Bastille before he'll end up in front of a priest. There are probably a dozen *lettres de cachet* out there with his name on it. They just haven't caught up with him yet."

"Lettres de cachet? Royal warrants of arrest?" Eleonora asked. Were his murders not to be condoned, after all? she wondered, then added with feigned nonchalance, "I would have expected to find clutches of females clinging to him, not jailers."

"No one clings to d'Agenais, my dear. Which is not to say they don't try. The foolish ones, anyway. Handsome as the devil—he *is* the devil, if you ask me—he was a wild youth who did not improve with age." Geneviève shrugged. "And a *lettre de cachet* is a convenience, something to be used or not used, depending on the whim of the person holding it. D'Agenais answers to no one's whims, though there are jailers aplenty waiting for him."

And those jailers were not all in France, Eleonora thought. "You imply a great deal, Tante."

Geneviève patted her hands. "You are an innocent, my dear. It's best you stay that way."

Eleonora turned away to hide a bitter smile from her aunt. "No, Tante, I am not. Can any woman be innocent who has seen her husband's dead body on a field of battle?" *Or her lover's after the Turks have captured him?* she added silently.

Her aunt shook her head and *tsk*ed at the horror of it all. "At least I am comforted knowing your Miklos wasn't fighting the French when he was killed."

"No, the honor of fighting the French went to my brothers. Two of them, anyway. Christophe was too young at the time, to his eternal irritation, but Endres and Gabriel fought at Philippsburg." Eleonora picked up the box of her mother's notes and stroked the smooth polished surface with her fingertips. *Where they saw d'Agenais, the devil's son, fighting with all the bloodlust of his father. How else would I know to be here?*

Geneviève gasped. "They weren't hurt, were they?"

"They found their wounds most satisfactory. None were mortal. It was left to Miklos to die in battle. They were quite put out with him for upstaging them."

"D'Agenais fought at Philippsburg," Geneviève said. "The stories are endless about his valor. You'd think after all those duels he keeps fighting, that someone would have figured out that he was hardly shy with a sword!" She pursed her lips. "But no, gossip about his courage eclipsed that of his sins for nearly a year. His Majesty even raised him from chevalier to comte—the nobility of the sword ever rewards itself, I've noticed!—and he was fêted wherever he was still received. Which was almost everywhere." Her aunt lifted her eyebrows and sighed, as if to wonder at the world's foolishness. "And envied. Oh, how he was envied! Until that business in Paris with the Rachands."

"What business, Tante?" *The business of murder?* she wanted to ask.

Geneviève snorted. "By the saints, *I* don't know the truth of it. No one does, I'd wager. Ask *him!*" She screwed up her face, as if thinking hard. "Three men dead. The king's mistress put it out that they were fighting over *her,* though everyone knows d'Agenais had turned down her 'invitation.' I'd bet my best ruby earrings that no woman had anything to do with it." Tante's hand went to her ears, and she reassuringly rubbed the pearl and red stone drops. "Well, at least my garnets."

Eleonora wanted to ask more, but a maid scratched at the door and slipped in at her mistress's call.

The wide-eyed girl curtsied deep, then held out a folded and sealed note. "I was told to deliver this to your hands, madame la comtesse."

Geneviève abruptly stood. "By whom, girl?"

Brown eyes darted to the marquise du Peyre, then back to her mistress, but Eleonora had turned the seal to the afternoon sun and ignored her. The girl curtsied again. "Your pardon, madame, but I do not know. A footman gave it to me." Eleonora looked up and forced a smile of thanks before nodding the girl's dismissal.

The door clicked shut, leaving Eleonora alone once again with her aunt. "Well?" Geneviève asked. "Aren't you going to open it?"

Eleonora rubbed her thumb over the seal. *The d'Agenais lanner falcon.* "Perhaps later, Tante."

Geneviève smiled with satisfaction as she made her way

to the door. "A *billet-doux* already, my dear? How lovely."
A frown creased the woman's brow. "It isn't from one of
those married scoundrels, is it? You must be careful of
tho—"

"No," Eleonora interrupted, "no, it isn't from one of the
married scoundrels." She put her fingers to her forehead as
if she had a headache. "Please believe me, Tante. I am not
here to find a husband. I merely came to find peace." *The
peace that comes from retribution won—for a family that
has been denied it for too long.*

Geneviève nodded knowingly. "Of course, of course,
my dear. I'm sure you'll find what you're looking for at
château du Peyre." The door clicked closed behind her.

Eleonora collapsed onto the bed, the unopened note in
her hand. There was still a faint taste of the juice from the
orange in her mouth, and she swallowed. Damn her for a
fool! Being in the bower with d'Agenais had been but another hand in the deadly serious game she played, but she
remembered it all too vividly, and she did not want to remember; it was exactly what d'Agenais would expect.

She looked up. On the silk lining the inside of the bed's
canopy, a picturesque tableau had been painted of a de-
mure wood nymph fleeing a pursuing satyr. She and
d'Agenais? In the background was another pair, a laughing
nymph this time, one who was successfully keeping her
pursuer at bay.

How she envied that nymph. She glanced at the clock
on the mantelpiece, the porcelain portrayal of Artemis van-
quishing her audacious lover. She looked back to the note
in her hand. "How do I play it, d'Agenais? You think this
a game—but it's a duel." She narrowed her eyes and
tapped her bottom lip with a corner of the folded paper.
"A *duel* . . ."

She rose to her elbow, her brother Christophe's voice
loud in her mind. *"Feint and retreat, El! Feint and retreat.
Make your enemy come to you."*

She gave a derisive laugh. She had certainly managed
the "retreat" part. *Now,* she thought, sliding her finger

under the d'Agenais seal to break it, *if only I can manage a "feint."*

She unfolded the thick white paper. Petals of a damask rose drifted into her lap, their scent perfuming the air. The note was blank—except for the scroll of an elegant *A* written in the lower right corner.

Touché, she thought, *but no first blood, d'Agenais. That honor will be mine.*

There were two harpsichords in the château du Peyre, and Achille made his way through the halls toward the second of them. The first, an elaborate German one, was in the grand music room, a room usually full of chattering, flirting men and women, a room he knew the Hungarian countess would avoid.

Strains of an unfamiliar melody filled the air as he neared the paneled door. He lifted the latch and entered, neither overly careful to be quiet, nor raucous enough to be deliberately noticed. It was a habit with him, to give free rein to Fate: he courted her as much as any mortal woman, for Fate's gifts were precious and rare and often provocatively unexpected.

The room was a small one for the château, made smaller by a screen set against a far corner to shield the sight of accompanying musicians. He sat on a nearby chair and was content to listen as the countess Batthyány continued playing. He regarded her, intently studying the written music in front of her as her fingers moved over the keyboard. He noticed a bowl of rose petals set to one side on the harpsichord, and he raised an eyebrow at it. She must have had a servant gather more to add to what he'd sent. It was a gesture neither coy nor sentimental, and he was more impressed than he wanted to be.

A false note made her stop. She canted her head to one side and played the phrase again more slowly. Even though she was practicing a new piece, her fingering was firm and sure, and she played the notes again and again, increasing their tempo each time, until the music flowed allegro as it had been written. Then, seamlessly, she began to play the piece once more from the beginning.

It was a piece he had not heard before, but the style was familiar. Speculation flitted through his mind about the obscure countess who must have connections at the far-from-obscure court of Vienna, where Bonni was court musician. He frowned, an uneasy feeling niggling at him that all the pieces of their game were not yet on the game board.

Another false note. "Bah!" she exclaimed, and switched to the last few bars of the extravagant and extremely difficult ending of Fux's *Gradus ad Parnassum*. At the end, her hands flew into the air. "You see, Master Bonni, there are a *few* pieces I can play."

"More than a few, I would wager," Achille said, and had the satisfaction of seeing her start with surprise. She had not known he was there. Good. A woman who could become absorbed by music could be guided into becoming absorbed with him. For a short while, at least. "Madame, you play with skill and inspiration," he added. "Two attributes of which I am most fond."

The countess rose and stood by the harpsichord, one hand touching it like a singer beginning a recital. "Inspiration? Temper is more like, monsieur," she said. Her eyes slowly lowered to the floor—did they pause almost imperceptibly on the bowl of petals?—then she raised them to him. "Are you fond of that, too?"

"At times, madame." He rose from the chair and went to the instrument. "Anger can warm the blood as satisfactorily as any other emotion." He stirred the rose petals with his finger, spilling some of them onto the polished surface, then crushed a petal between his fingers and waved it beneath his nose. "So long as it isn't *only* anger that warms the blood."

He thought he saw her flush, but it was difficult to tell in the late afternoon light. She turned away and then, to his surprise, she chuckled. "Anger is more likely to stir up apoplexy than passion, I should think. But music, now . . ."

"Ah, madame, you read my heart." He sat down at the

harpsichord and began to play the Fux piece from the beginning.

She spun around at the sound of the first measure. "You play?" she asked, astonishment clear in her voice.

"As often as possible, madame." His fingers raced over the keys allegro. "Occasionally, I even play music." This time she *did* flush, and he stopped in midmeasure.

She leaned on the polished wood lid. "Please continue."

Her face was closer now, her lips slightly parted as she waited for him to resume. "I shall," he said with a slight smile, his gaze brushing the full breasts that mounded above the tight bodice of her pale blue gown. "Lean closer," he coaxed, and she did.

He played a short piece full of minor thirds. It was easy to let the sound flow over him, through him. Alone, he would have closed his eyes and savored the delicious visions the notes conjured in his mind.

Her head rested on her hand, and her beguiling green eyes were softly focused, her lids slightly lowered as she took in the music he played. Her ivory skin had been flushed to gold by the long rays of the late afternoon sun. A curl of her hair lay against her graceful neck.

He fancied a droplet of juice slowly making its way down that exquisite length, and he fancied himself licking that sweet droplet from her flesh. He had kept himself from tasting her in the bower, but soon that restraint would be rewarded, he promised himself, for the taste of passion on her flesh would be sweeter than any fruit.

"Do you know this?" he asked, playing a chord, a minor third. He watched to see if she knew what that particular progression of sounds meant.

She shook her head, still absorbed in the music. He ended abruptly. "Do you know what it means?"

"Means?" she echoed. A languid smile slid over her lips, and he imagined such a smile on her face after a long, slow crescendo to ecstasy. "Is it a pastoral?" she asked. A delicious laugh bubbled from her throat, as if she'd drunk a glass too much of wine. "Not more cavorting nymphs!"

"Not a nymph, madame countess. These three notes mean a mortal woman awaiting her lover's touch."

"And what notes portray a man, monsieur le comte?"

He played a major third without taking his eyes from her face. "A mortal man—fulfilled."

Her eyelids lowered and a fingertip began tracing the edge of the harpsichord. "In music as in life. The woman waits, the man is fulfilled." She straightened. "Better the nymphs, I think," she began, digging her fingers in the rose petals. She scattered them over the keys as he played. "They, at least, occasionally enjoy themselves."

She swept him a deep curtsy. "I am most grateful for the music lesson. Good evening, monsieur le comte."

He nodded, letting her walk from his sight. He waited for her to reach the door before he played a minor third followed quickly by a major third. "Good evening, madame la . . ." the door latch clicked closed ". . . nymph."

Achille stared at the silent keyboard, his hands still resting on the petal-covered keys. Maddening, she was. But not a lowly nymph. No . . . He smiled. Nothing so lowly as that. His fingers struck a minor third. "You are Artemis herself, aren't you, my countess? The goddess of the hunt, ever elusive—until she met Orion the hunter. Beware the hunt, Madame Batthyány, because, unlike Orion, I shall not lose."

Another evening of cards. Eleonora swallowed a groan and kept her smile pasted in place as she sauntered in the wake of Tante Geneviève through the Green Salon. Tables had already been set up; apparently her aunt, flush from her previous winnings, wasn't about to let dancing take up precious time that could be spent so much more profitably.

"Oh, dear," Geneviève said, stopping in midstride and turning back to Eleonora, "it's most unfortunate, but I really must introduce you to those arrivals from last night." She led Eleonora to a group of three standing by a far table partially obscured by a potted orange tree. One of the three, the gossipy Vicomte de Vigny, she already knew, and Geneviève introduced the other two as the marquis and marquise de Rachand.

The marquis was the man d'Agenais had played cards with the night before, the one who had called the comte a murderer. A man in his mid-thirties who seemed to bulge from his too snug clothes, he squinted at Eleonora with the look of someone who'd missed a meal and was now gazing at a stuffed pheasant. Eleonora returned only the most banal pleasantries; he gave a shrug and excused himself.

His wife, Joëlle, the marquise de Rachand, smiled graciously if a bit distractedly. "Lovely, Madame du Peyre," she said to the older woman. "Quite lovely. A pity we're not at court just now. I know a desperate fellow who would pay a most handsome *gratuitie* for such a prize as Madame Batthyány. Even if she is a foreigner."

Geneviève looked uncomfortable. "Most handsome?" she asked with a glance at Eleonora that was full of guilty avarice. French courtiers and their wives were notorious throughout Europe for their greed. The court at Paris was ruinously expensive, and they had learned to turn everything to profit. Matchmaking, Eleonora had heard, had proven one of the more lucrative ventures, as was doing favors for the king's mistress.

"Most handsome," Madame de Rachand repeated absently, her eyes scanning the crowd behind Geneviève and Eleonora. Vigny chuckled, and Joëlle sent him a glare of disgust.

A servant came up just then and took Geneviève away to deal with a minor crisis. Joëlle watched her go, then hissed at Vigny. "Where is d'Agenais? He hasn't bolted after that paltry game with my husband last night, has he? I'm not traveling another league, even if I am on the king's business."

Vigny smiled at the marquise. "The king's *mistress's* business is more like. She still hasn't forgiven d'Agenais for turning her down, has she?" At an impatient glance from Madame de Rachand, he went on, "Oh, he hasn't bolted, I promise you, madame. But he's hardly likely to dance on a table so you can espy him." The vicomte's smile turned sly as he bowed toward Eleonora. "Forgive my rudeness, Madame Batthyány, but the marquise searches for a former . . . ah, *attachment.*"

Joëlle swatted Vigny with her fan. "The comtesse is not a child, Vigny." She let her gaze focus on Eleonora for a moment. "The comte d'Agenais and I were lovers, madame. I have come here to speak to him about . . . an urgent matter."

Eleonora's life had taught her too well to keep her emotions hidden, so her shock did not shake her outward composure. Out of the corner of her eyes, she saw skepticism flash across Vigny's expressive face before it returned to its usual blandness.

"If the House of Rachand is expecting an heir," Vigny said, glancing as nonchalantly as he could at the marquise's small waist, "I should perhaps mention that the comte d'Agenais left the château de Gemeaux, the site of your last meeting, more than seven months ago."

"An heir! My God, what a notion." La Rachand shuddered, then snapped his arm with her fan again. "Don't be an ass, Vigny. I *know* when he left Gemeaux. Why do you think I'm here, fool?"

"To recoup your husband's losses, perhaps?"

"Recoup? For what? So he can lose again?" La Rachand asked, not quite convincingly. "I'm sure you've heard about last night."

Vigny bowed to her. "Luck smiled on Monsieur d'Agenais."

"She smiles much too often, if you ask me," the marquise said. "Though that, too, can change." She leaned toward Eleonora and squeezed her arm. "One way or another."

Eleonora gave her a polite smile. The marquise seemed disappointed and pulled back. "One way or another," she repeated, then scanned the assembling crowd. With a huff of disgust, she excused herself and moved on.

Vigny gave Eleonora a sympathetic glance. "Madame de Rachand has much on her mind."

"Her husband's losses must be a great worry."

The gossip ran his eyes up and down Eleonora, a knowing smile curving his lips. "Perhaps. Though Joëlle's . . . interests . . . are rumored to be varied."

There was a subtle change in the hum of the crowd, like a change of key in a melody, and Eleonora instinctively looked at the entrance. D'Agenais stood there dressed in burgundy velvet trimmed in black, making her think of a heady wine to be tasted in the dark of night.

Vigny waved to catch the comte's attention. No, she thought, she didn't want to be seen with him in so public a place. Little could be accomplished before so many watchful eyes. She made to move off, but Vigny detained her with a hand on her arm.

"I don't believe you've been formally introduced to the comte d'Agenais," he said, the light of mischief bright in his eyes.

"I . . ." Eleonora averted her eyes from the approaching comte, as was proper for a man and a woman who had not been formally introduced.

"Here he is," Vigny said, bowing to d'Agenais. "Madame, though your aunt should perform such a service, I know she will not, so may I? Here is Monsieur d'Agenais, a well . . . respected hero of the last war. And, monsieur— here is Madame Batthyány, a charming visitor from Hungary, though I believe she lives in Vienna, as do so many of her countrymen."

The comte gave her a bow of the greatest disinterest. "Madame," he said, his voice flat.

"Monsieur," she answered back as flatly, and gave him as impersonal a curtsy as she could, considering his rank. Vigny looked disappointed.

"Look! Everyone is settling into play," the gossip said. He gestured toward an unoccupied table nearby. "Perhaps a game of mort?"

D'Agenais slid him a glance of the utmost disdain.

Eleonora snapped open her fan and said, "I do not like any kind of whist. Even three-handed."

"Ombre, perhaps?"

Eleonora opened her mouth to refuse, but d'Agenais

forestalled her. "A short game," he said, then gave her the briefest of nods and turned back to Vigny. "If Madame wishes."

Vigny eagerly pulled out a chair for her. She graciously acknowledged d'Agenais and sat down. "It might prove more amusing than watching others play."

As their self-appointed host, Vigny signaled for wine to be brought, then arranged for a pack of cards. She and the comte sat at right angles to each other and remained distantly polite. No one would ever guess that she had eaten fruit from his fingers, or that she had strewn rose petals across his hands.

The cards were presented on a silver salver, but when Vigny picked them up, he scowled at them and then at the servant. "These are the wrong cards. We require a Spanish pack, you fool!" He rose and bowed to them. "Excuse me a moment," he said, and marched off.

D'Agenais sipped his wine and studied a chandelier hanging above a nearby table. "And how does your search for a husband progress?" he asked, not changing his pose.

"My aunt talks a great deal too much," she said, her insipid smile never faltering. "I do not wish to find a husband. A husband is an annoyance, and marriage is a cruel penance imposed on schoolgirls for sins not yet committed."

"And what of the sins of Mother Eve?"

"Those have surely been paid for in full. And what of the sins of Adam? He could just as easily have declined that bite and saved us all a great deal of trouble."

"Ah, the tempter versus the tempted," he said, his voice musing and seductive, though she knew no one could discern that from his apparent indifference. "The seducer or the seduced. Who is to blame?"

"The one who falls. The one who is weak."

"You are harsh. One has already fallen—the seducer. Is she weak?"

"She? Women are rarely seducers."

"A rarity, to be sure. But not unknown."

Vigny returned then, and the comte diverted their conversation to the banal and once again became the bored guest. She had wanted their . . . game . . . to be kept private, but why did *he?* Surely it wasn't kindness that made him spare her becoming the object of lascivious gossip.

He could have easily insinuated a great deal to Vigny, yet he had not. His manner had made it clear that they were strangers, and that they were destined to remain so.

Such noble consideration, she thought sarcastically. *A devil's son would never be so—*

"Your play," the comte d'Agenais pointed out with a haughty fatigue only a Frenchman could convey.

—so full of subtleties and stratagems.

She played her card. And lost.

D'Agenais smiled blandly. "It seems you have underestimated your opponent."

She met his gaze. "It seems I may have. Another hand?"

Chapter 4

Achille rose early the next morning. He slipped naked from between the silk sheets and stretched his tall, lithe body in the long rays of sunshine. There was a spice of anticipation in the air, as if he had trod upon a curl of cinnamon.

He bathed in water scented with sandalwood, then dressed in his black robe before settling down to a cup of thick, sweet coffee and the verses of his favorite troubadour, Bernard de Ventadour.

The old poetry was a link with his father. The two of them had sat for hours by the window in the library, reading through the aged manuscripts, the boy stumbling over the archaic French, the father smiling. The works of the troubadours were little known, but Achille had had the manuscripts transcribed by monks still learned in the art, and bound in the finest leather. Those, and a few more recent books, by Voltaire and Montesquieu, he always carried with him.

Once, his books had been a source of joy. But over the last year, after Paris, after what he'd done, his books had become a refuge from the darkness of remorse. They had seemed his only refuge, but recently it had seemed that lightness was beginning to creep into the darkness. Perhaps salvation would not prove as elusive as he'd once expected.

Oh, good and desirable love, he began reading, and an image of an exotic dark-haired beauty had begun to form in his mind when a scratch on the door interrupted him.

Beaulieu answered it, then came and bowed to Achille. "Monsieur du Peyre," the steward said with a roll of his eyes. Achille reflected unpleasantly on the duties of guest to host, then put his book and his imaginings aside and nodded.

A moment later, the door slammed open on a cursing marquis du Peyre, who hobbled in with the aid of a walking stick.

The marquis swatted at the helpful Beaulieu. "Leave me alone, you cursed fool." The steward departed without a trace of reluctance. Du Peyre dropped himself into a chair opposite the comte's. "Wives should be put away in the country."

"This is the country," the comte said reasonably.

"Preferably *another* country." Du Peyre snorted, then smacked the table with his fist. "Damn fool woman. Tells that blighted niece of hers she can use my best hunter. Tonnerre!" He shifted in the chair with an embarrassed glance at the comte.

"So, d'Agenais, I've had to call off the hunting for today." Du Peyre wistfully gazed out the window at the beautiful morning. "And on such a day." He sighed. "Stubborn old— Never marry, d'Agenais. Never, never, never—" He smacked the table again. *"Tonnerre!* Can you believe it? If he comes back with so much as a strained . . . Why that precious cat-eyed *niece* of Geneviève's had to pick *this* morning . . . Well, I told her! 'No horse of mine,' I said, 'no horse of mine goes out before *nine!'* "

Du Peyre stood, leaning heavily on his stick. "Good talkin' with you, d'Agenais. Don't know why that fool woman complains you're such a devil. Damn fine thing for a man to be." He looked glum and started hobbling out. "An *unmarried* man. Damn fool woman . . ." He bent his knee to kick at a heavy chair, then stopped with a curse. "Already did that. Damn toe's probably broken . . ." The door closed on his mutterings.

Achille took another sip of coffee, studying the day outside. A few moments passed before he glanced at the clock. Eight-twenty. He rang for his valet, who entered silently and bowed.

"I shall be hunting as planned," the comte told him.

A half hour later, Achille was walking through a gilt-mirrored salon on his way to the stables when a woman rushed up behind him.

"Monsieur!" she called. It was Madame de Rachand.

Achille was tempted not to respond. They were alone in the room. He glanced out the doors to the terrace, already anticipating meeting the Hungarian countess. The glint of excitement he'd seen in her green eyes when he'd mentioned riding flashed through his memory. He had plans to divert that excitement to himself.

"D'Agenais! D'Agenais, you will acknowledge me!" The marquise's voice shook with indignation.

He turned and gave her a slight bow. "Will I, madame?"

"You black-eyed—" Her eyes narrowed with anger at the affront he'd given her. She spun away from him, her wide hooped skirts following after a moment's hesitation. "You have been silent for over seven months. You haven't even tried to see me. Did our time together at Gemeaux mean nothing to you?"

"An hour in the hedges?" His stomach clenched in disgust at the memory, though he lifted only an eyebrow. "Do you think I would go to so great an inconvenience as to follow a woman merely on the promise of her bed? Little that is memorable can be accomplished in shrubbery." Unexpectedly the scent of damask roses and the taste of oranges came to mind. "Though occasionally . . ."

"I told Madame de Chateauroux you wouldn't listen," La Rachand said, scowling. "But the king's mistress wanted to give you one last chance. She is no fool, though, d'Agenais. She knows you think of no one but yourself."

Some might think that La Rachand's scowling face under the overwhelming powdered coiffure was pretty. He considered it tedious, a perfect reflection of the woman underneath. "At the moment, I am thinking of my ride, madame." He nodded and turned to go.

"Think of this, monsieur—the king's mistress wants you back in Paris. She's forgiven you. Think of the power that awaits you. The . . . opportunities for your devil's amusements. La Chateauroux can make sure anything is forgotten. Even *your* transgressions, d'Agenais."

"*I* have not forgotten them." He smiled slightly. "Nor do I mean to."

She looked disgruntled. "Can you never be satisfied? Do you even know what *would* satisfy you? How can a man as selfish as you turn down money, power, influence? It is all any man could want."

"I am not *any* man, madame." He studied her face, but she would not meet his eyes. "How little you know of me." He rubbed his thumb across his fingertips, the black suede of his riding gloves molding itself perfectly to his hand. "How little anyone knows of me. Or of my transgressions. My selfishness is of its own kind. It is not *pandered* to by a king's mistress . . ." his voice took on a finely honed steel edge ". . . or her procuress."

La Rachand sucked in her breath at the insult. She picked up a porcelain figurine—"You go too far!" she screeched—and threw it at him.

He didn't move. It missed him and crashed into a wall behind him. "La Chateauroux must have offered to pay you a great deal," he said casually. "Ten, twenty thousand louis? Or is your husband to be paid with a lucrative appointment at court? With enough corrupt skill and graft, one could easily make fifty or even a hundred thousand."

She laughed bitterly. "Nearer two hundred thousand." She turned narrowed eyes on him. "La Chateauroux will not forgive you twice, d'Agenais. Refuse her this time, and who knows what may happen? It would be easier on all of us if you went back to Paris. Yes, Rachand needs that appointment, but you . . . you're alone, d'Agenais. Can't you see that? And unless you return to Paris, you'll always be alone. La Chateauroux will see to that."

"I shall be leaving shortly," he told her. She smiled with

both relief and triumph, until he continued. "To be with the army in Bavaria."

"No! Let me tell her you'll come back."

"You may tell the king's mistress that I heed the call of the king—not the king's whore."

"You fool!" she screamed. She pushed a chair out of her way, the delicate legs scraping loudly on the marble floor. "Think what you do—"

"Think what *you* do the next time you agree to be a whore's pander."

"*Bastard!* Rachand said you would never agree."

Achille closed up inside. His vision pulsed red, became a point of rage, hot and dagger-sharp. He started toward her.

"*D'Agenais, no!*" she cried, backing away. She dragged the chair in front of her. "I didn't mean—"

He grabbed the chair and flung it away. An ear-shattering crash resounded off the walls when it hit a mirror. Sparkling shards spun dizzily in the morning sunlight.

The marquise ran shrieking from the room. "You'll pay for this!"

It took but a moment before calm settled back on him, fading the red from his sight and returning the comfort of his senses to him.

"I agree," said a voice from the doorway. The countess Batthyány stepped into the room, nonchalantly lifting her skirts above the shattered glass. "That mirror did make the room much too bright."

He folded his arms and waited. How long had she been there? And would she now turn coy? The glass crunched under her riding boots as she walked toward the terrace doors. She gave him the slightest nod as she passed. "After all, monsieur, why would one want to reflect light into dark corners?"

He gave her a bow that managed to acknowledge her mocking question. "Why, indeed, madame? Light can be so distracting."

"You are easily distracted, then? A pity. But perhaps

that explains why someone in Paris scurries to be your keeper."

" 'Scurries,' madame?"

" 'Scurries,' monsieur. Like rats in a dark corner." She walked through the terrace doors and out into the morning sun.

Achille watched her go. He smiled and followed. After all, it was du Peyre's hunt that had been canceled, not his.

At the stables, the countess lost some of her composure when Achille's bay-colored horse was led out to stand next to du Peyre's hunter.

"No, I'm sorry, you mistake the matter," she told the groom saddling her horse. "I ride alone."

The groom looked shocked, but Achille forestalled the man's protests. "It's foolhardy to ride alone," he said. "What would happen if your horse stepped in a rabbit hole and came up lame?"

"Then I would walk."

"What if *you* came up lame?"

"Then I would *crawl,* monsieur. I wish .to ride alone."

He lowered his eyes to hide a stab of pique. "Why, madame? A tryst, perhaps?"

She mounted with the groom's help, then turned to Achille while expertly controlling the impatient beast beneath her. Green eyes dark with anger scoured his face. "You insult me, monsieur. Do not judge others' actions by your own." She wheeled the horse around and bounded away toward the east.

Achille cursed under his breath. "Groom," he said with steel in his voice, his eyes never leaving the countess's retreating form, "a louis d'or if you have Chiron saddled before she's out of sight."

The groom's eyes widened at the promise of such riches, then he rushed to comply. Achille mounted just as the telltale puff of dust from the countess's horse reached the crest of a hillock. He flipped the groom one gold piece, then another. "You did not saddle my horse and you did not see where I went." The groom grinned his understanding and nodded, gripping the money tightly.

Achille heeled Chiron into a leaping gallop toward the sun and the hillock where the countess had disappeared. The animal thundered down the road, dirt and mud from a spring rain flinging out from his hooves. Achille's blood pounded with the chase. His breathing deepened, became faster; it needed only his sword in his hand to kindle the bloodlust of a cavalry charge.

He rounded the crest of the hillock at a full gallop. A racing horse was barely discernible on the road far ahead. Tonnerre's power and swiftness had never been thoroughly tested under the inept hands of the marquis du Peyre, but now it seemed the animal was finally tasting the glory of beast and skilled rider becoming one.

Achille leaned further over his horse's neck, urging the animal on even faster. His senses responded, immersing him in that glorious dream state of wind whipping his unpowdered hair, gloved hands on the reins reacting with instant precision, the muscles of his body extending, contracting, in concert with the great power he controlled beneath him. The smells of horse and fresh-turned earth were headier than the finest wine.

He followed her still, through the shallow valley and up a high hill. The road skirted the edge of an ink green forest to his left, the brown trunks of the trees blurring as if he saw them through rain-smeared glass.

The road began to twist and turn. Again and again he lost sight of her, only to regain it an instant later. Did she know he was following her? Did she care?

He crested the hill and started to descend, then pulled up sharply when he saw no sign of her. His eyesight was keen, but nothing moved on the steep road that led down to a river that cut through the floor of the valley.

A steep escarpment ran along the edge of the valley. To the south was mostly open country with a few scattered trees. To the north, the trees were thicker, and the escarpment rose ever higher to a promontory that jutted out over the river valley.

Movement caught his eye. There. She rode just inside the line of trees, heading for the promontory. He sat watching her, breathing hard from his exertion, and without realizing it, his right hand curled into a fist. The horse lifted his head in protest at the unexpected tug on the reins. Achille looked down. Of itself, his body had taken on the position of attack.

He kneed his horse into the forest and made his way toward the promontory.

Eleonora spread her arms out toward the sun and smiled. The promontory was covered with soft grass and a few large, smooth boulders whose tops barely broke the surface of the ground. In the shade of a magnificent plane tree, several pools of rainwater had formed in pockets in the stone, and the horse that had given her such an excellent ride slurped noisily behind her.

Her smile widened in satisfaction. She had outridden the devil comte. A feather-light touch of pride swept over her, then left her. She had *had* to outride him; she needed to be alone to think.

The comte d'Agenais. The demon apparition she'd formed in her mind, and meant to conquer, was coalescing into the comte d'Agenais, the full-blooded man, and it troubled her. It was easy to scheme against the apparition, an unrelentingly evil straw poppet she'd been sent to entice, but the man . . .

When they'd been alone together in the bower, instead of forcing himself on her, he'd merely been provocatively teasing. And again in the music room, he'd seemed to genuinely enjoy listening and playing, though even then he'd turned suggestive. It still niggled at her that, when they'd played cards, his distant manner might have been borne of kindness to keep her from being stained by gossip.

No, she scolded, and shook off her doubts. He was cleverer than most, yes, and more subtle, but the blood of the devil ran deep in him—his rage in the mirrored salon had proved that. And she must remember the men he had murdered. France's king may pardon deaths from dueling, but

Eleonora knew d'Agenais killed because it was in his blood.

The horse nickered behind her. The ride had helped to drown out all the distractions the comte had thrown at her and let her concentrate on strategy. She needed to slow down, to rethink her approach, for the ride had not drummed out d'Agenais's overheard words to Madame de Rachand: *Do you think I would go to so great an inconvenience as to follow a woman merely on the promise of her bed?*

Was that male bluster? she wondered, then waved away the question. The d'Agenais she was coming to know was not the kind of man who blustered over anything. In fact, the man she was coming to know made it seem foolish that she could have ever thought that a few enticing smiles, a sidelong glance here, a delectable pout there, would *voilà!* turn him into a drooling puppy that would follow her wherever she led.

But what would make him follow her? She hugged herself. His touch in the bower had already made her . . . uneasy. What if she had to go even further—to know him more, to know what *would* cause him to . . . so inconvenience himself?

Her mind balked at the images that thought conjured, images of her husband and his pawings. She shuttered off the memory, as if against an ugly storm, and thought instead of the beacon of her duty to her family. The glow of that beacon comforted her, and she straightened her shoulders, ready to return to the château and the task at hand. She would do whatever needed to be done.

She turned back to the horse—and discovered the comte d'Agenais watching her from the shadowed edge of the trees.

It took her only a moment to recover. "Monsieur le comte," she began, putting her hands on her hips, "when a woman says she wants to be alone—"

"It usually means she doesn't."

She canted her head to one side, studying the elegant figure holding his horse's reins, then grinned. "Usually, monsieur. Not always." She wanted to chide him for following, but she had recovered her equanimity, and her voice came out sprightly. It was too wonderful a day to scold.

He led his horse to one of the pools of rainwater, then looked at her from the shadows. "And today?"

She laughed. "Had the horse not been such a splendid ride, I would have answered you with a termagant's scold so fierce, it would have sent a dervish scurrying for cover."

"Or a rat to a dark corner?"

"A *very* dark corner."

"But it was a splendid ride," he began, and stepped out into the sunlight. She stared at him as he took off his gloves. His long, dark hair had come unbound from its queue as he'd ridden, and the straight, thick strands fell well past his shoulders.

His sensuous mouth was lifted in a slight smile, the taut angles of his face sharply delineated, and his black eyes spoke of pleasures sought and pleasures grown wearisome.

The exhilaration she'd felt from the ride and her resolution to trap him evaporated like a flower's perfume on a too hot day. Her body was reacting in unfamiliar ways, and she did not like it.

"Splendid ride?" she echoed, hugging herself again, this time to keep the warmth in her suddenly chilled body. "Yes, yes, it was." She turned away from him to look out over the river valley. "My uncle was most kind to let me ride what must be a prized animal."

D'Agenais came up behind her. "Kind, indeed," he said. Her arms were crossed in front of her, hands on her shoulders, and he drew his fingertips down the length of her fingers, the touch light and tingling.

She took a step away and let her arms fall to her sides. She waved at the view before them. "The valley is beautiful."

"Is it?"

Startled by the question, she glanced at him. His eyes

were on her. "Of course it is," she answered, then turned back to the view.

He came around in front of her and sat down on a boulder a few feet from the edge. "What makes it beautiful?" he asked, his gaze steady on her.

Puzzled, she said, "The trees, the river . . ."

"Come here," he said.

"I can see well enough from here."

"No, madame, you cannot see well enough. Your own words condemn you." His tone challenged her.

She mentally ran through her mother's notes. There were responses aplenty for a man who was raving dementedly about the beauty of her eyes, but nothing for a man who was telling her those eyes couldn't see. She imagined the disinterest that would be in his own dark eyes if she should lose courage and run.

She stepped closer to the edge and craned her neck to peer down. She was used to heights—but not to him. "There's a road leading to the river," she began, then looked at him hopefully.

He rose, more graceful than any man had a right to be, led her back to the boulder, and sat down, bringing her to stand in front of him. "Madame Batthyány," he said in that intimate, caressing voice of his, "I have seen landscapes with trees, a river, and a road that Virgil might have led Dante through on his visit to the Inferno."

He covered his eyes with her hands, the flesh warm under her fingertips. There were no notes to aid her now— and her instincts had fled.

"Tell me what you see." He idly brushed her fingers back and forth as he held her hands to his face. An unfamiliar heat sparked and caught along her nerves like a droplet of resin that had seeped from burning wood and fallen into a flame.

"Do we play a child's game, monsieur?" she said, piqued by the unwanted sensations rippling just under her skin.

She felt the muscles of his face move in a smile. "Not

a *child's* game, madame." She made to pull away, but his light touch was unexpectedly firm. "What do you see?"

How mobile, how telling, is the movement of a face, she thought. What truths about him were even now skittering under her fingertips? She forced her gaze away from him. She did not need truths; she needed only to—

"I see a foolish man sitting on a boulder in front of an even more foolish woman, and both are on a promontory above a *singularly* beautiful river valley."

" 'Beautiful' is an easy word," he said. "It slips out at the slightest provocation. A garden, a statue, a song, all may be called beautiful." He lowered her hands from his eyes, but did not release them.

"Some would call an exotic Hungarian countess beautiful," he murmured, "with her delicate cheekbones canting a hairbreadth more steeply than most, with her eyes slightly slanted, hinting of feline mysteries, with her auburn hair the color of a priceless spice from the East." He rubbed the inside of her wrists with his thumbs. "And with the scent of amber perfuming the pale ivory of her flesh."

Eleonora knew she should answer him in kind, a low, throaty murmur hinting at intimacies beyond mere sight. *Saint Stephen, but I never thought I'd need the skills of a courtesan!* She pulled her hands from his grasp for fear he would sense her unease, and smoothed back a loose curl. A step back, then another. She plucked a broad leaf from the nearby plane tree and crushed it between her fingers, letting its aromatic perfume mask the masculine scent of his sandalwood.

"A fine lesson in the French art of *seeing,* monsieur. Shall we see how attentive a student I am?" She put her hands on her hips and melodramatically swept her gaze over the valley to take in the panorama. "A man sits on a boulder . . . no, a man with long, dark hair sits on a gray boulder . . . mmm, no, still too plain—I need to compete with 'canted cheekbones' and 'feline mysteries'—"

She broke off, caught up in her own game. How difficult it was to describe the black-eyed devil who sat watching her, amusement and patience—the patience of a predator stalking prey—on his too-handsome face. The face was all too familiar; her mother had drawn it a thousand times from memory until the face, if not the man, had haunted Eleonora's every nightmare since childhood ...

Her gaze drifted beyond d'Agenais's shoulder and into the distance—and into the past. "It should be night. A gibbous moon casts deep velvet shadows. A man, taller than most, and sublimely graceful, sits on a pale gray boulder that gleams in the moonlight. The smoothness of the stone's surface, worn by water and wind and time, is at odds with the sharp angles of the man's face. Angles that have been chiseled into marble by the Greeks and bas-relief by the Romans, angles that have been piously drawn by scribes in precious inks made with ruby and lapis and gold, and carved by master woodcutters ...

"Rendered again and again throughout time, the angles and the features are dark and familiar, a constant in our lives, a reassuring image of what all men, everywhere, pray ... *against*. It is a face without peace, without the repose of innocence, without—"

"Without patience, madame."

He came toward her. She put out her hands to stop him. He grabbed her wrists, one in each hand, and closed on her. She stepped backward. He stepped forward. He used his body to press her backward still until she smacked into the trunk of the spreading tree.

"Your imagination sees more than your eyes, Magyar." He held her arms straight out from her sides, pinning them against the heavy branches as his body pinned her against the trunk. "You have been too long in a country whose blood-soaked soil feeds the crops you eat, and whose water runs red in the seasons of war."

She struggled to free herself, but he held her fast. "I am a poor student, then, d'Agenais. You asked me to tell you what I saw." She was breathing hard, her breasts pressing into his chest. "And I did."

His face hovered over hers, his breath puffing warm and moist against her skin. "There is no peace because you give me none," he said, his voice losing its chill. He nipped along her jawline. She tried to twist her head away, but he bent further, his mouth at her ear.

"And, madame," he murmured, "you mentioned innocence, but do you truly *want* innocence?" His tongue flicked inside. She gasped, and her body jerked at the unexpected sensation. He traced the edge of her ear with his tongue, then nibbled at the lobe. "I find it quite banal."

She had ceased seeing anything but a blur of dark hair against white clouds. Without volition, she closed her eyes, as if her sight were now on the inside, sparkling warm and potent. There were no visions of the nightmare devil or his son as his mouth trailed kisses, tiny licking kisses, down her neck, then suckled the delicate flesh he found there.

A moan, her moan, drifted deliciously on the morning breeze. He drew his lips across her face, rubbing lightly against her eyelids. His mouth drifted to hers, and her lips parted, a tiny whimper escaping, but he only touched them, breathing in her breath, then exhaling it back into her. Then . . .

Nothing. His touch was gone. Her skin still pulsed with the feel of him, but it was a memory that warmed her, not his lips. Her body yearned for more, for the completion of a kiss. She blinked her eyes open.

He had backed away, releasing her. His breathing seemed more unsteady than she remembered, but he was watching her coolly. Everyday sounds returned to her in a rush: the horses grazing, the breeze whispering through the treetops, the song of a warbler . . .

"Thank you, monsieur le comte, for the lesson," she said. She straightened, bit by bit, as if she were pulling taut a string that held her together. She made her way to the horse, pressing her lips together to still the insistent tingling, then mounted quickly.

His teasing lips had awakened sensations she thought never to feel again, illicit, wine-drunk sensations. She tightened and loosened her fingers on the reins.

He rested one hand on the saddle's pommel in front of

her, the other behind her. "A lesson of taste, a lesson of sight," he said with a smile.

She let her gaze drop to his face, his mouth. His damnably delicious sensual mouth. *Saint Stephen, help me.*

"What other lessons shall I teach you?"

She watched the teasing words come from his lips. *Saint Stephen, the promises they held . . .*

"Perhaps I am not always to be the pupil," she said, and then before second—rational—thoughts could stop her, she leaned over and kissed him.

She put a hand behind his head and slid her lips over his, parting them, dipping her tongue in to taste his. Then, as quickly as she'd begun, she pulled back.

A quick pressure of her knees, and she and the horse were bounding into the trees.

She reached the road, her heart pounding in her ears. Tufts of grass and dirt flew as she wheeled the horse west, toward the château. In seconds, they were flying down into the shallow valley at a dead run.

Chapter 5

Thunder. The thunder of pounding hooves came from behind her. Trees, then meadow, smudged past like a ruined watercolor. Eleonora urged the horse on. She risked a glance over her shoulder.

She saw a darkness—horse and rider—against the ruddy dirt of the road. A darkness that was gaining on her.

She cursed du Peyre and his stables for not having animals that could outrun a trained cavalry horse. She cursed again—herself, this time—for not realizing that d'Agenais had let her stay ahead of him on her ride out. She'd ridden her brothers' horses often enough, and if French army officers had ones half as good, she was in trouble.

Rousing Magyar curses snapped into the wind like a pennant. Fool! She cursed her traitorous body; she'd known love once. However briefly, however wrong, she'd known *love*. But now the hunger, the burning, the unquenchable ache, shot up inside her like flames rising from stirred embers.

No! How could her body defile her memories like this? No, no, no, she could not believe that the yearning of love could be so easily counterfeited by d'Agenais's skilled artifice.

The thunder of hoofbeats behind her grew louder, nearer. Eleonora leaned lower over the horse's neck, urging him on. The beast had great heart and was giving her his all, but the sound of the approaching storm told her it would not be enough.

She glanced back. D'Agenais was two horse-lengths away. One and a half. One. Blood and hooves pounded in unison. The nose of his horse was at her stirrup.

They were even. He matched her pace, the horses bounding together. He moved his horse closer. His leg pressed just behind hers.

"What are you—" she shouted at him, but the wind stole her words away. His arm snaked out toward her. Her eyes widened. *"You're mad!"* He hooked his arms around her waist and tugged. "D'Agenais, for God's sake!" He tugged again, and she felt herself slipping.

She'd underestimated his strength. There was a powerful soldier's body beneath the silks and the velvets and the brocades. She hissed a curse at him. She tried to hang on. But d'Agenais knew how to judge the motions of her riding exactly.

He pulled her free.

A scream welled up her throat. He propelled her body across the open space between the two speeding horses, the road blurring dizzily below. He threw her into the crook of his other arm and immediately began slowing the horse. Du Peyre's hunter continued down the road at a gallop, heading for home.

"For God's sake, d'Agen—"

"For *my* sake, Magyar," the comte said, and covered her mouth with his.

He kissed her. Hard, thoroughly, his tongue sweeping into her mouth and possessing it. His mouth took demanding sucking kisses from her lips, then plunged in again and again. She wanted to resist, to fight him, but her hands were around his neck, her fingers spread into his hair, holding his mouth to hers.

She sucked his tongue into her mouth. Twined hers around it. Rivulets of sensation flowed and coiled hotter and hotter through her body. She curved into him as if to absorb the heat of him, the promise of him.

A rumble came from low in his throat. His arms tightened their hold. The horse slowed to a walk, the movement rocking them, rousing them, all the rhythms of their bodies swaying together in an elaborate sensual dance.

He nipped sensually at her bottom lip. "Eleonora," he whispered, drawing his open mouth along her jawline. Her head fell back, her eyes closed. Her breath came ragged and uneven. He kissed the base of her throat, then the soft flesh under her chin. His kisses warmed the blood in her veins like brandy held over a flame.

"Achille," she murmured, and drowsily opened her eyes. She drew the strands of his hair through her fingers, then watched the breeze pluck them from her grasp. She traced the angles of his face with a fingertip, touching each contour and wondering if this was indeed a face that had personified darkness to generations of the fearful, or if she had read into it what she wanted to find. Had she not known better, she would have thought his was a face that could be like no other.

He smiled a slow, sensuous smile. "I do not find you banal, my comtesse. I am pleased."

"Banal? You mean you do not find me innocent." She should be insulted, but she laughed instead. "I am a woman, Monsieur d'Agenais. An innocent adult is a simple-minded one. Innocence is best left to children."

His eyes left hers for a moment and stared unfocused into the countryside. "Not to all children."

She had a glimpse then of the man behind the face, a man who had once been a child. An unhappy one? She straightened as best she could, still seated in front of him on the horse. Her mind seemed fuzzy, as if the brandy-warmth in her blood had brought brandy's cloudiness as well.

"I am sorry," she said, putting a hand on his chest to steady herself. Through his shirt, she could feel a solid sheet of muscle. "I did not mean to bring back unpleasant memories."

His gaze returned to her. "You will bring me only pleasant memories," he said. "Very pleasant memories."

His tone was bantering, but she could think of nothing to say. It was her turn to look away into the fields. The

memories she would bring him would be far from pleasant
. . . after Vienna.

He put his finger under her chin and drew her back to
face him. "Why have you come here, Eleonora Sophia
Juliana, Countess Batthyány?"

"Perhaps I came to seduce you."

"And perhaps I might believe you if we had not just
met."

She dropped her gaze. "The marquise du Peyre is my
mother's half-sister. My grandmother married twice. First
to a Frenchman, then to a Hungarian."

"You tell me strategy, madame. I ask for the objective
of the strategy."

"You talk as if I'm Frederick of Prussia maneuvering
into Silesia!"

"As bold and as wily a man as Frederick gives anyone
pause—and so should the daughter of a half-French
mother and a Hungarian father."

"Bold and wily? I would prefer, I think, to be called
'banal.' "

His intimate smile was back. He gave her a quick,
heart-stopping kiss. "No, madame, I think you would not."

The horse crested the last hill before the descent to the
château du Peyre. D'Agenais kneed the horse into the
shadow of a tree and kissed her again, hard and deep, as
if stirring waters he did not want to let settle for a long,
long while.

He raised his head from hers and said, "It will be as you
wish. Strategy alone. The objective I will come upon soon
enough."

Without warning, he dismounted, then set about adjusting the stirrups for her. "Chiron will obey you. He ap-
preciates skill. You may trust that the groom will not
mention the change of horses," he told her as he finished.

"I do trust it, Monsieur d'Agenais. I would guess that
few dare to idly mention anything about you." The horse
bobbed his head and friskily danced to one side until
Eleonora settled it with expert control. "Your horse is worthy of a Magyar."

"It is worthy of a soldier, madame."

"You call me a soldier? Do you think me so full of stratagems, then?"

"I call you a woman. Of course you are full of strategems. That is the game of it, to reveal them one by one . . ." He paused, rubbing her ankle just above the boot tops, his fingers caressing the swell of her calf. "The way a lover's body is revealed in the heat of—"

"The heat of the day has gotten to you, monsieur," she interrupted quickly, and kneed the horse ahead. When there was a safe distance between them, she looked back over her shoulder, and called, "Be careful you don't confuse an 'apt' student with a 'rapt' one!"

"I confuse nothing, madame la comtesse. Nothing at all."

Eleonora arrived back at the stables and quickly dismounted. She saw the look of knowing speculation in the groom's eyes and kept her expression blank. A curse welled up her throat.

Strategy, stratagems—the words, in d'Agenais's voice, hammered in her brain. She had a new enemy now. She had to plot out a strategy to defeat it, to defeat the traitor her own body had become.

She bit her lips to scatter the memory of his kisses with pain. She rushed through the halls and salons, barely nodding in response to polite greetings from the other guests. Their eyes followed her, the curious foreign countess nearly running through the château—and in her riding costume, no less.

She reached her rooms and threw open the door. She rang for the maid and had the girl hurriedly help her change into a casual, unconstrained morning gown of simple linen.

"No powder, Martine," Eleonora said when the maid began arranging her hair. "I need to . . ." She broke off, her mind blank. "I need to . . ." Her gaze frantically searched her room, stopping on a neat stack of paper on the writing desk. The music she'd left in the harpsichord salon had been returned. ". . . practice. I need to practice."

Martine frowned. "Perhaps Madame would enjoy a rest before—"

"No!" Eleonora interrupted sharply. "Thank you for your concern, but the part I am to play is much more difficult than I'd expected." She caught herself up. "I mean the *piece*, the *piece* I am to play . . ."

Martine shook her head, but said only, "As you wish, madame," then quickly finished her task and left.

Elbows on the dressing table, head in her hands, Eleonora tried to gather her scattered thoughts. Memories flitted in and out of her mind: her husband, Miklos, in one of his rages, the bellowing resounding off the stone walls of their castle in the mountains. Then the image grew softer, quieter, and she again remembered the lover she'd once had. Bálint, with his sweet voice and his sweeter kisses.

But the kiss turned demanding—and much more recent. She touched her lips and squeezed her eyes shut. "Bálint, Bálint," she called softly, but it was Achille's kiss that flooded her memory.

"No!" She stood abruptly, sweeping the table clear of its cosmetic pots and badger brushes. "I've known a man's kisses! A man's, do you hear? Not a devil's! And I've heard sweet, gentle whispers of devotion, all pledged in a stolen moment . . . I know what love is. *Love,* do you hear? Love, not . . . not . . ."

She shivered; it was not Bálint's murmurs she kept hearing in her mind. She grabbed the stack of paper from the writing desk. Music. She wanted to drown in music. She wanted to hear no words at all, neither her dead lover's nor the comte d'Agenais's, she thought as she left her rooms and rushed to the salon. The very much alive comte d'Agenais.

The door to the small music salon was slightly ajar when Eleonora reached it, and she hesitated a moment before silently pushing it open. She stepped inside, expecting to see another guest, but she saw no one. She made for the harpsichord.

Thank God those damned petals were cleaned— The sound of a slap brought her up sharp. It came from behind the lacquered musicians' screen in the far corner of the room. Voices began with whispered hisses, then grew louder with anger.

Eleonora grimaced; interference was a cardinal sin in France. She would likely be denounced by both parties involved if she gave in to her compassion. Still, she took a breath to call out when another slap made her stop.

"You stupid bitch!" the marquis de Rachand's voice spat out. "Recall what is at stake, madame wife," he went on sarcastically. "It was your blundering with d'Agenais at Gemeaux that forced us to travel to this rustic blot on the countryside."

The mention of d'Agenais had Eleonora rooted to the spot, unable to move.

"Don't call me bitch, you stupid cur!" the marquise de Rachand spit back. "I did what I could. He is not the kind of man to be lured by mere availability. Even with the added incentive of cantharides in his wine, he was not so easy to attract as you seem to think."

"He is a man, madame wife. You acted well enough in *my* bed when I still wanted you there. You know how to at least *pretend* that you like a man's touch."

The marquise hissed at him. "Watch what you say, husband. I could entrap a Jesuit if I chose. Or is that jealousy talking? Jealousy that it was not *you* in the shrubbery with him instead of me."

The marquis hesitated, then said, "He is too old by half."

His wife gave a sharp bark of laughter. "But when he wasn't too old by half, how you must have coveted such a dark and handsome Ganymede—"

Eleonora stared at the screen, eyes wide with shock.

"Monsieur le Bâtard had already killed a man in a duel by the age of fifteen," de Rachand said. "I want the

d'Agenais *lands,* madame wife. I want revenge for what he's done, not a d'Agenais sword through my gullet."

"And I want considerably more than that," the marquise said, her voice full of venom. "We must find another way to ensnare him. No woman could hold him the way we need him held."

"If not a woman, then what?"

"I have a *lettre de cachet* from La Chateauroux, signed by the king. It remains but to have d'Agenais arrested, and he will be in the Bastille within a sennight. I've already set things in motion."

The marquis snorted. "Have you now? And do you think an intendant within a hundred leagues of du Peyre would carry it out?"

"Perhaps not, but . . ." The marquise was silent for a long while.

In the quiet, Eleonora suddenly realized she could hear the sound of her own breathing. Entranced as she'd been by the Rachands' revelations, she'd forgotten how precarious her position was. She began to inch her way back toward the door.

"But what?" the marquis asked impatiently. "I still think a simple hunting accident—"

"No. Or at least not the kind he would expect. If the intendants here will not cooperate, then we will conduct d'Agenais to one who will."

Eleonora reached the door, but she couldn't make herself leave. *Think of the risk!* she chided herself—yet stayed to listen.

The marquis laughed. "Conduct him—by accident, of course. Excellent. Excellent. I must go see du Peyre. I'll have him reschedule the hunt for the day after tomorrow. That will be perfect, don't you agree?"

Eleonora rushed back into the hall. She took a couple of steps, then spun around and began humming the melody to the piece she'd come to practice. "La-la, la-a-a, la, la . . ." She put on her best guileless smile and entered the music room, still humming loudly.

The marquis and marquise were just emerging from behind the musician's screen, and Eleonora brought herself up with feigned surprise. "Monsieur, madame, hello!" she said brightly. "I came to practice ..." The words trailed off, and she shook the music she held as if to prove the veracity of her statement. The paper was limp with damp. She'd clutched it so tightly that even some of the ink had smeared. "I do not mean to interrupt. I can return later."

"No, no, no," the marquise said, coming toward her. "We need to prepare." She patted Eleonora's arm a bit too long. "Such a beauty you are. And such a waste it is for you to be imprisoned in this wretched place. A pity we're not in Paris. There are so many more amusements—"

"As you said, my love," her husband interrupted, "we must prepare—for dinner." He gave Eleonora a bow more suited to Versailles than a modest château in eastern France, then held out his arm for his wife to take.

With a tiny moue of disappointment, the marquise took her husband's proffered arm and walked to the door with him. There she paused, and said to Eleonora, "I'm sure you won't mention you saw us here, will you, madame? It's so unseemly to be caught in a tryst with one's husband."

"Who would believe me, madame?" Eleonora said with a knowing laugh. The couple smiled benevolently and sauntered out.

Eleonora staggered to the stool in front of the harpsichord and collapsed onto it. Enemies of a man such as d'Agenais were bound not to stay idle or to rely on the turn of a card. She straightened and busied her hands with arranging the music.

But such revenge as the de Rachands planned could be dealt with, she assured herself, and began to play the piece by Bonni. She would tell d'Agenais of the scheme against him. He would be grateful to her for that, surely. He would believe her to be an ally, an accomplice; he would believe her to be trustworthy.

And will he thank you with kisses? a voice in her mind taunted. *And will his hands caress you with gratitude?* She hit a false note.

A minor third.

Her fingers began to tremble and she clenched them in her lap. "No," she whispered to the empty room. "I do this because I must. It is but a ploy to bring him closer." *Closer* . . .

She squeezed her eyes shut. "Bálint, Bálint," she called softly, pulling a memory of her dead lover from its hiding place. A tall, dark-haired man sat near a deeply cut castle window, the low, masculine sound of his voice warming her, soothing her, as he read ancient poetry. Eleonora let the image calm her, and she resumed playing.

Music filled the room for an hour or more, music of yearning, of passion, of desire. And when she finished, she sat contented in the ensuing silence. Until she remembered—

Bálint had been blond.

The day had turned unexpectedly warm, and the evening, like a stubborn fever, was refusing to cool. All the windows in Eleonora's rooms had been thrown open. She drooped against the frame of one, eyes closed, futilely fanning herself in the still air. Her dress clung to her, and the hair piled on her head seemed almost too heavy for her neck to bear.

In the distance, she heard the forced gaiety of the château's guests gathering for a late supper in the garden. Her aunt had invited her, but Eleonora had pleaded malaise and declined. There was a tray of food untouched behind her.

She had not seen him since his kiss. She roused herself and turned back to the room, frowning at the tray. He would know her for a coward if she did not show up for supper; only the foolish or the timid would remain indoors on such a night.

She snapped the fan shut, threw it on the bed—it was useless anyway, for it neither cooled nor enticed—and left her rooms. She would face him if she had to, casually, even offhandedly, perhaps make a trifling conversation . . .

and oh! by the by, she'd—accidentally!—overheard the oddest thing. Did he perchance have any enemies?

At the terrace doors, two impeccably dressed servants bowed to her as she passed through. All the others must have already gathered, for she walked alone on the soft, grassy pathway lit by an occasional flickering torch. It was still overly warm, and she ran her fingers just inside the low neckline of her gown in a vain attempt to loosen it.

"I would offer to cool you," d'Agenais's voice said from the shadows to her left, "but I prefer you heated."

She halted to avoid letting him see her falter. "Wilted is more like, monsieur," she answered.

He stepped from the shadows, gave her an elegant bow, then stood beside her. "A hothouse flower, are you? I would not have guessed." He pulled something from his coat pocket. A fan. *Her* fan. He must have sent a servant into her room to retrieve it from where she'd left it on the bed. "But even a tender wilting shoot can be coaxed into opening her petals and . . ." he slowly opened the fan a petal at a time ". . . blossoming."

D'Agenais began to fan her, but she reached out to stop his hand. Her fingers curled over his wrist, the powerful swordsman's muscles working under her touch. "No, please—" she started to say, then bit off her words.

He carried her hand to his lips and kissed it. "Say 'please' again," he said, not taking his regard from her hand. He kissed the base of each finger.

"Your pardon, monsieur," she said, slipping her hand from his wrist. "I am expected at supper." She turned away from him toward the muffled sounds of the gathered guests that came from just beyond the tall obscuring hedges.

A firm, unyielding hand grasped her elbow. "Indeed you are, madame." He gave her a graceful nod, using his free hand to gesture to her left to a gap in the hedges. "But it lies this way."

Eleonora struggled not to gulp in the heavy, suffocating evening air. He was forcing her hand. Go or stay? Her next step would be irretrievable.

His kiss on the ride could be explained away—words like "stolen" could soothe a prickling conscience—but what he was asking of her now . . .

There was a sharp burst of laughter from beyond the hedges. A crowd of people flirted and giggled and cursed just a short distance away: Tante Geneviève, the gossipy Vigny, the Rachands.

She glanced at the comte waiting beside her. But here there was only silence. He seemed at ease in the fading light, as if the growing darkness was familiar and known, but his eyes were unreadable. The torchlight gave an otherworldly cast to the angles of his face, like the cunning, seducing devils carved on a thousand stone columns.

Did he perchance have any enemies? her own voice mocked archly in her head. And she remembered her false dark-haired memory of Bálint. The easy path of revenge she'd expected was turning into a quagmire beneath her feet. But duty beckoned. She looked at the dark opening in the hedges that d'Agenais had indicated—and prayed that the quagmire wouldn't suddenly become an abyss.

She drew in a deep breath. "You are most kind, monsieur," she said with the best smile she could manage.

"No. I am most hungry, madame," he answered, drawing her arm through his. "Most hungry."

Chapter 6

⟨━━◦◦◦━━⟩

The path was a long one, longer than Eleonora expected. In silence they walked, her arm tucked around his, through greenery lush and abundant. The sounds of the guests soon faded, leaving her feeling as if she and the comte d'Agenais had left the world of the château du Peyre far behind them.

The quiet was almost too companionable. The cadence of their steps matched, making their bodies move to the same rhythm, as if they danced a simple country dance to music only they could hear.

Ahead of them, a wall made of mortarless piled stones marked the boundary of the park. A lantern glowed near a break in the wall, making the forest seem even darker in the gathering twilight. She expected d'Agenais to stop there, or to turn right or left and remain in the gardens, but he swept up the waiting lantern without breaking their sauntering stride.

"How fortunate," she murmured as they crossed into the woodlands. The path was still clearly marked, but less ... tame. "Imagine, a gardener—by the veriest chance—just happened to leave his lantern there. Such luck."

"Such *Fate*," he corrected.

"Ah," she said. "How obliging of Fate to favor you with light. Stumbling about in the dark would be so ..." She paused and gave him a sidelong glance. "So un-French."

She felt the muscles of his arm tense. Vines that, in the park, would have been neatly clipped, here climbed in spreading trees and spilled down from the branches. He brushed one aside with more vigor than was called for.

"Darkness does not always make one stumble," he answered as she felt his tension seep away. He covered her hand on his arm. "Darkness can beckon, madame. Tantalize."

He stopped, withdrew his arm, and shuttered the lantern, plunging them into the night. "Sight can be a tyrant," his voice said from beside her, rich and deep, "which must be dethroned for the other senses to be relished."

She drew in a breath to protest. "Monsieur—" she began, then felt him stroking his finger along her jaw.

"I hear the sound of your quickening breaths," he said.

Nervous, she licked her lips.

"A-h-h." He drew his thumb over her just-moistened mouth. Her lips parted. "Such a small, delicious sound," he murmured. There was pressure on her skirts as he moved closer. "But I want to hear more." He caressed her neck, his fingers slipping around to stroke her nape. "So much more." Her head tilted back and her eyes closed. There was a luxurious warmth radiating from where his fingers touched her. The heat of the late spring night no longer seemed . . . unpleasant.

She heard the snap of tin against tin, and the darkness behind her closed eyelids glowed suddenly golden. He'd unshuttered the lantern.

"But how can the tyrant Sight be condemned when such loveliness rewards it?"

She grimaced at being caught, and she looked into the forest. "You spoke of hunger when we began this journey," she reminded him. "Am I to pull roots from the ground?"

He drew her arm through his again and began walking. "And I speak of hunger still," he said.

A flush rose up Eleonora's cheeks, but she said nothing. The circle of light bobbed slightly with their walking, but she saw little of the ferns and low-growing plants along the path.

Tremors of shimmering heat still teased where

d'Agenais had touched her. It was just the sultry heat of the night, she told herself, and as if to catch up loose strands of hair, she rubbed her neck to make the sensations go away.

She tried to force her mind into hardheaded calculations to deal with what might lie ahead, but his words from the night before sounded in her head. *The seducer or the seduced. Who is to blame?* he'd asked.

The one who falls. The one who is weak, she'd answered.

They neared a bend in the path, and to her right, Eleonora could see a faint glow as if the trees had begun shining of their own accord. She glanced at d'Agenais. She must not be weak. At the bend, a new path had recently been cut, wide enough for the two of them to walk down side by side. The glow in the trees was closer now, and directly ahead.

Lengths of gauze had been stretched from tree to tree, to both the right and the left, forming a room amid the forest. A curtain of ferns fanned between two trees in front of them like the guardians of a gate, and there he paused.

Achille set the lantern on a nearby stump and closed the shutter, watching the crescent of dimming light and shadow crossing her face. In the moment before his eyes adjusted, he heard her breaths quicken with anticipation, and he watched with satisfaction as curiosity replaced the distress on her face.

She eyed him for a moment, a smile threatening to curve her expressive lips. "What have you done?" she asked, a hint of excitement tempering her wariness.

Good, he thought. Soon she would be oblivious to the old memories that haunted her eyes; soon she would be oblivious to everything but him.

"Monsieur! What have you done? Tell me. Show me."

Indeed, my countess Eleonora, he said silently, *I shall tell you, show you . . .* Pinpoints of light sparkled through the leaves of the ferns, illuminating her face with a soft glow. Does she realize how much her face reveals? he wondered. Even in the subdued light, he could see her wit, her courage, and a light brushstroke of the innocence she scorned so much. He remembered her kiss and felt himself stir. Her eyes narrowed and she sent him a knowing look. "Not a lover's grotto, surely?" She gave a moue of disappointment. "I would not have expected such an *ordinary* thing of you."

Achille let his gaze drift into the distance over her shoulder, as if considering a weighty subject. "You wish a grotto? Du Peyre has one near here, in the ruins he had built." He bowed and gestured back down the path. "However," he said, ripping the fronds away, "there is gilt here, and satin." He took her hand and led her through the opening. Her eyes widened. Her lips parted.

He smiled at her astonishment. "But it is the gilt of a hundred candle flames, and the satin of a flower's petals."

She walked away from him as if in a trance. Surrounding her were hundreds of small crystal globes, each one holding a flickering votive candle. They had been set on mirrored silver trays, some on vine-covered stumps, others suspended between branches.

Nestled in the shadows between the sparkling trays of candles were silver tubs planted with night-blooming flowers, their scent drifting through the enclosure like a sorcerer's spell.

"Oh, monsieur," Eleonora whispered, opening her arms and turning round and round.

Achille made his way to an alcove set between two trees near the entrance and pulled away the concealing ferns to uncover a traveler's sideboard already laden with food for supper.

He poured the vin du champagne, letting the movement ease the tension of anticipation. Soon he would leave for the front—accompanied by a magnificent memory of the passion of Eleonora Batthyány.

"Vin du champagne, madame?" he asked, holding out a glass to her.

Eleonora's smile was composed, and she reached out to take the proffered glass. *The one who falls,* she silently reminded herself through the wonder at the enchantment around her. "Thank you, monsieur," she murmured.

"You may rest there, if you wish," the comte said with an elegant gesture toward another shallow alcove, this one with a velvet counterpane laid over a soft mound of leaves, the illuminating candles all around.

"Rest?" she asked, dismay fluttering in her stomach. An image flashed in her mind of her sprawling there, a provocative smile on her lips and her eyes half-closed. "I am not fatigued."

"It is cooler there."

She took a sip of the champagne to give herself time. There could be no mistaking what he planned to have happen on that velvet, but then—wasn't that what she needed to happen? Though only up to a point ...

"Thank you, monsieur," Eleonora repeated, giving him a brief nod. "The night does seem unseasonably warm." She lowered herself onto the velvet, the leaves rustling under her as she sat down. She tucked her feet under her, careful to keep from looking like one of the too amiable maidens in a pastoral frolic painted by Boucher. She wanted to tease his palate, not become dessert.

To her surprise, he did not immediately join her. He leaned against a nearby tree, arms crossed, contemplating her while his thumb rubbed the condensation on the side of his champagne glass.

She lowered her gaze to her own glass, unable to meet that intense scrutiny. Tiny ripples disturbed the surface of the liquid, and she took another sip to hide her trembling.

She looked around her, her gaze flitting here and there, anywhere but at those dark, enigmatic eyes watching her. In her mind, she tried to recall herself to her duty. But the resolution shimmered like a mirage, an illusion, while his presence burned away everything but the very real *now*.

"All these candles!" she said, making her voice as sprightly as she could. "The sight is intoxicating. I've never seen so many—not even in a church."

He raised his glass to her. "Consider this another altar then. To a goddess."

She laughed. "And does that make you Silenus or Jove?" she asked, then waved her hand to forestall an answer. Myths could be dangerous; there were too many amorous adventures at every turn. "Your pardon, monsieur. I am being excessively silly." She shook her head. "This is lovely, though. No one's ever done such a thing for me before."

Her eyes flew to his face; she was appalled at what she'd just revealed. "That is—I mean—No one's ever had servants diligent enough to do this. Such patience yours must have!"

The comte shrugged. "They do what I require."

"And what else do you require?"

He gave her a long, steady look. "I require stamina, madame."

The heat of a flush crept up her neck. "And if they do not have . . . stamina, do you discard them?"

"I have them rest." A smile played around the corners of his sensuous mouth. "And I require skilled hands. If they are not skilled, they must be taught. And they must be diligent at their lessons." His gaze lowered to study the last sip of champagne in his glass. "And I require that they be true."

"To you? And if they are not?"

Silence answered her. He straightened and returned to the sideboard. She heard the gurgle of champagne being poured, then the subdued clatter of lids being lifted from serving dishes and of silver clicking against porcelain plates.

His back was to her, but she could see the subtle shadows of candlelight moving on the velvet of his jacket.

"And if they are not, monsieur?" she called out. The noise stopped. He turned to face her, but did not leave the sideboard.

"Anyone who betrays me, madame, meets the same fate. *Anyone.*"

"And do you feel no remorse, no regret, when you mete out this fate?"

A shadow of grief and sadness clouded his face for an instant, then was gone. "Duty to honor is rarely without its sting," he answered.

There was silence between them then. In a few moments he brought her a plate of food, and she was disconcerted to find he'd had her favorite dishes prepared. How had he discovered them?

She murmured her thanks and began to eat mechanically, preoccupied with why she'd pushed him to talk of betrayal. She needed to know how far she could goad him before he lost his temper, she told herself. But doubt crept in.

It was possible that he enjoyed the feel of anger as much as the feel of silk or the scent of a rose, yet the anguish she'd seen wash over his face had been real and unmistakable. He was so complicated! She'd expected the evil of the devil's son to be simple and straightforward. But d'Agenais was a labyrinth—and there was no thread to lead her out of the maze, no guide through the convolutions to keep her from becoming irretrievably lost.

She raised another bite to her mouth, but he put a restraining hand around her wrist. She gave a start at the contact and had to struggle to keep from pulling away.

"The food does not interest you," he said. His dark eyes were steady on her, but they seemed . . . disinterested. It shocked her.

"Monsieur?" she managed to say. "I don't underst—" She broke off, his hold on her wrist becoming uncomfortably tight. She struggled to keep hold of her composure. "The food is delicious," she managed to say.

"How can you know that since you have not tasted it?" he asked, adding, "Do you forget all your lessons so quickly?"

Eleonora lowered her gaze to her plate, struggling to maintain control. In a moment, she raised her eyes, then leaned toward him, deliberately letting her bosom strain at the low neckline of her gown and regarding him through sultry, half-closed eyes. "How would you have me answer such a question?"

He smiled appreciatively and set their plates aside. "Like this," he murmured, bending much too close. " 'I fear, Achille, that I shall need to be taught again and again.' "

His mouth hovered over hers. "So very tiresome for you," she managed to say.

"Indeed. And so very many lessons." He pulled her to him, and kissed her.

His lips slid over hers, coaxing them to respond. He kissed her upper lip, then the lower, sucking lightly on the delicate flesh. The warmth of the night became an inner heat, tingling, tantalizing . . . terrifying.

"Monsieur," she said, somehow finding the strength to push away. Shaking, she rose, her knees nearly buckling, and made her way to the sideboard. She reached for the bottle of champagne, desperately wanting to rinse the provocative taste of him from her mouth. Her lips quivered uncontrollably, and she bit her bottom one to still the trembling. *Saint Stephen, help me!*

The dishes rattled when she clumsily picked up the champagne. *Who am I? What kind of woman . . . ?* The neck of the bottle clattered against the rim of the glass as she splashed the sparkling wine into it. She set the bottle down with a thud, then cupped the glass with two hands and held it to her lips.

She drank and drank, letting the cool liquid flow over her tongue and down her throat. *Wash away the feel of his touch* . . . Wash it away, so she would no longer feel it. The last drops spilled down her chin, but she didn't notice. Wash it away—so she would no longer crave it.

Eleonora wanted to run away. Not just from the candlelit grotto, not just from France, but from herself. There had been nothing of passion in her husband's gropings. Passion was something best kept in poems, safely tucked away in books. Bálint had read to her of it, but the words had been meant to warm her on a lonely winter evening, nothing more. His kisses had been sweet, but in the end they had been only kisses.

And d'Agenais wanted more, so much more.

She glanced at him. He stood in stark relief against the candle flame behind him, his dark hair and coat seemingly outlined by fire. He radiated power, ruthless power, power that would not be crossed, like Lucifer himself standing in front of the flames of hell.

"To what god does the priestess give thanks?" d'Agenais asked.

"To the god of deliverance," she answered, pouring herself another glassful of champagne. Her hand still shook.

His laughter was deep and rich and full. "From what?" he asked. "Me? Passion? You've had a husband in your—"

She shot him a warning look.

"—bed," he finished. "And you're too beautiful not to have had lovers."

She drank the second glassful of champagne even faster than the first. "Frenchwomen may be so bored as to think lifting their skirts in the shrubbery exciting, but I am Hungarian, d'Agenais. We have more to keep us busy than amorous intrigues. The nobility of Hungary are true aristocrats. We do not let ourselves be bled of every last sou by our sovereign, then be made to slaver at his feet like dogs. We have not docilely handed over our rights as hereditary seigneurs to a—"

"And yet you are here."

She made a moue of irritation at his interruption. "I am in France visiting my mother's dear half-sister to enjoy a few weeks of rest," she said with feigned loftiness. She kept hoping that the champagne would dull the pricking of the memories of his touch, but it seemed to be acting far too slowly.

"And yet you are *here*," he said again.

"If you recall, it was the lure of supper that brought me *here*." She broke off a piece of bread and popped it into her mouth.

"Was it?"

Piqued, she turned to face him, eyeing him over the rim of the crystal as she drank. "Why do you keep teasing me? What do you want me to admit? That I came here to be seduced in your bower of bliss?" She finished the champagne and giggled.

"I want you to admit the truth, Eleonora."

That brought her up sharply. The fuzziness from the champagne that was just beginning to dull her brain suddenly dissipated. She looked into the empty glass, then set it aside.

"The truth?" She crossed her arms in front of her. "Obviously there's no doubt that you expect us to become lovers. But why, d'Agenais? Why me? You have all the sophistication of the French court, while I have all the experience one lout of a husband could give me."

"No lovers?"

"I'd thought—" She closed her eyes. Looking at him made her eyes hurt, the enticing devil in front of the fire, but he burned there still, in the bright afterimage behind her lids. "I thought I had. But you make me doubt even that." She looked at the hundreds of tiny flames around her, and thought those points of light and fire could be inside, making her burn in a way she'd never experienced. Bálint's kisses had soothed, not . . . not *seared*.

"Doubt?" d'Agenais asked. She remembered when she'd first heard his voice on the terrace, thinking it a sound she could listen to forever. "Either you have felt a lover's kisses, or you have not. Felt a lover's arms around you, or not." His voice grew rough. "A lover's hands caressing you. His body poised above yours. Then merging. Either you have felt ecstasy in a lover's arms, or you have not. It is not a thing which allows much doubt."

She felt a stab of shock at his bluntness and could think of nothing to say in reply.

He'd resumed his earlier stance, leaning against a tree, arms folded, one leg casually crossed in front of the other. "No answer," he said. "Interesting. But no answer is response enough. No answer means you *do* doubt your lovers." He straightened and came toward her. "But rest assured, madame—you will have no doubt about me."

She wanted to turn away from him, but could not make her body follow her commands. D'Agenais came close and began stroking her neck, his fingers rubbing where her pulse beat just below the surface. His gaze greedily drank in the sight of her face, and she grew more uneasy.

"I can take—and have taken—what I want, Eleonora," he said, deliberately letting her see the hunger there. Carnal. Blatantly erotic. And impatient.

"I will wait for you to give me what I want," he said, and she relaxed a bit until he added, "but I will not wait for long."

She swallowed, then regretted it, knowing he could feel the muscles of her throat working beneath his hand. She pushed free of his hold, and he let her go. She had no illusions; she knew the strength, the power that was—for now—quiescent under his velvet coat.

"What you want," she said, looking away from him and wrapping her arms around herself. "You want in my bed. All this—" She flung her arms out to take in the enchantments of candlelight and sparkling silver and the night-blooming flowers. "All this, because you want in my bed."

From behind her, he seized her shoulders and gave her a lingering sucking kiss on her neck. "No, I do not want in your *bed,"* he murmured against her wet skin. He gripped her shoulders tighter. "I want *you.* All of you.

"Do my words disturb you?" he asked. "Would you prefer lies or pretense?"

She hesitated, then shook her head.

"I did not think you would," he said. "Truth is always best." He bit her neck again, then nipped at her hairline. "And, my sweet countess, it is so very true that I want you to give me this enticing, voluptuous body."

She shuddered, and felt him smile against her flesh. He turned her to face him, his head hovering close. "And you will."

Where are my schemes? she wondered in a haze. He had caught her off guard. She had no experience with a man such as he. With Miklos's soldier's crudeness she had had no need of words, and Bálint had had soft words, but nothing more.

D'Agenais drew his lips over hers, and the promise of that moist warmth befuddled her. She had expected seductive French lies—and had found the truth more seductive than any lies.

"Monsieur," she murmured against his mouth, not sure if the word was a protest or an invitation.

"Achille," he corrected, then fit his mouth full on hers.

His tongue was hot, slippery, insistent. He explored the sensitive inner flesh of her lips. She savored the heat that sparked from his quest.

He picked her up and carried her to the counterpane, then kissed her again. Was he giving or taking? Confusion fogged her head. It was so easy to slip into mindless delight. He'd taught her that. How had his lessons so quickly become a part of her?

His tongue spiraled around hers, drawing forth a luxurious fever from deep in her body, a fever that seeped into her blood like water into parched soil.

Her hands slid up his arms, across his wide shoulders, reveling in the feel of sculpted iron muscle moving beneath the velvet. She felt him stroking her sides, her back, then pressing her against his hard chest. Skilled fingers began loosening the laces of her bodice.

She moaned a feeble protest. His mouth lifted from hers, and he began tasting the soft flesh beneath her jaw, slowly making his way to her ear. Her eyes finally closed, and her head fell back. She wanted to let go then, to give in to the weakness inside her, to let him be her strength.

The pressure around her eased, and she knew he'd loosened her bodice. He drew the linen off her shoulders. His thumbs caressed the soft flesh he'd just revealed as his lips trailed down her neck.

Her arms crossed behind his head. Was she urging him on? She moaned again, almost tasting the sweet sugar-heat that dripped like honey left in the summer sun.

"Eleonora," he whispered against the hollow at the base

of her throat. "Such beauty pleading to be . . . taken."
There was a sudden wetness on the tops of her breasts.
Champagne. He'd poured the last of his champagne on her
and . . . *m-m-mmm* . . . he began to suckle, lick, and kiss it
away.

"Monsi—"

"Achille." His tongue dipped into the valley between
her breasts. *"Achille."*

"No," she whimpered. He trailed kisses up the mound
of her breast, then paused. "No, Achille," she said again,
her voice deep and sultry. "Not while you deny me . . ."

Her eyes, half-closed now from desire, looked into the
black unreadable depths of his gaze as she untied the neck-
band of his shirt.

A sensual smile grew on those talented lips of his. "I
would deny you nothing, mada—"

"Eleonora," she interrupted with an answering smile. "I
would deny you nothing, *Eleonora.*"

He slid his hand over her breast, slipping under the
neckline of her gown to pluck the hidden nipple. She
sucked in her breath at the exquisite shock that flashed
through her.

"I would deny you nothing, *Achille,*" he said, his black
eyes flashing with an unyielding sensual hunger.

He freed her breasts from the confines of her gown, his
fingers caressing, stroking the soft globes. Then his
thumbs brushed against the stiffened peaks. A cry escaped
her. A moan. She squeezed her eyes shut. *No, no* . . . She
steadied herself with a hand on his shoulder.

He plucked, swirled— *Oh, God* . . . Her fingers dug into
him. *No, this wasn't how— How can he— He—* The words
drifted away in a senseless tangle.

She was confounded. It should be she enticing him. *But,
oh-h-h, yes, oh, yes* . . . She floated in the half-light of
pleasure. Her head fell forward. It was a winding, tightening pleasure coalescing low in her body. Insistent, promis-
ing . . .

An errant thought drifted by. A devil's hands were
giving her this devil's pleasure, this devil's promise . . .

Oh, if he were the devil, she mused, near-drunk on voluptuous desire, there would be many more witches in the world.

She put her hands into his hair, then hungrily kissed his mouth. She dragged her lips across his face and pressed her cheek to the side of his head. A primitive sound, half growl, half moan, escaped her.

"Please, Achille. I can't . . ." She shook her head. "I am so lost. Oh, please. I do not want to be so. . . ."

His hand moved slowly up her body to cradle her head. They pulled slightly apart, and he looked into her face. "My sweet Eleonora, how can you be lost? We have barely begun the journey. There is so much more that awaits us."

She drew in deep, ragged breaths. She knew her trembling body gave the lie to her pleas for him to stop. "Barely begun," she said with a self-deprecating laugh, "and the widow begs for mercy."

She ran her hands up his arms and gently pulled away. "Forgive me," she said. "You must think me a fool."

To her surprise, he tugged her gown back into place, then embraced her to tighten the laces. "I think you a beautiful . . ." he broke off and stole a quick kiss from her lips ". . . arousing woman. And I want you to give yourself to me with no doubts. No regrets."

With his hands, he once again cradled her head, his thumbs rubbing the soft flesh in front of her ears. His hold tightened. "I give you mercy—for the moment, Eleonora. But do not think me merciful. I am not."

Chapter 7

Achille lay awake in his bed. A few minutes earlier, a clock had softly chimed the hour. Three o'clock in the morning. The château was quiet, the walls seeming as slumberous as the owners and guests.

Naked beneath the silk sheets, hands folded behind his head, he moved his hips and felt the smooth material slide over his erection. He'd wakened from a delicious dream, his loins tight with a man's hunger, and had deliberately kept that passionate image of a certain Hungarian countess vivid in his mind.

He moved his hips again. It had been years since he'd dreamed of a woman. The muscles in his arms, his shoulders, his ridged stomach, grew tight and solid. He should have taken her tonight. There amongst the candles, her head thrown back in a delirium of sensation, she could have been a sacrifice such as would have lured the most reluctant god from Olympus. A sacrifice to Eros, she would have been, her moans the sweetest benediction ever heard.

How she had responded! He could feel again her full breasts, her taut nipples against his palms. It would have been the work of a minute to slide his hand under her skirts and caress the silken thighs, feel her moistness on his fingertips, inhale the intoxicating perfume of her aroused womanhood. The tightness in his loins intensified. His blood thrummed with the primal compulsion of a man.

He wondered at himself, at his restraint. Sweet Christ, he wanted her.

Her kiss had taunted him, nearly pushing him over the edge. Her body had flushed with its hunger, and her hips had almost imperceptibly begun the tensing, and releasing of that most ancient of dances. And her tongue, of its own accord, of its own sweet wanton accord, had twined with his.

Her tongue ... with her hips ... *Jesus, Jesus, Jesus.* He'd nearly taken her right then. He threw the sheet off him, letting the night air cool his heat. He sucked in deep gulps of air to free the tension coiling so tight in him. Did she realize how much her body had promised? It was only that that had kept him from ravishing her. Only that.

But, Sweet Christ, his pleasure would have been great.

The next evening, Achille stood alone on the balcony, watching the other guests gather for supper. The warmth of the day before had turned into an afternoon of drizzling rain, though now it seemed but a heavy mist. Eleonora, he knew, had spent the day practicing the harpsichord piece she was to play at the recital later in the week. He would bet that she had perfected the music long since, but that, like him, she had found the music had a calming effect on her overwrought nerves.

A smile came unbidden to his lips. He liked the notion that the cool countess had needed calming. And last night he had glimpsed just how much heat simmered below that cool surface.

A servant came out bearing a glass of wine. He held it out to Achille on a salver while hunching against the dampening mist. From inside the salon came the commotion of a grand entrance. "The duc de Cassian," the servant offered, then left.

Achille studied the tableau through the glass. Eleonora, he noticed, entered the room following the duc's entourage. Madame de Rachand rushed to her and tugged the protesting countess toward the surly duc. The sullen duc, the scheming marquise, and the reluctant countess, Achille mused. Eleonora reached for a glass of vin du champagne to evade the marquise's touch on her arm, but she only succeeded in putting herself closer to the duc's grasp.

Achille absently set his wine on the wide stone balustrade. Perhaps it was time to end his solitude.

A footman bowed and held the door open for him. "Send for my man to bring me a dry coat," he told the footman. The man nodded and left, and Achille began making his leisurely way to the other side of the room.

Du Peyre hailed him from near the door, limping only slightly. "A moment, d'Agenais," du Peyre said, and put a hand on Achille's arm to draw him aside. "The hunt's on for tomorrow morning. I don't care if we have to ride through mud a man could sink into over his head. What's this? God's life man, you're *wet.*" The marquis shook his hand. "What have you been doing outside? No, don't tell me, I don't want to know. Even the thought of doing it outside makes my bones ache."

Instinctively Achille moved closer to the wall so that his back did not face the open doorway. "Perhaps I prefer solitude," he said.

Du Peyre snorted. "My guess is that you're just being damned discreet." He narrowed his eyes and scanned the crowd. "The bitch of it is, you disappear for ages on end, and I never notice any of the ladies absent! I remember that even as a pup, you scorned the maids, or else I'd be taking a closer look at the staff."

A shrill note of laughter scraped through the room, hushing the other voices. Achille's gaze went to the trio of Eleonora, Madame de Rachand, and the duc de Cassian. As he watched, the marquise glanced in his direction, blanched, then forced another laugh. Eleonora's face was carefully blank, a slight stage smile curving her lips.

"If you'll pardon—" Achille began.

"That swollen cow's hide," Du Peyre spit out.

Achille tensed like a suddenly taut wire, and his hand balled into a fist. "What did you say?" His voice was flat and deadly.

Surprise and fear lashed over the marquis's face. "No

need to get testy, man. I-I just meant she came here uninvited and seems to have brought half of Paris after her!
You can see where that would put any host into a bit of a
snit."

Achille relaxed. "You speak of La Rachand."

"Of course I do. Detestable woman. Who do you
think—?" Du Peyre shot him a look of disgust. "Geneviève's niece?" The marquis grunted. "God's life,
d'Agenais, you are severe! I'm her uncle, mind. She's a
strange one, all right, but I'd never call her *that*. You may
have excessively developed tastes, monsieur le comte, but
I think she's more than passably pretty." Du Peyre gave a
sharp tug to his coat. "Quite a bit more than passably
pretty. Looks a lot like Geneviève, in fact. Not so delicate,
of course. And I doubt she can sing as well—no one can
match my Gen when she sings. Her hair's a lot like Gen's
was, though."

Achille frowned, watching the softness of reminiscence
give a dreamy look to the marquis's eyes. A suspicion
lurked in the back of Achille's mind. Absurd, he thought,
chasing the notion away.

Du Peyre's smile deepened. "I remember when I first
saw her hair unpinned, lit by firelight. Oh, my Lord, she
was beautiful. And her smile . . ." Du Peyre cleared his
throat. "That was a long time ago. Just a green boy, you
know."

"You were in love with her," Achille said, taken aback
by the idea. "You were in love with your own wife."

"Sh-h-h! Someone might hear you," du Peyre said. He
snapped his head right, then left, checking to see if anyone
had overheard. He lowered his voice to a whisper. "No, of
course not. Of course not. What a thing to say! I have a
mistress, d'Agenais. You know that. Everyone knows that.
That chevalier's fat wife. Er, plump wife." Beads of perspiration formed along the marquis's upper lip.

"I am wrong," Achille said. "You *weren't* in love with
your wife."

Du Peyre visibly relaxed. "Of course not."

"You *are* in love with her."

"D'Agenais!" the marquis said with a suppressed squeal. "I should call you out for that."

"And lose your life defending a lie?"

Du Peyre pulled out a handkerchief and wiped the perspiration from his lip. "Please don't tell her. She'd die of embarrassment. She loves being fashionable, you see. It's what's done."

"I won't tell her, du Peyre. I prefer to ignore what is fashionable, not set it."

Du Peyre looked thoughtful for a moment. "W-what do you mean 'set it'?" he asked.

"Being in love with your wife is a novel idea, is it not?" Achille couldn't recall ever hearing about it before. He'd heard rumors, of course, about some distant provincial baron or other, but like rumors of talking horses and showers of toads, no one could ever prove them. He shrugged and added, "And what is novel one season is often fashionable the next."

"Do you think so?" Du Peyre chewed on his lower lip, his eyes watching his wife across the room as she gracefully nodded to her guests, occasionally stopped for a brief moment of chatter, then continuing on, slowly making her way toward the duc, La Rachand, and Eleonora. The marquis sighed. "She's still a petite little morsel, isn't she?"

Achille said nothing. *Morsel*, he thought, his eyes on Eleonora. *No, my countess, you are not a morsel, but a feast, one I shall partake of soon.*

Madame du Peyre smiled brightly at the trio and patted her niece on the arm. When she said something to the duc and La Rachand, Eleonora's stage smile abruptly turned genuine, and the two of them, aunt and niece, nodded their au revoirs and left.

"Perhaps Geneviève needs my help," du Peyre said as the two women slowly came toward them. "I think I'll go see what . . ." The marquis's words trailed off as he went to join his wife.

The tread of a familiar footstep behind Achille made him turn to Beaulieu. The steward bowed. "Your coat, monsieur." The man smoothed the velvet garment draped over his arm.

Achille glanced around to see the marquis and marquise du Peyre walking jauntily toward him. Eleonora followed more slowly, her eyes looking everywhere but at him.

"D'Agenais," du Peyre called, then his eyes lit on Beaulieu. "Excellent, your man is here with a dry coat. De Cassian's arrival has stirred everything up, and my poor Gen's had to rearrange everyone for supper." He patted the hand on his arm, and Madame du Peyre beamed up at her husband. "But my Gen ... that is, madame my wife has, of course, managed to put everything to rights. That is, if you don't mind sitting with my niece."

Madame du Peyre's smile faltered, and Achille saw her cast a quick look of apology back to Eleonora.

Eleonora gave her a reassuring smile. "It's all right, Tante," she said. "I've had countless suppers with my three quick-tempered brothers. Monsieur d'Agenais would have to try very hard indeed to match them."

Achille gave her a courtier's bow. "I shall try to my utmost, madame la comtesse."

Her aunt sucked in a shocked breath. "Eleonora!"

He smiled at the older woman. "I shall be pleased to partner Madame Batthyány for the evening."

Madame du Peyre nervously clutched her husband's sleeve. "Oh, not for the entire evening, Monsieur d'Agenais! I mean ... it's only for supper ..."

"Come, come, Gen," du Peyre said. "We have other guests, and supper is about to be announced." He leaned down and whispered something about "set the fashion" in her ear. She looked delightfully confused for a moment, then nodded and let her husband escort her away.

Beaulieu softly cleared his throat. "Monsieur ..."

"Help me change my coat, Beaulieu. I'm sure Madame Batthyány will forgive me a few moments in my shirt-sleeves."

Eleonora gave him a shallow curtsy. "Of course, monsieur," she said. "They do say clothes make the man. Now I am to see how."

In only seconds, Beaulieu was settling the dry coat on Achille's shoulders. The steward smoothed out the charcoal gray velvet, then departed.

"I . . ." Eleonora began, but had absolutely no idea what to say to the man who last night had . . . had . . . She wanted to ask him what he'd said to du Peyre to make him so attentive to Tante Geneviève, but she seemed unable to form the words.

Achille held up a hand as if to stop her, though her voice had trailed off long since. "There is no need to make polite conversation on my account, Madame Batthyány," he said. He nodded to a passing couple. "I am fatigued."

"Yes, of course, monsieur," she said, disturbed by his kindness. "I will gladly accede to your wishes."

"Of course you will, madame," he answered.

At that moment, the doors at the end of the salon were thrown open, and the maître d'hôtel entered with all the pomp and grandeur of royalty. He bowed to the marquis and marquise du Peyre, and grandly gestured for them to enter through the open doorway.

It was the signal for the supper crush to begin. Achille offered Eleonora his arm, and after a moment's hesitation, she accepted it. They began the slow process of moving toward the room where supper was to be served. Men nimbly maneuvered between the huge hooped skirts, each one vying for more space than was available, while the women dipped and canted to avoid crushing their skirts.

In a grouping of sofas and chairs near the center of the room, Eleonora saw Tante Geneviève's sister-in-law coyly prompt a gentleman who had strayed too near to help her rise while she ostentatiously cradled her slightly protruding belly. Eleonora felt a stab of soul-deep envy. To be able to have a child . . .

There was a snort of derision from Eleonora's right, and she turned to see one of the solid matrons to whom her aunt had introduced her. "I daresay she won't be quite so coy when it's time for her confinement," Madame de la Cheylard said. "I had fifteen, you know."

She tilted her head toward Eleonora and lowered her

voice so that it was difficult to make out over the noise of the crowd. "And I knew who the fathers were of each and every one of them. Which is more than can be said of some of these 'ladies.' "

"Fifteen," Eleonora said. "They must give you great joy." On the other side of her, Achille seemed oblivious to the mass of people around them. She felt awkward being paired with him, afraid someone might comment on it, though she knew that, unless one maneuvered mightily, couples, married or amorous, were usually kept apart.

"Joy?" the matron said with a laugh. "Ha! Children are the bane of a mother's existence. They *always* manage to disappoint." She shook her head sadly. "I only have eight left. Five of the girls we packed off to the Claires."

"That must be a source of pride for you," Eleonora said, then added when Madame de la Cheylard looked puzzled, "that your daughters are so pious as to want to become nuns."

"Pious? What's that to say to anything? The upkeep for their lives in a convent—even if they live to ninety—is piddling compared to what their dowry would be. Though I do have a pious one, all right, but she's the one we kept. Do you have any children, madame?"

Eleonora's fingers involuntarily dug into Achille's arm. "Children?" He did not look at her, but seemed to let the crush push him closer to her. He became her anchor in the churning sea around her. "No. No, my late husband and I had no children."

"How long were you married?" the matron asked, giving Eleonora's figure a sidelong glance.

Achille's hand was warm as it lightly covered hers. "Almost four years."

The woman shook her head regretfully and make a *tsk*ing sound. "Ah. Well, that at least explains it."

"Your pardon, madame, but it explains what?" Eleonora asked. They finally crossed the threshold into the dining room, though she was careful not to show her relief.

"Why your dowry is so high, of course. Five hundred thousand louis! I nearly fell off my chair when I heard. A man usually has to marry a tax farmer's daughter to get that kind of money."

"Five! No, it's . . ." She let her voice trail off, aware of the held breaths around her. How could they all not help but overhear? *The dowry is nothing!* she wanted to shout. *Don't you understand it? I will never remarry.* "That is, I'm sure my family could never come close to what a tax farmer might pay for his daughter to marry."

The current of the crowd diverted Madame de la Cheylard away just then. After allowing herself a deep breath of relief, Eleonora let her gaze skate over the room to discover the footman who would lead her to her seat. Ahead and to her right, one waited patiently, his eyes on Achille, and she realized the comte had been guiding her in the proper direction all along.

And she'd let him.

It had all happened so naturally, so comfortably. She glanced at Achille. Amongst so many people, his face was closed, features that she had seen shadowed with desire now making him appear unapproachable. But she had seen him smile, had heard his laughter, had felt the lure of those dark eyes and the touch of those skilled hands . . . and had been near him when he'd been dangerously approachable.

Uneasy at her thoughts, Eleonora considered putting more space between them, but any movement other than toward the waiting footman would be noticeable.

The flow of the crowd brought Madame de la Cheylard closer for a brief moment. The woman chuckled. "Oh, dear, whatever can Geneviève have been thinking of?"

"I beg your pardon?" Eleonora said.

The matron looked at her and nodded her head sideways. "There, being seated at your table. Don't you see? It's Madame de Tauves!" Her eyes gleamed with anticipation. "O-o-o-h, I wonder what she's going to do when she discovers she's at the same table as d'Agenais?"

Eleonora couldn't keep her eyes from going to the petite blonde just sitting down at the round table that she and d'Agenais had been heading for. *Another former lover?* First Madame de Rachand, and now . . . *Unless there is no "former"* about it. Her stomach knotted. She tried to snap her hand from Achille's arm, but his touch had gone from light to firm an instant earlier.

She swallowed hard, not sure if the lump in her throat was distress or merely pride, but wanting it to be neither. "Madame de la Cheylard," Eleonora said, just as the matron was moving away. The older woman paused, her eyebrows raised in surprise. Eleonora leaned toward her. "Who . . . ? That is—"

Madame de la Cheylard gave her a knowing look. "Don't worry, madame," she said comfortingly, "you won't have an old lovers' tangle on your hands." She looked thoughtful for a moment. "Come to think of it, I don't think any of his former, ah, liaisons would dare that sort of thing. Not with *him* anyway."

"But what—?" Eleonora began, but the woman acknowledged a footman's gesture and moved away toward her table before Eleonora could stop her.

Beside her, Achille lifted her hand from his arm and gracefully maneuvered her into her chair. He leaned over, his head near her ear as if making a courteous inquiry as to her well-being. Only Eleonora heard what he actually whispered.

" 'But what?' madame la comtesse?" he murmured, his breath warm and moist against her ear. "A minor incident, nothing more. Madame de Tauves's brother had the pleasure of being run through the heart by the comte d'Agenais in a duel."

Eleonora held her breath to keep from crying out. He straightened, and she looked up at him. *"You killed her brother?"* she rasped out in the barest whisper.

He withdrew his touch, and her anchor in the crowd was gone, then she realized it had already been taken from her, the moment he'd breathed those words in her ear. Through dazed eyes she saw Achille subtly gesture to an old abbé about to sit down at a neighboring table. The old prelate looked surprised until his gaze fell upon Madame de Tauves. With a minimum of fuss, the two men traded places.

The abbé bowed to Eleonora and sat down next to her, but her eyes were on Madame de Tauves. *Achille killed her brother.* Eleonora's hands went cold at the thought of Endres or Gabriel or Christophe lying dead on the hard ground of a dueling field. To never hear Christophe's carefree laughter again, or to never smile again at Gabriel's gentle teasing, or to never see Endres's somber brown eyes lighten with contentment as he watched his darling little daughter . . .

"Your pardon, madame," the abbé said graciously.

She forced her attention back to the table. "For what, monseigneur?" Her lips formed a semblance of a smile. "It is I whose wits have been wandering."

"Your wits or your eyes, madame la comtesse?" He gave her a genial grin. "I deprive you of so handsome a supper partner as Monsieur d'Agenais, so it is only fair that I pay penance by not having your attention."

"No, it's not that," she said, shaking her head.

He chuckled. "Not to worry. I don't mind. I listen to the ladies complain that he ignores them, but they do, I notice, rather like to look at him—and hope he'll look back, I'd wager."

"Not all ladies, monseigneur," she answered. "He is a . . . difficult man."

The abbé's expressive eyebrows shot up. "Difficult, you call him. Hmmm. Exactly right, I'd say, unless that temper of his is riled. But, of course, you would know nothing of that."

"No, of course not." She let her glance slip down the table to Madame de Tauves. Was that the crime Madame's brother had committed? Had he riled Achille's temper?

A servant poured their wine, and the abbé beamed his thanks. He lifted the glass in a toast to Eleonora. "To a beautiful and perceptive young woman." He downed half the liquid in the glass, then discreetly smacked his lips. "Excellent wine. Excellent. Du Peyre's cellar is unequaled in eastern France, I'd say."

He chuckled, and she heard him mumble "difficult" under his breath, then chuckle again. He finished the rest of his wine in a huge swallow and signaled the servant for more.

He laughed to himself, making his shoulders shake. *"Difficult.* Oh, indeed, indeed. Most would call him something rather stronger, I believe. Ha! But not to his face, of course. He's killed I don't know how many men, including, of course, Madame de Tauves's rascally brother. They were keeping tally in Paris, but I hear he's already outlasted all their bets. And then there was that matter with Rachand's family . . ." A shadow of a frown crossed his cheerful face.

He laughed again. "Difficult! I'm surprised you could see that on such short acquaintance with him."

"You mock me, I think, monseigneur," she said, and began picking at the turbot she'd just been served.

The abbé ate with gusto. "No, my dear, I don't think I do. You are quite right about him. The comte d'Agenais *is* a difficult man. The fact that you don't call him all the other things he has been called makes me think highly of you. But don't mistake the matter. He is also a dangerous man. All men are who are willing to back up their word with their lives."

"You sound as if you admire him!"

He paused, his fork halfway to his mouth. He appeared to study the turbot, then lowered his fork back to the plate with a sigh. "Madame Batthyány, we are talking of a man you know only from his escorting you into supper." She, too, put her fork back onto her plate, but the abbé didn't seem to notice. "No doubt you've heard gossip about him," he continued.

"Some," she managed to say.

He nodded as if that was what he expected to hear. "Sometimes I think there isn't a woman in France who isn't aware of him. But the gossip won't tell you that, buried under that temper and formidable exterior, there is great nobility, and great honor."

"Honor and nobility!" she gasped. "What of Madame de Tauves's brother? How honorable was that?"

The abbé lifted his glass to the silent Madame de

Tauves, who sat down the table from him, then he turned back to Eleonora. "It was a duel, madame. D'Agenais could do nothing less, given the provocation the wretch gave him. Quite honorable, I assure you. Though not particularly legal."

He pursed his lips and studied her. "You surprise me with your question," he said. "You are a Hungarian, a foreigner, I realize, but your aunt has said you live most of the year in Vienna. Hardly a place where dueling is unknown."

She shifted uncomfortably in her chair. "It is known, of course, though most *provocations* are not so numerous as Monsieur d'Agenais's." And what of those murders in Paris? she wondered. What could have provoked him to such an extreme?

" 'Judge not, that ye be not judged,' " the abbé intoned, then set about consuming the next course. "I knew his father," he told her between mouthfuls, "and I knew him as a child. Such a boy, he was! Constantin—his father—used to strut around with such pride that he had sired so extraordinary a son. 'A son worthy of Charlemagne!' he'd brag. But when Constantin ... died ... it was as if a light went out in young d'Agenais. Now a darkness fills him that, I fear, will keep him forever separated from his nobility and honor—and the boy he was."

Eleonora discovered she had to blink to clear her blurred vision. "It—it is hard to imagine the comte d'Agenais as anything but a man."

"He was not a child for long. His mother saw to that." The abbé took a long swallow of wine, though Eleonora had a feeling he hardly tasted it. "I must say that, *officially*, I have to disapprove of Monsieur d'Agenais. His impiety does, after all, border on the blasphemous. But his is a troubled soul, and perhaps one day, he'll remember how to pray. It is the only thing that will save him, I fear."

No, monseigneur, not even that will save him, she said to herself, taking a sip of wine. Once he reached Vienna, her family, her brothers, would see to that. She lowered the glass to the table with an unsteady hand; the reminder of Achille's fate did not comfort her as it should have.

The old man leaned toward her and put his hand lightly on her arm. "Don't tell a Jansenist *or* a Jesuit I said this," he whispered, "but sometimes I think we have to find Providence in our own way. Or perhaps it's Providence that finds us."

It is not Providence that will find the devil that is comte d'Agenais. It is justice.

But the words rang hollow in her mind. She thought not of the raging devil, but of his wit, of amusement lightening his dark eyes, of his subtle unspoken considerations—

She brought the disturbing musings to an abrupt halt. How could she let herself forget what he was! Imagine Christophe dead by that devil's sword. Imagine Christophe wounded, defeated, kneeling before d'Agenais to yield up his sword as demanded by the strict code of a duelist's honor, his life forfeit or pardoned at the whim of the victor.

Her hand began to shake as the dueling field in her mind became more and more real. She could almost feel the blades of coarse grass jabbing though the soles of her slippers, smell the taint of blood on the breeze, see her brothers falling one by one to the devil's sword.

"No," she cried, but the word came out as a choked whisper. She couldn't let that happen. She couldn't—

"Are you quite well, madame?" the abbé asked, patting her arm reassuringly. "Perhaps another sip of wine?"

"Your pardon, monseigneur. I . . . I'm fine. Yes. Thank you." She raised her eyes to his understanding gray ones. "Monseigneur, I need to ask you a, ah, professional question."

"I'll answer if I am able, my child."

"Which is . . . Which is the greater sin, monseigneur, keeping a vow to one's family, a sworn vow, a vow as holy as if it had been taken on the blood and crown of Saint Stephen while bringing harm into their midst, or breaking that vow and keeping them safe?" *Or wanting a*

*devil near me, wanting his hands on my body, his lips, his
laughter—*

He hesitated, then took his hand away. "It is a difficult
question, Madame Batthyány."

She managed to maintain her composure, though her
mouth trembled. "I'm damned, aren't I? No matter which
I choose, I'm damned."

Chapter 8

The next morning, Eleonora's maid had to take extra time to hide the smudges of sleeplessness beneath her mistress's eyes. Already Eleonora could hear the baying of the hounds for the hunt. The sound set her teeth on edge. She waved away the box of patches her maid held out to her.

"No, none of that," Eleonora said. "Just keep it as simple as possible." The maid clucked her disapproval, but Eleonora wanted nothing but the sweet oblivion of sleep, where no dark-eyed seducers made her body burn with the most exquisite aching . . .

Her mind was befuddled. It had been too easy. It should have been harder to catch his eye, to entice him. But from the beginning, he had been there, waiting for her to fall.

She had caught herself a devil, it seemed. And now she was damned.

She stood abruptly. "I must go. I hear the horns," she said, then flushed when the horn sounded belatedly, revealing her lie. She picked up her riding crop, and began to search for her favorite fan when she remembered d'Agenais still had it.

"Martine," she said, addressing the maid. "Who entered my—" She broke off with a shake of her head. "Never mind."

The maid curtsied. "Your pardon, madame, but nobody else pays me to watch your rooms for comings and goings, so I don't." The girl rolled her eyes in disgust. "Except for

112

Madame de Rachand, but if she thinks I'm missing my chance with the wine steward for a paltry sou, she's very much mistaken!"

She curtsied again. "So if you'll excuse me, madame?" Eleonora nodded, and the girl strutted to the servant's door. "That wine steward is about to learn my virtue is going to cost him pretty! The head groom paid forty sous for it, and so can he." The door shut with a snap.

Eleonora sat down hard on the dressing table stool. Was that what it was all about? Forty sous. Or maybe that was for an hour. She wondered what the going rate was for a nobleman—did a duc pay more than a marquis? A vicomte more than a baron? Then she wondered if they paid at all.

She almost envied the maid. No disturbing dreams, no insistent hunger, no devil who wanted . . .

The call to the hunt blew again. She looked outside at the crisp, bright morning. The maid's mention of Madame de Rachand had made Eleonora remember the woman's malevolent plan to destroy d'Agenais. She almost envied the woman the ease of a *lettre de cachet*.

So easy then to simply let them arrest him and whisk him out of the country. So easy then not to have her resolve clouded with his passion and unexpected kindnesses.

Is that why she hadn't warned him of the danger? And was that why she was thinking of not telling him this morning? It would not redeem her own lost soul. She rose, thought of her missing fan, and snapped the riding crop against the skirts of her hunting costume. She looked at the tall wardrobe in the corner and considered. Even if she didn't tell him, it wouldn't hurt to be prepared.

She quickly went to the wardrobe and dug out one of the small pistols her brother Christophe had slipped to her. In a matter of minutes, she loaded it and tucked it into a pocket. She left then, her step lighter than it had been since she'd arrived at the château du Peyre.

Chaos hit Eleonora like a palpable force. Dogs howling, men cursing, a shrill woman's voice complaining of a too frisky horse.

"I trust your sleep was undisturbed, madame," d'Agenais's voice said quietly from behind her. "No, don't look around. It is no one's concern that I address you."

"I slept like the proverbial sinless Dutchman, thank you," she answered softly, pulling on her gloves. "And you?"

"I slept the sound sleep of a not-so-sinless Frenchman."

"I'm glad to hear it, monsieur," Eleonora said as she smiled and waved at Tante Geneviève, who was trying to keep the chattering women who were not riding from scaring the horses. "I should hate to have your sins intrude on your rest."

"Sins never intrude, madame." He stepped beside her as if passing by chance. "And speaking of sins," he added, sotto voce, "I have decided that I do want you amongst gilt and satin." He nodded to her as if to a slight acquaintance and walked toward his groom, who stood holding his bay horse.

Her eyes narrowed as she watched his lithe, muscular body mount the powerful horse. It was suddenly easy to recall her duty. *And I want you in chains, d'Agenais.*

She stepped off the terrace and entered the chaos. Several of the other male guests, all married if she remembered Tante Geneviève's whispered injunctions when they'd been introduced, bowed and begged her to ride their horses. A joy, they assured her, an honor to see such a beauty matched with an animal worthy of her.

There were double and triple entendres in their unctuous words, all flying around like burrs in an untilled field. She understood a few of them, guessed at a few more, and was certain one or two completely passed her by. She seethed inside, and silently cursed the smirking lot of them—still she nodded her gratitude for the kind offers, and politely declined.

A groom scurried by, and Eleonora called to him to bring her a horse—one with spirit, mind!—and stood waiting. Many of the group were already gathering down near a line of poplars, and she worried she would miss the first ride.

Another Frenchman, the gossip Vigny, bowed and offered her his inexhaustible services. Why couldn't the devil's son be one of this lot? she wondered.

Eleonora felt a hand on her shoulder. The touch was light, but stayed a fraction too long. "Don't frown so, my dear," Madame de Rachand said.

The woman shooed Vigny away with a coy smile, but as soon as he had gone, she turned to Eleonora. "Don't mind him. He's a vile little pest, a necessary evil that one tolerates because he can be useful."

Eleonora felt herself being studied again. "He has been most amusing to me," she said.

The marquise absently waved the subject away as if she were batting a fly. Her eyes narrowed. "Haven't you been sleeping well?" she asked. Eleonora felt her chin being grabbed. "You're not bedding one of these stinking little wretches, are you? To think of their hands on—"

"Madame!" Eleonora said sharply, and wrenched out of the marquise's hold.

La Rachand looked away, her mouth a thin, hard line. "I've convinced the duc de Cassian that the joys of the rustic life away from Paris might be more pleasant than he expects. The beauties of the countryside, I told him, can be quite bountiful."

"What has that to do with me?"

The marquise's smile told Eleonora that the woman was much too pleased with herself. "Don't play the child with me, comtesse. Unlike your dear aunt, I am not so deceived by a beautiful face and figure.

"De Cassian is looking for a new wife," she went on. "His last one died as the result of an unfortunate tragedy, and left him with nothing but girls to pack off to a convent. He needs an heir. And you, my pretty green-eyed foreigner, look sturdy enough to give him one."

"You have taken too much upon yourself, madame," Eleonora said, struggling to control the flash of pain at the mention of children. She let her temper seethe instead. *Is the entire country of France mad?* "I do not wish to marry again."

"Don't do any stupid tricks," the marquise went on.

"I've assured your aunt that the rumors surrounding de Cassian are just nasty jealous lies, but you would do well to keep those rumors in mind and not refuse him."

The groom led a prancing black gelding to a nearby mounting block and signaled to Eleonora. "Why are you doing this?" she hissed to the marquise. "We have no ties."

The woman patted Eleonora's face before she could pull away. "Don't frown so, my dear comtesse. A woman must always think of her face." She gave Eleonora a bright smile. "And just think, when you marry, we shall be neighbors. There is but a garden separating our *hôtel* from de Cassian's." And with a jaunty wave, she walked away.

Eleonora stalked to the waiting horse, thinking how delightful it would be to wring the woman's neck. *Saint Stephen, forgive me, for I have committed murder in my heart.* She wanted to go home. She wanted to return to sanity. Even her mother's rantings and her brothers' arguments were preferable to *this!*

She mounted the gelding and kneed it toward the baying hounds. In the hubble-bubble around her she saw tiny finger waves of lover to lover, kisses puckered into the air, or lips deformed with snarling bloodlust urging du Peyre to release the dogs. Gone were the feigned—or real—ennui, the studied gestures, the languid poses, she'd come to expect from the guests of the château du Peyre.

And in the midst of it all was the comte d'Agenais, an island of serene elegance on the other side of the boisterous crowd. Only he, it seemed, was himself.

Madame de Rachand insinuated her horse next to Eleonora's. "Du Peyre says you're an expert horsewoman," the marquise said, shielding her eyes from the early morning sun.

"My uncle is being kind."

The marquise gave an unladylike snort. "He said it in a fit of pique, which means it's probably true. I would counsel caution. Expert horsewomen have a habit of riding off where they will, but today you would be wise to stay close to the pack, comtesse."

"Indeed, madame la marquise," Eleonora replied evenly, though dismay was rising up her throat. "And why is that?"

"You are new to riding with us French. You might become . . . lost." The woman's gaze narrowed on d'Agenais, and her mouth turned up in a bitter, triumphant smile. "I would particularly recommend that you avoid the old charcoal burner's ravine just south of those Gothic ruins du Peyre built last year. The unwary can often find such abandoned places rather perilous."

"I shall keep mindful of your . . . advice." Eleonora kneed her horse forward, making her way through the prancing, stomping horses.

So, she mused, she was being warned away, was she? She found herself near the front, close to her uncle. Du Peyre saw her and paused in his shouted orders to grunt at her, but he did not ask her to leave, apparently willing to acknowledge that she wouldn't slow them down.

She casually rearranged her skirts, glancing behind her as she did so. To her right was the comte d'Agenais, and just behind him was the marquis de Rachand.

Warn d'Agenais, a voice screamed in her mind.

No! Let the devil's son be ensnared. Let him be tamed! Then he will follow me.

She felt a stab of unease at leaving even a man like the comte to the wolves. Under her hand, buried under several thicknesses of skirts and petticoats, was the reassuring solidity of the pistol. That, at least, was something she could count on.

The horn sounded, and the dogs were released. Almost as one, the lead horses bounded away, Eleonora's among them. Exhilaration drove everything from her mind as she let herself be caught up in the glorious blood-pounding ride.

Awareness of the other riders faded as if in a dream. She cared nothing for the barking dogs or the stag they searched for, only the ride. The instincts of generations of Magyar horsemen were in her blood. The power of the horse was *her* power; the glory of muscle and sinew reaching, straining with each stride of the gallop, that was *her* glory. There was no doubt here. No uncertainty. No unease. She was not a stranger in this special world made by human and beast together.

On and on she rode, nearly oblivious to those around her. A momentary glare blinded her and she winced, breaking the spell and bringing the barking, shouting, cursing cacophony crashing into her ears.

Her uncle shouted a curse at the hunt master. The dogs had lost the scent. Everyone slowed.

Ahead, sunlight glared off the mirror surface of a small lake. The hunt master led them all toward the western shore, evidently hoping that the dogs would pick up the scent in the brush there. On the far shore, set against a cliff, were the Gothic towers of du Peyre's fanciful ruins.

She studied them, doubt assailing her. She glanced toward the south. Open forest grew right up to the edge of the lake. It had the look of being as carefully groomed as any garden. There was little underbrush, and it had nothing of the wild, terrifying menace of the Black Forest that she remembered so vividly from her journey.

D'Agenais could hardly be taken by surprise in there, she thought.

Warn him!

The marquise had said the charcoal burner's ravine was to the south. Eleonora frowned, knowing from her homeland just how quickly the forest could become dense and dark and secretive.

Warn him!

She looked behind her. The corpulent de Rachand was already wheezing from the exertion, while ahead of him sat the lean figure of d'Agenais, unruffled by anything so incidental as a spirited ride. She smiled at the notion that d'Agenais could be made to go anywhere against his will.

That should have been a calming thought—except that d'Agenais, too, was studying the forest to the south.

Warn him! the voice in her head cried a third time.

Why? Why should I warn him? I would look the fool. There's no reason for him to go south.

Ah, the voice answered, *you know him so well that you know the reasons for his actions?*

Of course not.

Then why don't you warn him?

Because I do not want to fail my family. And I will fail them . . . Think of the night of candles! How easily his hands wove a spell I nearly could not break.

Could not? Or did not want to break?

Could not! How could I want such—

Pleasure?

Eleonora shook her head to clear away the stinging voice of her conscience. *Don't you see,* she told it, *once I fall, he will never follow me. This way, when he sees how uncomfortable things are for him, he'll come with me.*

Are you so sure he will be free to follow?

Of course! What could chain a man such as he?

Treachery. Much as you plan to use.

The dogs suddenly began howling. They'd found the scent. Eleonora sighed in relief as the hunt master pointed north. She wanted to be gone from this place. Once she and the comte were on their way north, she thought, darting a look over her shoulder, her ambivalence would cease its sting—

D'Agenais wasn't there.

Her heart seemed to stop, and she sat frozen. It took a long moment for her mind to thaw enough to admit to rational thought. Maybe he had just moved farther up in the pack. Her gaze careened through the bustling crowd that was beginning to bound off after the dogs.

Eleonora maneuvered to the edge. By twos and threes they rode past, Vigny, a flirting wretch named Fleury, even Rachand, all intent on the elusive prey—but d'Agenais was not among them. Soon everyone had gone by. She looked south, into the trees. There, a dark shape was just disappearing into the shadows.

Turn north, a part of her urged, *turn north to ordinary men and their ordinary lies. Turn north. Follow the men whose kisses don't burn, whose caresses don't trail fire . . .*

She squeezed her eyes closed. The baying of the hounds

faded as she listened. A breeze caught uneasily at tendrils of her hair that had come free. The air smelled damp. The morning sun was warm on her face, but a storm was coming. She shivered. She hated storms.

Seemingly of its own accord, her hand tugged the reins toward the south. A whimper of protest escaped her, and she opened her eyes to stare at the path that led into the forest, a path that grew ever nearer.

No, a storm wasn't coming, she thought with a shudder. She was going to it.

Achille led his horse, Chiron, down the ever-narrowing forest path, toward a meeting with Beaulieu's son, Jean-Baptiste. In the chaos of readying for the hunt, a groom had pressed a note into his hand. He ducked a low-growing branch, the rustling of the paper in his pocket indistinguishable from the sound of the leaves.

There had been a moment, a fleeting moment, when he'd looked at the folded paper and had felt a surge of anticipation. A billet-doux from the countess Batthyány? He had no doubt her body would be his when he chose to have it, but a letter would mean he'd captured more.

Then his sense had returned. The seal was a plain one, hastily stamped. He had discerned enough of the countess's spirit to know that whatever she might send, she would openly acknowledge it by using her own seal.

Impatiently he'd ripped the missive open and had recognized the handwriting of Jean-Baptiste. What could the boy have discovered about the countess so quickly? The script, though even more tortured than usual, urged the comte to meet him at the old charcoal burner's camp south of du Peyre's ruins.

It was unlike Jean-Baptiste to be so secretive. It made Achille wary, and he wondered what it was about the countess Batthyány that could be so damning the telling of it required such an odd meeting place. Was she indeed involved with Rachand? And if so, how was he going to make her pay?

The path curved from south to east. It would lead

through the old charcoal burner's camp, coming, eventually, to du Peyre's Gothic ruins east of the lake.

He smiled at the irony of that. Less than half a mile north from the camp was the entrance to the lovers' grotto. His muscles grew taut with the image of having Eleonora there, of her responding to his caresses, of them reaching complete passionate fulfillment.

What was there about her that made him pursue her so relentlessly? To want passion with her to be the last memory he would take into battle with him, possibly into death?

She was fully a woman, a complex woman, and that complexity tantalized.

A muffled *crack,* like a shod hoof striking a stone, made him bring Chiron to a halt. He scanned the woods behind him with narrowed eyes and alert senses. There was no telltale movement, no unnatural shadow. Whoever was trailing him was skillful at not being detected.

It could be just a poacher waiting for him to pass. But once, outside Philippsburg, he'd been ambushed in just such a forest, and by just such a silent, invisible enemy.

He raised an eyebrow. Enemy? He smiled grimly and kneed his horse back into a walk, listening carefully for signs that he was still being followed. They were there. Barely discernible, but there.

He gave bitter thanks to those Hungarian hussars who had ambushed him so long ago. If not for them, he would not know what to watch for, he would not know that he was being tracked by the countess Batthyány.

Disappointment stung him. So she was working for Rachand, after all. Why else track him? No doubt that was what Jean-Baptiste waited ahead to tell him, but Achille's attention remained on the shadow behind him.

The stinging surged to anger. The beautiful Eleonora had caught him off guard. Had fooled him with her lies, with her consummate artifice. That raised the stakes. That raised the stakes very high indeed.

And he would see that she paid—in full.

* * *

Eleonora peered through the obscuring foliage at the comte d'Agenais. Half an hour earlier, he'd stopped, and she was sure he'd seen her—or heard her, though she wasn't sure which was louder, the horse's hoof cracking against a stone or her own heart nearly beating out of her chest. But he'd gone on, and her heart had settled down to a deafening drumroll.

She'd tried to keep track of distance the way her grandfather had taught her, but it was the increasing number of stumps amongst the underbrush that told her they were nearing the abandoned charcoal burner's camp.

A vine had killed a tree just ahead, and its long, dangling vines concealed d'Agenais from her sight for a heartbeat. She carefully edged past, concentrating hard on not disturbing the vines.

"A tryst, madame la comtesse?" The comte d'Agenais sat on his horse at the edge of a clearing—watching her with cold black eyes.

"Hardly, monsieur," she said, trying to see past him into the clearing. It appeared deserted. She let her horse move closer. "At least not for me. But perhaps you . . . ?"

He studied her with a narrowed gaze. "Perhaps I what, madame? Do you think I meet a whore to sate me until you're in my bed?" He leaned toward her, making less than an arm's length between them. "Why have you followed me?"

The harsh words made her wince. The birds had gone silent, making it seem as if there were no sound in the forest but the pounding of her guilty heart. It was proving difficult to maintain her bravado.

"I have followed you for nothing, it seems." She glanced at the peaceful clearing. She'd been a fool. She should have known the Rachands would be more talk than action. "I thought to—"

D'Agenais grabbed her head and covered her mouth with his hand. *"Down."* He swung his leg over and dropped to the ground, yanking her off her horse just as a pistol shot exploded into the silence. The bullet *thwack*ed into a nearby tree. The comte pushed her behind the trunk, then smacked the horses, sending them into the forest.

His back against another tree, he drew his sword. He looked at her across the open space between them. "You thought to *what*, madame?"

"D'Agenais, I—" she began, but was cut off by rough laughter coming from the clearing.

"No hidey-hidey, m'sieur!" a coarse voice called out. "You's come to meet w' your fa-a-aithful serv'nt, ain't you? Well, c'mon, then! He's waitin' mighty patient-like."

The comte spit out a harsh curse under his breath. "Jean-Baptiste." His gaze held hers for a long moment. She shivered at the anger, the scorn she saw there. "Are you worth a man's life?" he said bitterly.

"No! I—"

"I agree, madame." He tensed as if to spring.

"Wait," she called in a hoarse whisper. "I think he has another pistol."

"As do I. Is there anything else I should be warned of?"

The heat of a flush stole up her neck. She opened her mouth to say something—what?—then merely shook her head.

He stepped from behind the tree, sword at the ready.

"Be careful," she whispered, knowing he couldn't hear.

She peered through the foliage. Three stout men waited for d'Agenais. They formed a half circle around the center one, who held a knife at the throat of a young man. Her stomach tightened. The men were the sort she'd seen all too often after the wars. Ruthless, swaggering with the arrogance of survival, they had chosen to live with the easy comforts of brutality.

Sick at heart at what she'd allowed to happened, Eleonora swallowed hard to clear her tight throat.

"You see?" the man holding d'Agenais's servant said. "Here he is. Waitin' like a good 'n' proper slave."

"He is a servant, not a slave," the comte said, his voice almost conversational.

The man *harrumph*ed and spit. "One's t'other. Now, drop the pretty apple peeler and let Tyllo there show you some nice hempen rope we picked up in Marseilles." He indicated the man holding another pistol.

D'Agenais's blade did not move.

The man sneered. "That fat old boy-lover what paid us said you was to be tied up sweet and pretty like a New Year's present." He held the knife closer to the servant's neck, so close that if the young man even swallowed, the blade would draw blood. "But accidents happen. Don't they, m'sieur? Tyllo—"

"No," Eleonora gasped under her breath. Why hadn't she warned him? Overriding guilt twisted mercilessly inside her. Her hands shook as she reached into her pocket and dug out the pistol she'd hidden there.

D'Agenais held his ground, a firm, wide-footed stance. To the eye, he didn't move at all. And yet he suddenly seemed a spring that had been wound too tightly. Fine hairs at the back of her neck stood on end.

She held the pistol up, eyeing down the barrel. The comte's tall, muscular body partially obscured her line of shot to the one called Tyllo. That left the brute holding Jean-Baptiste. She closed her left eye and squinted.

He wore layers and layers of old, stained clothes. It was a shrewd defense, she thought. A bullet could become lodged in the layers, or an aim could be misjudged and miss the actual body underneath altogether. But there was one place he couldn't hide. Between his eyes. She took aim.

And fired.

The man's head slammed back.

Through the acrid gray smoke of the powder, she saw that d'Agenais didn't even flinch. He leapt at Tyllo, the sword sweeping aside the pistol. Shock barely had a chance to register on the man's face before the blade plunged into his heart.

The other wretch attacked the comte with a sword. He was unskilled, but that made him dangerous. D'Agenais was quick, able to parry the crude slices aimed at him. Their boots kicked up clumps of rotting leaves; their curses and grunts filled the clearing.

Jean-Baptiste had slumped to the ground when the dead man's hold had suddenly been released. He staggered to his feet just as the man d'Agenais fought fell lifeless at his feet.

A curtain of silence dropped on them. Eleonora began to shake uncontrollably. From nearby came the unmistakable sounds of retching. She closed her eyes and clenched her teeth against her own nausea. *Saint Stephen, I've killed a man.* Now she knew what it was to be provoked to murder.

"Jean-Baptiste," she heard d'Agenais say.

"Your pardon, monsieur," the young man said. "I am recovered now." She'd unconsciously braced herself, prepared to hear fear, even terror—not respect—in the boy's voice. She turned to watch the master standing solicitously over his servant.

The young man rose to his feet, wiped his face, and gave his master a wobbly bow. D'Agenais sat on a nearby stump, and he waved to Jean-Baptiste to do the same. "Sit, boy, and put your head between your legs."

After another unsteady bow, the servant did so, but he gingerly sat on the edge.

"Head down."

"But, monsieur!" Jean-Baptiste exclaimed.

"Down!"

The servant complied, then added in a muffled voice, "I would never have forgiven myself if you had been harmed!"

The comte brushed at a slight cut on the back of his hand. "Nor would I have forgiven you. Tell me how this came about."

The young man lifted his head, his color returning now. "Oh, monsieur, I have failed you miserably. I did not get much beyond Epinal before I was taken. A very pretty girl . . ." He paused and glanced at Eleonora, a blush stealing across his cheeks. "A very *friendly* girl, if you take my meaning, monsieur, came up to me and . . . and boldly asked me if I was traveling to Passau. I didn't tell her—I swear I didn't. But later, she knocked on the door to my room at the inn and said that since I was going on such a long journey, maybe I needed someone to, ah ..." His voice trailed off, and he swallowed guiltily.

"L-later, three men, pounding and yelling that I'd besmirched their daughter and sister, broke open the door and dragged me away. I expected to be beaten and robbed, but just outside of town, they paid off the girl, trussed me up like a sack of millet, and brought me back here!

"And, monsieur, the oddest thing. You'll never guess who I heard talking with these villains. The marquis—"

"De Rachand," Eleonora finished.

"Yes, madame!" Jean-Baptiste said, a look of innocent surprise on his face. "How did you know?"

D'Agenais held up his hand. "That is something madame la comtesse and I will be discussing shortly."

The chill in d'Agenais's voice when he'd spoken *of* her, not *to* her, made Eleonora apprehensive. "You can't think I was a part of this!"

The comte stood, ignoring her. "Help me drag these bodies into that hut," he said to Jean-Baptiste. "The intendant can send someone out to bury them."

She turned away from watching the comte's grim task and began walking toward the path that had led her here.

"Do not go far," d'Agenais warned her.

"The horses—"

"Jean-Baptiste will retrieve them."

"Monsieur!" She spun around in time to see the two men swing the last body into a ruined daub-and-wattle hut. She winced but held her ground.

"We have unfinished business, madame," d'Agenais said. "And I mean to finish it."

Chapter 9

～⌒♊⌒～

The comte went to the pile of coiled rope that had lain at the feet of the man called Tyllo. Eleonora's nerves wound even tighter. "Why are you acting like this? I saved your servant's life!"

"You nearly cost him his life," he answered, condemnation in his words. "Or perhaps that was the idea."

"What? How dare—"

"Jean-Baptiste, see to the horses. They should not be—"

"How dare you! How dare you suggest such a thing!"

"—too far up that path." Jean-Baptiste scurried out of the clearing.

"Monsieur le comte." Eleonora faced him, hands on hips. "You are damned lucky I don't have another pistol, or I'd shoot you where you stand."

A pistol lay on the ground where Tyllo had dropped it. D'Agenais kicked it to her. "There, madame. You're a passable shot when aiming at an unmoving target." He held out his arms. "I am unmoving."

"Bastard!" She kicked the pistol away, turned her back to him, and began to stalk out of the clearing.

He grabbed her wrist and spun her around, nearly jerking her arm out of its socket. He pressed her back against a tree.

"Let me go!" She squirmed to be free of his hold, but his arms were bands of iron.

He looped the rope he carried around one of her wrists,

127

then tied it to a low-hanging branch. She pounded on his shoulder with her free fist.

"You wretched— Release me!"

He caught her other hand and tied it up the same way.

"No!" she screamed. "No, don't bind me! No, please— Why are you doing this? D'Agenais—d'Agenais—" He tied her ankles to the tree so she couldn't kick him. She struggled and strained at her bonds. "For God's sake, *Achille!*"

Jean-Baptiste returned at that moment, leading both horses. His eyes widened and his mouth gaped.

"Oh, God. Jean-Baptiste, help m—" But even before she finished her plea, the blood of generations of French servants that ran in the boy's veins asserted itself, and he quickly recovered. In seconds, he stared stony-faced into the distance.

"The horses, monsieur."

"Thank you, Jean-Baptiste," d'Agenais said with infuriating calm. "Now take the gelding—"

"No!" Eleonora cried.

"—and ride it back to the château du Peyre. Talk to no one, Jean-Baptiste. Especially not to accommodating young women. Go to your father and tell him you are to be kept close. No one is to speak to you, and you are to speak to no one."

"Yes, monsieur." He bowed, still not looking at Eleonora, and mounted the gelding. He reined it toward the path, then paused.

"Monsieur?" He stared straight ahead of him into the forest.

"Yes?"

"In Epinal I heard of a foreign noble lady who, when passing through, paid for a surgeon to visit the sick girl-child of the miller. She paid for prayers to be said to Saint Stephen."

"On your way, boy."

Jean-Baptiste gulped, possibly at his own temerity, then kicked his heels. In moments, Eleonora and the comte d'Agenais were alone.

"And now, madame . . ."

"Achille, please. Untie me. Why are you doing this? I came to warn you!"

He wrapped his hand around her neck, forcing her head back. "Did you? I heard no alarm."

"Achille . . ."

"And what of this morning? I heard no words of warning from you when I passed you on the stairs."

"I meant to—"

"You meant for me to be attacked." His black-eyed gaze bored into her. The fire of anger she saw there seemed to be the flames of hell itself.

"No!" She tried to look at him through her lashes. "Achille, how can you say that of me?"

"How can I not? You tracked me with the skills of a Hungarian hussar, Eleonora. Why would you do that if not at Rachand's bequest?"

Why? She opened her mouth to answer, but she slumped against the tree when she realized she could not. A tear slipped out. It trailed down her cheek and dripped onto his hand. He flicked it away as if it burned him. "By Saint Stephen, Achille, I do nothing for the Rachands."

She sucked in a breath. The bonds that held her seemed to slacken when she stopped straining at them. Had he noticed?

His black eyes told her clearly that he didn't believe her words, but he didn't move to tighten the rope. Was he going to kill her? The nobility of most countries could kill with impunity, but not noble killing noble. Was that true in France? A bitter bubble of laughter stuck in her throat. As if that would matter to a man like Achille. Hadn't he killed men of rank in Paris?

She glanced at the hut concealing the bodies of the brutes who had held Jean-Baptiste. She, too, had killed. Provocation to murder knew no rank, it seemed.

She let her head fall back against the tree. "I thought somehow it would all be so civilized," she said. "So *French.* An intendant, perhaps, or a priest would ride up, hand you a letter written in the most elegant script, you would bow in acknowledgment, and ride off with them. The Rachands wanted you in the Bastille, but I was certain that a day or so later, you'd return as if nothing had happened."

He put a hand on the trunk above her head and leaned on it. With the other, he began to caress her neck. "You still have not said why you wished even this simple-minded scene to come to pass." He undid the knot of the cravat of her hunting costume, dragging the ties through his fingers.

"The night before last . . ."

"Yes?" His fingers worked at the top button on her jacket.

"Achille, please. I was confused. I—"

"A man kisses you, and you want him put away in the Bastille?" He unbuttoned the rest of the gold medallions. "Is that wise, do you think?" He pulled open her bodice, exposing the nearly transparent chemise she wore over her stays. "Is it, Eleonora?"

"Achille," she whispered. Her face grew taut as she struggled for composure.

"Do you know what manner of man I am?" He ripped the chemise open to her waist. Her breasts mounded above her stays. She gasped and turned her head away, her breathing harsh and shallow.

He stepped back and tore open his own jacket. Cold fear coiled like a snake in the pit of her stomach. *No, please, God, don't let him—*

"Do you know, Eleonora?" The protest of linen was loud in the clearing as he ruthlessly pulled his shirt aside to reveal his hard, muscular chest. There was a scar high up near his right shoulder.

"This is the kind of man I am. This is a reminder of my time at Gemeaux. When I played rough in the shrubbery with that whore La Rachand. I am a man who has sated himself on life. I am a man who seeks—"

He spun away from her, dragging his hands through his hair, and seemed to gain some measure of control. "God, what a fool I was. I thought you were one more game among many. Someone to stem the weariness, the godfor-saken eternal weariness. But you ... you've raised the stakes. Damn you, Magyar, you've raised the stakes very, very high."

"*I* have raised them?" she asked. "They cannot be so high as when you dallied with Madame de Rachand. You knew both of them hated you for what you had done in Paris. Did you think to turn that aside with your atten-tions? It didn't work, d'Agenais. They still hate you for it."

"I daresay they are not alone in that, madame." He kept his back to her, but she saw him shrug. Many might have thought it a casual dismissal, but she could see his tension in the taut way he held his shoulders. "I did not 'dally' with La Rachand. At the time, I did not even know who I was with. A careless glass of wine, and grief can be pushed over the edge into madness."

"And *this* is madness!" She ruthlessly crushed an unex-pected tendril of empathy for him. He had bound her! Saint Stephen knew she could never feel anything for him, she told herself. But as soon as the thought formed, she knew it was a lie. *No!* No, she mustn't feel for him— Her plans, her plans ...

"Achille, I-I am not part of their schemes. I only over-heard them talking," she began while trying to wriggle her gloved right hand through the loop of rope. She had to get away. "I did think to warn you, truly."

She froze when he sent a disbelieving glance over his shoulder, then he went back to staring into the forest.

The bark tore through the back of her glove and into her hand as she tugged on it. She set her jaw and pulled. Her hand slipped free of the glove. She quickly set to work on her other hand. "But I ... that is, I didn't understand much of what they said."

During her struggles, her skirts had pulled free of the rope, loosening it enough for her to slip her boots out.

"You dissemble, madame. I have known from our first moments together on the balcony that you are far from being a fool. I do not believe that you understood none of what they said."

"No-o-o," she said, gingerly taking a step away from the tree. She studied the path that led away from him, toward the east, and licked her lips in trepidation. She was not at all sure her legs would carry her. "No, I understood some of it, of course."

She silently gave thanks that he had not tied her bonds very tight, then felt a stab of cold fear. What if he hadn't *meant* to tie her bonds tight? What if he wanted her to run? She mentally gave herself a shake. *What if you turn into a pool of melted marrow and soak into the ground?* she mocked.

She grabbed her skirts in two handsful. "I understood some of it all too well," she said.

And ran. In three long strides she was at the edge of the clearing, then beyond it.

"Madame!" d'Agenais bellowed after her.

Leaves whipped into her face, branches snatched at her hair. She held her skirts high, her feet nimbly leaping over the treacherous exposed roots that were all that remained of the cut trees. She ran hard, her heart pounding, her boots thudding on the solid-packed dirt path.

Ahead, she caught a glimpse of yellow stone through the trees. The ruins! Could she hide? Her breaths were ragged.

She ducked a low branch. As a child, she'd run just this hard, but then it had filled her with exhilaration—not foreboding. Air blew against the sheen of fear on her skin, exposed by her torn chemise, chilling her.

From behind her, she heard the sound of a horse's hooves. She risked a glance backward. Achille was riding toward her at a trot. A centaur he seemed, one with the horse, implacable, adamant. And he was close. At any second she expected to feel the hot breath of the horse on her back.

Damn him! She rounded a bend in the path. Just ahead was an arched opening in the stone wall. Yes! She urged her burning legs to carry her faster. Let him try trotting behind her on those ramparts!

Her boot heels hit the paving stones with a crack, and a shock of hope went through her. There! To her right, wide stairs spiraled up the outside of a stone tower. From behind her came the hollow clop of shod hooves on stone.

She leapt toward the stairs, trying to take them two at a time. Her foot slipped. She stumbled, caught herself, and kept climbing.

"Madame!" d'Agenais called. "*Eleonora.*"

Her heart thudded with exertion. She kept running upward.

"Eleonora, come down," he said calmly. "You have no choice."

She reached the top. She leaned against the stone wall, gasping for air, her legs trembling. A narrow stone walkway circled the rampart of the tower—and led back down the same stairs she'd just come up.

D'Agenais's voice drifted up to her. "It's a false tower, Eleonora. You have no choice but to come down."

"I can see that, d'Agenais," she called down to him between gasps, her jacket and chemise hanging open.

The tower she'd climbed was one of two that fronted an enclosed courtyard. To the back, where the ruins had been built into a cliff, were three arched doorways set in an unadorned wall, though only one seemed to actually have a door. Her fingers clung to the stone. "False tower, false doors, false manners, false . . . everything. Is nothing genuine here?"

He was looking up at her, a dark figure against the surrounding pale yellow stone. The centaur's shadow he cast stirred with his horse's impatient movements, which he didn't bother to control. Or perhaps the impatience was his.

"My anger, Eleonora, is genuine enough." The centaur shadow became still. "If you are a part of the Rachands'—"

"*No*, I tell you!" She spit out one of her brother's curses under her breath. She glared down at him. "I overheard them, yes! As I told you. Accidentally! But I didn't know about Jean-Baptiste. I swear I didn't."

"I hear your words, Eleonora. I want to see the truth of them in your eyes. Come down." His voice was velvet-deep and carried easily up to her.

Her mouth was dry. His tone was caressing, but she could feel the glove of steel beneath the velvet. She opened her eyes and studied the figure of darkness below her. His terms were clear enough: If he believed her, she would be unharmed.

But if he did not see the truth in her eyes . . .

"And I hear *your* words, d'Agenais." *And your threat. But I have no choice, do I?* "But I will not be bound. Do you hear me? *I will not be bound.*"

"Agreed."

She swallowed, her tongue sticking to the roof of her mouth, as if to prevent her from saying more.

She edged along the tower's walkway to the stairs. "Then I shall come down, d'Agenais."

"I shall be waiting."

Eleonora dragged her hand along the gritty stone as she went down the endless turnings of the spiral stairs. The descent seemed to take forever, her legs slowly managing one shaky step at a time.

The sun was bright, and she had to squint against the glare. Months, years, seemed to pass as she made her way downward toward the waiting comte d'Agenais, but the shadows told her the morning was not yet half-over.

She rounded the last turning. He waited, still mounted on his horse, his torn jacket and shirt revealing the sculptured muscles of his chest and stomach. She stopped when she was still a few steps from the courtyard floor.

Keeping her eyes carefully level with his, she said, "Look closely, d'Agenais, and you'll see the truth of my words. I was not and am not a part of the Rachands' scheme. I am not guilty of their crimes."

He regarded her steadily. "Then what are you guilty of?"

She took another step, then another, until she reached the floor of the courtyard. "Stupidity, for one thing."

"And for another?"

She paused. Careful, careful, she told herself. She could feel wariness creeping into her, wariness that would show in her eyes. She tried a smile. "Stupidity takes up a great deal of room, monsieur."

"That, madame, is conjecture on your part." He swung a leg over and dismounted in one smooth motion. He closed the space between them, his face inches from hers, but he did not touch her.

"Your eyes are Delphic," he told her, his voice low. "And like the ancient oracle, they hide as much as they reveal. I see much, madame, but there is a great deal more that I do not see. I see truth, but what truth? And nowhere . . ." he trailed a finger along her jaw ". . . *nowhere* do I see stupidity."

She took a step back. Her heel hit the bottom step. "Look, d'Agenais, I *was* being stupid. The marquise said she had a *lettre de cachet.* I thought . . ."

She rubbed her forehead. Why did he have to stand so close? To intimidate her, of course, to confuse her, to keep her from dissembling. And it was succeeding. She shook her head to straighten her thoughts. *Saint Stephen, how have I come to such a pass?* "You know what I thought."

She heard him step away and she looked up in relief, but it was short-lived. He untied a wineskin from the saddle. "And so you followed to watch the arrogant French lord receive his deserved punishment," he said, handing her the bag.

Her thirst was too great for her to decline the offer. "Not exactly, monsieur." She lifted the corners of her mouth in a weak smile of thanks and took the bag. In seconds her head was bent backward and a stream of cool, dark wine was sliding down her throat.

"And for what did you wish to see me punished, madame?" d'Agenais asked, the undertones in his voice deeper now, more complex. "The presumption of wanting you?"

With a gulp, she swallowed the last mouthful of wine. "And then who would be the arrogant one?"

"Who, indeed?" he asked, his eyes still on her.

She grew uneasy under his dark regard. The sun grew hot on her exposed bosom, reminding her that she stood before him revealed to her stays. She curled her fingers into a ball, determined not to clench her jacket closed as she so desperately wanted to.

She lowered her gaze to the view of his naked chest and waist. A trail of silky black hair disappeared provocatively under the band of his breeches. She rubbed her forehead again and made to look around the courtyard. "Is there somewhere cool . . . ?"

"There is a place," he said, "out of the sun."

"Yes, yes, thank you. I'm sure that would be more comfortable."

"Infinitely more comfortable," he said, taking the winebag from her.

He led his horse to a shaded corner with a pool and looped the reins through a ring set in the wall. Then they walked toward the back of the courtyard to the only real door in the archways. When they reached it, he put his hand on the latch, but she reached out to stop him. He paused.

"I was wrong not to warn you," she said. "But please believe me, the only part I played in their scheme was in overhearing it."

"Convince me, Eleonora."

He opened the door, and a puff of cool, perfumed air enveloped her. He bowed slightly and gave an elegant gesture for her to precede him.

She nodded to acknowledge his formality, then walked in. It took a moment for her eyes to adjust to the sudden dimness. Behind her, d'Agenais entered and closed the door. She could see clearly then. All too clearly.

It was a cave. Had been a cave. Now, wax candles burned in elaborate silver sconces set into the rough-hewn walls. Rich Oriental carpets covered the floor, and everywhere glittered gilding that had been laid on with a lavish hand.

Heavily upholstered chairs and ottomans had been set around the room in groups of two, three, and four, and there were chairs that tilted back with arms longer than necessary, sofas canted at unusual angles, and, at the far end on a dais, a bed. A huge gilded bed, a royal bed, mounded thick with down, and draping over it, a crowning canopy of gossamer silk suspended from the roof of the cave high above it.

Eleonora squeezed her eyes shut. *"Fool,"* she gritted under her breath. She spun to face d'Agenais. He was leaning negligently against the door, arms crossed, a slight smile playing over his mobile mouth.

His smile widened. "The candles are lit every morning when the wine cabinet is replenished," he said. "A bit excessive for my tastes. It is, however, quite cool."

"Cool! Excessive!" She turned her back to him. "God, what a fool I've been. You *led* me here. You deliberately led me here." She grabbed a small statue from a nearby table and held it in front of her like a weapon. "Didn't you? Didn't—" Her gaze suddenly registered what it was she was holding. It was a satyr; a rampantly ready satyr.

D'Agenais took it from her grasp and set it back on the table. "No, Eleonora. You led me."

She flushed and stalked into the middle of the room. "So the game is ended. I made a foolish mistake and now I am to pay."

"And how did you think the game would end when you began it on the balcony?"

"Not like this. Not so soon."

"I am an impatient man. I also don't have a great deal of time. A courier will arrive shortly with my commission."

"Commission! You go to war?" *He is leaving!* She tried to gather the tangled threads of her composure. Time, time, she had no time. "I had not realized." She had to turn this situation around; she had to *think.* "Perhaps you would find it more accommodating to resort to one of your more accessible ... admirers," she said, feeling hollow at the thought of another woman in his arms.

He laughed. "One more tryst in the shrubbery? That is not the kind of memory I mean to take with me."

If only he wouldn't laugh, or smile like that, she thought. *If only his eyes didn't glint with enjoyment when they bantered. And if only his voice didn't go through me ...*

"Eleonora, it is you I want."

She wandered about the room on unsteady legs, moving away from him, from his words, studying the contraptions and accommodations as if they truly interested her. *It is you I want.* Her thoughts clouded. She should be exultant, but while she should have plans, strategems, she had only images of him.

"What if I do not want the game ended?" she asked, struggling for control. She paused in front of a bizarre chair whose high arms were shaped like the open claws of a lion. "What if I wanted to cool your ardor, just for a while? I could play the ingenue. You have no taste for innocents." She held her arms out wide and made to back into the chair. "Would you lose inter—"

D'Agenais was in front of her in a heartbeat, grabbing her by the shoulders and pulling her forward. "Your pardon, madame," he said, holding her close, not appearing to want her pardon at all. He turned her around to face the chair, pressing her back against his chest. With his free hand, he plucked a candlestick from a candelabrum, blew it out, and used it to push one of the chair's arms.

There was a nearly inaudible click, then the lion's claws closed with a snap faster than lightning. Two more claws snapped closed around the chair's legs, then the seat tilted back, spreading the chair's legs apart as it did so.

"It works by levers and counterweights," he said, his voice low and caressing. "And I'm not sure how soon I could have found the key to unlock it." He caressed her shoulders. "Or how soon I'd have wanted to."

She stared wide-eyed at the obscene chair, aghast at

what her own naïveté had almost led her into. "I don't think I want to play the ingenue."

"I am relieved," he said.

She left his hold and walked on, glancing at the bed as she passed, then thoughtfully traced her finger along the edge of a japanned cabinet. "Or perhaps it's not a game at all, but a chase? Is that what entices you?"

She sent him a knowing smile. "So it follows that what would *not* entice you—is not to have a chase! Of course! The answer has been before me all along—Madame de Rachand herself even mentioned it. 'He is not the kind of man to be lured by mere availability,' she said. By the way, did you know she put an 'incentive' in your wine when you were at Gemeaux?"

"Yes, Eleonora, as soon as I'd carelessly drunk that glass of wine. It is difficult not to notice the . . . effects."

"Ah. Yes, well, I'm afraid you will have to be satisfied with mere availability. I have no 'incentives.' "

"Actually, you're leaning on a cabinet full of them. But I am sure I will be most satisfied without their inducements."

She stepped back from the cabinet a little too quickly. "Not if I become amiability itself," she said, slipping her torn hunting jacket off her shoulders and letting it fall to the floor. "Now, what am I to do first? Pose, perhaps?"

She thrust out her bosom to emphasize the mounding of her breasts above the stays, then turned her head slightly to look at him through half-closed eyes. "Or perhaps that isn't provocative enough for you."

He straightened. "Eleonora . . ."

She undid the waistband of her skirts. With a *whoosh* of cambric and lawn, they fell into a heap on the floor.

"Stop this."

"No, wait!" She began yanking the pins from her hair. The long, thick auburn tresses were heavy as they fell to just above her knees, and she shook her head to tousle them.

She heard his quick intake of breath, and thought perhaps undoing her hair had not been such a good idea. His eyes were avid on her.

Her clothes were scattered about on the rugs, a green crumpled heap that was her jacket, and the concentric ripples of her skirts looking like a green pond that a pebble had been thrown into.

Dressed in only her stockings, stays, and torn chemise, she went to an innocent-enough-looking chair. With hands on hips, she tilted her head inquiringly toward d'Agenais.

"It's safe," he said.

"Can I trust you?"

The corners of his lips lifted in a suggestive smile. "No."

She swallowed and looked away. As soon as she'd asked the question, she'd known the answer. She *could* indeed trust him. It made her uneasy to realize that, unlike her, he had never tried to deceive. Just the opposite, in fact, since from the first moment they'd met, he'd been blatantly honest about what he wanted. And she had not.

Gingerly she lowered herself into the chair, alert for the tiniest clicking sound. None came. The chair remained just a chair. She slowly let some of the tension seep from her muscles. "So many traps for the unwary," she said.

"So many traps for the *amiable.*" Achille's body thrummed with awareness as he let his gaze drink in her soft contours settling into the rose velvet chair. With the mindlessness of habit, she had flipped the breathtaking fall of her hair in front of her shoulder before she sat down, and now it partially covered her body like a meandering brook caressing the lush curves of a bank.

He shrugged out of the torn remnants of his shirt and coat, and deliberately dropped them on top of her skirts. A symbolic gesture, but an explicit one, and when he saw her flush in the candlelight, he knew it had not been wasted. He, too, could be amiable.

He went to the japanned cabinet and opened it, revealing decanters of wine and potent cordials, and a few small vials of liquids usually only whispered about.

"You said—"

He held up a sealed bottle of wine. "No incentives."

She was his. He had no doubt of that. Didn't she realize that by playing this "act," she made herself all the more enticing? She had finally hit upon a game he had no doubt of winning. And that meant he could take his time, keep his head clear, and savor her fall moment by moment.

There were two chairs near hers, one a bit closer than the other. With a quick calculation, he made his way to the one farther from the delicious Eleonora. He held out a glass to her and watched her lean forward to take it, as he knew she would. "A Mantes wine," he said, his voice huskier than he'd expected.

Some of her hair tumbled free of its caress of her body and spilled to the floor. What he would give to have that silken curtain caressing him.

"Thank you," she said, accepting the delicate glass from him.

With his booted foot, he pushed an ottoman closer to her chair, then relished the sight of her stretching her long, slender legs out to rest on it. She raised one knee and relaxed against the back of the chair as she sipped the pale wine.

Candlelight glinted off the highlights of fire in her hair and made the subtle ivory of her skin glow golden. His loins tightened with a primitive hunger.

"You puzzle me," she said, a half smile on her tantalizing mouth.

"Do I?" He watched her lips conform to the curved shape of the glass as she took another sip of wine, and his blood pounded harder at the thought of those lips curving . . .

Slow, slow, he admonished himself, but made no move to hide the blatant desire straining against his breeches. The more his body responded, the more he knew the prize was going to be well worth the winning.

Her shoulders lifted in a brief laugh. "Yes, you do." She leaned her head back and closed her eyes, revealing the most nearly perfect profile he'd ever seen. Proud, aristocratic, resolute, yet uncompromisingly feminine.

He remembered the taste of the soft flesh under her chin, and of her neck, and that small dimple where her blood pulsed so near the surface. He wanted to taste that very spot when he took her.

"But lately I've been puzzling myself as well," she said. He heard her words through a haze of sensual musings. "Here I am, sitting here with you, drinking wine with you—"

"Being most amiable," he interrupted.

"Now, but earlier . . . I actually thought you might—" Through half-closed eyes, he saw her turn toward him, her breasts mounding higher. Sweet Christ, he wanted her.

"I thought you might . . ." Her words faltered. She licked her lips. ". . . might rape me," she finished with a whisper.

"And now you think I won't?"

Her eyes were troubled. The wineglass trembled ever so slightly in her grasp. His body tensed for a moment until he convinced himself that her distress came from her confusion and not her situation.

"What kind of woman am I to sit here like this— drinking *wine* with you!" She set the glass on a nearby table.

He let his gaze travel over her luscious body, then thought of the woman he'd played cards with, of her quick wit as they'd sat feigning such disinterest, and he thought of the way she'd gripped his arm when he'd led her into supper and she'd been asked about children. Image after image of her flashed through his mind . . .

"What kind of woman are you, Eleonora? A beautiful woman. But your beauty is not just in your face and your form, but in your wit, intelligence, strength, passion, courage—"

"Courage! I ran from you in terror!"

"Was it terror, Eleonora? Was it?"

She averted her eyes. "Yes, damn you. Why else would I have run? Answer me! Why else?" She stood and began to pace. "Look at you! You resemble that damned satyr more than a man." She crossed her arms under her breasts.

"Of course I ran from you in terror. You tied me to a tree, you tore my clothes—"

"I'm a man of many passions."

She was magnificent in her agitation. Hair swirling about her exquisite body like a nimbus of fire ... Such passion she had in her. It almost matched his own.

He went still at that. Perhaps it *did* match his.

"Passion," she spat out, her eyes flaring as bright as any flame. "Is that what you—"

"Look at me, Eleonora. Tell me what you see." Would she tell him the truth?

Her gaze darted to him, traveled from his head down his body as he reclined on the chair. A flush stained her cheeks, and she twisted her head to look elsewhere. *"Look at me,"* he demanded. "What do you see?"

"Is this another of your infernal games? What do you think I see? Surely there's a mirror here somewhere. Then you can see for yourself."

"I want you to tell me."

"Tell you what, damn you?" she asked in exasperation. "Why does it matter?"

"Truth, Eleonora. Truth matters. In a world of artifice and posturings, the eyes are the only gates to truth. What you see."

"What I see? A man. Sprawling on a chair."

"Forget the chair. Tell me of the man."

She glared at him. "He *unfashionably* chooses not to wear a wig, but wears his own black hair to the middle of his back, and leaves it *unfashionably* unpowdered."

"Artifice, Eleonora. That does not matter to you."

"It is not artifice that his black eyes are those of the devil's own so—" She broke off, turmoil filling her eyes. "Saint Stephen, Saint Stephen, how did I get here?" She ran to the pile of clothes, snatched up her jacket, and held it to her.

"Why did you stop?" he asked.

She shook her head, but did not answer.

"What is it that you see that you don't want to tell me?"

"Why do you taunt me with these games of yours?" she whispered.

"This isn't a game anymore, is it, Eleonora?" He rose and went to stand behind her. He caressed her shoulders, reveling in the warmth of that ivory skin. "What you see when you look at me is passion, isn't it?" He rubbed his face against her hair. "Isn't it? But it isn't my passion for you that you see—though that's unmistakable—it's *your*—"

"Don't say it," she begged.

"Why not? Why not say that your own passion is as great as mine?"

"No, no, saying it makes it real." She reached up and touched his hand, the warmth from her fingers seeping into his own. "I don't want it to be real."

He drew his hands down her arms, then back up. Did she know how much she gave away with just the tiny movements of her body? "You want it to be real, Eleonora, but you're afraid it won't be. That's it, isn't it? That's your terror."

He kissed her neck and felt her flesh quiver in response.

"No, Achille," she whispered. "My terror is you."

He embraced her, her back to his chest, his arms wrapping around her breasts. "I don't want to be your terror. I want to be your lover."

She rocked her head back and forth, her hair rustling against his skin with tantalizing softness. "No," she said, "I can't. I can't."

He kissed the tender place below her ear.

"Achille, no . . ."

He kissed her there again, and slowly rubbed his lips up and down her neck. "Tell me you don't want me," he murmured. "Then I'll stop."

He lightly drew his fingertips across the enticing mounds of her breasts. *Take her!* his body roared. He was nearly trembling with the effort to keep from ravishing her. He craved *all* of her, and by the blood of his fathers, he swore she would give him all of her—body, mind, and soul.

"No, not again," she whimpered. "You make me so lost. You make me forget. How can you do this to me?"

He forced his roaming hands to stop their caresses. Soon he could not have stopped, any more than he could have stopped a full cavalry charge. She swayed against him, but he steadied her, then stepped away.

"Now who plays the game, Eleonora?"

"What? I don't understand."

"Don't you? It's an easy enough one to play, isn't it? Call me devil while you melt in my arms. And then later, revile me, cast me in the role of your evil seducer."

She wrapped her arms around herself as if she were suddenly cold. "Unless you take me by force, the fault would be mine."

"From innocent to martyr. Nicely done."

"Stop mocking me! What do you want me to say?"

"I want you to say, '*Yes*, Achille, I want you. I want to kiss you and touch you and caress you and become one with you and fly to heaven with you.' I want you to say, 'I want to be your lover, Achille. I want your body to merge with mine. I want to fall asleep with the sound of your heart under my ear, and I want to wake with my body twined with yours.' *That*, Eleonora, is what I want you to say."

He looked at her from beneath his lashes. She clearly had not expected so direct an answer, and she hovered between shock and indignation. "That's what I *want*," he added. "I'll settle for a clear and distinct 'yes.' "

A chuckle bubbled from her, and she shook her head ruefully. "My head is in a spin! How did I ever think I could . . ."

He held out his hand to her. "Lovers, Eleonora. A man and a woman pleasuring each other."

"You make it sound like little more than an alfresco dinner. Once done, it cannot be taken back. Or forgotten."

"You have already proved sublimely discreet. And I shall not wish to undo it, or forget it."

"Devil's words, Achille," she said, but the jacket she held slipped from her grasp and fell to her feet.

Anticipation pounded in his veins. "Then be this devil's lady."

She reached out and touched her fingertips to his. Exultation flooded him. *Body and mind . . .*

Their fingers twined. "And later?" she asked quietly.

"Later, I will have memories of you. I leave for the front when the courier arrives. What happens now determines the memories I will take with me."

"And nothing can change that?"

"Nothing, Eleonora," he answered, pulling her to him. "Nothing but Fate herself could change it."

Chapter 10

Achille cupped her face and felt Eleonora's tremor, the sensation arcing from her cheek to his palm like a spark from a spinning sulfur ball. He slid his lips over hers. Her mouth parted as if in a plea for him to deepen the kiss.

What was there about her that made *him* spin inside? That made him want her, made him dream of her instead of his own satiety, made him want to know her, made him want to pleasure her, *her,* not for his own sake, but for hers. Always before, before Eleonora, a woman had been ... just a woman. Now ...

He sent his tongue into her mouth. A sortie it was, quick, sweeping. He returned, as he would in battle, winded, his blood singing. Again she met his raid, equaled it, matched it, twining, exploring, tasting.

Her arms were around his neck, her hands in his hair. He stroked her back, pressing her into his body, feeling the points of her breasts against his chest.

His hands slipped the chemise from her shoulders, down her arms. It draped on her hips, concealing her intimate dark curls in one last lone protest. He did not push the garment away. He knew it would fall.

He kissed the exquisitely soft flesh under her ear, tasted with his lips and tongue the column of her neck, feeling her respond, absorbing that response into himself. With his fingers, he began unlacing her stays, but his hands fell still again and again whenever he kissed her, not willing to

147

spare even the smallest part of his consciousness to anything but the taste of her.

Eleonora let her head fall back as if its weight were too great to bear. A delicious heat shimmered wherever his lips touched her. *So good, so good . . .* Her stays and chemise fell away. She caressed his shoulders, his chest, hungry for the hard, masculine feel of him.

She wanted him, wanted him to make her burn as he had amidst the enchanted candlelit trees. Thoughts swirled with desire, like leaves dancing in the rising heat above an autumn fire. What could it matter if she were to be with him once, a woman with a man? Passion, he'd said, there was passion in her.

He drew his hands up her body as if the contact fed him, nourished him. A moan spilled from deep in her throat. A man, a woman . . . *Once, please, once,* she pleaded silently. Once, she wanted a man's passion to speak to hers. What could it matter? It would be his body, and hers. Nothing more, nothing more . . .

His fingers traced the outline of her breasts, under the soft globes, to the sides, as if he were reading her with his fingertips. Her pulse surged, consumed by his touch.

He stared enthralled at the place where the backs of his fingers followed the swell of her breast, an enchantment seeming to have taken hold of him. "You bewitch me," he murmured. "Isolde to my Tristan. But she needed . . ." he kissed the hollow between her breasts ". . . a potion for her . . ." he swept his hand around a breast, then fanned his fingers across a deep rose peak ". . . sorcery."

Flame licked out, as flint struck to priming powder. Eleonora sucked in a breath. "Yes . . . oh, yes. Such sorcery," she said, leaning into his touch, her eyes fluttering closed. "A soldier's sorcery. Spells of fire, of siege . . ."

"Of surrender." His mouth took hers again, tasting, coaxing, as if to draw the secrets of her into himself. The scent of his sandalwood filled her head. And the only sound she heard was the pounding of her own blood.

Achille carried her to the bed, murmuring of her beauty, her hair, her eyes, of the truths he wanted to see in them.

For a moment, reflected in the huge gilt-framed mirror at the head of the bed, a ravishing satyr held his soon-to-be-ravished nymph. Then he laid her on the white satin sheet that covered the down mattress, and she sank into a cloud.

He knelt over her, his lips nipping at the pulse of her neck, his hands sweeping over her breasts, plucking the buds. She moaned, wanted to touch him, but he brushed her hands away. "I am a selfish man, Eleonora," he murmured against her skin. "I want the pleasure of pleasuring."

He drew his hands down her stomach, over her hips, cupped the globes of her behind, then stroked her thighs. Of its own accord, its own hunger, her body moved, strained to wherever he touched, like music made yearning flesh. Her pleasure was to be of his composing.

"*Ah-h-h.* What you do ..." she murmured, the words sliding from her with a deliciously sensual slur. "Achille, Achille, I am fevered. I am—"

"You are mine," he rasped, nearly mad with the feel of her. He closed his eyes and kissed the flesh low on the feminine plain of her abdomen, suckled it, slid his open mouth over her, as if he could taste the tremors of her nascent passion.

A sweet cry slipped from her parted lips. He kissed her thigh, then again, nearer the hidden enchantment of her womanhood. Her scent intoxicated him. He nuzzled her luxurious auburn curls.

"Achille?" she asked, the word caught between a moan and a whimper. "Achille, what are you ..." The words trailed off in a moan.

He kissed her thigh again, so near, so near ... She drew up her knee to protect herself, but ended by revealing herself to him. He groaned.

"El—" he ground out. His hands tightened on her hips. She beguiled him. He kissed the auburn curls, then tasted lower.

He heard her gasp in surprise. "Oh, God, no, you mustn't ... No, no, you—" Her hands flitted to his hair, then away, like a frightened bird. "What do—?"

He drew the tip of his tongue along the intimate rosy swollen edge of her, like a mage tracing the letters of a spell. A moan of questioning protest tumbled from her throat, and a shock of surprise broke through the sheen of pulsing hunger in his brain. She was questioning the unknown.

His lips pressed against her in a gentle kiss, then stroked and nipped. He slid his tongue over her. Her hips rose. His mouth took her.

"Ahhh," she cried, her body arching into him. "Oh, God, what are you—" Her words slurred into a long moan, a sensual melody of surprise and wonder. He kissed her deeply, intimately . . . and oh, so slowly.

Her hand clenched in his hair. Her body, following the rhythm of its own inner music, began to move against his mouth. He heard her breaths quicken, luscious sounds of hovering expectation.

"What is h-happeni— Oh, God, please," she pleaded, not knowing what she implored him for. Her hands curled and uncurled in the sheet.

She tensed. A sob broke from her, *"No, no, no."* Her head rocked back and forth. She strained against him. *"No, no—oh, God, oh—"* She shuddered. She cried out. Her body arched, held, as wave after wave of her moans filled the air.

When the rapture receded, her body fell limp onto the sheets. Achille rested his head on the sweet pillow of her thigh, struggling to maintain control of his own body. He was shaking with the effort. If he took her now, he would finish almost before he began.

The passion of her. Sweet God, the passion of her. Dangerous thoughts drifted, of long days, months, years, with a lover such as Eleonora. He ran his hand over her other thigh, up to her hip. And thoughts of salvation, thoughts that a man might not always find it on a battlefield. A sound intruded.

Weeping.

He raised himself onto his hands. "Eleonora?"

She wiped impatiently at her face. "This cannot be, this cannot be," she said, her eyes closed. "I am in an abyss."

He kissed the tears. "After passion it can seem so," he told her. "But it does not have to be 'after' just yet." Hunger for her thrummed in his blood, barely under his control. He kissed the swell of her breast, the base of her neck, the softness below her ear. His hands roamed her body.

"No, no," she said, rocking her head on the satin sheet. "I can't feel this— Sweet God, what have you done to me? I shake. I'm frightened. Saint Stephen, help . . ."

Under his hands, he felt the rhythms of her body change, become remote, as if she were withdrawing from him. "Eleonora," he whispered. Eyes half-closed with passion, he raised his head to see her face. "Eleonora! Look at me."

She opened her eyes and looked at him. There was a wall inside her. Hiding her, keeping her from him.

Achille sucked in a labored breath. He wanted *all* of her. "What do you do?" he asked harshly. He balanced himself on one hand, one knee. "Why are you keeping yourself from me?"

"Why am I . . . ?" She blinked at him, her eyes showing him hurt and confusion. Her eyes, her eyes, her eyes . . . She closed them and laid her head back on the pillow, then curled up on her side. "What are you saying? What do you mean? I am here for your taking."

Her fingers fisted into the soft sheet, pulling it toward her naked body. He grabbed it and held it to keep her from covering herself. She lay supine on the white disheveled sheet, an odalisque who could tempt the most sated of sultans. His body thundered with hunger for her. The arch of her neck, the swelling of her breasts, the softness of her thighs— *Take her!*

"You have *everything* more to give me," he said.

"Damn you," she whispered. "Do your games never end?"

He yanked the sheet toward him. "Do yours?"

"Achille—" she cried, and rose to her elbows.

"I had not taken you for such a coward, Eleonora."

"Coward! How can you say such a—"

"Did you think I wanted nothing more than to spill my lust into you? Is that what you thought? Is it? I am no boy, madame, willing to dip into anything that can take me!"

She scrambled to her hands and knees, backing away from him until the mirror set at the gilded bedstead stopped her. "Achille, you're unbalanced. You're raving. Look at me. Look at us! How can you say I'm denying you anything?"

"How?" he asked, closing the distance between them. She straightened, her back flattening against the mirror. The image pulsed before his eyes, a doubled temptation of lush, creamy flesh and streaming hair. He pressed her head between his hands. "Look, madame," he said, forcing her to face the mirror, "look and see how I can say such a thing."

Once again her back was against his bare chest. The luscious swell of her behind pressed into his loins and his rampant desire. Sweet God, the promise of her! How could he not . . .

Inside him, the sword of his will began to waver. *No,* he roared silently, the sheer terror of that wavering giving him strength. He wanted all of her; he would have all of her. He would not waver.

Do not feel the silk of her hair against your hand, he commanded himself. *Nor the cream of her passion-warmed skin. Feel nothing, nothing, but the sting of what she is denying you.* He steadied his breathing, silencing the deafening clamor of his insistent hunger.

Her eyes . . . green and wide, composed—those things he could command himself not to see. But the wall in them, the wall that separated, that kept her apart from him. That he saw, that he could not be blind to.

"I don't know what you expect me to see!" Her gaze met his in the reflection. "Saint Stephen, you're as unstable as priming power. Are you mad?"

"Do not blame madness for your reserve, Eleonora. We are both all too sane. Look again."

Her eyes snapped open, and her gaze stared at his in the mirror. "Reserve! My God, look at this place. We are both all too *in*sane. What do you want me to see? What do you want of me that I have not offered you?"

"Look into your eyes, Eleonora." She glanced briefly at her own reflection. *"Look,"* he ordered, then waited until she complied. "There is a wall there, high and strong in those green eyes of yours, and you are behind it."

He loosened his hold on her head, letting the silken strands of her hair flow over his fingers. "Part of you is here, with me, animating this beautiful body, smiling with these tantalizing lips, touching me with these long, supple fingers. But there is much of you that is not with me. I have glimpsed the fire behind that wall. I have seen the flames of that which you deny me. And I want it."

She leaned forward, splaying her hands on the mirror, earnestly looking at his reflection. "You mistake me! There is nothing more. I am the same woman who looked back at me this morning at my dressing table. I have never been with a man this way before, Achille. Never! I don't even know what you are asking of me."

"Never? How could your husband have glimpsed such a fire and not yearn to be seared by it?" Achille caressed her shoulders, the scintillating warmth of her skin rushing to heat his blood. "How could your lover have felt such sizzling heat and not crave to burn in those flames?"

"There is nothing, I tell you!" She bent her head and rested her forehead on the cool glass. "My husband only saw, only cared to see, that I was female. To Miklos, I was a readily *accessible* female." Her hand on the mirror balled into a fist. "That is what wives are. *Accessible* females to husbands in rut." She sobbed and hit the glass, though not hard enough to break it.

"And my lover . . . sweet golden Bálint . . . He read poetry to me. Sang bittersweet songs of star-crossed love. And in the spring, he kissed me. Again and again, kisses tasting of wine, of ripe apples, of candied violets." A tear slid down the silver surface like a liquid diamond. "And I thought it passion."

Achille watched Eleonora raise her head from the mirror and turn her eyes to him, eyes that sparkled with unshed tears. He discovered his jaw had tightened, and his stomach had knotted. "Why do you tell me this?" he asked, unpleasantly aware of a new sensation beating in his blood, just out of time with his desire: jealousy.

"Achille, I'm sorry if I have disappointed you. What seemed like such a sin at home, here seems but an innocent dalliance. I never even broke my marriage vows."

"Your husband is dead," he said roughly. "Your vows, dust." He yanked the sheet free of the bed, the end snapping in the air. "But your precious blond Bálint—is that what you hide behind that wall in your eyes? Thoughts of *him?*" He threw the sheet around her and wrapped her tightly. "Do you dream of his lips when mine are tasting yours? Do you?"

He kissed her hard, thrusting his tongue deep into her mouth. Desire sluiced fresh in his veins, but it pounded with jealousy and anger, a full chord of passions that roared like a waterfall.

She twisted her head to free herself from his punishing kiss, and he let her. "No!" she cried. "You misunderstand."

"Do I? Do I misunderstand that you think of him when my hands caress you?"

"Yes!"

"When my touch pleasures you, is it his touch you are thinking of?"

"Achille, no!"

He pulled the ends of the confining sheet tightly around her, pinning her arms to her sides, and molding the white satin to her breasts and her slender waist. "And when we join as one, will it be *he* who you feel entering—"

"No, no," she said, shaking her head. "Stop this. Bálint is dead. *You are jealous of a dead man.*" Her face contorted in pain. "He is dead. Bálint, too, was a soldier. Three years ago, there was a battle with the Turks. It had rained. There was mud everywhere. We lost badly. There was a retreat. One of the survivors told me that Bálint . . . that Bálint's horse had been killed. He was on foot. The

Turks swarmed over the retreating men, capturing scores of them trying to slog through the thick mud.

"Six months later, an old family steward whispered to me that Bálint had been found. And before he could . . . explain . . . I ran to him. I burst in, before they could stop me. He was dead. He'd died of exposure, somewhere out on the plain. It was winter, and he'd been left there to die. And I saw— God help me, I saw what those Turkish dogs had done to him."

Her forehead had dropped to Achille's shoulder, and, as if of its own accord, his hand had begun stroking her hair. She went on in a whisper, fighting the pain, but wanting, finally, to tell someone, to tell *him*. "He'd been visciously beaten. They'd cut out his tongue. And—and—" She choked down a sob. How it hurt to remember. She lifted her head and stared into his eyes. Achille's hands were warm, soothing, comforting, and somehow she managed to say the words. "And, sweet God, Achille, they'd taken his manhood.

"I felt such sorrow, such grief, at what had been done to him, at how he must have suffered. Think of me what you will, but I had cared for him.

"And then, in the following summer, Miklos was killed. But his was a clean hero's death, and he was buried with a hero's honors. And me they honored as the hero's wife.

"Those are the men I have known, Achille. And I do think of them." She brought her lips to his and kissed him lightly. "But I think of no one's lips except yours when you are kissing me."

Eleonora began unwrapping herself from the loosened sheet, and her curves were soon obscured by the folds.

"Then what are you hiding from me?" he asked.

She went completely still. The faint rustling of the satin fell silent. "H-hiding?" she stammered.

"If you are not dreaming of candied-violet kisses, what is behind that wall I see in your eyes?"

She did not meet his gaze, but tugged repeatedly at a stubborn corner of the sheet. "That damned wall again. I tell you my deepest anguish—not even my brothers know how Bálint died! And you ... Why won't this wretched sheet come loose?"

Achille stopped her hand with an iron hold. "What are you hiding, Eleonora?"

"At the moment, less than I want to, obviously," she snapped, pulling the sheet tighter around her. The sheet tangled in her legs, but she managed to kick free.

"You evade the question," he growled, fast losing patience.

"Please! No more anger. My head is pounding already." She slipped off the bed and began gathering her scattered clothes. When she came to the coat he'd so mockingly dropped on top of the pool of her skirts, she threw it aside. It hit a chair upholstered in blue and gold brocade. She heard a faint click, then a second later the chair tilted back, a small, padded plank slid out to each side, and, about shoulder height, two handles appeared, shaped like a man's—

"Saint Stephen," she muttered under her breath. She shot a look toward Achille. "I should hate to know what sins could match those of the French."

He reclined on the rumpled satin sheet, propped on one elbow, and watched her. "Sins, Eleonora? Is that what you hide?" He rose to his knees in one fluid motion, the perfectly sculpted muscles of his half-clothed body gleaming in the candlelight. "How long have you been a widow?"

She could sense a tension in him, an alert anticipation, like a warrior preparing to strike as he listened to the approach of his enemy. She licked her lips. "Two years."

"Seven hundred days." He wrapped his hand around the gilt bedpost and leaned forward. "Seven hundred days, Eleonora, without your husband. Without your golden lover. A woman may commit many sins in seven hundred days. Is that why you came to France? To hide your sins among so many?"

"You know why I came! I told you ..."

"I know *what* you told me."

She fumbled hopelessly with the tangled sheet wrapped around her and the bundle of clothes she wanted to put on.

It didn't help that she felt his intent gaze following her every movement, her every breath.

She went to the japanned cabinet and opened the door to use as a screen. "Between you and Tante Geneviève, I might as well try to convince a rose to bloom in winter! *She* believes I came here to find a husband. No matter that I've told her a hundred times that I have not." With shaking hands, Eleonora fastened the ties of her skirts, then buttoned her jacket over her stays. The torn chemise was useless.

"Freedom, I tell her, it has to do with freedom. I followed you to the charcoal burner's camp of my own free will. Just as the . . . rest of this . . . was of my choosing. Or at least of my not denying. Free will! Tante doesn't understand that I will *never* give that up. Never!"

"You will never become a Jansenist, either, with that kind of talk."

"Surely you're not a Jansenist. Surely you don't believe our lives are preordained. That everything we do has already been set in a fixed, unchanging course. That even what happens in this wretched room was planned.

"Bah! Nothing is fixed. Not even sins." She slammed the cabinet door closed, and stood as dressed as she could be. "God knows what kind of sins you've conjured up for me in that black-haired head of yours. I don't know what you want of me." With firm strides, she went to the door to the courtyard, then paused. "It obviously isn't what I thought you wanted."

"It's simple," he told her. "I want *all* of you, including what you are hiding. And you'll give it to me."

"Don't be so sure of that," she said, throwing the bolt to unlock the door. The metallic *clack* emphasized her words. "You spurned what I was willing to give you. I may not make the offer again."

She opened the door, bracing for bright sunlight to blind her. But storm clouds had gathered, and the sky had turned to an overcast gray. She could not even tell where the sun was. *How fitting,* she thought.

"I did not spurn you, Eleonora. I merely postponed my acceptance."

Bitter laughter stuck in her throat. "You yourself said your commission will arrive any day now. Do you think I am some camp follower who will trail after you to the front? Think again, Achille."

She stepped outside and pulled the door closed behind her. "Think again," she whispered to the empty courtyard. "It is you who will follow me."

The blustery wind tugged at Eleonora's skirts as she made her way up a hillock half a mile from the château du Peyre. A farmer who lived near the ruins had given her a ride to the last crossroads. She'd been grateful that she hadn't had to walk the whole distance—she didn't think her legs would have carried her—but the farmer's constant chatter had made thinking difficult. His lack of surprise at seeing a highborn lady trudging along a dirt track had made her wonder at just how inured the local residents must be to the château's goings-on.

At the top of the hillock, she paused under the canopy of a spreading oak and studied the distant vista. The château was new and fashionable, proclaiming the wealth and status of its owner even in the dull gray light.

She sat on a low-growing branch, then stood again. There was a restlessness inside her that she couldn't calm. Her hand curled over her stomach. She wished that she had walked now. She would rather feel tired, then this . . . Saint Stephen, what he had done to her! She glanced at where she guessed the sun might be behind the clouds. Early afternoon. She began pacing, then stopped herself. At least she hoped it was early afternoon. If it was, she could get away with the horse-shying story she'd concocted. Much later, and eyebrows would raise and mouths would smile knowingly, and the only question in their minds would be who her assignation had been with.

She idly began plucking off leaves. At least she hoped that that would be the question.

From behind her, she heard the faint whinnying of a

horse, and her fingers halted their denuding of the branch. She wasn't up to facing Achille again so soon. She grimaced at her remembered bravado in the empty courtyard. *I want . . . what you are hiding,* his voice said in her mind. She wasn't sure she was up to facing him again—ever.

But she would have to. For her family's sake. For the sake of what she was hiding from him. The memory of her responses to his caressing hands made her flush, and her skin grew warm with a heat the breeze could not blow away. What he had done to her body had frightened her, had made her body not seem her own, had shackled it with chains of fire, imprisoned it with a luxurious hot liquid . . . terror.

And yet, for a brief, fluttering moment, she'd been bathed in a peace such as she had never known, a peace wound up with Achille, with his laughter and his smiles and his words that could challenge or caress. A peace wound up with . . . something else. Something that had been the most frightening of all. She licked lips suddenly dry at the realization of her own hypocrisy. It was not her family she would be thinking of if he kissed her again the way he had in the grotto, or if he touched her, or stroked her, or—

"M-madame?" a hesitant voice said.

Eleonora nearly staggered with relief to realize it wasn't Achille. Her fingers dropped the leaf they had been shredding and she turned around. "Jean-Baptiste," she said, surprised. The young man stood a few paces down the hillock from her, his hands tightly gripping the reins of the gelding she'd ridden. He seemed to weave a little in the wind. "Did you lose your way back to the château?" she asked.

He bowed, then had to steady himself. "No, madame. I been waitin' for you at a farmhouse back by the crossroads." He put his hand to his head. "I think . . . I think *I* had too much wine. It was thirsty business . . . waitin'."

She frowned. The tightness in her body made her irritable, impatient. She should have walked, she thought, she should have walked. "Waiting for me? Why?"

He cleared his throat and shuffled his feet. "To give you your horse back," he told her, holding out the reins. "The ladies in Paris aren't like ... that is, Monsieur, my master, he isn't used to ..." Jean-Baptiste bent his head, then peeked up at her through his lashes. "Why did you give money to have prayers said for that little girl?"

"Prayers for—? Oh, in Epinal." Eleonora spread her hands wide. "Her mother seemed so distraught. Prayers can be comforting," she said, then added with as gentle a smile as she could muster, "and sometimes we're given what we pray for." *And sometimes not,* she added silently.

He started to nod vigorously, then winced. "That's true, that's true. My mother, she was sick, an' monsieur le comte, he paid for many prayers, an' she became well again an'—"

"D'Agenais paid for prayers to be said?"

"Yes, madame. As long as the priest wasn't a Jesuit, monsieur said. He hates Jesuits. Papa says it's on account of his tutor an' ... an' all that. But monsieur paid handsome. That's why I told him what you did."

"I'm far from being a saint, Jean-Baptiste," she said. An image of Achille, half-naked and magnificent, filled her mind, and she felt her body stirring with an unnameable hunger. She steadied herself with a hand on the tree trunk. Oh, she was far, far from being a saint.

The young man hunched his shoulders in a shrug. "Don't know much 'bout saints. Saw a finger bone o' Saint Florentinus once, though ..." His words trailed off, and with the quick movement of someone who has barely managed to work up the courage, he wrapped the horse's reins around the low branch.

He bowed unsteadily again. "But I do know it's best if you ride in on your horse. I've heard how they all talk. In Paris. Before—" He flushed and stood at attention, his eyes taking on that blank, unfocused look that she'd seen so often in French servants. "I don't know why monsieur is so angry with you, madame, but even if he flogs me, I want you to take the horse."

"Flog you? Does he?" Eleonora asked, silently scolding herself for pumping a servant for information.

"N-no," Jean-Baptiste answered. "Not yet anyway. He does roar, though. Sometimes."

"When he's angry . . ." The young man nodded, and Eleonora smiled. "Well, thank you for the horse," she said. "I don't know how much talk it will stop, but it was kind of you to do it. Now, you'd better go on to the château before your master discovers that you've disobeyed him. He still has his horse, remember, and I'd guess he'll be in a fine pet for roaring, too."

He bowed and began a sort of stumbling trot down the hillock.

"And stay away from farmers who are so generous with their wine!" she called after him. He waved good-naturedly and kept on toward the château.

She crossed her arms under her breasts and leaned against the trunk, staring at the horse. "I wish I had a few bottles of that farmer's wine myself," she muttered to the gelding. It shook its head from side to side, rattling the bridle. "You're right. Getting drunk around Achille is a bad idea."

She thought about his skilled hands and his beautiful devil's face and his glorious devil's body and his . . . "Getting drunk around Achille is a very bad idea." She uncrossed her arms and tugged at her skirts, wishing it were the coiling ache inside of her that she was straightening.

"Stop thinking about what happened in the grotto!" she scolded herself. She went to the gelding, and using the low branch to give her a leg up, she mounted. "I have to keep my head. I can't give in to him." She kneed the horse toward château du Peyre. "I can't give in to . . ." *a devil's son who pays for prayers!*

A devil's son whose dark eyes had devoured her as she'd reclined on the chair in the grotto. A devil's son who had shown her heaven and the peace that could be

found there. "No! No, don't think of that. Just think . . .
'I can't give in to him.' " *I can't give in to his lips, his
eyes . . .*

"I can't give in to . . . me."

Chapter 11

Eleonora heard the remnants of shouts in the wind as she neared the stables. As she rode closer, the bustle became clearer and she could see grooms darting into and out of the horse barn in a blur of livery. She groaned. Not another hunt! All she wanted to do was dismount, go to her room, and shut the door behind her.

"Watch it there!" a rough voice called just as a groom emerged from the shadowed doorway of the stables, trotting two horses out to a waiting coach.

Another carriage stood next to it, an impatient coachman banging his whip handle against the seat to attract attention.

"*Here,* you blighted rascals! Bring me some horses."

"Have a care!" she heard, and managed to rein her gelding out of the path of a groom leading two beautiful white horses to yet another coach.

Nearby, a young stable hand struggled to keep a spirited horse from shying.

"What's going on?" Eleonora shouted to him over the din.

He gave her a quick nod and grinned. " 'Tis *war!*" he cried, his eyes wide with excitement.

"War?" she echoed, her gaze taking in the frantic crowd around her. On the far edge she saw Achille, sitting calmly astride an aloof Chiron. She flushed and looked away, then ice shards of panic pricked her skin. *He isn't going to leave? No, not yet!*

Fleury, a nobleman whose flirting she had found distasteful, strode up, clearing a path for himself with the liberal use of a riding crop. "You, there," he snarled at the boy. "I want that horse *now*. Bring it here." The stable hand tugged on the horse's reins, the once jittery animal suddenly reluctant to move. "*Now*, boy! Plum staff assignments don't wait for dawdling stable brats. The army is already marching through Bavaria."

He yanked the reins out of the boy's hand and jerked his head in an order to help him mount. In seconds he was at eye level with Eleonora. "Madame la comtesse," he said with a nod. He sawed on the reins to keep the horse from skittering away.

She nodded to Fleury, but her eyes were on Achille, riding past on the other side of him, a dark sea of composure in the middle of the storm swelling around her. Achille seemed indifferent to her presence.

"Duty calls, madame," Fleury said. "A pity. Du Peyre said your dowry was worth four hundred thousand louis. A prize well worth the winning." His appreciative gaze traveled up and down her body. "And a form well worth the taming. But who knows what I will win and tame when we carve up Mother Austria!"

"Try for Vienna, Fleury," Eleonora told him with disgust. "I trust there you'll at least win some manners."

His lip curled in contempt. "Had I time, madame, I would enjoy making you regret you ever came to France." His horse gave a sudden start and leaped away. Fleury gave all his attention to fighting for control.

"You would be too late, Fleury," she said to herself. "I already regret it."

Something dark caught at the corner of her eye, and she turned to see Achille a horse-length away, holding his riding crop as if he'd just used it.

The stable boy ran up to her, and she forced herself to smile at him. She swung down from the horse—and discovered her legs trembled in their effort to hold her upright. The boy steadied her with a knowing look.

"Wipe that smirk off your face," she told him with a shaky smile. "I'm not drunk."

A horse backed into her, and she jumped to keep from being stepped on. She staggered and caught herself on the gelding's saddle.

"Whatever you say, madame."

"Oh, how I wish that were so," she murmured, and glanced at the wide doors of the horse barn. Achille was just disappearing into the shadows.

She turned and started making her way toward the château. So it was war. She had hoped it would not come so soon.

Three excited young men strode past her, openly admiring her, as if they had already donned their soldiers' manners. They tipped their hats to her, but less than a step beyond her, their talk returned to the glory and spoils of war.

The leaves of the hedges rustled in the fickle wind, first blowing one way, then another. The heels of her riding boots dug into the soft grass path with each step. Once, she'd heard her brothers talking about the new cadence marching of Frederick of Prussia's armies. Did it keep fear away? she wondered. Step ... step ... Did it make it easier to face the killing lead and the bayonets?

A few minutes walking brought her to the château, and she made her way to her room. She paused in front of the door, her knees shaking as if with a palsy.

From her right came muted but frantic voices: Tante Geneviève surrounded by servants. "Eleonora!" her aunt called, waving to the servants to wait while she greeted her niece. "Thank heavens you've returned."

"I'm sorry I'm late, Tante. I—"

"That doesn't matter, dear." Geneviève absently patted her arm. "This is a disaster. Half a dozen men are leaving. Only the desperate ones, of course. Poor St. Juste even left without his linens! Can you imagine?" She gave an irritated shake of her head. "Oh, what does that matter? The rest will follow at their usual leisure—and I still have to entertain them. It's this storm. What it's done to my beautiful garden supper! I must have the recital this evening. I have no other choice. You can see that, can't you?"

Eleonora barely had time to nod before Geneviève began again. "There, I knew you would understand. What a dear you are." Her aunt gestured to the clutch of servants to follow, and bustled down the hall. "We should all have such dutiful daughters," she called, and disappeared around a corner.

"Of course, Tante," Eleonora said to the empty hallway, "this *dutiful daughter* will be glad to play this evening." She stood there dazed for a moment, then let herself into her room.

Once inside, Eleonora gave herself over to letting the maid coddle her. But the luxury soon turned into a trial. Nothing was said about how Eleonora had left that morning with an elaborate coiffure and had returned with her hair in a simple spray of pinned-up curls.

The maid met her eyes in the mirror. "The wind," Eleonora said weakly.

"The wind," the maid repeated. "Of course, madame. Happens rather often, it does. I'd just like to know where it blows all them pins. Must be quite a pile of 'em somewhere."

Eleonora blushed, but the corners of her mouth tilted up. "I-I'm sure," she said.

The maid helped Eleonora out of her riding habit. A loose button fell off, and Eleonora gave a start. "I can explain that," she began.

The maid rolled her eyes and sighed. "Pardon me for saying so, madame, but ladies stopped explaining loose buttons, torn petticoats, lost chemises, and tousled hair in my grandmother's time. Them that had done something tried to say they didn't, and them that hadn't done something tried to say they did."

She shrugged. "Don't much matter to me," she added, hanging the riding habit on a peg in the wardrobe. "Raymonde was offerin' pretty good odds on monsieur Fleury, but I didn't take him up on it. Told him you weren't like the other ladies. Told him you was a lot wilier than any of *them,* and that you'd probably surprise us all."

Eleonora rubbed her forehead. "I suppose I shouldn't be shocked, but I can't like being betted upon."

"No, madame, I guess not," the maid said, holding up an afternoon gown for approval. "But iffen you'd care to drop a hint about the, uh . . . wind . . . today, I could make a bundle off Raymonde."

"Monsieur *Zephyr,*" Eleonora snapped. A puzzled frown creased the maid's brow. "Never mind, Martine. Never mind." In minutes, the expert hands of the maid had dressed and coiffured her back into impeccability.

Eleonora went to the window and looked out on the stormy landscape. The sky had darkened even more; it would rain soon. She felt a stab of pity for the men racing to Bavaria to clamor for the scarce lucrative positions. And she felt a greater stab of pity for their horses.

Beside her, the maid lit a small candelabrum to compensate for the failing light, then went into the other room. The sudden solitude made Eleonora want to call her back. She rubbed her arms, uneasy.

The window glowed with the glittering candle flames, a crescent of three bright points of light curving around the reflected image of her face. She stared into her own eyes. "What a fool you were," she whispered to the woman staring back at her in the window. "You thought yourself clever for having snared him so easily." She winced at the memory. "I thought I knew you, Achille. Mother told me so many stories . . ." She drew an arc on the glazing, connecting the bright points of reflected candle flame.

"When I was small, those stories used to scare me. Deep in the night, I'd wake up, staring into the darkness, expecting a devil to snatch me away. When I was older, I'd wake, but it was with thoughts of vengeance. That's why I had Gabriel teach me to shoot, and Christophe teach me to fight with a sword.

"I never doubted that I knew my enemy, Achille. I never doubted—until I met you. And now I doubt even myself."

She turned away from the window. His father had hurt her family so badly, but where had her hate gone? She thought of Achille's devil's eyes, of how much they told of the man. She'd seen them half-closed with passion, and shadowed with sorrow, and glinting with appreciation at one of her barbs, and then shining with unexpected laughter. She smiled to herself. Or flashing in one of his rages!

He was so *intense*. There was so much fire in him. And so much . . . honor. The kind of honor that did not manipulate with deceit or lies or false promises.

And what was in her? She turned back to the window and stared at the reflection of her own eyes. Deceit. Lies. Schemes and stratagems, exactly as he'd said.

But what did *he* see in her? What was it he wanted to see? She ran her hands down her body, remembering the pleasure Achille had given her. A soft smile lifted her lips. How his eyes had glittered at her when he'd so blatantly told her what he wanted of her. No deceit there! *That's what I want,* he'd added. *I'll settle for a clear and distinct "yes."*

He certainly wanted to see consent! she thought with a lighthearted laugh as she lifted her eyes back to her reflected gaze.

And suddenly she knew what Achille wanted to see. There it was, filling her eyes, staring back at her.

Her heart.

She froze in horror. *No!* No, she couldn't— She snapped her gaze away. No.

She staggered to the writing desk and snatched up the music she was to play that night. "I shall be in the small music room, Martine," Eleonora called out to the maid, then added to herself, "where I should have been practicing this morning instead of . . ." But it was already too late for regrets.

She made her way to the door, a carefully pleasant smile curving her lips. But inside her mind, she heard the distant echo of mocking laughter, and she crunched the music in her hand to keep from faltering. *What is it you regret, El?* the voice taunted.

The tension Achille had engendered inside her still had not eased. God help her, but she had wanted him to complete what he'd begun. Still wanted him to. *"No,"* she whispered, opening the door. She squeezed the ridges of the latch deep into her hand. "I can't . . . I don't . . ."

The door closed on her lies. She had failed her family, yes, but she had done worse. A hundredfold worse. She had betrayed them.

She was in love with the devil's son.

Coldness drifted through her like a low-lying ice fog, and she stumbled in the corridor. She could never let him know, never let him *see* that awful truth in her eyes. That would be the ultimate betrayal of her family. The faces of her brothers, her mother, her grandfather, swirled in her mind, all indescribably sad. A claw of ice squeezed at her heart. Her pain felt nearly mortal.

She reached the music room and settled at the harpsichord, then began playing the Bonni over and over again to perfect it. What could she do? What could she do?

Her fingers increased their speed. She couldn't betray her family; they meant everything to her. She was desperate to fulfill their plans. But there were no options left to her.

Except one, a chill voice said in her head. Her mother's voice. *Show him what is on the parchment, my most dutiful daughter. Show him that, and he will not leave for war.*

The music stopped abruptly. A cry of denial escaped her. Terrifying images tumbled in her mind: of Achille humbled and in chains; of the waiting covetous Turks always slavering for another slave; of Bálint's maimed body, the golden hair turning to sable in her fevered imaginings. She put her hands to her head as if to squeeze out the horrible image of Achille's body mutilated as Bálint's had been.

No, Achille must never see that parchment! Let him leave for war without knowing, without seeing . . . He mustn't see it. He would feel nothing but hate for her. There would be no forgiving her then. Ever.

* * *

Achille stood alone near a window in the gaming room. He'd changed from his hunting clothes into deep indigo velvet, as if he wanted to blend into the night outside.

Beyond the far door, the guests still remaining at the château du Peyre sauntered past, heading for the grand music room for the coming recital. Only four or five men had actually left for the battlefield, but their bustle had made it seem as if the entire château was being deserted. Now everyone chattered like shrill magpies with the news of war.

A servant came and held out a salver with a glass of burgundy on it, and Achille took it. "Will there by anything else, monsieur?" the servant asked.

"Bring the bottle," Achille said. "And then . . . and then send word to Madame Batthyány that I wish to settle our debts."

The servant bowed and left.

The tension in Achille's shoulders didn't ease until he was alone. Or as alone as one could be when scores upon scores of people swarmed just beyond the doors.

He should join them. He should play the proper guest. But he wanted solitude. The glass stem felt delicate in his fingers as he twirled it round and round. He could snap it like a chicken bone. Some men liked their women like that—frail, fragile things to be displayed like a collection of Venetian glass.

He took a long swallow of wine, feeling the astringency of the tannin along the edges of his tongue. It was a dry, full-bodied wine, redolent and complex.

He studied both the glass and the wine. The one like a fragile woman, the other like . . . Eleonora. He smiled and took another swallow.

He much preferred the wine to the glass.

Memories of her in the grotto made his body stir, but he clamped down on the rising hunger. His restraint with her astounded him. When she'd gone from the grotto, he'd remained staring at the closed door, his knuckles white from gripping the bedpost as he'd struggled for control. He had never gone so far with a woman and pulled back. He hadn't even known he *could,* until . . .

He'd felt her glorious body shudder with her ecstasy and had risen to kiss her tears away. Once or twice before, a woman had cried when the physical release of pleasuring had released other, more fundamental tensions. But when he'd looked into Eleonora's eyes and had seen the distance still between them, something had snapped inside him. It was then that he'd realized what he'd wanted to see, what he'd expected to see, what he had *craved* to see in her eyes.

Achille looked down into the wine and saw the ruby red liquid ripple ever so slightly with his trembling. He was a fool. A fool drunk on a boy's fancies conjured when he'd listened to his father's stories of knights and their ladies, of the honor of a man fighting for the woman he loved.

Achille had baited du Peyre that the man was in love with his wife, but that was a caprice of the moment. But love, the sweet, tormented enchantment that Constantin had told him was the only thing that really mattered in the world, that did not exist. It was the only falsehood he'd ever discovered in what his father had taught him. Love did not exist; therefore, it could not be fought for, and Achille had had to settle for the battlefield to honor his father's memory. Lust certainly existed, as did passion and, rarely, affection. But not love.

So why had he so desperately wanted to see in Eleonora's eyes what did not exist?

A door set unobtrusively in a corner opened and the servant stepped out, bearing Achille's bottle of wine on a silver salver.

"Your wine, monsieur," the man said with a bow. "Word has been sent to Madame Batthyány. And Monsieur Beaulieu said to tell you, 'The courier has arrived.' "

Achille's hand tightened around the neck of the bottle. "Indeed?" was all he said. The man waited. Achille drained the glass, the wine filling his mouth with its complex tastes.

"Tell Monsieur Beaulieu that no doubt the courier is

tired," Achille told the servant. "I shall meet with him in the morning." Achille waved a hand at the servant in dismissal. "Early."

"I shall give Monsieur Beaulieu your message, monsieur," the servant assured him, then left.

A few moments later, Achille heard Beaulieu discreetly clear his throat from behind him. Acknowledged with a nod, the steward bowed and said, "Monsieur, perhaps you would care to return to your rooms to refresh yourself. You could speak to the Chevalier Gillon's courier while you are there."

"And how often shall I refresh myself in Bavaria?" Achille asked. His commission—his salvation—awaited him in his rooms. The war beckoned, offering the peace that comes from chaos, where the outside din drowned out the sensory demands of his seeking, restless body. He *had* to go, to save himself, but a tension coiled inside him like the chain of an anchor. A chain that held him where he stood.

"Monsieur?" Beaulieu asked uncertainly. His weight shifted from one foot to the other. "Monsieur, it is the courier you've been waiting for. From Chevalier Gillon."

"I heard you, Beaulieu. Begin packing," Achille told him.

"I have already begun, monsieur," the man said, taking a step toward the door. "You said you wanted to leave the moment the courier arrived. Monsieur, you must come and talk to him."

Achille raised an eyebrow at Beaulieu's "must," and saw the steward flush. He leaned closer to his master and lowered his voice to a whisper. "Your pardon, monsieur, but the chevalier has put certain, er, restrictions on your commission. You need to talk with the man."

Achille felt his face grow hard. "What restrictions?"

The steward swallowed thickly, and his voice became even more subdued. "It—it's about Paris. It seems the chevalier heard of, uh, some . . . of what . . . happened, and, that is, he has told the courier that he feels honor-bound to offer you the commission as he agreed. But if you delay . . ."

"Go on."

"If you delay . . ." Beaulieu hesitated, nervously licking his lips, then went on. "It is not to be sold to you."

"I see," Achille said. "And how long am I to be given?"

The steward hesitated, then said, "Till dawn, monsieur."

A footman entered the room, leading Eleonora toward Achille. The man bowed and departed, and she nodded graciously but distantly to Achille, keeping up the pretense that they were the most tenuous of acquaintances.

"Monsieur," she said with the tiniest hint of disbelief in her voice. "You wished to see me? I had thought our debts settled."

Beaulieu cleared his throat. "Monsieur, please," he whispered, "the courier."

Eleonora froze. Achille sensed her abrupt transition from animated to still, as still as an animal who has smelled the scent of a predator. In her eyes he saw a bleakness that hadn't been there before—and the wall. "That will be all, Beaulieu," he said, and the steward bowed his head in acquiescence. "And tell the courier to sleep well. I shall meet with him first thing in the morning."

"At dawn, monsieur."

"I shall be there, Beaulieu."

Achille faced Eleonora. She had turned as white as a snow marten.

There was a fraction of a moment, no longer than the single beat of a nightingale's wing, when Eleonora felt the disorienting swirl of vertigo. The floor beneath her feet seemed suddenly not to exist. The burning candles blurred into a streak of light.

"Eleonora?" Achilles' voice asked in a whisper, distant and fuzzy. She grabbed something steady and hard, and abruptly the world was back in place.

"Your pardon," she said, and realized her hand was tightly clutching his arm. "I must have stumbled."

He frowned, and covered her hand with his. "You were not walking."

"That's because I was too busy stumbling," she snapped, and pulled her hand away.

He bent toward her, his face the careful mask of a solicitous gentleman. "Then perhaps you wish to stagger to a chair?"

"No, thank you," she said, giving him the most gracious nod she could muster. "I prefer to collapse where I am."

"As you wish," he said, though his steadying hand remained on her elbow for a long moment before he let it drop.

He reached into his pocket and brought out her fan. "You misplaced this, I believe. I wanted to return it to you."

"How kind," she said flatly, and took it from him. She nervously began opening and closing it, then forced herself to stop. "Is this your way of saying good-bye?" The corners of her mouth tilted up in a tiny smile. "And here I was expecting what they call 'French leave.' "

"Were you?" he asked, his voice low. "How could I leave without seeing you again after the . . . promise . . . of this morning?"

"There was no promise made this morning!"

"Ah, but my Magyar, there was. A long, sweet, fulfilling promise."

She flushed and turned her back to him. "I must go to the recital."

"Think of us when you play. A woman awaiting her lover . . . a man fulfilled."

"Damn you, Achille. Why are you doing this? Does it amuse you? If you want me so much, why not throw me on a gaming table and take me?"

"A tempting offer," he said, then added with a voice tinged with surprise, "and a few days ago, I would have accepted it. But now . . ."

"But now . . . *what?*" she asked, turning to face him, though she already knew the answer. A few days ago, he had been but a man, a devil's son. But that was before she had come to know *him,* before she had come to know the dark angel that was *Achille.*

"Then," he began, and paused, his gaze lowering and his dark eyes narrowing as if he was searching inside himself for the answer. A smile seemed to suffuse his face, transforming it, and he raised his eyes to meet hers. "Then, you were an exotic, intriguing woman. Now I know you are like no other. You are *Eleonora.*"

They stared at each other for long moments. Her lips parted, as if to utter a denial, but no words disturbed the silence.

A snap of delicate wood broke her trance. She looked down at her hands and the broken fan they held. "I—I must go," she whispered, making for the door. "The recital . . ."

"Play for me, Eleonora," he called after her. She let the pieces of the fan drop to the floor in answer.

Chapter 12

The wind blew the rain against the window in a capricious rhythm no composer could imitate, but in Eleonora's room, Tante Geneviève clutched the sheets of music Eleonora had played that evening and beamed at her niece.

"My dear, you were wonderful!" Geneviève cried, giving Eleonora an impetuous kiss on the cheek. "I'm so lucky to have such a talented niece."

Eleonora fussed with the ribbons of her brocade robe and tried to smile her thanks. "I should have practiced more."

"No, no, no!" her aunt answered. "How could you have improved upon perfection?"

"I was preoccupied at first," Eleonora said, holding tightly to a bowl of rose petals. It had been on the corner of the harpsichord when she'd sat down to play, the petals so fresh that raindrops glistened on their velvety surface.

"My dear, you are an artist." Geneviève held the crumpled music to her breast and cast her gaze heavenward. "You were merely preparing for the Muse."

Eleonora giggled. "I was preparing my escape! I've never played before so many people." She sobered and dipped her fingers into the rose petals and let them drift over her hand. "And I'd never felt so alone amongst so many." Until she'd seen the bowl of petals.

She'd known immediately who they were from, and the thought had comforted her. She hadn't wanted it to. It shouldn't have. But this token from the son of a devil had made her feel less alone ... and closer to Achille than to anyone else in the room. And it had been for him alone that she'd played.

The corners of Geneviève's lips lifted in a secret smile. "The damask roses have always been my favorite." She inhaled. "Their sweet scent fills the room, doesn't it? And that bowl of petals was such a thoughtful touch. I wonder who sent them."

Eleonora set the bowl on the dressing table. "Perhaps a servant—"

Geneviève laughed. "I have an exemplary staff, my dear, but not one of them would go out in the rain to gather rose petals on a whim! No, someone ordered them gathered. I might suspect Fleury, but he left this afternoon, and he's not the type to leave mementos behind." Geneviève chuckled, though a flush rose up her cheeks. "Well, at least not the kind of mementos that show up before nine months have passed."

"*Tante*. I barely spoke to the man!" Eleonora pulled her robe closer around her.

Geneviève sat down on the chair next to her and patted her arm. "Oh, I'm not talking about you, my dear. There was some to-do about an intendant's daughter last year." Her aunt sighed with more than a hint of resignation. "You, I'm afraid, don't seem to be susceptible to anyone."

Eleonora took a breath to answer, but her aunt forestalled her. "I know, I know. You're not here to find a husband. All right, I'm *almost* beginning to accept that. But you are a widow, my dear, and a discreet lover is quite allowable. It's expected, really. And you don't want to appear too chaste—that only makes you the object of all sorts of distasteful wagers."

Yes, Eleonora, she mocked herself silently, *you don't want to be too chaste.* "Tante, you've been so kind to me here," Eleonora said aloud, trying to keep the truth about herself from showing in her face. "But I am not made in the French mold, I fear. I cannot ... give of myself ... lightly."

Geneviève shook her head sadly. "No doubt you're right. You have such a passionate heart. For most of us, they're just games and diversions, harmless ways to pass the time. But for you . . ."

She gave her niece's arm an affectionate squeeze. "Be careful, Eleonora. You are so like your mother. Don't repeat her folly."

"Folly?" Eleonora said, puzzled. "Mother?"

"She, too, could not give her body where her heart would not go, but she made the mistake of thinking herself safe because her heart was carefully hidden and therefore—she thought—incapable of leading anywhere." A look of infinite sadness dropped over Geneviève's face like a veil.

"Tante, what are you speaking of? Mother's heart is with her family. And it has always been. She thinks of nothing but the family." Eleonora closed her eyes, an image of her mother's angry face hovering just behind her eyes. "How well I know."

Geneviève rose. "You must forgive an old woman's babbling. I am sure you are right. I have not seen your mother in years. I'm sure she thinks of nothing but her family." She kissed her good night. "Eleonora, just remember, hiding something does not make it safe."

Eleonora looked out at the rain. "Hiding? What is there to hide, Tante? Only the usual bits and pieces of regrets and petty guilts, nothing more . . ."

"As you say, my dear," Geneviève said, her hand on the door latch. "But it's been my experience that what we hide from ourselves is what's most dangerous of all. Be careful, Eleonora."

The rain continued to pound at the windows, sweeping against the glass in waves like the ocean against a cliff. After Geneviève left, Eleonora strode restlessly from her sitting room to her bedroom, and back to her sitting room again.

She felt edgy, nervous. It was becoming more and more difficult to think. The fire in the grate had taken the chill from the room, but the air was still uncomfortably humid. The brocade of her *robe de chambre* pressed heavily on her shoulders, and even its soft rustle as she walked grated on her ears.

She sat down on a chaise in a *whoosh* of brocade and lawn. The warm air was suffocating, and she felt nearly buried alive under all the yards and yards of material.

"El, it's just late," she told herself, loosening the ribbons of her robe. "You're tired. And the fire is much too hot."

She picked up the book she had hastily taken from the library after her recital to help her forget how Achille's dark-eyed gaze had been on her the entire time she had played.

Her fingers stroked the smooth leather binding. The scent of the roses still clung to her fingers, and the sweet smell mixed with the deeper scent of beeswax from the polished leather.

Reading would help. It would take her mind off her failure and ease her anxiety. She flipped the book open and skimmed the title page. She groaned. She had meant to get La Fontaine's fables, but what she'd actually plucked off the shelves was the *maréchal* de Saxe's *Mes Reveries*.

She threw the book in front of the hearth and stood up. The last thing she needed to read was a *maréchal*'s scribblings about armies and battle lines. She wanted to be free of soldiers, free of Miklos, of her brothers, even of Bálint. But most of all she wanted to be free of Achille.

She went to the windows and pressed her hands against the cold, damp glass. She let the chill seep into her flesh, wishing it could flow all the way inside her. How she craved a cool, rational head, and a body cold to being touched and caressed . . .

She turned from the window and went to stand in front of the fire. At her feet was de Saxe's book, and she picked it up again, the fire-warmed leather chasing the cold from her hands, the way Achille's touch had.

A knock on the servant's door gave Eleonora a start. She hastily put the book on a table, as if being caught holding it would somehow give away the secrets of her body.

She called for the maid to enter, and the girl came in and dipped a curtsy. She carried a package wrapped in a length of embroidered Chinese silk and tied with a ribbon the color of a damask rose. "The steward sends you his profound apologies for this being so late, madame. Its arrival was not brought to his attention."

Eleonora stared at the package the maid was holding out to her. A gift. She was not used to gifts.

The maid's eyes widened with anxiety. "It—it's so pretty, madame. See? All the flowers, and the tiny birds ... It must've come before the rain started. There's not a water stain anywhere. I swear it."

Eleonora smiled with a reassurance she didn't feel. "Yes, it is pretty, isn't it? Why don't you set it on the dressing table?"

With a reverence Eleonora wasn't sure it deserved, the maid set the package down, then went to the servant's door. The girl paused. "Oh, and the steward said there's a note addressed to you. There, tucked just under the bow." She curtsied. "Will there be anything else, madame?"

"No, Martine," Eleonora said, staring at the silk bundle. "That will be all."

A gift. She sucked in a breath of warm, humid air and forced her steps to take her to the dressing table. Her fingers reached out to the note tucked under the ribbon, hesitated, then pulled it free. She held it to the light of a candle. It had been formally addressed to her at the château du Peyre, as if it had come from far away. But the script was familiar. She turned it over. And it had been sealed with the lanner falcon crest of the comte d'Agenais.

Before her courage could falter, she broke open the seal and unfolded the letter. A single damask rose petal fell to the floor, leaving a stain from a raindrop on the paper.

Though you hide your soul from me, Eleonora, hide nothing from my sight so that I may see you in my dreams. A.

She let the letter tumble from her fingers. "Do devils

dream, Achille?" She picked up the package and hugged it to her chest, then went to stand in front of the fire. The cloth was a beautiful piece of work. She thought of someone painstakingly stitching each flower, each bird, the vines and leaves, and . . .

. . . and she thought of that stitching burning in the flames, the blues and yellows and greens all turning black as the fire consumed them. She loosened her hold. It was a devil's gift. It should burn.

She pulled the rose-colored ribbon, untying the bow. It slithered sensuously over her fingers before falling to the hearth. An end fell too close to the flames and caught, sending a tongue of fire sputtering out along the ribbon like a fuse of gunpowder. In a heartbeat, the ribbon was nothing but a line of ash.

Lightning flashed. She gasped, and spun to face the window, staring out at the violent night. A crack of thunder made her jump. The rain beat down incessantly. Lightheadedness stole over her, and she stumbled to a chair.

She was hot. So hot. But she wanted to be cold, so cold that she would shiver from it, shake from it, like ice on a tree in the wind. She should have had the maid scatter the coals. No, she thought, closing her eyes and rocking her head on the back of the chair, no, she couldn't do that. They would find out her weakness. Discover her susceptibility to heat. The devil's heat.

She lowered her gaze to her lap. Without its confining ribbon, the embroidered package had unfolded in her lap, spilling out a pool of transparent rose silk.

She sucked in a breath. Her hand, of its own accord, reached out to it. She lifted it, and it flowed over her fingers so softly that it felt as if the petals of the damask rose had somehow been spun and woven into gossamer.

There were seams in the silk, smooth and even and sewn with the tiniest of stitches. She stood, the Chinese embroidery falling from her lap unnoticed, and held the silk out in front of her. It was long, and there were sleeves, long ones that would taper from her shoulder to her wrist, and tiny ribbon ties.

A robe? The *robe de chambre* she wore felt unbearably heavy. No, she shouldn't. Couldn't. She bit her lip. It was a devil's gift.

She threw the silk robe onto the bed. She stepped back, clutching her hands tightly in front of her. The heat must have addled her wits. The heavy brocade she wore somehow slipped off one shoulder. Then the other. She unclasped her hands, and it crumpled into a heap on the floor.

Clad only in a long-sleeved nightgown of fine-woven lawn, she lifted the silk robe from the bed and began putting it on.

Her arm wouldn't go through. The sleeve was too small. She bit back a cry of disappointment. She held it up to her nightgown, pressing it against her shoulders. It seems a perfect fit. Then why . . .

She went still. Lightning flashed, and in that split second of daylight, everything was illuminated, the robe, her nightgown . . . and she knew how to make the robe fit. Thunder crashed. She did not hear it. She felt as if the storm outside had moved under her skin.

Her hand slowly went to the ties that held the nightgown closed, and undid the snug neckline of her gown. She pushed the cotton lawn and the chemise she wore underneath off her shoulders and down her arms. Naked, she stepped out of the pool of white at her feet.

The daughter would throw the rose silk into the fire. The sister would watch the flames catch and consume the fragile gossamer in a single breath.

But the woman . . .

She picked up the robe and slid one unclad arm through. It fit perfectly. She slipped her other arm through and let the sublime softness settle on her shoulders.

It had been cut to fit her unclothed form exactly, molding over her shoulders, her breasts, snugging in to her waist, then flaring slightly to conform to her hips. It fastened high on one shoulder, enclosing her in a cocoon that seemed made of cloud silk and mist.

She smiled. It felt so soft and wonderful. She began

humming the melody of the music she'd played earlier that evening. And she danced. Through the bedroom and sitting room, dipping and spinning, lost in the enchantment of the music and the caressing silk.

She spun around and around until she made herself dizzy, then she collapsed in a soft upholstered chair. Her head lolled, her body tingling deliciously from where the silk robe had brushed against her breasts and thighs.

Her own misty reflection stared back at her from the window. She jumped to her feet and preened in front of the image. The rose silk gave her skin a sensuous blush. Her nipples showed as two circles of darker blushing rose, and the vee of her intimate auburn curls seemed a damask shadow.

She ran her hands over her breasts and waist and hips, then did it again, much more slowly, imagining that Achille's hands were stroking her. Soon her hands fell limp to her sides. "Ride out, Achille, ride out to your battles and your war.

"And your dreams . . ." she said to herself, her voice wistful. She buried her face in her hands. "How can I desire a man whose hands kill as easily as they caress? The strength I am drawn to comes from battles he has fought. The deft touch that so entices is the deftness of a man skilled in fighting duels. What kind of woman am I? What kind of woman am I to know all this and still long for him?"

Thunder crashed in the distance. Devil's laughter.

She made her way back into the bedroom and slumped against the bedpost. "Saint Stephen, I'm so confused. I've failed. I've failed Mother, and Grandfather, and my brothers, yet all I feel is this giddy relief because he is going into battle and will be spared our vengeance. How could I have ever contemplated doing such evil to him . . . ?"

Her voice trailed off when her gaze was caught by the roll of parchment propped in the corner by the wardrobe. She stared at it, her eyes full of bitterness.

She snatched up the parchment, angrily untied it, and unrolled it with shaking fingers. A man's face stared back at her, dark, breathtakingly handsome, every harsh angle etched with cruelty. A devil's face. A devil known as El Müzir.

"You're dead, dead before I was born, dead before Gabriel was born, yet your hate still poisons us. I thought that coming here, entrapping your son, would exorcise you. Instead, I realize now how evil our intentions were!"

She thought of Achille condemned, chained deep in the labyrinth of cellars below her house in Vienna, chained until the Turks came for him.

She couldn't bear to see El Müzir's face any longer, and she flung the parchment from her. It landed on her dressing table, toppling pots and scattering bottles. One delicate lotion bottle teetered on the edge, then fell to the floor and shattered.

"The sins of the father," she whispered, "have become our sins."

A bolt of lightning flashed, its brightness washing the room of color for a hairbreadth of an instant. Eleonora gave a start, then slumped onto the bed. "In the end, you'll get us all, won't you?" Thunder rumbled, and the devil's laughter seemed to go on and on and on.

Rachand leaned back in his chair and smirked. "You sure you want another hand, d'Agenais? It's late, and you'd find your bed more profitable." He snickered and dug his fingers into the pile of gold coins in front of him.

"Deal." Achille let his hate for the man rise closer to the surface. It was late into the night, and few remained in the game room. Almost everyone had slipped away to the arms of a lover or to sleep. A snore punctuated his thoughts. He glanced behind him. Of course, some hadn't bothered to slip away first. Vigny for one.

The gossip sprawled on a chair, an empty wineglass dangling from his fingers, mouth agape and emitting an odd sort of whistling snort with each breath. Achille had thought to have the man carried off to his rooms, but he knew Vigny's snores irritated Rachand, so he had done nothing.

Achille waved away more wine, but the marquis de Rachand finished dealing and had the servant fill his glass. Rachand drank sloppily, then grunted, the sound falling somewhere between pleasure and censure.

"Du Peyre must've gone to bed. Can't think why else they'd still be pouring such respectable stuff. Everyone's too drunk to notice *what* they're drinking. I'd bring out a second pressing by now."

"No doubt," Achille said, "but perhaps du Peyre is running low on vinegar."

Rachand sent him a look filled with malice. "Play, d'Agenais."

Rachand picked up his cards, and for the briefest instant, a look of agreeable surprise flashed across that ruined face. His jowls sagged from dissipation, but Achille knew it was more than too much wine that had lined that wasted face and had reddened that nose and made the corners of those eyelids droop.

Achille glimpsed into a future mirror when he looked upon Rachand's face. The direction his own life was leading would take him there—an endless dark tunnel, forever spiraling downward, with only a touch of flesh on flesh, or a fleeting taste or scent, telling him he was still alive. He had craved sensation merely to know that he yet lived. Until Eleonora had diverted him.

He remembered her as she'd played the harpsichord earlier that evening. She'd been absorbed in the music, not realizing what he alone could see in her face—that she was playing for him alone. He wanted her. All of her. Everything she had to give.

But to go to her now would mean that he would want to stay with her, to bask in her passion, to absorb all her complexities into himself. But even that would not save him. He looked across the table into the mirror of Rachand's face. No, she was but another shard of his fracturing life. Salvation would only come from war.

Rachand snorted. "Look at your cards and play, damn you."

Achille gave him a level look, then—without looking at his cards—he threw in a thousand louis d'or.

The marquis sucked his teeth and scowled. "You must like teetering on the edge of ruin," he told Achille with a sneer. "You're already meat for the Bastille, after what you did in Paris, but now you want to be bankrupt meat. Very well, I shall be eager to oblige you." He threw in two thousand.

"One might even say overeager," Achille said, and added more money to the pile.

They both grew silent as the pot swelled into a cascading mountain of gold. Rachand's eyes glittered with feverish excitement, his fingers clasping and unclasping the cards.

Achille pulled off a ruby ring and tossed it at the base of the gold. "Odd that you should mention the Bastille." he said. "This morning hired thugs tried to 'oblige' me into that renowned retreat for meditating on one's sins."

"Obviously they did not succeed." Rachand licked his lips and took off nearly all his rings, the total of them barely equal to Achille's ruby.

"Obviously." Achille nonchalantly pulled off the d'Agenais crest. He held it up to the candlelight, the deeply carved lanner falcon seemingly restless to fly away. He could almost hear the flutter of wings. Was that the sound of the goddess of Fate hovering nearby?

He set the ring next to the bloodred one he'd put down earlier. The whites of the marquis's eyes showed with shock—Achille was betting not just the ring, but all that it represented.

"Obviously," Rachand echoed hoarsely, then cleared his throat. "How . . . how very disobliging of you, d'Agenais. Now someone is going to be put to even more expense by having to hire those thugs all over again."

"No one will be hiring those thugs again, Rachand."

The marquis went pale. "You killed them? You bastard! Do you have any idea how much I spent—"

Achille had gone deadly still.

Rachand's eyes widened with the realization of what

he'd said. "A figure of speech, nothing more!" he cried, fumbling for his glass as if to hide his alarm. The wine seemed to calm him, and he added with only a tinge of insincerity, "I meant nothing by it, I assure you, monsieur. Let us finish playing this hand."

Achille rose. "So the 'honorable' marquis de Rachand shakes at the thought of meeting me in the field, but readily hires others who are less timid."

Angry purple splotches discolored Rachand's dissipated face. "The field? Such courtesy! I don't recall hearing of such punctiliousness when you killed my uncle in his own library! Or when you ran through his sons in the Grand Salon. One of whom you had even called friend."

Rachand rose and faced Achille across the table. "You are lucky, monsieur le comte, that when your father met his *timely* end, you were known to be a hundred leagues away—or the curse might not be bastard, but patricide!"

"You stupid fool!" Madame de Rachand screeched from the doorway. "My idiot husband means none of it, d'Agenais! None of it, I swear. Tell him, you moron! The man has a brain fever, monsieur le comte, brought on by too much wine and too many nights spent reading all those bloody Roman stories of Tacitus."

A loud snuffling came from behind them as Vigny woke from his stupor and looked blearily around him. "Rachand does 'spend' too many nights, my dear, but it's in emulating Petronius rather than reading Tacitus."

"Shut up, you son of a bitch."

Vigny *tsk*ed. "Such language, my dear. And here I thought your new dresser was proving so accommodating."

"Vigny!" La Rachand grated, pressing her fingers to her temples.

Achille glanced at the gossip behind him, wondering why he had let Vigny diffuse the situation. "You interfere, monsieur le vicomte," he said, the tone one of observation rather than a command to back off. That surprised him.

Vigny winced in reflex, then cautiously reassumed his air of idleness. "It seems I do, monsieur. Your pardon." He gave Achille an obsequious bow, then straightened and rubbed under his chin. "Having so recently been a . . . uh . . . recipient of your . . . quickness," he said, carefully choosing his words, "I, perhaps, was startled into speech by the fact that Monsieur de Rachand remains alive."

"Now that you mention it, it *is* odd that he is still alive, isn't it?" Achille mused. The wings of Fate beat louder.

"You're mad," Rachand whispered. He turned to his wife. "He's mad."

The marquise snatched her husband's cards from the table. Her vehement hiss could easily be heard. "You *ass!* By the blood of God, how dare you let your temper get away from you." She shook the hand in front of Rachand's face. *"Look at what's on the table.* Play!"

"He hasn't even looked at his cards!"

"What has that to say to anything?" the marquise asked, grabbing Rachand's hand and clawing at his ring. She snarled a gutter oath. "Get this thing off."

She twisted Rachand's crest ring from his finger. He yelped with pain and began rubbing his reddened hand.

La Rachand flung the ring onto the table. "Your cards, d'Agenais."

There was a stillness inside Achille. He made a bet, inside himself. If he lost, he went straight to the courier and rode out to war at the first lessening of the storm.

But if he won . . . *Eleonora.* Sweet Christ, he wanted her. For the hundredth time, he cursed himself for not taking her in the grotto. If he had, would he now be standing over this table that was laden with all he had come to be, his hand hovering above the card that could call his fate?

He could barely hear for the flutter of wings. Fate was here. Next to him. At the turn of a card.

Salvation—or Eleonora.

The marquise snickered. "What's this? Is the great imperturbable comte d'Agenais feeling fear? Are your knees shaking? Is your stomach a tangled knot? Do your—"

Achille raised his hand, and her words abruptly halted. "As always, madame la marquise, you mistake the matter. I am savoring the anticipation."

He flipped over a card. There was a nearly inaudible squeak of surprise from the marquis. Achille turned over another card. The smile on the marquise's face stiffened. Another card. The muscles of Rachand's face began to twitch uncontrollably.

Achille stroked the back of the last card. He felt a sudden urge to pray. To Fate? To God? He did not know. He turned over the last card.

For a single compressed moment of time, there was no sound, no eye blinked, no heart beat, no lungs drew in air. Then Rachand slowly crumpled to the floor. The marquise stared unblinking at the cards Achille had turned over, her head going from one side to the other in stunned denial.

"No," she whispered, then repeated the word over and over again, her voice rising to an unintelligible shriek. She kicked her fallen husband. "You fool. You idiot. You cretin. You've ruined us. You've ruined us. You've—"

Vigny stepped to Achille's side, ignoring both the Rachands. "I believe you've won, monsieur," he said conversationally, though Achille could see his hands were shaking as if with a palsy.

Achille retrieved his crest ring from the table and slid it on his finger. "I believe I have," he said. He clenched his hand, seeing the falcon appearing to move in the candlelight. Fate, it seemed, had granted him his unsaid prayer. He closed his eyes and savored the anticipation building inside him.

He turned his back on the table and headed for the door, his long strides quickly covering the distance. He had won.

"Monsieur!" Vigny called after him. "What of your winnings?"

"I go to collect them."

Chapter 13

"**M**ama, Mama, I'm scared," little Eleonora cried, running into the salon where her mother sat sketching by the fire. Thunder rumbled. The five-year-old screamed and clambered into her mother's lap. Hands squeezed against her ears, Eleonora begged, "Make it stop. Make it stop." Lightning flashed, and her small body jerked in terror. She tried to hide her face against her mother's shoulder.

"Hush, my pretty angel," her mother murmured, patting her back to comfort her. The touch was rhythmic and soothing, and some of the tension drained away, easing the trembling of Eleonora's limbs.

"M-make it go away, Mama. Please."

Her mother had tucked an orange blossom into her hair, and the sweet scent enveloped Eleonora, making her remember it always as the smell of comfort. "I would if I could, darling," her mother said, wrapping her arms around the little girl and rocking her gently. "Thunder is the devil's laughter. He's come to snatch a soul tonight, and the laughter doesn't stop until he's found his victim."

Mama's long fingers coaxed Eleonora's clenched fist to relax. "You were a good girl today, weren't you?" Eleonora nodded vigorously. "You did everything Nurse asked you to do, didn't you?" This time the nod was considerably less vigorous.

"I-I was going to!"

"Oh, dear."

190

Eleonora began trembling again. "I was going to! Truly, Mama! I was! I was! Don't let the devil take me!" *Thunder rumbled, farther off now, but she screamed.*

"Now, now, angel, he's gone off for someone else tonight. He must've heard you." *Her mother wiped away her tears.* "But you won't disappoint Mama again, will you, darling?"

"No, Mama! Never, ever. I promise."

"That's Mama's little angel." *The comforting pats and the gentle rocking resumed, and Eleonora snuggled closer into the crook of her mother's arms.* "Mama was drawing a picture of the devil when you came in. Would you like to see?"

Eleonora's nod made her whole body shake. Whatever Mama wanted.

Her mother reached down beside the chair and brought up a bound book almost as large as Eleonora. The arms encircling her moved as her mother began flipping through the pages. To Eleonora's surprise, all of the pictures looked to be of the same man. Some in full face, some in profile, some of his whole body. A few had been painted with watercolors.

Her mother turned to the last drawing, about halfway through the book, and held it open for Eleonora to see. It was of his head and shoulders. He faced to the left, but had been drawn just as he'd turned to face the viewer. His intense dark eyes seemed to stare right out of the page and into her soul. She tried to squirm away.

She peeped up at her mother's face. There was an odd look on it. "He's p-pretty," *Eleonora said hesitantly.*

"Handsome, El," *her mother said absently.* "Men are called handsome, not pretty."

"I thought he was a devil. He scares me."

"He should."

"His hair is so long. Wouldn't it burn up in . . . in that other place? How come you never painted it? It looks white."

The tips of her mother's fingers stroked the fine charcoal marks, smudging them. "It was white."

Eleonora stiffened. "You mean you saw it? You mean he was here?" She screamed. "He was here! He came for me! He came to take me away to hell! He—"

"Stop it!" Her mother slapped her cheek, making it sting. "He didn't come for you. You hadn't even been born yet. Endres was still with his wet nurse, for God's sake." Lightning flashed, revealing her mother's intense stark face. Eleonora had never seen it like that before, and she began to whimper.

"He didn't come for you, Eleonora. He came for me."

Thunder began rumbling loud and close. "He's coming back," the little girl screamed. "No, no, don't let him—"

"—take me!" the adult Eleonora cried and sat bolt upright in the bed. She sucked in great gasps of air. Her body quivered almost out of control. She put a hand to her head to steady the dizziness that threatened her.

There was a movement by the fire. A dark shadow obscured the flames.

Someone knelt there.

She choked down her terror. Her heart pounded, still caught in the web of her nightmare. She pushed herself deeper into the pillows, her hands clawing at the counterpane she'd fallen asleep on top of.

A head turned, putting the shadow's profile in sharp relief against the red-orange flames licking up as they caught. It was a scene from hell, the devil's face outlined by fire. A recognizable devil.

"Achille," she breathed. "Thank God—"

"Thank Fate," he said, rising, his gaze hotly devouring her nearly nude form as she lay on top of the counterpane. Nearly nude, but for the robe he'd sent.

The movement brought back Eleonora's panic. He was not the creature from her dreams, but he was still dangerous. She scrambled off the bed to the side opposite from him. "What has Fate to say to ... Never mind, never mind, you must leave. You shouldn't be—"

"You received my gift," he interrupted.

"Yes, I—" She stammered, her hands fluttering as she

tried to find a way to cover herself. There was none. "You shouldn't be here."

He went to stand next to the bed across from her. He leaned toward her, his fisted hands supporting himself on the counterpane. "And you should not have troubled dreams, Eleonora."

"It was the storm," she told him, plucking at the counterpane to pull it up in front of her, but his weight held it in place. "Ever since I was a child, I remember . . . It's silly. I should—"

"This isn't the time for a child's memories," he said. He stepped back and began throwing pillows into a pile by the hearth, then he yanked the bed covering off and laid it on the floor in front of the fire.

"Achille!"

"It is time for *our* memories."

"Yours, you mean."

He stood at the edge of the soft down blanket and held out his hand to her as if he meant to begin a dance. "Mine," he agreed. "And yours."

She backed away. "What happened in the grotto was a mistake."

"I agree. I was a fool to stop."

"No!" she said bitterly. "I was a fool to think I could—"

"Have you never been made love to, Eleonora? Completely?"

"What?"" She turned her back to him. "Of course I have. What a question. I'm widow! You know that."

"I do not doubt that you have been taken. But surely with your precious Bálint—"

"Achille!" she cried, whirling to face him. "I told you I never broke my marriage vows. I am not a courtesan!" She pulled at a dangling ribbon tie on the robe in irritation.

"Are only courtesans allowed to feel pleasure?" he asked.

"Yes. No . . ." He began taking off his coat. "Stop that!"

He threw the coat onto a chair, the way a husband might. Or a lover.

"Get out! Do you hear? Just get out." She moved nervously around her side of the room, stepping to avoid the crumpled pile of her discarded nightgown and heavy robe.

He took off his cravat and began unbuttoning his waistcoat.

"I don't want you here! Can't you see that?" She went to the dressing table and started to straighten the toppled jars and bottles, her mind busy with trying to cope with the powerful presence behind her. Her hands reached out to the rolled parchment.

"You needn't clean that up on my account," Achille said, unperturbed. "A tiff with your maid?"

Eleonora froze, her hands still outstretched. *Saint Stephen, what am I doing?* She spun to face him, keeping her body between him and the table. "No," she snapped, "I just indulged myself in a fit of pique."

"I would much rather you indulged yourself with me. You did this morning." He slipped off his waistcoat and threw it over his coat.

"Stop this!"

With a single tug, he undid the tie of his shirt, and it fell open to a deep vee, revealing his hard-muscled chest.

She pushed off from the table, making the bottles rattle. "Put your clothes back on. I'm not some soldier's strumpet! I'm surprised you didn't come dressed in full officer's regalia. All that gold lace might have blinded me into submission."

"Gold lace?" he asked, his eyes narrowing. "Or would you prefer the bearskins of a Hungarian hussar?"

"Yes!"

He strode to her and grabbed her shoulders. "A hussar named Bálint, perhaps? How old was he when you knew him? Twenty? Twenty-one?"

"Twenty-two. He was a year younger than I."

"A boy soldier."

She pulled away and went to stand by a bedpost, holding on to it like an anchor. "I should have had you thrown out the minute I saw you by the fire."

"But you didn't, did you? You thanked God instead."

"This is what I get for trying to play the French sophisticate," she said, more to herself than to him.

"No," he murmured. *"This* is."

Something in his voice made her skin prickle. "What—?"

He wrapped his cravat around her wrist and the bedpost, and knotted it.

She tried to jerk her hand free. *"Achille,"* she cried. She struggled to free herself, to kick him. He stood behind her, and grabbed her other wrist. "Damn your tricks! Release me."

"Welcome to the real France, Madame Batthyány," he said harshly, his mouth at her ear. He grabbed her hips and pressed her against him. Her knees threatened to buckle. "Were you a soldier's strumpet, I would take you like this. A quick release of pleasure for me. Nothing for you."

"Then do it!" Anger threatened to choke her. Her vision pulsed red.

"I do not need your consent. You wear my gift. That is assent enough." He yanked at the binding cloth and it fell away.

She turned on him. "God in heaven, *I will not be bound. I will have my freedom, do you hear?*" she screamed, swinging at him.

He caught her arm in a iron hold. "Never—"

"Never what? Never deny you? You can take this body, damn you. You can return from war stinking of horses and dead men's blood, and you can throw me down and you can tear into me and you can grunt like a *pig* when you finish."

"Did I grunt like a pig this morning? *Did I?"* He released her. "I am not Miklos."

"You are a man," she spit at him.

"Yes, Magyar, I am."

She put her hands on his chest and slowly curled his shirt into her fists. "And you wanted a pretty seduction, didn't you? All coy smiles and rapturous sighs. Have I disappointed?"

She pressed her body into his and brazenly moved her

hips against his breeches. "Did you expect, perhaps, faint little die-away sighs?" Her hands uncurled, and she slid them up into his hair.

Achille grasped her shoulders. "Do you think to repulse me, madame, by your forwardness?" His hands began making slow circles down her back. "I am not repulsed." He cupped the globes of her behind and held her tightly against him. He looked down into her eyes. "You forget, I have seen your body as it trembled with pleasure. The promise of that has not been fulfilled. And I am selfish, Eleonora. I want much. I want that promise fulfilled."

"Has the wall gone from my eyes?" she asked.

"No."

"But it does not bother you now?"

"I would have it gone," he said, his voice low. "But even then, I think, I would not see what I wish to see in your eyes."

She closed her eyes to block out the sight of his seductive gaze. He slid his arms around her to warm her with his embrace, then kissed her temple.

"A beast in rut is not how it should be between a man and a woman. Let me show you the pleasures a man can give a woman, and the pleasure she can give him," he said. "I leave soon, Eleonora. I can ask for nothing more than this night with you."

He pressed his lips to her closed lids. "I want the taste of you on my tongue again, and the scent of you on my skin. And I want you fully."

She was scarcely breathing. "Is it for your soldier's memory that you want all of this? I have had my fill of soldiers and of war."

"It is deep in the night. I will not be a soldier till dawn." His thumb stroked her cheekbone.

Eleonora trembled. "I shake, Achille. This morning you made me feel turned inside out, as if my blood did not heat me from within but needed you to ignite it. Intimacy can be as binding as chains. And yet . . . and yet, I glimpsed the peace of heaven in your arms this morning, and—just once—I would like to go to the heaven the poets sing about."

She looked levelly into his eyes. "But know what you ask, Achille. I am not one of your Frenchwomen who trysts merely because it is fashionable. I am Magyar. I can be no other than who I am."

His chest moved with his breathing, still controlled but more rapid than it had been. A shadow of a smile lightened the angles of his face. "Come to me," he said.

She reached up to pull a pin from her hair.

Achille's breathing seemed to halt for a long moment, then came out in a rush. "Fate is kind," he murmured.

His fingers buried themselves in her hair and began pulling out the remaining pins. Heat danced just under her skin. Her hair tumbled down her back.

"Do you know how you test the limits of a man's control?" Achille asked. He gazed into the green depths of her eyes, and though the wall was still there, passion simmered, a woman's passion, strong and powerful.

She smiled wickedly. "I know how to try." She brought a finger to her lips and slowly licked it with the point of her tongue, then she began tracing along the opening vee of his shirt.

His loins grew tight. She bent her head and kissed the wet trail she had just left. *The promise of her* . . .

With a growl, he picked her up and carried her to the counterpane he'd laid in front of the hearth. He knelt over her on the fire-warmed linen. She wrapped her arms around his neck and pulled him down to her side. He took her mouth with a sweeping kiss.

It took all of his willpower not to devour her. The exquisite taste of her, the responsive lips beneath his, the tips of her breasts pressing through his shirt, all fueled the blaze that had ignited the moment he'd seen her sleeping in the rose silk robe. He had not been with a woman since Gemeaux, and after this morning, his body roared for a quick coupling. But he would not give in to it.

He slowly drew his hand down her silk-wrapped body, the feel of her skin through the gossamer fraying the bonds of his control, then he undid the ribbon ties and opened the robe to feel her warm skin against his hand. Her hands began rubbing his back with long, slow strokes. And while her tongue eagerly twined around his, her fingers tugged the shirttails from his breeches.

Her hands slipped under the linen. "Mmmm," she hummed, and the sound reverberated deep in his body. She explored the muscles of his back, his arms, his chest.

She seemed to want to touch him with her whole body. He rose to his knees and swept the shirt off. She smiled and reached up with her hand to stroke the ridges of his stomach. "There is such steel under the velvet."

"And such passion under the silk," he said.

Her hand roamed lower, stroking the evidence of his desire through his breeches. He sucked in a breath through his teeth and found his hips moving against her hand. His pulse drummed in his ears. The hot molten tyrant of lust begged for completion.

He removed her hand. "Later," he said. "Later, this will satisfy. Not now." He slid his open mouth over her palm, then kissed his way up her arm. "Now, only you will satisfy." His mouth found the peak of her breast through the robe. She moaned, and her supple back curved toward him. "Only you."

He settled next to her, their bodies touching from shoulder to hip. The warmth of her skin glowed through the silk into his hand as he caressed her. The dip of her waist, the swell of her hip, the long, slender length of her thigh. Under his touch, she stretched and writhed as her body woke from its sensual slumber.

Eleonora gave over to the shimmering, insistent heat his hands conjured. She nipped at his powerful arm, and lightly ran her teeth along the shape of it. She felt the swell of him against her thigh, so close . . . A bolt of anxiety shot through her. He kissed her neck, her breasts, twirling his tongue around the sensitive peaks. Her blood turned to flame-warmed brandy, intoxicating in its driving heat. She moaned, and her anxiety seemed suddenly to vanish.

His hand stroked her stomach, then lower, into her intimate curls. A finger traced the moist pink place of her womanhood, and a deep exhalation puffed from her. Her body tensed. Waiting . . . anticipating . . .

He dipped in. A whimpering moan came from her throat. His finger circled, explored, probed deeper. "Ahhh," she cried, tensing at the invasion. Her fingers gripped his arm.

"Sweet El," he murmured, returning to his earlier gentler soothings. "Do I hurt you?"

"N-no," she whispered.

"Do you want me to stop?" He kissed her mouth, her eyes.

"This morning," she gasped out. "Will it be like this morning?"

"It can be. But more."

She stared at the ceiling, a shaky laugh escaping her. "Poor Achille. This is not so diverting anymore, is it?"

His hand left off its gentle fondling, and he took her by the chin. "Look at me, Eleonora. What is between you and me stopped being a diversion a long while ago. But I will not lie to you. I am selfish. I want you. There is a promise in you that I have seen in no other woman. I want it."

He gave her a rueful smile. "But this is, after all, a seduction. I am not a small man and I do not want to hurt you."

She propped herself up on her elbows, let her hair fall back, and closed her eyes. She shook her head and laughed. "I suppose a Frenchwoman would be as red as a pomegranate from embarrassment right now. So why am I not?"

He traced her profile. "You are Magyar."

She raised her head and grinned at him. "I am, indeed. Perhaps it is the breeches that are . . . intruding."

"Breeches, thy name is patience," he said sardonically.

"Meaning without them . . ."

He raised an eyebrow in acknowledgment.

She rolled onto her side to face him, her hand sneaking

down to undo a button. He kissed her deeply. She undid another button.

"Think what you do, Eleonora."

She suckled kisses along the hard line of muscle of his chest. "No," she murmured against his skin, "no, I am through with thinking."

He let her finish undoing the buttons, then he pulled away and quickly discarded his breeches. She bit her lip at the sight of him.

"Are you thinking, El?"

"No," she whispered, looking away, then looking back. "It's just that I've never seen a completely naked man before." She peeped up at him through her lashes and grinned. "Do you want me to tell you what I see now?"

"Witch!" he said, gently pressing her back to the soft counterpane. "But I will tell you what *I* see. A luscious, voluptuous, sensual woman who's about to be seduced."

His hands returned to their caressing, and his lips returned to their kissing. He teased the inside of her thighs with his fingertips, slowly going higher and higher.

Eleonora let herself be carried away by the sensations. His hand reached her again, and she felt him hesitate. "Mmmm, yes," she said, closing her eyes and raising a knee.

"My Magyar," she heard him whisper. His touch swirled, then slowly sank into her.

She purred, basking in the radiating warmth his fingers were engendering. "So sweet . . ."

The heat intensified, as if it were the glow from a lantern whose shutter was slowly being lifted. And like that, it was an illuminating heat, letting her see things clearly for the first time. The chains of intimacy were soft indeed.

Achille shifted his body. She felt a momentary swell of trepidation, but his touch gentled her. "El . . ." She nodded, keeping her eyes closed.

"No, El. Open your eyes."

She looked at him, into his dark gaze, then let herself see all of him. He raised himself above her, and she moved to accommodate his long, powerful body. He slowly lowered his hips toward hers, moving against her without rushing. His breaths rasped unevenly. His eyes were half-closed.

Her hips rose and she began matching her movements to his. "Yes," he groaned. He trailed tiny kisses across her face.

The circle of rhythm took hold of her, spinning her, spinning her . . . The glow of beckoning heat brightened, expanded. A longing built inside her, making her yearn for completion.

She wanted him. Her hands slid down his back. She wanted him as fully as a woman could want a man. A moan slipped out. "Achille. Fill me." *Make me whole again.* "I want you."

He kissed her mouth, as if he wanted to take her moans inside of him. He adjusted himself. She felt him enter her. Slowly, slowly . . .

"*Sweet God* . . ." he said into her hair. "Oh, God, El . . ."

The movement of her hips increased its tempo. Her fingers dug into his back. Her breaths came in gasps. Oh, sweet invasion . . . He filled her completely.

She held on to him, her face against his neck. It felt so good, so good. A delicious tightening coiled in her. Her legs wrapped around him.

A long, low groan came from deep inside him. "El . . . El, I can't—"

"Don't stop. No. Please. Don't . . . *Yes, yes*—" She shattered. A cry tore from her throat. Her body trembled, over and over and over.

Achille sucked in his breath. "God, *God, God!*" He plunged into her—and found paradise.

Chapter 14

"**M**mm?" Awareness slowly broke through the pleasured sleepiness of Eleonora's mind and she rolled onto her side, facing the fire. Achille knelt in front of it, gloriously naked as he stirred the coals to flare into heat. She snuggled her head on her arm and lay watching him.

"There's no need for a fire," she said, her voice seductively low. "I'm already warm." *And complete.* Her hand stroked the indentation in the counterpane where he had been.

He smiled lazily at her. "I needed the light to see you more clearly," he said. "Before I go."

Her heart thumped. She darted a glance at the window. It was still dark. She felt his fingers caressing her ankle as if to comfort her, and she turned to see him.

"It won't be dawn for an hour or more." He stretched out his long frame beside her and drew the backs of his fingers along her jaw. "I wanted to leave before many of the servants were up."

She brushed a thick strand of sable hair from his temple. "Don't mind about the servants," she whispered. "I want you to stay."

His smile was soft and sensuous. He leaned toward her, the linen rustling beneath him, and kissed her. It was a lover's kiss, lips touching lips with infinite tenderness. "Were I any other man, the world would merely shrug to know I'd been with you tonight." His smile fell into a line, and he rolled onto his back and stared at the ceiling. "But I am not another man, Eleonora. And the world will not easily dismiss my being with you."

A laugh escaped her, and she began rubbing his chest, wanting her fingertips to memorize the feel of him. "What do I care if they gasp instead of shrug? I am queen of my domain in Hungary. Nothing French can touch me there."

Her fingers drew swirls and arabesques on his stomach, and she felt his muscles contract beneath her touch. She tipped her tongue out, wanting him again but not knowing how to tell him. "Or will they burn me at the stake for being a witch who has known the devil?" she teased.

She lightly tugged on the line of black hair that led down to his only partially quiescent phallus. It started to respond and his hand snapped around her wrist.

"You *are* a witch, Magyar," he said, smiling again, pulling her hand away.

The loss of that smile had stung her, the very sting of it a surprise, and she realized that when he did smile, there was no look of the devil about him at all. She propped herself on an elbow and traced that smile. "And you are a devil," she answered. "Except when you smile."

He kissed her fingertip. "And what am I then? An angel?"

She burst out laughing. "You?" She tilted her head and squinted at him. "Let me see," she said. "Smile." He bared his teeth. "You look like a wolf grinning at dinner!" She prodded him in the side. "A real smile this time."

His gaze slowly skimmed over her body. His eyes darkened and his mouth curved with sensual anticipation. He ran a hand up her arm and pulled her on top of him. "Real enough?" he asked, his lips so close to hers that she could feel his breath.

She licked his mouth as if tasting something exquisitely sweet. "As real as the heaven you took me to, dark angel. Take me there again." She lay outstretched, her curves conforming to the uncompromising hardness of the body beneath her.

His eyes turned serious as his gaze crisscrossed her

face. "You do right to call me dark," he said, weaving his fingers into her hair. "And it has nothing to do with the color of my hair or my eyes. The darkness is inside me, Eleonora. When I was young, my father read to me of battles and deeds of honor a knight would do for his lady. I wanted to become that kind of man. The kind of man who rode tall and straight and proud, proud of his accomplishments, not merely for the blood that flowed in his veins.

"After he died, I still read the books, studied them, memorized them. I was careless once, and my Jesuit tutor discovered me. I became more careful after that. But I still read them.

"I grew into a man. The memories of my father became misty phantasms, and the deeds of honor I had once so desired to do became, in manhood, deeds of war, of battle, of . . . death.

"It is good that I am leaving, my passionate Magyar. I have done too many things that cannot be undone. Your fire wakens the boy's dreams in me." He caressed her face. "But it is too late. And I would not have you harmed."

She rolled, sliding one knee over him, then sat upright, her legs astride him. Once, his words might have frightened her. But not now, not after he had taken her to heaven. "I am Magyar," she said, knowing that the hunger sluicing in her veins showed clearly in her eyes, her voice. "Dark angel, I will not be harmed."

She curled her fingers around his shoulders and dug in. Her eyelids fluttered half-closed, and using the power of her knees, she opened herself over his engorged desire and let the slippery heat of her slide over him.

He groaned. His hips lifted to meet her. "Eleonora . . ." he breathed, the sound undulating between a warning and a plea.

She kept moving over him.

"Sweet Christ, woman, think what you— Ahhh." He grabbed her thighs and controlled her movements. His eyes closed. When he opened them again, he looked at her with a devil's gaze. "You shall reap what you have sown."

With an iron hold on her hips, they moved together. She bent lower. He placed a hand in the small of her back and pressed, molding her as she slid over him. "Yes," she moaned, feeling him against her. Her nails dug into his flesh. "Fill me."

"Beg, Magyar."

She grinned wickedly and tossed her hair back and forth. She undulated her hips so he just slipped into her, then out. He sucked in a ragged breath.

"Beg, devil."

His hands cupped her breasts, his thumbs flicking over her erect nipples. She shuddered and cried out at the sudden intensifying of sensation. What before had been a slow mounting toward an unknown pinnacle became . . .

"God," she whimpered, "sweet, sweet God . . ." Consuming flames licked up from where she slid so intimately over him. Her entire body flared with blinding intensity, as if too much powder had been put in a priming pan.

The sound of his breathing was harsh and ragged. Through eyes blurred with passion, she saw his jaw clench and unclench as he struggled for command of his body.

A sense of power burst through her, like oil thrown on a fire. The devil was hers. Hers to control. Hers to send to heaven.

She leaned over further still, rubbing her breasts on the hard, sculpted muscle of his chest. A growl exploded deep in his throat. His arms wrapped like bands across her back. Her fingers dragged up to feel the contracting of his muscles as he held on to her.

"I want you, devil," she rasped, adjusting her sliding body. "I want you—*now.*" With one sure movement, she engulfed him.

A roar tore from him. His body arched again and again. His hands gripped her hips. "Witch! Witch. Wi—"

She tensed herself around him to glory in the feel of that delicious invasion. A shock went through him that pounded into her.

She did it again. His head rocked back, air hissing through his clenched teeth. "God, *yes.*"

The coiling, pulsing heat inside her wound tighter and tighter. Her fingers slid into his hair without her being aware of it. Control was slipping away. Conscious thought seemed a misty, faraway dream. She buried her face against his neck, mindlessly kissing, licking, nipping at his flesh. Hot tension danced faster, faster—

And exploded. She cried out. Wave after wave of fire rolled through her. Her body clenched around him.

His arms tightly claimed her. "El, my El," he breathed. His body rose to meet hers, and held. A cry burst from him. His fingers fisted in her hair. He groaned, a long ribbon of sound.

Slowly the tension drained from his body, but he did not release his hold on her. Their breathing was labored as she lay limp on top of him.

Sensation throbbed in her body. Time ceased to be. No past haunted her with its devils, no future loomed with its failure. She felt cleansed and free.

Achille's fingers began to trace slowly up and down her spine. "You have given me dreams, Eleonora." He kissed her temple. "It is a precious gift."

She folded her arms on his chest and rested her chin on them to sleepily study him. "What kind of dreams?" she asked, the words slurring with the delicious lethargy from their lovemaking that still warmed her.

He smiled at her, as if pleased that he'd caused the purring satisfaction in her voice. "The kind of dreams a man has when he is leaving a woman he doesn't wish to leave. The dreams of anticipation that won't be assuaged. Of nights—and days—of passion that won't be fulfilled." He drew his thumb along the tender flesh below her eye. "You are an extraordinary woman, Eleonora. If I could but stay awhile longer . . ."

She closed her eyes to block out the entrancing sight of him. "I am not worth your praise. I am an ordinary woman, Achille. Perhaps my foreignness has led you to think I am more than I am, but if anything, I am less than other women. It was safe to be with you—you were leaving, and I had nothing left to lose."

His arms tightened and he rolled them over together until he was kneeling astride her. "Tell me you would have been with any other man the way you have been with me," he demanded, gripping her shoulders and staring down at her with black eyes that had grown fierce. "Tell me you would have lain with another man who was *safe* who could pleasure you. Tell me. *Convince me.*"

"Achille, no, I did not mean . . ." She winced. "Please, my shoulders." He lessened his iron grip just enough not to hurt her. She fluttered her hands uselessly at her sides, wanting to touch him, yet hesitant. She drew in a deep breath to try and answer him. "I do not know what I mean. I did not speak rightly. My wits are addled."

Her hands finally lit on his arms. He stared down at her, his face shadowed by his hair, yet she could see his eyes glittering with frightening intensity. "I am not yet convinced, Eleonora."

"Achille! How can you change so easily from angel to devil? Of course I would have lain with no other man. It is *you* who made me wonder, you who gave this flush to my skin . . ."

His hold eased into a caress. "And you," he said, lowering his face to hers, "who have given me wonder . . ." He kissed her. "And delight . . ." He kissed her again. "And the unfamiliar sting of something I do not wish to name . . ."

His lips slid over hers yet again, taking her mouth with a slow, languid questing. She felt his desire stir against her thigh, and her own hunger began to grow insistent once more.

He broke off the kiss with a surprisingly tender smile. "There are so many parts of you that I have only glimpsed, Eleonora. You're like a forest where, with each turning, a new glade, a new vista, is revealed. I want to see them, feel them, experience them all. You are a woman like no other."

She returned his smile, though she knew hers was bittersweet. "Like a forest, am I?" With the tip of her finger, she traced the curve of his mouth. "So terrestrial, when you roam between the heavens and the inferno."

"How could I have demanded that you give me what I cannot give?" he asked. "You call me a dark angel. If so, it is a dark and fallen angel. I would that salvation could be found in a woman's arms, but it cannot. I must go."

In one fluid motion, he drew back to his knees, heels, then rose to his feet, towering above her. She made to rise with him, but he put out a hand to stop her.

"I shall miss you, devil," she said, surprised at how deeply the words rang true inside her. She glanced toward the window, where the remnants of the night's storm still blew against the glass. "Now, at least, not all of my dreams will frighten me."

He went to where her brocade robe lay crumpled in a heap and picked it up, then brought it back to her. "Know that when this devil dreams, Eleonora," he said, bending down to cover her, "he will dream of you."

Achille dressed quickly while she watched him from the counterpane, so rumpled from their loving. The heat of their passion lingered on her skin and in her blood, and she pulled the robe around her more to cover herself than for warmth. Her hair still unbound, her shoulders bare, she stayed where she was, reluctant to move, as if leaving the counterpane would shatter the bubble of enchantment Achille had so skillfully conjured.

Fully dressed now, it was Achille, the comte d'Agenais, who came to her one last time. He sat on his heels in front of her. "Dawn is moments away and I must leave you." He drew the back of his hand over her flushed cheek. "Good-bye, madame la comtesse."

"Good-bye, monsieur le comte," Eleonora whispered, and then he made for the doorway between the bedroom and the sitting room.

He paused by the disheveled dressing table, his sword hand curling into a fist. "So strange that I am loath to go. It tugs on me like a homesickness for which there is no home. Perhaps a token would ease the reluctance." He picked up the roll of parchment to free a ribbon, the roll catching on a badger brush and partially unrolling before snapping closed.

"No!" Eleonora cried, the thudding of her heart drowning out her gasp. "No, you mustn't . . ." Her words choked off, and she put a trembling hand over her mouth.

He had lifted the ribbon to his nose and closed his eyes to breathe in her scent on the silk, but her cry made him turn to her with a frown. "Eleonora? It is but a small—" He broke off, looking at the roll of parchment he still held in his hand. "Did you think I meant to take this?"

Achille regarded her for a long moment. *Don't look!* she wanted to shriek. *Don't look at the parchment.* She knew she should appear nonchalant, uncaring, but she might as well try to control the moon as her watery muscles.

"I—I— Take the ribbon," she said shakily. How to keep her fear from showing on her face when it seemed to have been smeared on her like a too thick cosmetic? "You must hurry, Achille! It's nearly dawn. I didn't mean— I'm sorry. A remnant of my nightmare . . ."

"Why are you so concerned, Eleonora?" he asked, his eyes narrowing. "Why are you so concerned?"

"No, it is nothing. Please, just take the ribbon and go," she said. Clutching at the robe wrapped around her, she rose unsteadily.

Almost unthinkingly, he stuffed the length of silk into a pocket and began unrolling the parchment.

"Achille, no!" she cried. She ran to him, reaching out to take it from him, but he turned and kept it from her grasp.

Inch by inch, Achille revealed the face on the parchment in all its beautiful, magnificent cruelty. He stood staring at it, at the dark eyes, the long hair, the chin and cheekbones so like his own. He paled.

She wanted to touch him, to bridge the chasm that was opening between them even as they breathed. "Achille . . ." she said on a thread of sound. "It is—it is but a picture. It's old. It means nothing."

He slowly turned to face her, his eyes black and haunted. "Is this how you see me? Is it, Eleonora? Ruthless, cruel . . ." His gaze returned to the drawing. "The nights—I've spent so many long, starless nights staring into my own tainted soul, but never did I see such evil as you have drawn. No wonder you call me devil," he said. "How you must hate me."

Eleonora teetered on a precipice. He did not realize what it was he held. That could save her. *Leave it be,* a voice screamed in her head.

"I do not hate you." And she realized with heart-stopping clarity just how much she loved him.

He held out the picture to her. "This refutes that."

"No," she whispered, turning her head to keep from looking at the face that had haunted her dreams since childhood. "No, it does not."

She took a breath—and stepped off the precipice. "The picture is not of you."

He shook the parchment, making it rattle. "I am not blind." In his eyes, she could see anger beginning to replace shock. She could only shake her head in reply.

"Eleonora, I am not blind," he spit out. He strode to the cheval mirror, then held the picture up to one side so he could look at it and his own face at the same time. "If this is not me, then who . . ." His eyes narrowed, darted back and forth as if seeing the differences for himself.

To her surprise, Eleonora could see both the startling similarities—and the differences. The two faces had nearly merged in her mind, but now, seeing them side by side, the picture was clearly of a different man from Achille. She held on to that thought, fervently wanting them to be different.

"Achille, leave now. Turn your back and go. Don't ask any more questions."

His eyes met hers in the mirror. There was no softness in them, just the ice of a harsh winter. "Who, madame?"

She was scarcely breathing. She started to shake her head, but it stopped halfway, as if it had forgotten how to move. Was this how a duelist felt when he saw the blade plunging toward his heart?

Hoarsely, as a penitent confessing a mortal sin, she said, "I know only what I have been told. He died before I was born. I do not know his true name, but he was called El Müzir."

Achille's eyes held hers. She had seen hares held in much the same way, just before a wolf's jaw closed on their necks. She closed her eyes to break the spell.

"He was a Turk. At one time, a sultan of Temesvár." Behind her eyes, like a series of moving paintings, she could see the story unfold as it had unfolded a thousand times in her mother's telling. But it was not her place to reveal all of the story. She opened her eyes.

"He traveled to the west," she said, her heart fluttering like a captive bird's. "To France."

His face grew closed, hard. For a heartbeat, the two faces looked identical. "And what else was this man, this *Turk,* this onetime sultan of Temesvár?" Control made his breath come evenly. "Be careful how you continue, madame la comtesse. Men have died for not being careful. Many men, madame, *many men.*"

She wanted to hide from him, from the turbulence of his building fury. She felt bruised and buffeted, as if she'd stood for hours in a strong wind, but she kept her back straight and faced him.

"El Müzir . . . was your father."

Cold silence engulfed her. He stood in front of the mirror as if trapped in ice. He said nothing. The muscles of his jaw clenched and unclenched.

"Achille?" she whispered.

He stared at her with eyes that seemed windows to hell, then turned his gaze back to the drawing. With taut precision, he began rolling up the parchment. He went to the dressing table, his boot heels thudding against the carpet with a soldier's stride.

He set the parchment in the exact place where it had been. "How long?" he asked, his voice clipped, strained. "How long have you believed this lie?" His hand balled into a fist. It arced out to sweep everything from the table.

Jars and bottles shattered against the wall, sending perfumes and lotions and cosmetics dripping down the wall like blood from a wound torn open.

He snapped his head to her. *"How long?"*

"I have known of El Müzir since childhood. He . . . visited my family before he continued on to France," Eleonora answered. She pulled her robe tightly around her and shivered. "We did not know of you until my brothers saw you at the battle of Philippsburg."

"Is that it?" he demanded. He picked up the table and threw it against the wall. Gilded legs cracked and splintered. She winced, struggling to keep from cowering. He turned toward her. "Is that it? You lay with me, then call me *bastard* because I resemble a man your family once knew?"

He closed on her. "Achille, *no*—" She backed away, but she collided with the bed and fell backward. He gave her no chance to escape, but straddled her, pinning her to the bed.

His hands encircled her throat, his thumb rubbing the soft flesh under her chin, rubbing, rubbing. Her mouth worked, but terror clogged her throat. She clawed at his tightening fingers. She struggled to throw him off her, her movements a mockery of their earlier lovemaking, but he held her fast.

"I tell you again, madame la comtesse—be careful how you continue. Now, tell me again how my resemblance to this *Turk* makes me his bastard son."

"Not just resemblance," she gasped out. "We checked. Father—" She broke off, a sudden wash of grief diluting her panic. "Father left . . ." Eleonora tugged on Achille's hands. "Achille! I can't—" The pressure lessened slightly. She nodded her gratitude and sucked in a deep breath.

"After Philippsburg, my brothers returned home. They had discovered your name, but nothing more. By then, though, it was too far into winter. Father left the next spring. He traveled to France, to the village of Agenais."

She squeezed her eyes to shut out the rage blazing on Achille's features.

"Father wrote to us, to Mother, and said yes, yes, El Müzir had been there. He'd posed as an astrologer . . . and had gone to Agenais, had been invited to the château d'Agenais by the wife of the chevalier."

Achille released Eleonora and rose from the bed. "The wife of the chevalier," he mimicked bitterly. "She . . ." He knelt back onto the bed before Eleonora had a chance to straighten. Strong, insistent fingers spread into her hair and held her immobile. "But your story has holes, madame. No one named El Müzir has ever been an astrologer at d'Agenais. There was an old laboratory in a closed-off wing of the château. When I was twelve, I broke into it, played there, read all the old books. I would remember a name like El Müzir. It is a name a boy would remember, don't you agree?" He held her head tight, and his thumb stroked her neck. "Don't you agree?"

"He did not use the name El Müzir when he was in France. He called himself Oncelus."

Achille's hands went still. There was a stab of surprise, of pain, in his eyes, but he remained motionless. It felt as if she were being held by a statue of marble.

He swallowed. "That, too," he said hoarsely, "is a name a boy would remember."

He focused on her again, the pain masked. "But it was nothing more than a name in an old account book. I will not believe what you say. Because a boy also remembers his father—and that man was not a Turk!"

Achille caressed her neck, but there was no tenderness in his touch. Fear rushed through Eleonora, cold and biting. "Clever Magyar," he said silkily. "I'm impressed. Such an elaborate game you play, gathering bits of twigs and twine like a magpie—a battle where I fought, a name from an old account book; you even called my father—*my father*—'chevalier' and not comte, for that title was conferred upon me after the oh-so-eventful Philippsburg. But why? Do those Hungarian winters pass with such unrelieved boredom? Or did I skewer one of your precious brothers?" He took her hands and pulled them out to either side of her, his fingers twining with hers.

"Stop this," she pleaded. "Please—"

He bent closer. His tongue slid out and licked her lips. She turned her face away, but he went on lapping the sensitive flesh below her ear. "Is that your game? A subtle Hungarian revenge for damage done? My reputation could not have been too difficult to build on, though the Turk is innovative. And how to resolve that my mother had never gone to Turkey? Have the Infidel come to her! Brilliant, Magyar."

He kissed her neck, a long, slow kiss. "But you haven't won the game yet, have you, my clever, clever comtesse?"

"Stop this, Achille. Look at me! See how clever I am," she spit out at him. "I submit." A sob escaped her. She hated weakness. She drew in deep, heaving breaths to control the shaking fear inside her that bit at her sanity. "You won, you won—is that what you want me to say? Burn the damn picture! End this."

He snarled. "So. You would hold on to the last card. I have gambled twice this past night and won. I will win again. Confess your lie. *Confess it.*"

"It is no lie," she said.

He gripped her hands tighter. "Confess it!"

"No lie, Achille. I cannot change the past! If I could, I would erase my ever having come to France. *But that is no lie.*"

He abruptly released her. "Damn you, woman. There was no Turk! That picture could easily have been drawn from your brothers' description of me."

"My mother drew it when I was five. The Turk was real."

"Lies."

Eleonora pushed herself to her feet and stumbled to where the roll of parchment had fallen. "Here, burn it. Burn it!"

He faced her with fury swirling around him like a night

wind. The power of his body wound taut and deadly. It was the duelist who stood before her, the duelist who had killed.

"Achille, the sun has already risen. Burn this and go." He did not move. "Damn you!" she cried, and went to the fireplace herself. She lifted the parchment to throw it into the flames. "Your salvation awaits you on the battle-field, remember? Hate me if you will, but you must go—"

His hands closed around her wrist. "What need has a bastard of salvation?" he asked, pulling the drawing from her grasp. "I, too, have a last card to play."

"What do you mean?"

"There is one person who can prove this slander false," he said, dragging her toward the servant's door.

"It isn't fal—"

He pulled the door open and roared for her maid.

"What are you doing? Stop!"

"Courage faltering, Magyar? Don't you want to play out the hand?"

"Achille, don't do this."

The maid scampered into the room, hastily arranging her clothes. She skidded to a halt, eyes wide, when she saw Achille. She stared at Eleonora.

"Dress your mistress for travel," Achille ordered.

"No!" Eleonora countered.

"Then pack her things," he went on as if Eleonora hadn't spoken. "Quickly."

Bobbing her head in a frantic nod, the maid backed away. "Y-yes, monsieur. At once, monsieur." Her heel kicked into a splintered table leg and she glanced down. Eleonora saw the girl's face go white as her gaze darted to the destroyed table, then around the shambles of the room.

"Don't listen to him, Martine. Monsieur d'Agenais is just in a temper. He'll be over it soon."

Achille pulled her to a chair and sat her down. "What will be over, madame la comtesse, is this game," he told her in a voice that only she could hear. "In two days time. When you confront the woman so intimately implicated in your lies.

"My mother."

Chapter 15

Achille looked over his shoulder at the maid. *"Now, girl."*

The maid jumped. "Yes, monsieur," she squeaked, and hurried to the wardrobe. She grabbed two handfuls of satin and velvet and turned to throw them on the bed. She stopped in midthrow and gasped, looking from the empty mattress to the counterpane in front of the hearth to the tumble of pillows.

The girl began to shake. She hugged the dresses to her. "M-madame, are you un-unharmed?" she asked. Terror made the muscles of her face twitch uncontrollably. She closed her eyes, and tears dripped down her face. "Please say he didn't hurt you. P-please, madame. You've been good to me." She cast a watery glance toward Achille, then Eleonora.

"Saint Stephen," Eleonora said to Achille under her breath. "She thinks you raped me. Let me go to her. She's frightened."

"Your promise first."

"Promise?"

"To see this game through to the end."

"End? Taking me to your mother will not do that. Burn the picture. That is your end. Your mother will deny it. What woman wouldn't?"

"One can reveal much without words," he said, glancing significantly at the rumpled counterpane. "Your promise."

"And if I don't give it?" Eleonora asked, then shook her

head. "Don't answer. I have no doubt you would drag me through the château to your coach." She nodded. "My promise."

"Good." He released her wrist. "We will discuss later what you will forfeit to me when you lose. And don't think to run away. It is not only Hungarians who are good at the hunt." He bowed, turned, and departed, the roll of parchment firmly in his grip.

The clicking of the door latch behind him sounded like the closing of a prisoner's cell to Eleonora.

"M-madame?"

Eleonora rose and went to hug the trembling girl. "It's all right, Martine. Sh-sh-sh. It's all right. Monsieur d'Agenais did not hurt me. At least, not the way you mean. Not physically." She wiped away the maid's tears. "Truly."

"Your pardon, madame," Martine said with a sniffle. "I must have embarrassed you terribly."

"You were very brave to say that in front of him."

The maid straightened her shoulders and raised her chin. "If Monsieur d'Agenais has me whipped, I can take it."

"Well, I don't think Monsieur d'Agenais will have you beaten. He has . . . much on his mind. But it did take a lot of courage to face him. I hope I can be as brave."

The maid's eyes went wide again. "Are you really going to go away with him?"

Eleonora's stomach clenched, but she managed a smile and a nod. "I have to. I promised."

"But you'll be—"

"Ruined? Well I guess that means no more invitations to sit down to cards with the archduchess of Austria." Eleonora let her eyes roam over the rumpled counterpane, her mind and body remembering the ecstasy Achille had given her. She swallowed what seemed to be a rock lodged in her throat. "Such is the price of playing with the devil."

Achille strode through the corridors of the château du Peyre, cold black fury pounding in his veins like drums calling him to battle. A footman appeared in a doorway.

"Have my coach and horses made ready," Achille ordered as he passed. The startled footman jumped, then trotted alongside. "And one for baggage," Achille added. "Madame Batthyány will be accompanying me."

The footman stopped and stared, his mouth hanging open.

Achille did not break his stride. *"At once,"* Achille said, raising his voice as if to make it carry over the sounds of battle.

"Yes, m'sieur!" the servant shouted, and scurried off.

Memories of his father swirled through Achille's mind. Scenes of color and laughter and smiles, all blurry and far away, as far away as the man he had become was from the boy he had once been.

Those memories, a few trinkets, and his books were all he had left of his father. Now *she* wanted to take those memories from him as well, make them memories not of a loving father, but of a doddering cuckold. His mother had also tried to take his father's memories away—by tearing down the old château d'Agenais so that by the time he was twenty, there was not a stone left that his father had seen. But she had not succeeded in taking his memories.

And neither would the countess Batthyány.

When he reached his rooms, he paused, his hands hovering over the door latch. He thought of the night just past. Had the exotic countess taken him so high only so he would have further to fall?

There was a ripple of hurt, of regret, mingled with his fury. Last night, for the first time, he had glimpsed the possibility of a pleasure beyond sensual ecstasy, beyond the boundaries of the flesh, to one of an intimate friendship that could only be shared between a man and a woman. But it had been only a glimpse, like the flash of the sun on a distant lake. And then she had taken it all away.

His hand crashed down on the latch. The promise of her had indeed been fulfilled.

"Monsieur!" Beaulieu cried as Achille strode into the

room. "Praise God." The steward turned to a man standing near the door, impatiently slapping his hat against his leg. "You see? I told you he would come."

Achille threw the roll of parchment onto the bed. "Have that sealed in oilskin. Do not look at it," he told Beaulieu. He ignored the courier. "We leave within the hour."

The steward, catching Achille's urgency, hastily began pulling off his master's coat and waistcoat. "Of course, monsieur," Beaulieu said. "Captain Heraut here said the road east—"

"We will be traveling south," Achille said. "To Valeria."

Shock registered on Beaulieu's face before he could master himself. "Valeria, monsieur?" He glanced toward the courier in confusion. "You wish to visit the Holy Sisters of Saint Valeria? But Colonel Gillon awaits you in Bavaria."

Achille pulled his shirt over his head. "You will ride with Jean-Baptiste in the baggage coach. Madame Batthyány's maid will accompany you."

"Madame Batthyány?" Beaulieu asked, his voice rising in bewilderment. "The one from Hungary? Madame du Peyre's niece? I—I—"

The courier stepped forward, bowed stiffly, and held out a packet of sealed papers. "Monsieur d'Agenais, here is your letter of commission from Colonel Gillon. I must leave immediately. The rains have swollen the rivers, and I wish to be off before the bridges are flooded."

"Then be off now," Achille snapped. His desire for war seemed to lie in the distant past.

The courier looked taken aback. His gaze bounced between Beaulieu and the comte, then he stared at the packet in his hand as if at a loss. "But . . . but what about the five thousand louis d'or?"

"Nothing is being bought. Therefore, there will be no five thousand."

The courier turned on Beaulieu. "You mean I slept in that frigging chair all frigging night for nothing? You said he was anxious to get this! You said he was tearing up the turf waitin' for it. You said— Damn! I coulda been pounding some chambermai-ai-ai-ai—"

The point of a sword pressed against his throat, making it difficult to talk. Achille regarded him with deadly calm down the long blade. "And *you* said the rivers are swollen. *Be off,* or you may find yourself floating down one instead of crossing over it."

"Y-y-yes, monsieur," the courier gasped. Achille lowered the sword, and the man flew to the door. He paused there, seeming to gather a bit of false courage now that he was out of immediate danger. "You realize, I'm sure, that this means Colonel Gillon will not—"

Achille threw the sword like a javelin. The blade buried itself in the door a hairbreadth from the courier's hand. The man screamed and ran.

Beaulieu quickly recovered from his shock. "I take it, monsieur, that this means you will not be accepting Colonel Gillon's offer."

Achille braced his foot against the door and yanked the sword out of the wood. "You take it correctly," he said, his gaze caressing the honed edge of the blade.

His English uncle had given him the sword as a birth present. He'd wielded it as a child, under Constantin's careful gaze, killing the mythical dragons of Tristan, the apparitions of Parzival ... until his father had died. Then— Then, six years later, he had first used it to kill a man. Defending his father's honor.

He twisted the blade, letting the sunlight play over the blued steel. And now? The countess's words went beyond whispers, beyond gossip, and fighting her lies would demand more than a duel in the morning mist. But fight he would.

He turned to Beaulieu. "We leave within the hour."

"As you wish, monsieur."

No, thought Achille, it was not as he wished. He gripped the sword hilt. But it was as it would be.

* * *

In her rooms, the maid settled a traveling cloak around Eleonora's shoulders and smoothed the linen with shaking hands.

"Thank you, Martine," Eleonora said, smiling at the girl. "Are you sure you will be all right riding in the baggage coach with Jean-Baptiste and his father?"

"Oh, yes, madame!" the girl said, her eyes bright. She blushed and looked down. "I mean, Monsieur Beaulieu has been most kind, and Jean-Baptiste is ... is ..." Two shy eyes peeped up at Eleonora, and the girl's blush deepened. "He has been most kind, too."

"I see," Eleonora said. "Run along, then. I don't believe we should test Monsieur d'Agenais's temper by dawdling."

Martine curtsied, then asked with a frown, "Are you sure you don't want me to ride with you?"

"I'm sure that what I *want* has nothing to do with how things will be. Now, hurry. I'll be there shortly," Eleonora said, then scooted the girl toward the servants' door.

Alone for a moment, Eleonora looked around her rooms one last time. How much of herself was she leaving behind? The woman who had walked in had had so much self-assurance, so much arrogance, ready to fulfill the destiny her family had chosen for her.

But the woman who was walking out ... Eleonora pulled up the hood of the cloak. That woman had chosen her own destiny, and now she must fulfill it.

She could hear Tante Geneviève's screams for a full minute before the door flew open. "This cannot be!" Geneviève cried as she rushed in. "Tell me the servants have all gone mad."

Eleonora took her aunt by the hand and gently turned her back toward the door. "You've been so kind," she said, and kissed Geneviève on the cheek. "Walk me to the coach so I can say a proper good-bye." She led her out into the hall.

"No! How can you do this?" Geneviève tearily demanded, struggling to keep up with Eleonora's long strides. "D'Agenais, of all people. I had no idea! I mean, *d'Agenais,* for God's sake! Eleonora, he's dangerous. He has *killed!"*

"So have my brothers, Tante. It is what soldiers do when they must."

"But his duels! And what happened in Paris. He was utterly ruthless, Eleonora. Please don't go with him."

In the corridor, Eleonora stopped and hugged Geneviève. "I know this is all confusing for you. It is for me, too. But things . . . just happened. That's the way of it sometimes, isn't it? Don't worry, I'll be all right."

Tears welled in her aunt's eyes. "Oh, this is all my fault. All that empty-headed nonsense about you taking a lover. You don't have to. Truly!"

"No, no, it's not your fault at all," Eleonora assured her. Just ahead, over the older woman's shoulder, Eleonora recognized the window seat where she'd first seen Achille. A living, breathing, compelling man had sat there, not the devil-construct she'd made up in her head. She could still remember the feel of his eyes on her as he'd watched her walk toward him.

She should have turned around and walked back out the door, when she'd had the chance. If she'd ever had a chance.

"But—*d'Agenais,* Eleonora! The stories I've heard. He scares me so."

"There are always stories about men like Monsieur d'Agenais, Tante," Eleonora said.

Geneviève sniffled. "But you haven't even asked what they are!"

Eleonora looked up. She didn't need to ask. In her line of sight, as if caught between two mirrors, doorways within doorways within doorways, stood Achille in the open front door, hands on hips, feet apart, riding boots up to his thighs.

"I must go, Tante." She hugged her aunt again. "Don't blame yourself. You've been so sweet and good to me. Thank you."

"I'll light a candle for you in chapel."

Unexpected tears choked Eleonora's throat. "Thank you,

Tante, thank you. I'm going to need your prayers." She
turned and began walking the last long length of corridor
toward the waiting comte d'Agenais.

Achille let his body move with the sway of the coach.
On the seat next to him was the carefully wrapped portrait
of Eleonora's infamous Turk, while across from him,
Eleonora herself gripped a leather strap to keep from being
thrown about. His coachman had been ordered to spare
nothing to speed, and he was carrying out his orders with
his usual relish. The faster they left these storm-rutted
sidetracks behind and traveled on the main road, the
sooner this travesty would be over.

"Comfortable?" Achille asked her.

She shot him a glare, then went back to ostensibly
studying the landscape they were passing through at so
fast a clip. "Would it matter if I was not?"

"Not in the least."

"I'm quite comfortable, thank you."

He yawned and stretched, then put his feet on the seat
beside her and crossed his ankles. "Your pardon, madame.
I didn't get much sleep last night."

A flush crept up her cheeks, but he saw a tiny smile lift
at the corners of her mouth. "Neither did I. Some brute
kept me up all night with his groans."

"Ah, it was groans that kept you awake? For me, it was
the most delicious little cries. Over and over and—"

"Achille!" She glanced at him, and though her voice
was sharp, there was something in her green eyes that told
him his taunts were hitting their target.

He changed tack. "Perhaps it would have been wiser to
have read a book," he said. Using his booted toe, he
kicked a book that had been resting in the corner of the
seat toward her. "I believe you were reading this one last
night."

She gave him a look of surprise, and picked it up.
"Maurice de Saxe's *Mes Reveries,*" she said, reading the
title stamped on the spine. "Yes, I was looking at it last

night." She set it back down on the seat and added softly, "Before my nightmare."

"Brushing up on tactics?" Achille asked. "His ideas about deploying armies in battle are more fancy than real. Perhaps you should have read Caesar's *Conquest of Gaul.*"

She gave him a level stare. "I already have."

They came to the crossroads and turned south. Once they were on the main road, the surface became smoother. He stopped baiting her, and she returned to gazing out the window.

He watched her body move with the motion of the coach. She didn't hold herself stiff, fighting the sway as many would have, but rather rocked with it.

She made love the same way, moving with, not fighting, the sweet tyrant of desire. His taunts to her now taunted him. Her moans and cries had been delicious, spontaneous. His body tightened. The pleasure she had given him had been greater than he'd expected. Much, much greater. As had hers. It disturbed him to know how much her passion had augmented his own.

He silently cursed her. Her passions obviously went beyond the carnal. How else to explain her playing this cruel game? Study her as close as he might, he still could not see the ruthlessness that must be there. Had he been mistaken? Was that what was behind the wall he still saw in her breathtaking green eyes?

Outwardly she sat composed. The only hint of her anxiety was the hand in her lap that had curled into a ball. Was it vulnerability she hid from him? Or only ice?

Eleonora turned to him, frowning. "How soon will we be turning back to the east? There's another storm coming. We'll run into it if we continue south much longer."

"We do not go east."

"What?" she asked, going pale. "I thought château d'Agenais was directly east of here."

"It is."

"But we're going south."

"We are."

"Stop answering like a damned Jesuit! Where are we going? You said you were taking me to your mother."

"I am. My mother is prioress of the convent of the Holy Sisters of Saint Valeria."

"A prioress!"

Achille put his feet on the floor and leaned toward her. "Yes, madame la comtesse, the woman you have accused of consorting with an Infidel is now a nun. Do you wish to recant? We can return to du Peyre before the storm hits. Admit to this lying game, Eleonora!"

The hand in her lap trembled. "I cannot," she whispered. "It is not a lie."

He sat back. "You're willing enough to play this callous game," he said with a snarl. He kicked the seat next to her, and she jumped. "And I am more than willing to make you pay when you lose."

They rode south for hours. The storm caught up to them, but still the coachman drove on at a rattling speed. Eleonora sat staring at the pages of de Saxe's book as if absorbed, her eyes blurring on the descriptions of how to form a battle line, while Achille sat silently immersed in his own dark thoughts. Was he contemplating how he was going to make her pay? She shuddered. Perhaps she should have asked Tante Geneviève to tell her those stories about him after all.

The rain increased. Thick droplets splattered faster and faster through the window, and Eleonora reluctantly tied down the leather curtain. The light had grown dim; she could no longer even pretend to read.

Soon they were splashing through puddles, the sound punctuating the constant drone of water being thrown against the undercarriage by the wheels. She thought of her childhood home in Hungary, perched so high on the edge of a mountain. Europeans called the Magyar fortresses "eagles' nests," but to her the ancient citadels built to withstand Huns and Turks and Tartars meant safety. The stones had proved impenetrable to everyone but God.

And the devil.

The storm, the storm, she thought, *if only it would go away.* She felt caught in a waking nightmare, her girl-child's anxiety overlaying the adult Eleonora's like a smothering shroud. She shook her head, trying to rid herself of it. The rain, the stabbing light, the thunder . . . And over it all, she heard the maniacal laughter of the coachman.

Achille seemed to emerge from his self-absorption. "Hervé enjoys his work," he commented.

"Enjoys!" There was lightning, a space of five breaths, then the crack of thunder. She winced before she could stop herself. "Achille, this is getting dangerous. We left the baggage coach behind an hour ago. There's no one to—"

They rounded a bend in the road. She grabbed the leather strap. Rain poured down in sheets, and Hervé shouted with glee.

"Your coachman is insane!"

"Of course. Of what use is a sane coachman? He would only want to stop at every inconvenience."

Lightning and thunder struck again, this time closer together. Eleonora managed to keep a calm expression, but her stomach clenched in reaction. She hated being scared of storms; she *hated* it.

Think of home, she told herself. A mocking voice cackled in her head, *Think of it, but will he ever let you see it again?* She growled in exasperation and threw the book against the back of Achille's seat. *"You're insane. I'm insane."* She rubbed her face. "Why am I here? Tell me I'm having a nightmare. Saint Stephen, how could I have been such a fool?"

"Eleonora—"

"What? No 'madame la comtesse'?" Her hands fisted in front of her face. "Madame *l'idiot*, is more like!"

The blinding light flashed again. The coachman laughed. Thunder. Laughter. She put her hands over her ears and bent over. *"God, I hate storms,"* she screamed.

"Eleonora!" There was an arm across her back, holding her. "Eleonora, listen to me. There's no place to stop between here and the river. Eleonora, can you hear me? We have to cross the river before we can—" Thunder interrupted him.

"Make him stop laughing! Make him— Yes, yes, I hear you." She pulled away from him, hugging herself. "I hear you. I hear you. Get us across the river."

Achille pounded on the trap to the coachman. The man opened it and glanced in with a mad grin. Rain drenched him, drooping his leather hat. "Yeah, m'sieur?" he shouted. His two wildly bushy eyebrows seemed to move independently of each other. "You want I should go faster?" Eleonora couldn't believe how the man bubbled with good cheer.

"Cease cackling, Hervé."

" 'Tis the horses, m'sieur! Happy, happy—ain't been this happy since they flew out o' Paris! But I'll tell 'em. Don't know as they'll listen, but I'll tell 'em." The trap closed.

"We'll get to the river shortly," Achille said, turning back to face her. He remained next to her, though she couldn't see his eyes clearly in the dim interior. "End this, Eleonora."

"You end it," she spit out. "Forget you ever saw that picture." Pages of her mother's sketchbooks leaved through her mind. "I wish to God I could."

"I wish to God your brothers had come," Achille shot back. "What kind of men are they to send a woman to exact their revenge?"

"They are the kind who go to war. And this revenge is for all my family. We Magyars fight when we are wronged, Achille. For the last one hundred and fifty years we have fought the Turks—and when we're not fighting the Turks, we fight the king. Thirty years ago, Joseph, archduke of Austria, was king of Hungary. Prince Rákóczi and half of Hungary rose up to defy him. My husband was a boy of twelve. He was the only one of his family to survive. We *elect* our kings. We *consent* to being ruled. And we fight when we must."

Achille leaned toward her. "So do we bastards, Eleonora."

Eleonora stared at her hands in her lap. How much should she tell him? She'd gone over and over the question during the hours she'd spent in the coach. If she told him the whole of it, of the plans her family had laid for him, his anger would spill over into hate and contempt. He was a dangerous man, but it was the thought of contempt that stopped her, contempt for *her,* that she didn't think she could bear to see in his eyes.

"A wrong was done us, and we will be avenged." She unclenched her hands and splayed them on her skirts. "I was a 'second'—isn't that your duelists' term? I was to entice you to come with me and—"

"Meet your brothers at a venue of their choosing, not mine," he finished for her.

No, she answered in her mind. *What awaited you in Vienna was nothing so civilized.*

"What am I supposed to have done to cause such a thirst for my blood?" he asked, but his tone was idle, as if he didn't expect her to answer. He stroked her cheek with the backs of his fingers. "If their ire came now, of course, I would well understand it. I imagine no brother is comfortable with the notion of his sister in the arms of a man who is not her husband. Particularly in the arms of a man he has fought in battle."

"Their ire would be unwarranted. I am as much to blame as you."

"Yes, the Magyar did *consent,* didn't she?"

She had consented. And yet . . . Eleonora's hands had stopped shaking. She flexed her fingers. There was no hesitation, no tremble. Her terror had gone, cut down like a scythe through summer grass. She would not cower before him. She loved him, but it was an impossible love, to be kept hidden away forever.

She raised her head, straightened her shoulders, and turned to face him. "I consented. But it was my *body* I consented to give you last night. My *body* I consented to let ride in this coach. My body only.

"Look in my eyes, Achille. The wall is still there. I gave you my body, but the rest I have not given you. My mind, my soul—my Magyar soul—still belong to me."

Chapter 16

Eleonora sat alone in the coach at the river's edge. The roar of the rushing water drowned out even the sound of the rain hammering on the roof. Outside, Achille and the coachman stood at one end of the bridge and considered what to do next. The bridge had been damaged, but not destroyed.

She waited, staring at the wrapped portrait of El Müzir. If she had any courage at all, she thought, she would throw the abominable thing into the river. No, that would be cowardice rather than courage. It would not undo the last hours. It would not relieve the pain she had caused Achille.

A few moments later, the door swung open. Achille looked up at her, seemingly oblivious to the water sheeting down on him.

"We'll have to go across on foot," he shouted. "Hervé wants to try and walk the horses and coach over." Lightning flashed, quickly followed by thunder. Achille glanced over his shoulder, then turned back and held out his hand. "We don't have any choice. The lightning's getting too close."

She took his hand and stepped out of the coach. The weight of the sudden drenching made her stumble, but she recovered and went to the end of the bridge.

Water billowed around the ancient stone pilings. A ragged half-moon had been eaten out of one side, and as she watched, another block fell away with a white-plumed splash. An immense old willow sprawled at the far end in front of boulders that seemed to grow out of the ground. There was still a path, scarcely coach-wide, that looked solid.

She took a deep breath, almost of relief. Physical difficulty she could meet head-on. She scooped up her heavy wet skirts and started across. Her stockings were exposed to her knees, but better that than let her skirts trip her up.

Before she could take a second step, two hands gripped her shoulders. "Easy," Achille said into her ear. "Take it slow."

She nodded and continued on. The pressure of his hands was light but sure, and his presence behind her felt more solid than the stones under her feet. It comforted her, more than she wanted to admit.

The water was rising. A dirty brown slurry began washing over the already slick stones. Achille's hands gripped her tighter. That anchored her, let her narrow the focus of her awareness to each step, each stone where she set down her heel.

"Almost there," he said.

Soon she could see the spindly branches of the willow brushing back and forth in the rain and wind. Two more steps. Then one.

The pressure on her shoulders lifted. "Achille—"

"Over there," he said, pointing beyond the willow to the lee of a boulder. Behind him, Hervé had begun leading the skittish horses onto the bridge.

Eleonora started toward the boulder, then realized Achille was not following her. She spun around. He was already halfway back across the bridge, helping his coachman.

Two more stones broke off. "Hurry!" she screamed. "The river—"

Her scalp prickled. The air smelled burnt. *Lightning.* She crouched to leap toward the boulder— She couldn't breathe. *She couldn't breathe.*

The willow exploded.

A fist of air. Water. Wet, floating, gray, grayer, grayest . . .

Black.

The wisps of Eleonora's dreams, of laughing devils and dark angels, slowly faded into wakefulness. Her body began to feel again, and her ears began to hear again. She heard . . . quiet. Sweet, blissful quiet. No pounding rain. No thunder, no rumble of a river. She squirmed and stretched.

A woman chuckled. "There, you see, m'sieur?" an unfamiliar woman's voice said. "She was just tuckered out from all that commotion. A good night's sleep, and your wife'll be in fine fettle."

Wife? Eleonora opened her eyes. She was in someone's bedroom. It was small and plain, like the woman who stood watching her from the end of the bed she lay in.

"Achille?" she said, the sureness of sleep giving way to confusion. She felt her head; it had been wrapped in linen.

"I am here," he said, putting a hand on her arm. He stood next to the bed in his shirt-sleeves. "Lightning struck the willow. You were knocked into the water. Mrs. Fremyot here and her husband have been kind enough to take us in."

"The horses? Hervé?"

Achille flashed her a grin. He shouldn't do that, she thought groggily. It made her forget how dangerous he was. It made her forget everything but the night they'd spent by a fire.

"Hervé would approve of the order of your questions," he answered. "They are all at supper in the stables. He is unharmed, as are the horses."

At the end of the bed, Mrs. Fremyot beamed at them. "Think you could take a bit of soup, madame? It's mighty tasty. Ask your m'sieur if it ain't so."

"My monsi—? Eleonora broke off when Achille squeezed her hand. She smiled at the woman. "Soup does sound good. Thank you." Mrs. Fremyot curtsied and marched smartly out of the room, her wooden clogs *thunk*ing on the floor.

When she and Achille were alone, Eleonora turned to him. "What is this about a wi—"

"Sh-sh," he said, putting a finger to her lips. He glanced meaningfully at the thin curtain that hung across the doorway. He lowered his voice. "Some mistakes are not worth bothering about."

"I wish that thought had occurred to you back at the château du Peyre."

"I said mistakes, not lies."

She lowered her eyes and felt at her wrapped head again. "Did I get hurt? There isn't any pain."

"Mrs. Fremyot wrapped your hair to keep it from soaking the bed," Achille told her. He leaned over and began unwinding it. Long strands of auburn fell in great loops all over the both of them and became tangled in the linen. "You do it," he said in frustration.

She giggled. "It is a mess, isn't it?"

Achille slowly pulled away, letting the damp silken strands flow over his hands. He turned away.

He went to the fire and began stirring it up, ignoring the sting in his leg as he knelt. A horse's hoof had grazed him on the outside of his left thigh, slicing into him, and now blood stained his riding breeches.

He'd told Eleonora that lightning had struck the willow. Fact. He'd said she'd been knocked into the water. Fact. What he had not told her was how the horses had panicked, rearing and kicking, then charging across the bridge, the coach careening after them, one of its wheels missing her head by inches.

Gut-wrenching horror surged through him at the remembered scene; he clamped it down. He didn't want her to die. He just wanted her to acknowledge her lie.

But if she had been a man, dead is exactly what he would have wanted. Her games threatened everything he believed in, everything that he was. Dead is what he would have wanted. And dead is what she would have been.

From behind him he heard Eleonora's rustlings, the toss of linen, the toweling of her hair. He tried to ignore the sounds, but could not. He had never been with a woman this way, spending an evening in a room where he had not made love—and would not. He gave in and listened to all the intimate sounds of the woman behind him and found an odd sort of peace.

But peace did not sit easily on him, and he rose. "We will not reach Valeria till late tomorrow evening."

The rustlings paused, then resumed. "Inconvenient, am I?" she asked, her voice laden with sarcasm. "I trust you'll understand if I feel no great urge to beg your pardon. But thank you for bringing me here."

He stared into the flames. "Fortune smiled," he said, his voice twisting with irony. "This is an isolated farmhouse, and I do not believe the Fremyots are of a mind to ask too many questions."

"Would you answer them if— Achille, you've been hurt!"

He looked up to see her rushing toward him, dressed in her nightgown of nearly transparent lawn. "I was grazed by a horse's hoof. I've been scratched worse by incompetent barbers."

She went to her knees beside him, her unbound hair cloaking her shoulders, and the flushed cream of her skin showing through wherever her nightgown touched her. With gentle fingers she began prying away his breeches from the wound.

He caught her wrists. "It's nothing."

"Achille, this could be serious," she said, her earnest green eyes staring into his. "It should be seen to. We need to send for a physician."

Before he realized what she was doing, she rose, whirling to face the curtained doorway, and shouted, "Mrs. Fremyot! Send for a—"

Achille covered her mouth with his hand. "No physician. It needs nothing more than for Hervé to drench it in wine and wrap a bandage around it."

Eleonora squirmed free. "Don't be foolish! A physician— Where is that woman? Mrs. Fremyot!" She turned to go to the doorway.

Achille put a hand on her shoulder to stop her. "Look around you, Eleonora," he said, lowering his voice to almost a whisper. "Do you see a crucifix anywhere?"

"A crucifix?" she asked, looking impatient. "What has that to say to anything? You need a physician, not a priest."

"There are no crucifixes because these people are Huguenots, Protestants. They do not follow the church of Rome. That is against the law in France, Eleonora. Send for a physician, have their faith discovered—and you send these people to the galleys."

"The galleys?" she cried. "No, oh, God, no, I didn't mean . . ." She trembled. Her arms went around her stomach, as if she was queasy at the thought of what she had almost done.

"I do not know how it is in Hungary," he said, his hand slipping from her shoulder to her neck, "but in France, religion is the state, and those not of the king's religion are traitors."

"In Hungary?" she said harshly. "What does the wording of a liturgy matter, or the cloth of a priest's vestments, when Hungarian sons have been stolen from their mothers and their fathers and made slaves of the Turks?"

Outside the curtain, the hurried clop of clogs grew nearer. Mrs. Fremyot ran into the room with the peculiar gait of those accustomed to wearing wooden shoes. "Yes, madame, yes? I was fetching you some nice fresh butter for your soup." She stopped with a clatter when she saw Eleonora bent over with her arms around her stomach.

Achille helped Eleonora to the bed. "My wife is not feeling as well as she'd thought. Perhaps that soup you mentioned . . ."

"Oh, dear, oh, dear," Mrs. Fremyot clucked under her breath. "Why didn't you tell me, monsieur? Madame needs to be much more careful with a little one on the way."

"A little—?" It took a full second for Achille to understand what the woman was babbling about, but it was clear from Eleonora's white face that she had understood immediately.

"No, no, it's not that," Eleonora managed to say. "I'm still a bit shaky is all."

"Of course you are," Mrs. Fremyot said indulgently. She fluffed the lone pillow. "Here you go now. Lie down and rest a mite longer. There you go." The woman continued to bustle about the bed, tucking and smoothing.

"Is this your first?" she asked, but didn't pause long enough for an answer. "I've had seven myself. Lost only two, bless their souls."

"Thank you, Mrs. Fremyot," Achille said with a bow to dismiss her.

"This is women's talk, monsieur," she answered, waving away his dismissal. She turned back to Eleonora. "My babies were coming out one a year, don't you know, till me an' Jules figured out . . ." She cast a mischievous glance at Achille. "And your monsieur looks to be even *healthier* than my Jules."

She leaned over and whispered, "Iffen you want my advice . . . well, *I* say, what happens between a husband and wife is nobody's business but theirs. Lovin' don't always have to mean more babies, iffen you get my meanin'."

"Thank you, Mrs. Fremyot," Achille said, ushering her toward the curtained doorway. "At the moment, however, I believe Madame needs food more than advice."

The woman winked and waved at a pale Eleonora, but Achille pushed her through the curtain before she could say anything more.

The crackle of the small fire was the only sound in the room. Achille went back to bed and sat down, one hand covering Eleonora's clenched fingers. "I'm sorry," he said.

"She meant no harm," Eleonora replied, though she kept staring into the fire. "It is an insignificant hurt compared to what I've done to you. You have every reason to hate me."

"Many reasons, perhaps." He wrapped a strand of her

hair around his finger. It would be so easy to bend a little and kiss her. To taste her. To slide into her.

"Sweet Christ," he said, turning from her and running his hands through his hair. "What you have done to my life? When this is finished and I have won, you will have much to pay in forfeit."

"And if you do not win?" she asked softly.

"Then you would be little better than an enslaving Turk, little better than the man you claim is my father," Achille said.

He pushed aside the curtain and walked out.

Eleonora had slept fitfully. She thought she'd wakened several times during the night, thinking she felt Achille sleeping next to her, but when she'd awakened for good at first light, she'd discovered she was alone.

By the time she'd dressed with Mrs. Fremyot's help, Achille had had his mad coachman ready the coach and horses. A quick bite of bread and cheese was all she was allowed before Hervé hustled her into the coach with a grin and a wiggle of his bushy eyebrows.

"The horses seem to have recovered from their fright," she said to him from inside the coach. If she talked to him, she might not be so disconcerted by him. "You must have sat with them all night."

"All ladies like a bit o' coddling after a nasty start like that." The coachman gave her a considering look, then glanced over his shoulder to the waiting Achille. "Eh, m'sieur?"

Achille gave Hervé a glance sharper than any saber. "Valeria by nightfall," was all he said, and he followed Eleonora into the coach, the leather-wrapped parchment in his hand.

"Hoo-hooo," the coachman said, and clicked his teeth. He closed and latched the door, and Eleonora heard him mutter, "This is gettin' to be even better 'n leavin' Paris."

The ride was strained, the whole long, miserable day punctuated by Hervé's curses. The storm had covered the roads in debris from trees and brush, and even where they were clear, the paving stones had been loosened by the driving rain.

In contrast to this rushing dash south, her journey from Vienna to the château du Peyre had been leisurely. She'd stopped only at the bigger towns and had had the luxury of time to wait on the cooks and their bounty from the ovens.

She remembered how amiable she'd been when she'd disembarked from the boat that had carried her upstream from Vienna to Passau and had discovered she'd have to wait an extra day to hire a carriage. Now she knew it was not any goodness in her nature that had made her so amiable, but reluctance to meet the blackhearted devil she had traveled to entice.

But that reluctance had gained her nothing. How naïve she had been! She glanced at Achille, absorbed in his reading of Tristan in the seat opposite. Even in repose, the man had an energy about him, a sense of power, of control. To think that she had thought to tease and tantalize such a man into following her to Vienna, there to meet—

She looked away, letting her gaze travel unseeing over the lush hills of eastern France. Fool! She had indeed teased him and tantalized him—but he was hardly a man to plead for her favors through a closed door. He was not a man to plead at all.

They stopped briefly in the late morning for a round loaf of hard rye bread and a mild, creamy white cheese, washed down with a sour unaged ale. At around two or three in the afternoon, when most civilized people were sitting down to a normal dinner, Achille allowed them to halt only briefly, and this time added a slice or two of cold beef to the bread and cheese. The wine, at least, had not been too badly watered.

It was nearing dusk when Achille finally put his book aside.

"It's getting dark," she told him. "We'll have to stop soon."

He didn't answer her, but flipped the latch on the trap to the coachman. "Lanterns" was all he said.

"Awww, m'sieur," Hervé whined, "I can see just fine. The moon'll rise in an hour or so. It's almost half-full, an' the clouds ain't so bad that they'll cover it all the time."

"Lanterns, Hervé. And get stout boys to hold them. I don't want to lose one of them in the mountains."

"Now, I told you tha's just a story, m'sieur. I never did actually lose one. He was just kickin' up some spirits is all. Found him in a couple o' days. An' besides, the horses likes 'em small."

"Stout."

"Yes, m'sieur. Stout," Hervé said, then added in a mumble, "I'll find me some nice fat ones. Tall, too, w' their voices already crackin'. They'll get us up the mountain, all right. In a sennight." Achille closed the trap on the rest of the coachman's grumblings.

"We're going into the mountains?" Eleonora asked. "At night?"

"Surely the brave Magyar doesn't balk at a night ride."

"Of course not! I live in the mountains," she answered, feeling the sting of pique at letting him bait her. "But at night we ride on horseback. Here, we're in a coach without runners or torches, with only that mad coachman of yours—" She broke off and gestured angrily at the wrapped parchment. "This business is not worth risking your life over."

"You want to take away my past, all that I am," he told her. "Why quibble over my future? In war, there is a thing called *dégât*—completely devastating the earth to keep the enemy from finding food or forage or shelter. That is what you wish to do to my life."

"That is what El Müzir did to my family. He was an enemy who devastated us, who has kept us from ever finding peace. He killed my brother. He killed Imri."

"What is one more death on the battlefield?"

"There was no battlefield! Imri was five years old. El Müzir flew into one of his rages, and Imri got in the way—and died for it. My mother never recovered from that shock. Even after El Müzir had been gone from us for years, even after she gave birth to Gabriel, to me, to

Christophe. Even that did not diminish her hate—and her hate is ours."

He leaned toward her. "I do not doubt your hatred of this El Müzir. I do not doubt the evil he did your family. But he is not the man who sired me. Confess that lie."

"Damn you! Haven't you ever held on to something for so long that it seems to be the only thing real in your life?"

"Yes," Achille said, his voice low and calm and deadly. "What you would take from me. The Chevalier Constantin d'Agenais. My *father.*"

She closed her eyes and turned her head away.

He shifted onto the seat next to her. "No, madame, I won't let you turn away." He grabbed her chin and forced her to face him. "While he lived, my father was my tutor. The old France was best, he told me, when the true nobility of France rallied to the king's banner on a battlefield, not to the king's cobbler for the latest in fashionable buckles. He told me the stories of all the chevaliers, of all the d'Agenaises, at the side of Charles the Wise, and Charles the Mad, and Francis the First, and Henri the Fourth.

"And he sang to me the songs of the troubadours. He sang of Tristan, of Isolde, of Roland, and Charlemagne."

Eleonora's throat was tight. "And you believed in those stories, didn't you?" she whispered. "And took those songs to heart, and heeded their lessons . . ."

He released her and turned away. "Heeded? My father died when I was nine. It was then that I discovered the world was not as he would have it be. And all the ardent words I had shouted from the turrets became nothing but the rantings of men whose bones had long since turned to dust."

He shifted in the seat, and she could see his hand clenched as if holding a sword.

"Was it the words that were ardent?" she asked softly. "Or the heart of the boy who shouted them?"

"It does not matter. They are both dust."

"Are they? The words are still yours. If they could raise the heart of the boy, could they not do so for the man?"

"No, they could not." His voice had turned harsh and bitter. He put his hand around her neck, deliberately digging his fingers into the soft flesh under her ear. "The boy cried for his dead father, Eleonora. The man bears many scars, some that might make him a hero, others that damn his soul, but the deepest scars are of the whipping his Jesuit tutor gave him upon discovering the tears the boy shed for his father. *That,* madame, is when I began to heed my lessons."

Achille expected her to cry out at the pain, to plead with him to release her. She met his gaze straight on, only a slight tightening at the corners of her eyes telling of the pain he was causing her.

" 'That blast is blown for me,' " she quoted, " 'for I am the prize and yet I am not dead.' "

For a heartbeat, there was calm inside him, a solitude that for once was not lonely. "You have read of Balyn," he said, letting his hand lighten its hold on her.

"You see, monsieur?" she said softly. "The words are not dust."

He lowered his mouth to hover over hers. "But the heart *is,*" he said, his breath puffing against her lips. "Make no mistake."

"I mistake nothing." Her eyelids had half closed.

"Ah, but I say you do." He pulled away. "And that, madame, is why we are in a coach without runners or torches, riding up a mountain at night, with only a mad coachman between us and the edge."

She withdrew into the corner. "Damn you, Achille," she spit out.

"Isn't that what you have in mind?"

It was her turn to clench her fists. "No! Whatever you may think of me, that is not what I have in mind. Leave this be. Let me hire a carriage in the next village. I can ride far away. You'll never have to see me again. I'll go north, then east, to Regensburg, be in Passau in—"

"Eleonora." It was nearly dark inside the coach, but he knew her face, knew what emotions were flickering through her eyes and over her oh-so-readable countenance.

The notion of never seeing those emotions again pricked at him.

"Eleonora, we ride up the mountain to the Holy Sisters of Saint Valeria, then we ride back down again. And then we ride north. To the château d'Agenais. No Regensburg. No Passau. No Vienna."

Chapter 17

Mist swirled and thickened around them as they made their way up the mountain. The orange glow of the postboys' lanterns lit up the heavy white fog like an anteroom of hell. The coach wheels clattered against the stones in the road, the sound echoing as if they rode through a closed room.

Eleonora clung to the leather strap. *Truth, Eleonora,* he'd said to her in the grotto. *Truth matters. In a world of artifice and posturings . . .* What would he do when he learned that a man who could kill a child without remorse was truly his father?

"Don't go through with this," she said to the silent Achille sitting on the seat opposite. "Say nothing to your mother of that picture. Give her a present. Alms for the charity the sisters do. A thousand louis d'or. Two thousand. I'll pay it. Then let us turn around and go back down the mountain." She leaned forward in her urging, reaching toward him, almost touching him to convince him.

"The charity the Holy Sisters of Saint Valeria do is the taking in of unwanted noble daughters," he told her, his voice ironic and tinged with bitterness. "Daughters of France can be so expensive. They can 'lodge' at Valeria till they're ninety at a cost of no more than five or six thousand louis d'or. A dowry for the same daughter could be ten times as much."

She sat back. "Like Madame de la Cheylard's daughters," she said.

"Like Madame de la Cheylard's daughters." She felt his gaze studying her. "You seem disturbed by that," he said. "Is it not the same in Hungary?"

"There are not so many people in Hungary that we pack off inconvenient ones like winter clothing," she said, a dollop of self-righteousness creeping into her voice. "So many were killed during the wars. My grandfather told me he once traveled for three days across Hungary's great plain without meeting a single living soul. The Turks . . ." She fell silent, the words slicing into the air between them.

"Ah, yes," Achille said, picking up the cylinder of oilskin. "The Turks."

The coach slowed, then came to a halt. She looked outside and saw two giant wooden doors just discernible through the mist. Hervé jumped to the ground and gave a hearty yank to the bellpull hanging to one side. Its jangling sounded brash and out of place in the somber silence.

"It's so late," she said, glancing over her shoulder at Achille. "Perhaps they've all retired."

"Before the matins at midnight?" Achille asked sarcastically. "It does not matter." Hervé impatiently pulled the bell again.

One of the doors snapped open. A nun stood there, yawning, her headdress slightly askew as if hastily donned. "What is it?" she asked, her voice surly.

"Guests," Hervé state flatly.

"What kind of guests come skulking in after dark?" she said with a sneer. "Tell them to come back after prime tomorrow morning."

She started to close the door, but Hervé splayed his big, callused hand on it to stop her. "They don't want to wait till dawn. They want to visit the prioress *now.*"

The sister laughed. "They want to see the prioress, do they? Then tell them to come back after nones. She'll be busy till then."

"Nones! An' then you'll tell me she's at her dinner," Hervé snapped. "An' I'll tell you right now, Monsieur d'Agenais ain't gonna wait on his mama's dinner."

"Monsieur d'Agenais," the sister gasped. She stared at

the coach and crossed herself. "Oh, we're not . . . He's not . . . Oh, my. *Oh, my.*" She turned around and ran back into the mist, leaving the gate deserted and open behind her.

Achille threw the coach door open with a crack. Hervé rushed to unfold the steps.

"You don't mean to go on?" Eleonora asked Achille. "We're clearly not wanted."

He stepped down from the coach, the oilskin in one hand. He held the other one out to her. "Clearly," he said.

Eleonora looked at his outstretched hand. She suddenly wished she were back confronting the flooding river. Why had that crumbling bridge seemed so much easier to face than this one step out of the coach?

She took his hand and descended. He did not let go, but kept her hand in his and led her toward the night-shrouded priory.

To her surprise, he appeared to know his way around. "You must visit her often," she said. "A dutiful son—"

"My mother entered this order the day after I reached my majority. I escorted her here eleven years ago. I have not seen her since."

A lovely haunting sound, a lone woman singing one of the Psalms, came from their right. Achille led Eleonora to the left, past the arches of the chapter house, where the business of the priory would be conducted, through the staircase entrance and up old, worn stone stairs. At the top, they went through another door, traversed the open arcade, where tendrils of mist curled in past the massive stone pillars, and then through a final door.

Oriental carpets muffled their footsteps, and Eleonora heard the singing again, clearer this time and coming from her left. Achille had, purposefully or not, led her completely around the chapel instead of going through it.

They reached the end of the hall, and he pounded on an ornately carved door.

Eleonora heard a woman's muffled voice call, "What is it, Nicole?" Achille opened the door, and the voice became distinct. "Please tell me that precious Moravian princess has ceased crying! Why no one bothered to mention that the little wretch doesn't even speak Fren— *God save me!*"

"A difficult task, even for Him," Achille said, and stepped into the room. "Good evening, Mother."

A tall, slender woman, perhaps halfway between fifty and sixty, stood behind a white and gold writing desk and gazed at Achille, her face framed by her white and black nun's habit. She held several forgotten papers in fine-boned hands, and more were piled on the desk in front of her.

The first thing that struck Eleonora was the woman's beauty, the kind that mellows and transforms but never truly fades. The second thing was her eyes. Dark, enigmatic, and more like Achille's than Eleonora had expected.

That gaze slid from her son to Eleonora, and the similarity in the eyes became stronger, not from color or shape, but from the same keen wit behind them that Achille had. The fear Eleonora had managed to suppress started to claw its way out of its hiding place.

Her eyes on Eleonora, the woman who had been Madame d'Agenais said, "Why are you here?" She waved the papers at him. "I have three bawling German princesses on my hands, screaming to go home. In German, naturally."

"Let them," Achille said.

"Don't be a fool," his mother snapped. "You can't begin to know how hard I've worked to get them here. It's taken me nearly a year and a half! But the *rewards*. The eldest, for instance . . ." She threw down the papers she held and rifled through the rest of the stack.

She pulled a document from the bottom and began reading, "Siegfrieda, fifteen, fourth daughter—and twelfth child—of Count Reinhard Anhault of Moravia and his first wife, Dominique de Marcigny." She put the paper back in the stack.

"Dominique is dead, but *her* mother—the doting grandmother to Siegfrieda—lives but ten miles from this very spot. On some of the most fertile farmland in eastern France—fourteen thousand-*louis*-a-year fertile. I meet with her tomorrow to discuss her will."

She smiled with self-satisfaction. "This priory is going to be one of the richest in France. Already I've added substantial lands from some of the largest estates in Bourgogne—and already the bishops are starting to pass by here. *This* is where a woman can find power. Once, I was fool enough to think it lay . . . elsewhere." Her gaze traveled possessively around the room. "But now I know where it is."

"Indeed, Mother," Achille said, and went to the desk. He casually laid the oilskin on the corner. "And did you once think you could find power with astrologers?"

Surprise flickered across his mother's face, then vanished. "What are you talking about?" she asked. "And who is *she?*"

Achille turned and graciously held out his hand to Eleonora. When she took it, he drew her nearer the desk. "May I present—"

"God save me," his mother said, sinking into her chair. "You're not thinking of marrying—"

Achille ignored his mother's interruption. "May I present Eleonora Sophia Juliana, Countess Batthyány, of Hungary and more recently of Vienna." Eleonora gave her a formal court curtsy.

Madame d'Agenais shot her son a look of disgust. "You nearly gave me apoplexy."

"Forgive me, Mother," he said without a whit of sincerity.

The woman gave an unladylike snort. "Your 'forgiveness' is beyond my poor means. After that nasty business in Paris, you'll need at least an archbishop, or quite possibly a cardinal. The pope . . . no, I don't think even you could afford him. He's in the pocket of the Portuguese and the Spaniards—and we know how unforgiving *they* are. Now tell me why you've brought *her* here."

Achille bowed to Eleonora and led her to a chair. She hesitated, glancing at his mother. "Sit down," he whispered soto voce, and Eleonora sat. He turned back to his mother. "She brought me something I found . . . interesting. And we were speaking of astrologers. Particularly, your penchant for them."

There was a struggle for power going on in the room, the balance swinging back and forth between mother and son. Eleonora wanted him to stop.

"Who is she?"

"Particularly, one named Oncelus."

The woman behind the desk went pale. She gripped the edge. Her eyes became smoky and veiled.

Eleonora put a cautioning hand on his arm. "Achille . . ." she said.

His mother pulled herself rigid. "You *dare*— No maid, no respectable woman, would call you by your Christian name! I will not tolerate—"

"I suggest you become more concerned with what *I* will tolerate, Mother. Who is Oncelus?"

She sprang to her feet, hands curled into fists. "I knew no Oncelus," she spit out, then turned her back to him and began pacing. "How dare you brazenly bring your mistress here. Get out!"

"If you knew no Oncelus," Achille said, his voice the sweetest velvet, "then why was his name in the account book I found in that laboratory in the old wing at d'Agenais?" He splayed his hands on the desk and leaned on them. "You remember that laboratory, don't you, Mother? You had the whole of it torn down a week after I discovered it."

"Y-your father dabbled in—"

"Constantin hated anything to do with the arcane. He would let me read no books about it, ask no questions." Achille closed his eyes for a long moment. "It was the only thing he ever forbade me."

"I tell you, I knew no Oncelus! Now, leave me."

Eleonora saw the tightening of Achille's jaw, and his strong hands as they began stripping the wax from the oil-skin. She had seen a trial once where the verdict had been a foregone conclusion, and the accused had stood waiting for the death sentence to be pronounced much as Achille now stood, taut with control.

Achille pulled the roll of parchment free of the oilskin, letting the covering fall to the floor unheeded. "Then perhaps you knew this astrologer by another name, Mother."

"Why are you doing this? I knew no astrologers!"

"Not even one by the name of El Müzir?"

Madame d'Agenais missed a step. She caught herself on the wide stone window ledge. "No," she whispered, her back still to her son, her head bowed. "Not even ... not even by that name."

Eleonora put a trembling hand over her mouth. Achille already knew the truth. She was sure of it. He was being condemned before her eyes, and she could think of nothing to stop it.

There was the slightest shake to his hands as he unrolled the parchment. He stared at the face of El Müzir, as if burning it into his memory, then he held it out toward his mother.

"Perhaps a picture ..." He stopped and clenched his jaw, then began again. "Perhaps a picture will refresh your memory."

Turning, his mother said, "A pict—?" She went pale and still. Only her eyes moved, drinking in the portrait that Achille held out to her. One of her hands slowly reached out to touch it. A single finger lovingly traced the long line of El Müzir's hair, and a tear slid from the corner of her eye.

"He was so beautiful," she murmured in a voice barely audible. "And he had such strength, such power ... He was the sun. And as the world measures time by the sun's rising, so I measure my life by the time I spent with him."

Achille threw the picture from him, and his mother uttered a cry of protest. "And I, Mother, measure *my* life by the men I've killed. Killed defending the fact that the Chevalier Constantin d'Agenais was my father. De Neuville. Tournus. Vesoul. Montrevel. St. Julien. And— God have mercy on my damned soul—*Thierry*, Mother, let's not forget that I killed Thierry de Rachand! A man I had called friend. I killed them all defending a *lie*, didn't I, Mother? *Didn't I?*"

"No! No, I—"

"Your lies are done. The words may still spew from your throat, but it is too late. I have seen the truth on your face."

"What truth? What can you see?"

"Something I never thought to see in you." A calm came over Achille, a cold and deadly calm, the kind that buries the heart far from the shrouding distractions of emotions. He leaned toward her. "*Love*, Mother. Love remembered, love regretted, but still love."

His mother turned her back to him. "And how do you know what love is? Have you learned it from *her?*" She gestured angrily toward Eleonora.

His gaze rested on Eleonora for a long moment, two dark eyes set in a face of stone. Fear rose up Eleonora's throat like wine gone bad. Fear *of* him, fear *for* him.

"I have learned a great deal from Madame Batthyány," he said, then his winter gaze left her. "And now it is time, Mother, for me to learn from you. Of *this* man. Of whose seed I appear to be the fruit. My father."

Anger flushed his mother's face. "Leave this be, damn you! It is enough that he is dead."

"Then tell me how he died," Achille demanded. "Why did he come to d'Agenais? Where did he come from? *Who was he?*"

Madame d'Agenais wiped her eyes and began pacing. "He came from the East. I met him at an inn outside Agenais, on the road to Montagneux."

"The one that burned down soon after fa— Constantin died?" Achille asked, his voice flat.

His mother nodded without looking at him. "I used to go there, when I was bored. He was there one night, watching someone, but did not want to be seen himself.

"I know little of El Müzir's life before he came West. He once told me he was the first and most honored son of Pasha Mehmed Apafi."

"And his mother?" Achille asked. "Who was she?"

Madame d'Agenais shrugged. "A nameless concubine. It is how things are done in the East. El Müzir was brilliant. He'd been well trained by his father, but soon outstripped the old man, and others were brought in to teach the boy, including alchemists and astrologers. Such knowledge gave him power, and as a young man, he was elevated to sultan of Temesvár. And there he remained, consolidating his power, rising in the esteem of those who could help him, ruthless with those who could not.

"Until an *esir,* a slave who'd been taken as a prisoner of war, escaped him. Most Turks mutilated their slaves at the beginning, but El Müzir liked to break their spirit first. But this one he had not been able to break. He was ruined." Lece d'Agenais glanced at the blank face of her son out of the corner of her eyes, a look of calculation, as if wondering how little she could tell him.

"This ... prisoner," she went on, "had returned to his regiment and his army. How was El Müzir to reach one soldier surrounded by hundreds of thousands of other ones who were then laying waste to half of Europe?

"El Müzir, my magnificent and brilliant El Müzir, knew. He ... desired ... that I help him. And I did."

She stopped pacing and stood quietly in front of the window, hands clasped together, head bowed, the very picture of piety. "And he almost succeeded. Until, in high summer, he ... died." She squeezed her eyes shut, and tears fell unheeded and stained her habit. "And you were born eight months and three weeks later."

His mother faced him, her gaze unwavering. "El Müzir was shrewd and cunning, and he knew the value of deception. The world believes Constantin is your father, *and it will go on believing it.* He acknowledged you. Nothing can undo that."

"It is already undone."

"No! Ten years I spent with that wattled old man—so *you* could be a proud son of France. It was *I* who watched over your Jesuit tutors, *I* who made sure your every move told of your rank in the elite *Seigneurs Pairs.* I will not let you destroy all those years of work.

"And here! I've worked hard for the power I have—I hold *souls* in my hand. If it was to get out that I bore a child by an Infidel—I would lose it all. And I'll damn your soul to hell before I'll let that happen."

He leaned close. Eleonora watched, holding her breath. The air seemed charged. "Your lies have already damned my soul, *Mother*. Men lie rotting in the ground because I killed them."

"What do you care about souls—yours or any other?"

"As much as *you*, Mother." He scooped up the portrait of El Müzir and went to Eleonora. "Come, madame. We have far to travel before the sunrise." He took her by the arm and led her stumbling to the door.

His mother snapped out, "Achille! Your promise that this goes no further."

"How am I to pay penance for my sins—and yours—if I do not announce the truth of my father to all of Christendom? How else am I to pay for *his* sins, Mother?" He opened the door.

"*No!*" she screamed. "I'll have you followed. I'll stop you, Achille! I'll stop you—*forever*, if I have to."

She put her hands on the desk and leaned toward her retreating son. "El Müzir would understand," she called after him. "He would do it himself if he were still alive!"

Achille dragged Eleonora out into the corridor, not bothering to close the door behind them, then back through the chill of the open arcade and down the stone stairs. The singing had stopped.

Outside, the mist had grown thicker and colder. Wisps of it blew against her face like damned souls drifting in the haunted night. Silently she prayed for Achille to forgive her, the litany of self-loathing droning over and over in her head, but aloud she said nothing.

Ahead, a dim orange glow marked where the coach waited beyond the open gate. Their footsteps were muffled by the fog, and when they loomed out of the mist, Hervé jumped back from where he and the two postboys had been huddling around the feeble warmth of one of the lanterns.

"God's a'me," the coachman cried, "you're as silent as ghosts."

Achille opened the coach door and forcibly ushered Eleonora inside. She fell against the seat, her throat burning. "How can I ask you for forgiveness?" she whispered to him as he stood looking up at her.

"I'll leave word for Beaulieu in the village where we hired the postboys," Achille said as if he hadn't heard her plea. "He'll see that your baggage finds you." He closed the door without getting in.

"Achille?" she called. A tiny sound made her try the latch. Locked. She pushed the leather curtain aside. "Achille! You mustn't— What are you doing?"

Achille stood at the back of the coach untying Chiron. "Take her to Regensburg, then Passau, and down the Danube to Vienna," she heard him tell Hervé. "See that she arrives there safely, or you and everyone of your blood, everywhere, will pay."

"Y-yes, m'sieur," Hervé answered, very subdued, then turned and snarled commands at the two postboys who scampered to the front horses. The coach rocked as Hervé climbed to the driver's seat.

Eleonora reached out her hand to Achille through the small window. "Please, forgive me."

Holding his horse's reins, he began to give her an elegant courtier's bow, then stopped and bowed to her like a servant. His eyes seemed dead.

Emotion burned her throat. "I don't want to leave you like this!"

He stepped back and nodded to Hervé. The coach jerked into motion.

"Achille! Don't leave—" she sobbed to the dark, lonely figure who stood watching the coach drive away. Mist obscured him in less than a heartbeat. Eleonora sat back in the seat and closed her eyes. Tears fell unheeded. She had come to France to destroy the devil's son, and she had succeeded.

Two days later, Achille stood in the burned-out doorway of the inn outside Agenais on the road to Montagneux. He kicked at the threshold with a booted toe, the sudden movement making Chiron nicker softly behind him.

The stink of scorched and burned wood had long since disappeared, as had most anything salvageable. Whispers of evil spirits setting the fire had kept the inn from being rebuilt, but the whispers had not kept out the wind that blew the ashes away, nor the wild grasses that had crept in year by year. Now, after over twenty years, only the blackened stumps that had been the support beams remained.

"This is where Fate began the journey that would lead to my present life," he told the ruins. "Is this how Fate means to end it? With not even ashes to bury?"

He mounted Chiron and turned the horse toward Agenais. He thought of Eleonora, of her calling to him from the mist as the coach had driven her away, and for a moment it seemed as if the raging black emptiness inside him lifted. But, like water parting for a passing ship, it soon enveloped him again.

He rode on, through the village whose name he bore—had once borne—and turned up the long, tree-lined *allée* that led to the château d'Agenais.

He should feel ... something. There was little left of the building he had known as a child. The old wing had been destroyed when he was twelve. The entire main building had been given a fashionable new façade when he was fifteen.

And when he was nineteen—and away visiting his aunt and uncle in England—his mother had had the last of the turrets torn down, the high stone tower from which he'd shouted with such passion the songs Constantin had taught him.

Chiron moved restlessly under Achille as he sat studying the seat of generations of d'Agenaises. But there were no more left; the last of their line had died twenty-three years ago.

He rode up, and a servant rushed out to greet him, bowing as if the lord of the manor had returned home. Fool. There was no lord of the manor. There was but a *tenant*. "Remind me to send rent to my mother," he told the man. "I am quite in arrears. And she can use the money. There are all sorts of grandmothers of Moravian princesses to be wheedled into willing her their land."

The poor fellow looked completely confused. "M'sieur?"

Achille walked up the wide staircase. He felt disembodied, as if he was viewing himself from a far distance. At the top, a young servant waited, full of his own self-importance. "Welcome home, monsieur. I am Gérard. Monsieur Beaulieu appointed me—" Achille pulled off his riding gloves and slapped them into the man's hands, then continued on.

"Did Colonel Gillon's courier reach you at the château du Peyre, monsieur?" Gérard asked earnestly. Achille did not answer. "He seemed most impatient to get back to Bavaria," the servant went on, "now that the war has started. It seems they are to march into the bishopric of Passau, and the courier had plans to plun—er, that is, to, ah, inventory the bishop's possessions."

"Yes, well," Gérard said to Achille's back. The fellow motioned to another servant to follow, then scampered after Achille. "Perhaps Monsieur would care for a glass of wine," he said, panting, keeping up with Achille's long strides with a kind of walking trot. "To clear the dust from your throat."

Achille stopped abruptly, and the man nearly collided with him. The other servant rushed forward and held out a salver with a sloshing glass balanced on it. Achille took it and emptied it in one long swallow.

"That is your mother's favorite vintage," the steward said with a fatuous grin. "I thought perhaps you might enjoy—"

The glass stem snapped in Achille's hand. He let the pieces drop to the floor and walked on.

"Monsieur!" the steward called. "Monsieur, your hand. It's bleeding!"

Achille paused. He looked at his palm. "So it is," he murmured to himself. "Is the blood mine, do you think?"

"Monsieur?"

"How many cases of that wine are in the cellars?"

"F-four and a half, monsieur."

"Destroy them. Do not drink them. Do not give them away. Destroy them."

"As you wish, monsieur."

Achille mounted the grand staircase, taking the steps three at a time. From the top of the stairs, he called down, "Gérard! I will need a fire."

The young man appeared at the bottom of the stairs. "I'll have one laid in your rooms at once, monsieur."

"Now, why would I want such a thing on this nice warm spring day?"

Gérard opened his mouth to speak, hesitated, glanced over his shoulder, then said, "Then where would Monsieur like the fire?"

Achille stared down at the little man. "Underneath my mother's old bedroom window."

He walked down a long corridor to the suite of rooms his mother had used. He flung open the door, startling a dusting chambermaid. She squealed, then belatedly gave him a wobbly curtsy.

"Get out," he said. She fled.

His breaths came deep and ragged. His vision shimmered between red and gray. He went into her bedroom and began pulling drawers from cabinets and throwing them into a pile near the window. He toppled chairs and chests. Wood crashed against wood, splintering, shattering. Gilded fragments spun across the floor. Furniture upholstered in torn velvets, satins, and brocades released their stuffing into the air.

He saw nothing but what should not be there. What his mother had used, what his mother had touched, defiling the d'Agenais name. He lifted a stool upon which she had once rested her feet and snapped off the legs, one by one.

A cheval mirror reflected the image of a tall, dark-haired clockwork man. All must be destroyed. He threw the stool at the mirror. Glass exploded in deadly shards.

He went into the sitting room, to the writing table near the fireplace. He swept everything from its surface. A stationery box smashed against a marble column supporting the mantel. He lifted the table, prepared to heave it into the fireplace.

A frightened squeak came from the hearth. "Please, m'sieur!"

Achille locked his muscles. A small chimney boy covered in soot and ash peeped from inside the firebox. "Please, m'sieur, don't kill me! The housekeeper, she comes here to keep warm. I was just cleaning . . ."

Achille threw the table into a far corner. The boy winced at the sound of breaking wood. "Find another chimney to clean," Achille said, his voice cold and distant. "Now." The boy scurried away.

Above the fireplace was a father-and-son portrait of him and Constantin. Achille stood staring at the kindly old face of the man he had called father. The skillful artist had put Constantin's pale hair in shadow, while the boy's dark strands were lit by the sun, greatly lessening the apparent difference between them.

"No doubt that, too, was your doing, Mother," he said aloud to the empty room. He took a knife from his riding boot. His breathing was harsh, rasping.

He pulled the painting down and held the knife a hairbreadth above the canvas, ready to stab it, ready to cut himself out of the false, lying picture.

Remembered images danced before Achille's eyes. Constantin's gentle guidance when Achille had accidentally hurt a servant, his amused chuckles at Achille's little-boy cleverness, his genuine admiration for Achille's unskilled attempts at archery and swordplay.

"Watch me be Tristan again, Papa!"

"I'll watch, my brave knight, I'll watch. Careful, careful, don't pull my arm off. I'm an old man, remember? Younger now that you're here, but the years are still too many. But what's this, Sir Tristan? I see no Isolde."

"Aww, he doesn't always need her, does he?"

"What else does a knight have to fight for but his lady?"

"I can think of lots of things."

"Can you, my son?"

"Sure! Land, honor, and, and . . . the king!"

"And what true knight wouldn't give all those things for a token of his lady's favor? A lock of her hair or a soft smile from her rosy lips? Ahah! You laugh, do you, my boy? Well, Sir Tristan, one day a lady will touch your heart, and when you have felt the pain of love, and found its ease, then you will laugh—at yourself."

"You have been taken from me, Papa," Achille said to the picture in a raw whisper. "I am not your son. I am the son of a man who was all you taught me to fight *against.*"

Like a sword thrust, the thought stabbed into his heart. He'd been raped of his childhood, of his blood, land, title—even the *king* was no longer his. "Tell me this is but a spell cast on me, like the ones in the books. Cast by a beautiful sorceress sent to destroy me . . . She had no need of potions or spells; her eyes were deadly enough . . . and her spirit."

The image of Constantin's pale, kind eyes was transformed in Achille's mind into the cold, dark eyes in Eleonora's drawing, and again he heard the horror of his mother's words. "And now there is no laughter left to me," he said aloud. "There is *nothing* left."

Achille squeezed his eyes shut against the emptiness. Green eyes hovered in his mind, and a softly accented voice whispered there. For a time he'd thought—dreamed?—that perhaps he could find salvation, and that then he would return to Eleonora and claim her as his lady.

But one cruel portrait had taken everything from him. His past with Constantin was a lie. And although in those last days with Eleonora, he had dared to dream of a future, that future, too, was gone. It traveled in a coach heading east, through Passau to Vienna.

Passau. The word brought a spark of sanity. What had that servant said about Passau? Courier . . . impatient . . . war . . . *march into Passau.*

He looked again at the gentle old man in the picture. A spark rose inside Achille, like a flint to kindling. *What else does a knight have to fight for* . . . "I am no longer a knight, Papa. I can no longer ask for a lady's hand, or even for a token of her favor." His voice broke, but he clenched his teeth against the emotion surging inside him. "But a lady needs me, Papa. She is traveling to Vienna through a country threatened by war."

He set the painting aside and rose. "She needs me to keep her safe until she's back with her family. I have nothing now. Only a devil's heritage. No name, no title, no land. I can offer her nothing but that safety."

He strode out of the room and down the grand staircase, and ordered his horse brought round.

He mounted Chiron. He turned back to look at the château one last time. He saw it as it had been, the worn stone façade, the empty windows of the old wing, the turret towering over all ... and a boy standing on the ramparts next to a laughing, pale-haired old man, the wind blowing their hair, dark and light together. "I have heeded your lessons well, monsieur chevalier," he whispered. "The lessons of the last of the House of d'Agenais have not been forgotten."

He snapped the reins and spurred his horse away. Toward the east to Eleonora. To Passau. And to Vienna.

Chapter 18

Eleonora's coach rattled along at a breakneck pace through one French town, then another and another, until her head pounded with the drumming of hooves and rang with Hervé's mad laughter. But she welcomed it; it was all that kept the taunting of her conscience at bay. Her family was waiting for her in Vienna—waiting in vain for her to bring them the devil's son.

She had failed her family. She had failed Achille. No, what she had done was worse than failure. She might have forfeited a devil's son to save her family, but now Achille's life had been destroyed to no purpose. She thought of Bálint's body and shuddered. At least Achille was still alive and whole.

But my family will go on forever, she thought in despair, *slowly destroying ourselves—all because I fell with a dark angel.* Her family's wounds would never be healed—and neither would Achille's.

She'd spent the first day after Achille had sent her off, checking the roads behind her, braced for the telltale sound of a fast horse. But Achille did not ride up that day, nor the next, nor the next, and her relief warred with her disappointment. She had been led to believe him the devil incarnate, but instead she was leaving behind a man whose seduction she both craved and defied.

She had expected trouble crossing the border into Bavaria, but a coach with the arms of a French comte on the doors had no difficulty entering into allied territory. In

Regensburg Hervé offered to find them a barge that would take them down the Danube. He would watch out for her, he promised, and despite his madness, she believed him.

A woman traveling alone always aroused suspicion. But Achille's coachman harangued and cajoled each night's innkeepers into giving her the best cuts of meat for her supper and the softest beds for her sleep. There was a strong streak of loyalty in Hervé the coachman, to his master and his master's orders.

She declined his offer of water travel, and they continued on the roads through lush green valleys and hills that loosely followed the Danube. A week after the nightmare at the Convent of Saint Valeria, they reached the lands of the bishopric of Passau in eastern Bavaria, near the border with Austria.

Tensions were higher here, nearer the enemy, the people less friendly. Maria Theresa, the archduchess of Austria, was soon to be crowned queen of Hungary, and Eleonora had no illusions about her own fate should the skittish French army officers patrolling the roads discover who she was.

The road they were on skirted in and out of the edge of a forest, making it difficult to see ahead. It was late in the afternoon, the sun sending long shadows across their path. Though she could see nothing but trees and shadows on both sides, a light breeze carried snatches of German from a rough soldier's song. Hervé started whistling his own tuneless melody, the signal he had arranged to tell her to lower the leather curtains because there was possible trouble ahead. She did.

The coach slowed its pace, not an easy thing for Hervé to make himself do. Eleonora tried to peer between the curtain and the window. A long line of soldiers was marching in the same direction that she traveled, toward Passau. She shivered and sat back. Their officers would be riding at the front, the last she would pass before the border, and the most dangerous since they were the most likely to stop her coach.

She could feel Hervé try to pick up speed. The lateness

would give them a good excuse not to dawdle. Sunlight glinted off gold lace and jangling silver bridles and, to her surprise, off a bright white cross. These men were officers of the bishop's guards. She pressed deep into the seat to avoid being seen. Through the crack she could see a few men, lieutenants and captains, she guessed, lift their hats as her coach drove by, saluting the rank of the coach and its presumed occupant. They passed a major who studied the crest on the door with narrowed eyes. He did not salute.

Eleonora prayed. He spurred his horse to match the speed of the coach.

"Where are you in such a hurry to go?" he asked Hervé in German. The coachman grunted in answer.

Eleonora quietly opened the trap. The major called his question again. She hissed softly and saw Hervé's tiny nod. "Say 'supper'—*abendessen,*" she whispered. *"Ah-bent-ess-en."* That, at least, was something a man would understand.

Hervé repeated the word. The major laughed and waved them on their way. They rounded a corner and soon left the marching soldiers behind. Eleonora relaxed.

The coachman looked down at her through the still open trap. "Somethin' ain't right, madame," Hervé said. "Don't know what it is, but somethin's amiss."

"What do you mean? What's wrong?"

"That major, madame, he took a long time staring at monsieur's crest. 'Taint's what a stranger usually does. Most times a man'll just glance at it, like, so as he'll know what's due the rank o' those inside the coach."

"But what could he be looking for? Does he know Monsieur d'Agenais, do you think?"

Hervé shrugged, though all she could see was his great buff leather coat moving as if a sudden wind had caught it. "Hard to say, madame. Monsieur coulda fought with that major. Coulda fought against him."

"You mean he could be an old enemy?" she asked, thinking that if the major was an enemy of Achille's, the man had a lot of company. Could she explain that she was just a . . . a *what?*

Hervé chuckled with maniacal glee. "Old enemy be much more likely than old friend, I'd say. Monsieur, he ain't an easy man to like. Most o' them like it *easy.*" The coachman cracked his whip as if to say what he thought of such men.

"Well, *I* say," he went on, "none o' them *easy* men woulda taken a duc's surgeon from his cognac by the scruff o' his neck and dragged him to the muddy field where we was all full o' holes and stretched out like it was a priest we was wantin' 'stead of some physic." He cracked the whip again. "No, I tell ya, no, no, no, the monsieur ain't one o' them *easy* men."

Eleonora gave a wry look at Hervé. "I'm glad you straightened me out on Monsieur d'Agenais. I have—until now, of course!—often mistaken him for the gossip, vicomte de Vigny."

Hervé threw back his head and roared with laughter. "Ho, ho-o-o, you are a good one! No wonder M'sieur's taken with you."

Eleonora sobered and reached up to close the trap. "No, he is not."

The coachman snorted. "All I can say is, if—back at the river—iffen the Lord had decided it was your time to meet the angels, Monsieur woulda torn down the gates of heaven itself to keep Him from it. Cursed Fate, he did. Never heard him do that before. Cursed everything else, o' course, but not Fate."

She closed the trap. In Passau she would pay Hervé generously for his time and his unexpected kindnesses, and then take a boat down the Danube to Vienna, alone. She smiled, imagining the mad coachman trying to defend her against her family as efficiently as he had defended her against rapacious innkeepers.

There was a rap on the trap door. "Begging your pardon, madame," Hervé said when she opened it. "Don't mean to alarm you, but we still got one more ridge to

cross before we reach Passau, and there's a rider comin'
up fast behind us."

"The major!" she cried. "Let me handle him, Hervé.
Maybe he's impatient for his supper. He might ride on by.
If he doesn't, don't antagonize him. He can make you
wish you were back waiting for that surgeon, but I can at
least make him hesitate before he abuses a countess."
Hervé nodded.

The coach picked up speed, though Eleonora wasn't
sure how that was possible. The road had started to rise,
and its condition worsened. Ruts from the last storm had
not been worn down, and she was thrown from side to side
as Hervé tried to negotiate up the hill.

She heard him shout at the horses, curse them, cajole
them, trying to get more speed out of them. She hung on
to the leather strap, creating and discarding one explana-
tion after another in anticipation of being stopped and
questioned. Should she be a very distant d'Agenais
cousin? A discarded lover, no matter how true, might give
the major ideas, but what about a wife—

She broke off the thought. No, it would be simpler to
keep it believable. She was a Hungarian countess returning
home, and Monsieur d'Agenais had kindly offered her the
use of his coach. That would work, she told herself. *As
long as the major doesn't ask why,* a niggling voice in her
head added.

The coach began to slow; the hill was too steep. Were
those hoofbeats she heard? She longed for the pistol she'd
lost at the charcoal burner's camp. She should have had
Hervé buy a new one.

The coach swayed violently, then came to a jolting stop.
Hoofbeats pounded in the sudden silence. Near. Very near.

Eleonora braced herself. The rider came close, then
pulled his horse up hard. She stiffened her shoulders,
folded her hands in her lap, lifted her chin, and stared
haughtily at a spot well above head high. The coach door
flew open.

"Wie können Sie sich unterstehen?" she demanded.
How dare you?

She heard a man's chuckle. It was a sound she'd heard before. She swallowed and lowered her gaze. *"Achille!"* she gasped. He stood in the open doorway, a hand high on either side and leaning slightly toward her. The rays of the setting sun turned everything behind him gold. He was dusty and windblown from his ride, but his eyes on her were alert and intense. "Achille, you're here!"

"As you see," he said, and climbed into the coach. "Though it will take me a moment to thaw from your greeting."

Startled into retreat, Eleonora gathered her skirts close to her so that they didn't touch him. "What are you doing here? Why have you come?"

"I came to escort you to Vienna."

The chill, spidery fingers of her nightmare returned. "No, you mustn't! I need no escort. I shall be fine. I had no trouble on my journey to France."

"That was before war was declared," he answered with infuriating calm.

"Truly, Achille, I don't need—"

"Then let's say I have some unfinished business with your brothers."

"No!" she cried. "That is ended."

"Your part, at least," he said. "I have been challenged to a duel, didn't you say? And you are your brothers' second." He put his hand to his chest and bent toward her. *"Touché,* madame. I admit—you have first blood. And you have it so successfully that it is not even the blood I supposed it was. Perhaps now I shall meet your brothers on my knees, offering up my sword and my life to their mercy."

He had resumed the manner she remembered from that first night on the balcony of the château du Peyre, provocative, taunting, distant. The man she'd known so intimately in front of the fire was gone. "And perhaps not," she said, knowing that he could never be on his knees to anyone.

"And perhaps not," he agreed. "But I shall see that you reach Vienna safely."

The coach jerked free of its ruts and began lumbering up the hill. Moments later, Hervé pounded again on the trap. Both she and Achille reached to open it, and when their fingers touched, she flushed and pulled her hand back.

" 'Nother rider, comin' fast," the coachman told him. "An' this time it's the major, for sure. All that gold lace is nearly blindin' me."

"That damned German. Saint Stephen take him," Eleonora cursed.

"Major?" Achille asked, an eyebrow lifting askance. "And what has *he* done to your brothers? I'd think twice about questioning *his* parentage. Germans have an even nastier temper about that sort of thing than the French." He held up his hand and added, "Speaking in the abstract, of course, since I seem to be neither."

"Don't you go spilling such calumny about my brothers when it's *you* who is the problem here! That major took a long, *long* look at the crest on the door of this coach. No doubt he's part of your notorious past. I fully expected him to fling open the door, point his sword at my throat, and shout, 'Remember Strasbourg!' "

For a moment Achille looked at her with eyes as black as the smoke from a signal fire, then the corners of his mouth lifted. "I have not been to Strasbourg since I was seven," he said. "And it is in France."

She crossed her arms and sat back with a huff. "Heidelberg, then," she snapped. Apprehension and confusion made her temper short. "Though I don't doubt you were precocious enough at seven to offend any number of future majors. Whatever it is, deal with him yourself. It was *your* crest he was interested in. I've done worrying about him."

The coach cleared the top of the hill, and the strain was suddenly released. As Hervé shouted with wild glee, they began to career down the hill toward the gates of the city of Passau. Eleonora grabbed on to the strap and prepared to ride out the coachman's madness, as she had so many times before.

"We can beat him to the gates!" she heard Hervé shout.

The coach rounded a bend, tilting precariously onto two wheels. Fear rose up her throat. For a brief moment the leather flap swung out and she could see toward the east. Torchlight at the gates of Passau competed with the orange light of dusk and made the water of the Danube shimmer with gold.

But Eleonora hardly saw the golden river—her eyes were focused on the waiting troop of soldiers. Her gaze went to the man seated across from her. She discovered him studying her profile instead of the soldiers. "Any ideas?" she asked.

"One or two," he said, his voice like velvet.

"About the soldiers—what if they're waiting for us?"

A shout from behind the coach answered her. "Don't let them pass!" came the cry in German.

Achille dusted off his breeches, then straightened his lace cuffs.

"Saint Stephen, what are you doing? We're about to be arrested and you're—"

He stretched out along the width of the seat, tilting his hat over his eyes and managing to look ineffably bored.

"Pardon me for keeping you from your *nap!*"

"Have you learned nothing I've taught you?" he asked.

"I've learned you're spoiled, self-centered—"

"Demanding, and utterly impossible," Achille finished for her. "All the things which make the French aristocracy the most superior creatures in the world—and very difficult to arrest."

The annoying buzz of her outrage dissipated like a cloud of gnats. She fluffed her skirts until they took up the entire seat, then sat back with a pout. "Oh, la! This trip is so-o-o tiresome. My bathwater last night was positively *tepid,* I tell you. It took that wretched little man *four* trips to get it right." She gave a delicate shudder. "Imagine what tepid water would do to my skin. I would look twice my age." She shrugged elegantly and peeped at him from under her lashes. "I mean *thrice* my age."

"Excellent," he murmured as the coach began to slow.

"Remember, show no fear, no weakness—and be as insufferable as you can be."

"In other words, be like you," she whispered back. A light flared at the back of his black eyes. The sound of approaching hoofbeats forestalled his retort, but she knew it was only postponed, not forgotten.

"Don't let them pass!" the man called again. A horse whinnied as it was brought up sharp.

"Halt machen," another coarser, more self-important voice commanded.

She felt the coach shudder as Hervé dismounted. She heard snatches of a heated German-French argument between the two men, neither understanding a word the other said, yet each one more than understanding what the other *meant.*

A disgruntled silence fell, followed by a polite tap on the door. Achille locked it, then negligently lifted a tiny corner of the leather curtain. Hervé gave him an elaborate, self-effacing bow, and Eleonora suddenly had the suspicion that they had played these roles before. Oddly enough, that thought helped her relax. If they had survived once, they may well survive again.

"I most humbly beg your pardon, monsieur. I know you are most distressed about making the horses stand," the coachman said, shooting a glare over his shoulder at the sergeant-at-arms, "but this . . . *allemand* would have a word with you."

"Well, I would not have a word with him," Achille said in a court drawl that a prince of the blood might envy. "The man babbles."

"He is speaking German, monsieur," the coachman answered.

"Give the man my sympathies and drive on." Achille let the leather flap drop.

Eleonora tittered with amusement, making sure it was loud enough to be heard outside. She spread her hands in a silent gesture that asked, *What now?*

Outside, they could hear the jangle of bridles and the clop of hooves as the soldiers moved about. Achille leaned toward her and said, sotto voce, "I doubt they'll let us just drive away."

"It was worth a try," she said in the same nearly inaudible tone.

He frowned. "Perhaps, but those men aren't the town watch. They're the bishop's guards."

"So is the major."

"Ah," Achille said, and sat back, the light of understanding in his eyes. She could sense him withdrawing from their brief moment of intimacy. "That's twice now I've underestimated a . . . an adversary."

"An adver—?"

"My mother."

There was a sharp rap on the door. "Mmmm?" Achille managed to get out as he lifted the flap.

The major bowed. He held a paper in front of him. "You are the count of Agenais, are you not," the man stated rather than asked in stumbling French. "This crest, it is a lanner falcon, is it not, *ja?* The lanner is the crest of Agenais, *ja?*"

Achille gave the major a look of impatience, the very picture of French annoyance. *"Ja"* was all he said.

The major turned purple. "You come with us. Stop the falcon."

Behind him, a sergeant-at-arms opened the small side gate for foot traffic and then crossed himself as a long-robed priest walked through. The major turned to see who it was. "Monseigneur," he cried, and rushed to the priest's side.

A feral growl came from Achille's throat, and his eyes turned to black points of hate. Eleonora wasn't sure he even realized what he did. She touched his knees. He gave a start, then recovered himself.

"A Jesuit," he said under his breath, as a man might refer to a traitor or a murderer. Jesuits were rumored to be both.

The languidness returned to Achille's manner, though Eleonora knew the supreme effort the pose required. He was used to facing his enemies straight on in a duel of honor, but if he dueled with a Jesuit, death could take him before the challenge had been read.

The priest nodded at the major, then went to the coach. Eleonora tied the leather curtain completely open, fearing Achille would make the Jesuit talk to them through a barrier as if they were at confession.

The man bent his head in a priestly acknowledgment of Achille's rank. "A thousand pardons, monsieur," the Jesuit said, his French facile and easy. "I am Father Eduard." Without looking at the priest, Achille frowned and pulled at his lace cuffs as if straightening their disarray were of the utmost importance.

The priest went smoothly on. "I fear Major Freitag, a most diligent fellow, please believe me, has mistaken the bishop's orders. You are to be His Excellency's guest, monsieur. A hero of the last war!

"Please, please, I assure you, we are most honored. When everyone else is rushing north, we are doubly graced that you have chosen to visit our little outpost on the allied frontier, as it were." He ended with the most sincere smile Eleonora had ever seen. She suppressed a shudder.

She could see no way out. Achille sat silent, plucking his cuffs when, no doubt, what he wanted to do was pluck his sword from its scabbard and run the man through.

"Impossible!" Eleonora stated flatly. The Jesuit stared at her. "Thank His Excellency for us, of course," she added airily, "but you can see it is quite out of the question."

"Madame . . . d'Agenais?" the priest asked, glancing at Achille for confirmation. Achille said and did nothing. "Madame, I do not see—"

"Not see? How can you not?" she asked, her voice rising in outrage. She gave Achille a look of wifely peevishness. "Of course we cannot stay. *I have no clothes.*"

"His Excellency would never notice—"

"For days and days," Eleonora spit out, glaring at Achille while overriding the priest's mollifying words, "and leagues and leagues, I have been without a decent gown of any kind. *He* insisted on hiring the scrawniest little brats for postboys. I *told* him what would happen."

Achille rolled his eyes. "In inexhaustible detail, my lily among thorns."

"Madame, I—"

"And I was *right*," she said gleefully. "The little wretches—little cowards!—balked at the tiniest of streams. And *pouf!* Everything was lost."

"My voice of the turtledove, the Rhône is not the tiniest of rivers," Achille added, studying the ceiling of the coach. "And only two coaches were lost. The others merely had to be repaired."

"But everything got *wet!* Do you know what can be done with wet silk?"

He let his gaze drift down her body. "Wet rose-colored silk?"

The priest *harrumph*ed. "Monsieur, madame," he said, looking harassed, "I will instruct the sergeant to lead your coachman to His Excellency's guest house. I am quite sure you will enjoy His Excellency's hospitality for a few days and then be on your way."

He spun around and walked stiffly back to the sergeant. "To think I am to be nursemaid to those indulgent, extravagant little ..." His voice trailed out of hearing.

Achille released the curtain with one tug of the tie, and Eleonora let her shoulders sink. The coachman gave a single knock on the trap, and Achille opened it. No words were exchanged, just a look and a nod, and the trap was closed. The coach jerked into motion.

"Perhaps at the guest house someone will realize their mistake," she said, pulling her skirts closed. "At least we tried."

"Tried—and succeeded superbly, oh, thou fairest among women."

"Stop that nonsense. No one can hear you now," she said, feeling the sting of the mocking words. "And how can you say we succeeded? We were nearly arrested."

"Actually, Eleonora, we *are* being arrested."

"What? Are they taking us to prison? How can you be so calm?"

"A very soft prison, I'll wager. There are too many ways for Father Eduard to lose if he is too bold. He can't let us go free—that would snub my mother's request. And he won't risk confining us in shackles unless my mother specifically gave orders to do it. That might offend her. Who knows how many high friends the prioress might be able to call upon in retaliation? Though, of course, since he is a Jesuit, he will try to turn the situation to his advantage." He leaned back against the seat and crossed his hands behind his head. "Still, any time a Jesuit can be made to lose his composure is a success to be savored like the sweetest wine."

She had rarely seen him look so relaxed.

"Such a smile, Eleonora," he murmured, and she flushed to realize he was watching her. "Were Father Eduard to see you now, he would question his vows, not us."

"He is a priest," she protested. "He would question only our veracity."

"He is a man," Achille answered.

For a long moment, there was only the sound of the coach wheels echoing between them. The streets were narrow, and to Eleonora's surprise, Hervé guided the coach with slow care through the rows of closely spaced houses.

"Are you worried about the next days? I'll send Hervé to arrange for a boat downriver," Achille assured her. "The priest is blinded by his own petty hates. He sees what he expects to see. You played your part with great finesse— you have only to continue playing it as superbly as you began, and this intrigue will quickly grow tiresome for him. Then we can continue on our journey.

"However, madame wife," he added provocatively, "Father Eduard will not so easily shrug off such eccentricities as did Mrs. Freymot. I shall not stay in the stables for this night or any other."

Eleonora felt a stab of panic, then recovered enough to give him an arch smile. "Of course you shall not. You shall stay in one bedroom—and I shall stay in another. Every respectable establishment has separate bedrooms for husbands and wives."

" 'Tis a snug little place," the bishop's young understeward told them in fluent though heavily accented French as he led them through a lavishly gilded entrance hall. Brother Koln wore the long robe of the Cistercian Order, though he had not taken his final vows, for his hair had not yet been tonsured. "'Twas built for the late bishop's nephew's last mistress."

"And now?" Eleonora asked as they mounted the stairs, passing a score of Swiss guards placed at regular intervals, their pikes at the ready.

Brother Koln's face was carefully bland. "Now it is used occasionally for . . . particular guests of His Excellency."

Her hand was politely tucked through Achille's arm, though her fingers, unseen, were digging into him. Murals of naked, frolicking nymphs and satyrs filled each panel of the walls, reminding her of her bedroom at château du Peyre. But those had been private pictures in private rooms; these were brazenly public. She decided not to ask exactly what was "particular" about the bishop's guests.

"His Excellency is fond of cards," Brother Koln finished lamely, his cheeks flaming.

"I'm sure it's quite *respectable*," Achille said, apparently indifferent, though she caught the quick glance he shot at her through lowered lashes.

"I want a hot bath in *my* rooms immediately," Eleonora said, then added with a soupçon of a whine, "and make sure it's hot. Not tepid, mind, but hot."

"As you wish, madame," the understeward said, pausing for a second to bow sideways at them. Eleonora smirked at Achille.

Keeping his eyes on her, he said, "And we shall want supper in *our* rooms as soon as Madame has finished."

The understeward bowed sideways again. "As you wish, monsieur."

Achille raised an eyebrow in triumph, and Eleonora sulked picturesquely.

Brother Koln brought them to a pair of double doors and halted. He flung them open with a theatrical flourish, then stood back, looking abashed as the squeaks of a score of excited finches greeted him from a cage in a corner. "The, ah, late bishop's nephew visited Rome and returned with a few, ah, mementos."

The room was enormous, nearly the size of a ballroom. The room glowed—no, *pulsed*—with imperial purple and gold. Fluted columns lined the walls, interspersed with at least a score of statues. There were Roman athletes, Roman senators, Roman soldiers . . . and instead of nymphs, a statue of Venus herself.

Eleonora would have stayed on the threshold, dumbfounded, if she had not been holding on to Achille and been dragged along with him as he walked in.

"Veni, vidi . . ." he began. I came, I saw . . .

"Emi," she finished. I bought. "He must've had an entire Roman villa brought here."

Underfoot, rich carpets lay chessboard fashion to cover the floors. Fireplaces were set in three walls; huge wardrobes and tables and thick-cushioned Roman curved-back chairs filled the room. And at the far end, like an altar to a pagan god, was a gilded bed built in the shape of a temple.

She glanced at the understeward in the doorway, dwarfed between two red marble columns, then at Achille. She put the back of her hand on her forehead and said faintly, "I feel an uncontrollable urge to find a sacrificial goat."

Achille studied the tiny finches in the cage. "Or teach the birds to read the future." He glanced at her. "Though I trust there are no more secrets to learn."

Eleonora ignored the twinge of her conscience and began moving around the room. She was used to great wealth, but such eccentricity . . . "After this, I doubt Father Eduard would think you odd if you preferred the stables."

"But I certainly would." He looked at the understeward. "And whatever became of the late bishop's nephew?"

"He was made a cardinal."

"Of course. I should have guessed." The finches squeaked their agreement. "Have this removed," he said, indicating the cage.

Brother Koln cleared his throat and bowed, saying over the sound of the birds, "At once, monsieur. And, madame, I shall have your bath brought up."

She nodded absently, absorbed in examining a decorated Greek amphora set in the middle of a marble table. "Achille, what are these men doing?"

He didn't answer, but suddenly she felt a firm hand on her elbow drawing her away. "Achille, what—?" she began again, looking over her shoulder at the amphora.

"And have *that* removed *at once,*" he snapped at Brother Koln.

The young man jumped. *"Ja, mein herr!* I mean, yes, yes, monsieur. Right away. Your pardon, monsieur, the house is little used . . ." At a look from Achille, he scurried off.

She wrenched her elbow out of his grasp and went to the other side of the table, the amphora between them. "Now, what was that all about?"

Achille watched her with speculative eyes. "Surely it is not necessary for you to know all that goes on in the world."

She glanced down at the Greek vase and flushed.

"Once a thing is known," he went on, "the knowing cannot be undone."

Her gaze rose to meet his. "Nor can the doing be undone, no matter how fervent the prayers."

He raised an elegant eyebrow in doubt. "And are you prayers fervent, Eleonora?" he asked, his voice low. He took a step to come around the table, and she took a step in the opposite direction. "Do you pray that you had never left your mountains, your eagle's citadel? Or that you never traveled to France, to the château du Peyre, to that balcony where you went to cool your overwarm flesh?"

"I regret but a few moments," she told him, her finger-tips resting on the table's edge for balance. "Moments that occurred after a night of heaven by the fire in my room. The few moments that followed that happiness, I would undo."

"But they cannot be undone, can they, Eleonora?" Once again, he began circling the table, and she scurried to keep the marble slab between them.

"Why have you followed me?" she cried. "Why didn't you stay at your château?"

"The château is no longer mine. I am but its tenant," he answered. "What else is there for me to do but escort a lady to Vienna?"

"Leave this be! You are still the comte d'Agenais."

He lunged across the table and grabbed her. "Am I, Eleonora? *Am I?*"

His intense features were inches from hers. "Your mother said—" she began shakily.

"My mother cannot be trusted, even with the truth. I go with you to Vienna."

"No," she pleaded. "No, please—"

A scratching on the door disturbed them. She gave a start of surprise, and he released his hold. "What is between us is no concern of the Jesuit. A truce, Eleonora, until we are free of this place. After that—what will be, will be up to—"

"Fate?" she whispered. She nodded. "A truce, then."

He said nothing at first, his dark eyes staring into hers. When he did speak, his voice was unexpectedly uncertain, as if he'd been given something he was not sure it was safe to have. "A truce, then."

Chapter 19

The scratching came again at the door. "Enter," Achille called out.

Brother Koln opened the door, bowed, and motioned to a servant. A bow-legged footman walked stiffly into the room, bent in half at the waist, vaguely in Achille and Eleonora's direction, then grabbed the amphora by its two handles and carried it out of the room by holding it straight out in front of him.

"I most humbly beg your pardon, madame," the understeward said after the footman had departed, "but there is some problem with the bath."

"Problem?" she asked in her usual voice, then remembering her role, added sharply, "What kind of problem could there be with a bath?"

"The problem is not actually with the bath itself, madame. The difficulty appears to be in, er, *finding* it."

With a feigned huff, Eleonora turned her back to him, concerned he might notice her not-completely-successful struggle to hide her laughter. How could a contraption the size of a horse trough get lost?

Achille went to sit in one of the curved-back chairs by the cold fireplace. "Now, now, my dove," he said, managing to convey complete indifference by examining his fingernails, "don't give in to your pique. You know what that does to your complexion."

"What it does to my complexion is *nothing* compared to what I'm going to do if I don't get my bath, oh, my hart of the wildwood," she answered with purring sweetness. Achille gave in to a coughing fit.

"No, please, madame," Brother Koln squeaked. "There are only forty rooms. I'm sure the bath will be found at any moment."

Eleonora whirled on him with narrowed eyes. "You do have one, don't you?"

"Of course! Of course! The cook remembers when it arrived. She said the larder mistress fainted dead away into the fresh butter when it flew in."

"Flew in?"

"It is in the shape of a swan, madame."

"My dearest Leda," Achille shot at her under his breath. She shot a glare back.

"Your pardon, monsieur?" Brother Koln asked.

"My . . . heart of my heart has a penchant for swans."

Eleonora hugged herself and turned away, her pique becoming real for a moment. Why couldn't he keep to endearments about flowers and birds? "And a penchant for supper," she said. "Bring hot water and a basin for now. I will bathe later."

"Yes, madame. Do you, er, require swans for supper?"

"Good God, no!" she told him. "Anything you have in the larder will do."

"Anything but the butter," Achille added.

"As you wish, monsieur." The young understeward bowed gratefully and departed. Silence remained behind for the count of three beats, four . . . then Achille burst out laughing.

" 'My hart of the wildwood'?" he asked. "It isn't often I'm called a stag in front of a Cistercian novitiate."

She shrugged. "I couldn't think of any appropriate beasts of burden—at least none that I could mention in front him." *And what of 'heart of my heart'?* she wanted to ask. *It isn't often I'm called—* She broke off the thought, uncomfortable that the false endearment stung so. Uncomfortable that it stung at all.

A scratching on the door preceded footmen carrying in two tables of red marble with holes cut out of the tops and supported by a menagerie of fabulous sphinxes and chimera. More footmen carried in two enormous bowls of hammered gold and set them into the holes in the marble, and yet a third set of footmen solemnly bore tall, narrow-necked ewers made of lapis and gold, more suited to anointing a caesar than to washing one's face.

Both she and Achille watched the procession without comment, and the silence continued after the servants had gone. The only movements in the room were the two freshly laundered linen towels swinging from the side of each of the tables where a grave footman had draped them, and the steam rising from the ewers.

"They've forgotten a screen," she said, trying to keep her voice from revealing her sudden nervousness. "The drafts . . ."

"The windows are closed, and the curtains drawn," he said much too innocently.

"Y-yes, I know." She could think of no argument that wouldn't make her seem a silly schoolgirl. Reluctantly she made her way to a red-marbled table and poured the steaming water into the gold basin. The scent of roses filled her head. She inhaled deeply, remembering the damask petals in the bower and the ones he had had picked for her.

She needed to be separate from him. To place walls of stone and timber between them. How else could she escape the silken bonds of memory, forget the touch of his caress, the heated surrender to his kisses?

How else not to see his hand relaxed on the arm of the chair and recall the spell that hand had cast on the most intimate parts of her as he had led her to enchantment? Since childhood, in her nightmares the devil had come to find her; now in her nightmares he did not.

Eleonora plunged her hands into the water and drew it, warm and scented, up to her face. Her world had fallen into a hundred disparate pieces. Her life, her body, even her soul, could never again be what they once were. For the past could not be undone, as the taste of an orange could not be untasted . . .

. . . as Achille, once known, could not be unknown.

Achille watched Eleonora at her ablutions, unable to look away. She had hinted so strongly for privacy, but something deep in him had rebelled and denied her. A gentleman would have left the room, or turned his back. A gentleman would have—but then, he was no longer a gentleman.

He did not want to watch her, he told himself. He did not want to see the water dripping through her fingers like a goddess's tears, or her graceful hands stroking the dampness from her brow and cheeks, or envy the tiny curls caressing the nape of her neck.

She reached for the towel and, her eyes closed and her head tilted slightly back, began to pat her skin dry. He pushed himself out of the chair and went to the other basin, impatiently pouring water from the ewer and splashing it on his face. He doused himself again and again. He grabbed the towel and began to vigorously dry his face and hair.

In an unguarded moment, he looked over the edge of the towel and saw Eleonora standing next to him, watching him with a soft smile. She had returned order to her simple coiffure and smoothed the worse travel creases from her gown.

"May I?" she asked, bunching her damp towel. She took his silence for assent and brushed water droplets from the shoulders of his velvet coat. She seemed refreshed and at ease, her attention on her task.

It was a private moment between a man and a woman. Something roused in him down deep, deeper than the quick-to-anger gentleman he had been, deeper than the comte he had become, or the chevalier he had been trained to be; down and down, under the pain, under the memories, to a small, curled-up ball of something it took him a long moment to recognize.

It was a small child's memory, distant and fuzzy, made not of images or things seen, but of emotions long forgotten—contentment, happiness, and something so sublime and elusive that even in this moment of clarity, he could not name it.

He gently stopped her. In her eyes, for the briefest instant, like a falling star that is scarcely glimpsed before it is gone, he saw behind the wall she had so carefully built inside her. And the vision shook him.

"I'm not a very good valet, am I?" she said, looking sad, as if something precious had been taken from her.

"But a very beautiful one."

A bold knock at the door interrupted them. *"Again?"* he asked with a growl. "A Jesuit's revenge is subtle indeed. *Enter."*

The door swung open and hit the wall with a crack. Shoulder to shoulder, a man and a woman stood at attention in the doorway, identical in every respect—same face, same reed-thin body, same ginger-colored hair, ginger-colored eyes—except that one wore skirts and one wore breeches.

"The servants' door . . ." began the woman in German.

"Is locked," finished the man in the same language. "We had to . . ."

"Walk around." The woman curtsied. "I am to be *mein herrin's* maid."

The man bowed. "I am to be *mein sieur's* valet." They stepped into the room in unison.

Eleonora took a matching step forward and put her hands on her hips. "And we are to be fed," she snapped in her best High German. "Where is our supper?"

Achille understood the barest smattering of German and spoke even less, but he knew the voice of command when he heard it. Such a tantalizing chameleon was this woman Eleonora.

The two looked at each other, then took another step forward. "You must be tired from your journey," said one.

"We will help you refresh yourselves." They started forward.

Eleonora held up a hand, and they halted. "That's already been done." They looked taken aback, but Eleonora didn't give them time to respond. "Please see to our supper. And where are my chests? There were two in the coach. Have them brought up immediately. Monsieur's baggage was lost. He will need a change of clothes and some, ah . . ." To Achille's surprise, she faltered for a moment, then composed herself. "Monsieur will also need some nightclothes."

The two had brightened when Eleonora began her orders, and now they positively beamed with happiness. "Yes, madame!"

"At once, madame!"

The man bowed, then turned with a precision that would put Frederick of Prussia's infantry to the blush, and departed.

The woman bustled toward them. She lifted the damp towel from Achille's grasp, snapped it smooth, folded it, and returned it to its bar next to Eleonora's basin. Then bed curtains were thrown back, chairs arranged around a table . . .

Achille leaned over and whispered to Eleonora, "So my Magyar countess is fluent in French, Latin, German—and army. I'm impressed. You must have read de Saxe's book closer than I'd thought."

"You forgot Italian," she whispered back. "Ladies-in-waiting to the archduchess are required to read all four. It was she who told me that efficiency responds to efficiency. And I couldn't get through more than three pages of de Saxe."

"Indeed?" was all he said, then watched with satisfaction as a flush rose up her delicious neck when she realized that she'd just admitted that she'd not spent the long hours in the coach reading as she'd pretended.

Over the next hour, the chests were brought in and Eleonora's few gowns shaken out and hung in wardrobes. His small bag of books was brought in and set aside. Clothes were found for him, then taken away again when they proved too small through the shoulders and much too big through the waist.

The maid held up a wisp of rose-colored silk, a puzzled

look on her face. With a fiery blush, Eleonora gently took it away. The maid shrugged and returned to her work.

Eleonora, not seeing Achille watching her, laid the robe on the bed's sumptuous purple velvet counterpane and gently smoothed the silk. She drew the long ribbons through her fingers, her eyes soft with reminiscence.

In his imagination, he saw her lying on that imperial purple, beguilingly swoony in the afterbliss of lovemaking. Achille looked away, but the afterimage stayed with him as if he'd stared into the sun too long.

The ginger-haired valet strode in, carrying a barber's tools, trailing a servant struggling with a large screen. After shielding a far corner, he set about relieving Achille of the dark shadow on his jaw. Once, Eleonora peeked around the edge of the screen, but she blushed and went away when his eyes met hers.

Their supper arrived a few moments later. He thought it odd that they were not led to a dining salon—another subtlety of the Jesuit?—but when the laden dishes of roast quail and partridge were brought in, his thoughts were easily diverted to assuaging his hunger.

He bowed and offered Eleonora his arm, and escorted her to the table set with priceless porcelain and gold plate. There was more pressure than usual from the hand on his arm, and he realized she was weary. But he could sense her subtle efforts to summon her energy, preparing to once again play the part she was called upon to play.

He whispered into her ear, "Husbands and wives are not expected to converse at table."

"A delightful custom," she murmured, and the tension in her dissipated.

They sat at opposite ends of the long marble table. A large flower-filled urn blocked his view of her. He had it removed.

They ate lightly. A broth flavored with mushrooms was followed by roast partridge for him, quail for her, and salsify, all accompanied by a white wine.

She ate slowly, delicately, pausing to savor each bite. How had he ever seen anything of the clockwork in her?

he wondered. Her fingers shaped themselves to her wineglass with infinite grace, her head turned at a slight angle to give him a perfect view of the creamy flesh of her neck, her moist lips pressed against the rim—

"More cardoons with oil and lemon, *mein sieur?*" the ginger-haired manservant asked, as a footman proffered a salat.

Achille looked at his plate. He had not noticed what he'd been eating. He waved the man away.

After the remains of their meal had been cleared away, a fire was laid and chocolate brought in with due ceremony and poured into green and white porcelain cups. He went to his books and, feeling perverse, drew out a wellworn copy of the cleric-hating Voltaire's *Lettres philosophiques.*

He waited until Eleonora settled in a chair by the fire, then sat down in the chair next to hers, a small, round table between them for their chocolate. The servants departed, leaving them to their solitude.

He thought of the small, intimate table in his rooms at the château du Peyre, of how he had sat there with his coffee and his book . . . and an empty chair.

The Voltaire remained unopened on his lap. Somehow the words did not seem nearly as engrossing as watching the firelight on Eleonora's face as she struggled with de Saxe and his armies. She looked her most exotic at this three-quarter angle, he decided. Of course, her profile was one of classic beauty, well worth studying, particularly when her chin was raised in determination. And looking at her straight on meant that the lodestone of her eyes drew—

Someone scratched at the door. Eleonora looked up, glancing over her shoulder. "Not again."

Achille carefully set his book on the floor by the chair. He carefully stood, making sure not to snap off the arms of the chair the way he was going to snap off the arms of whoever was at the door. He carefully wrapped his fingers around the latch so as not to twist it off in his hand.

He opened the door. Brother Koln stood there, his eyes

growing wider and his skin growing paler the longer he stared at Achille.

"M-madame's bath . . ." he explained, gesturing behind him.

Achille slowly fisted his hand in Brother Koln's gray Cistercian habit and drew him over the threshold. "You will see that madame's bath is placed by the fire. You will see that the water for madame's bath is hot. Not tepid, mind you. *Hot.*

"Then you will see that the servants' door is securely locked. You will see that the servants leave this room. Leave this corridor. Leave this *wing.* And you will see that we are left undisturbed for the rest of the night. No more clothes. No more food. No more baths."

"*Ja, ja,* whatever you say, monsieur," Brother Koln said, his hands fluttering impotently at his sides like a flightless bird trying to take wing. "No more interruptions till morning."

"No more interruptions *until we call for you* in the morning."

"Please, monsieur . . ."

Achille raised him higher, forcing the young man to stand on his toes. "Till you call for us! Till you call for us!"

Achille released him. He staggered to the door, clutching his throat. "By the fire," he told the waiting servants. "Put that profane monstrosity by the fire." He ran out.

A few minutes later, Eleonora stood staring. Rose-scented steam drifted from the back of the brass swan facing the fire, its wings outstretched and its head arched over its shoulder to look at the bather in the hollow of its back. It appeared to be sailing into the center of the room without looking where it was going.

"My God, it's the size of a boat. There's even a reclining seat. And those wings!"

Achille turned a lever, and with an ear-piercing squeak, the two wings moved with clockwork jerks to cover the bather as if in an embrace. "Jove seems a bit gouty to me, Leda."

She shot him a glare, then asked the waiting ginger-haired maid, "Are you sure this thing is safe?"

The woman clutched a basket of sponges and soaps to her narrow bosom. She was shaking with fright. "H-h-heathen," was all she could stammer.

Achille flipped the lever back, and the wings began to jerkily return to position. There was a loud *thunk* and one wing wrenched to a halt halfway back while the other one continued on its path, so in the end it appeared that the backward-looking swan was saluting.

Eleonora giggled. "We who are about to bathe . . ."

The maid dropped the basket and fled.

Achille went to pick up the basket, then closed and locked the door.

"Aren't you going to call her back?" Eleonora asked.

"No."

"Achille," she said sternly, but he could hear the uncertainty beneath the façade.

"You played my valet," he said, walking toward her. "Now I shall return the favor."

"There is no need!" she cried, then gave him a badly rendered shrug as she tried to recapture her feigned nonchalance. "I made a very poor valet."

"And I shall make a very poor maid." He began setting out the towels and sponges and soaps on the small table that had held their cups of chocolate.

"You said you returned for my brothers," she said, evidently trying another tack.

"But of course I did, Eleonora. Why else would I travel halfway across Europe but to oblige men I have never met?"

He went up behind her and began softly stroking her neck and shoulders. Her eyes closed, as if to deny his presence, but she did not step away. "You are travel-weary," he murmured, changing the strokes into massaging circles. "The hot water will soothe you."

His fingers moved lower. He traced the neckline of her gown. Her head fell back against his shoulder, and he rubbed his jaw in her soft hair. She put a hand up to his, and he paused.

"Lie to me," she whispered. "Lie to me and tell me it isn't wrong of me to want—"

"Sh-h-h," he said, drawing a finger across her moist lips. "It is time for Madame's bath." Her back resting against his chest, he encircled her with his arms and slowly undid the front laces of her gown. The task held a delightful sting, for though his hands knew the movements, he had always done it in haste and impatience. Then, a gown had been nothing but an impediment between him and a woman.

But this woman was Eleonora. A woman such as he had never known. Complex. Sensual far beyond the carnal. Never to be completely known, yet always to be continually discovered. Being with her was like viewing a diamond revealed facet by facet, yet he always craved to see the whole.

Her gown loosened, he kissed the nape of her neck. He heard her tiny inhalation of breath. His blood quickened. His fingers tucked under the shoulders of her gown and slid it down her creamy arms, freeing her from the confinement of velvet and lace, leaving her dressed in only her petticoats and the fine cambric of her low-cut chemise.

He trailed tiny kisses along her hairline. For the comfort of travel, she had worn no stays, and his eyes drank in the maddening sight of her lush, firm breasts pressing against the thin material, the darker rose of her nipples showing through.

His breaths came more quickly. She turned and stroked his jaw, and he remembered when she'd peeked behind the screen to see him being shaved. He smiled. "I saw you peek around that screen," he teased. "Now you've witnessed the truth for yourself. I'm neither devil nor dark angel. I doubt either one requires a barber."

She returned his smile. "And I doubt either one would offer to be my maid." Her green eyes darkened to the deep emerald of a forest glade, and she began untying his cravat. "and you did promise me a bath."

"*You* get the bath, not me," he said with a laugh.

"Don't you want to save your only suit of clothes from water and ruin? You were so careful of them that night at château du Peyre."

"I was being careful to reveal why I was there. I could have thrown them in the fire as easily as over a chair." He cupped her face. "I wanted you—and I wanted you to know it."

She held his gaze and deliberately slid her hands under his coat. He let his arms fall to his sides, and she pushed his coat off his shoulders and threw it at a chair without breaking their gaze. He pulled his shirt over his head and discarded it.

He grinned at her, dressed in only his shoes, stockings, and breeches. "And now, madame . . ." He gave a quick tug to her petticoat ties and let them drop to the floor.

Blood pounded in his veins as she stood in a pool of white, in garters and pink stockings and her nearly transparent chemise. A keening lust rose up from deep inside him, swelling, thrumming, overpowering— It was right she should be his. *Take her.*

"And now, monsieur . . ." she answered, her voice rich with promise. She knelt in front of him and kissed his hard stomach just above the waist of his breeches. Her tongue tipped out and tasted his skin. He groaned, his control nearly shattered.

His desire was unmistakable, and she rubbed her hand over the hardened length of it, then began undoing his buttons.

Without warning, he bent over and picked her up in his arms. The heat of her skin on his inflamed him even more. Images flashed. Sensations from memories of her flowed and rippled. The rug would do; her petticoats would be enough of a pillow.

"Achille!" she said with a squeal and a laugh. It was the laugh that broke through his lust, a laugh of trust. Just a thread, a short, precious thread. But take her the way her husband had, and that thread would break and be gone forever.

"I want you," he rasped, somehow finding his voice, the words. The light of laughter in her eyes turned sultry. "Now, Eleonora, I want you *now.*"

She dug her fingers into his hair and kissed him. Her breasts pressed into his chest. "Take me," she whispered into his mouth. "Take me."

With a groan, he lowered her to the mound of petticoats, sweeping up her chemise to uncover her intimate deep auburn curls and her breasts. His mouth took a nipple, swirling his tongue around the hardened peak. A sweet cry escaped her.

"No," she whimpered. "Just take me. God, please take me. Fill me now, please now—"

"El, I don't want to hurt you."

"God, please! I hurt *now,* without you."

He pushed his breeches flap aside and covered her body with his. "El," he whispered, lost in a delirium. She had become his desire and his fulfillment. Her hips rose to meet him. He thrust into her.

A cry to heaven was torn from his throat. Her body moved with his. Her hands roamed his chest, his arms, his back, touching, urging. There was such a look of peace on her face. His awareness focused on the exquisite paradise of her. His soul saw her peace, blended with it ... the peace and the pleasure ...

Again and again, he withdrew and felt bereft. He entered, and returned to the sweet pleasuring of their joining. His vision blurred, but still he saw her, saw the peace that had become his peace, pleasure building on pleasure, heat and fire rising, rising, rising.

He plunged into her. "Sweet God, sweet God, sweet—" A long, shattering groan spilled into the air. His mind, his senses, were washed away, leaving only ... peace.

Long moments later, Achille roused from the honeyed afterglow. He still lay across Eleonora, his face nuzzled against her hair. He kissed her temple, then shifted his weight onto his elbows. He knew she had not reached her own pleasure, and he looked into her green-eyed gaze expecting to see disappointment or resignation.

She traced the line of his jaw with her finger and smiled at him, content and happy. "Thank you," she whispered.

"For what? Acting like your brute of a husband? I should hate myself." He kissed her neck under her ear. "I should," he added, "but, sweet Jesus, it was good."

She giggled and wrapped her arms around him in a hug. "Sometimes, for a woman, the need, the hunger, is to give pleasure." She hugged him again. "And it *was* good."

"Eleonora, you sound drunk."

"Maybe I am, but not on wine." She squirmed and stretched, a satisfied smile on her face. He was still inside her, and when he felt her tighten around him, he discovered that renewed desire was not far away. "I feel strong, Achille. And powerful. As if I could tame the world!"

He kissed her, then slowly pulled out. "No-o-o," she protested, and he tasted her soft lips again.

"Perhaps you can tame the world, madame," he said with a smile, "but I have set my sights much higher. I want to tame a Magyar."

"Tame," she spit out. She rolled onto her stomach, then sat back on her knees, her garters snug around her thighs. "Tame? Or break? Maybe you want to accustom me to the taste of the bit!" Her chemise was still in disarray, her proud breasts begging to be tasted and kissed and—

"Achille?"

"Mmmm?"

She leaned forward, putting her hands on her knees and inadvertently pushing her breasts together. His loins tightened. "Achille, look at me."

"I am." She moved and, oh, sweet God, she *moved* . . . "El, have mercy. A saint would sell his soul to look at you. Do you think I'm made of stone?"

Her pique faded and she glanced down to the base of his torso. She gave him a sly grin. "Well, now that you mention it . . ."

"Witch!" He sucked in two deep, controlling breaths. He'd be damned if she was going to be the only one to give pleasure tonight, he thought. And in that moment, he discovered that there was a limit to his selfishness.

To his infinite regret, she straightened her chemise, then stood. "I hope the water hasn't cooled too much," she said to herself. She went to the bath and dipped her hand in to test it. "Perfect."

An impulse came to him. He was not a man to have such impulses, but this one was strong and impossible to ignore. He got to his feet.

He scooped her up—

"Achille! What are you—?"

—and threw her into the bath. Water flew up the sides, then fell back on her in a wet embrace.

"You wretch!" she yelled through her laughter. The water swayed as it settled itself, hiding, then revealing her wet, cambric-covered breasts. "You are the worst—"

He leaned over and took her mouth with his. It was a deep kiss of exploration and possession. Her head fell back, her tongue meeting his, inviting his, drawing his, deeper and deeper into the discovery.

He broke it off, went to the table, and picked up the sponge and scented soap.

"And now, madame countess, the pleasure will be all mine."

Chapter 20

Eleonora tried to straighten on the bath's reclining seat, but she kept slipping back into the most abandoned position. She felt like an odalisque being readied for a sultan's pleasure. "Achille, I can . . ."

"Shhh." He removed her wet chemise, then dipped the sponge into the water and squeezed, the water spurting between his strong fingers. His gaze roamed over her body as his hands slowly rubbed the soap on the sponge.

She nervously licked her lips and tried to straighten once more, then gave up. Movement kept her from feeling the slide of water over her sensitive breasts, a sensual reminder of his lips and his tongue and the moist heat of his mouth . . . A tiny moan escaped her.

Achille trailed the backs of his wet fingers along her jaw. "Madame should relax," he murmured, tracing her neck and shoulders. His fingers massaged in tiny circles, making the water lap against her skin.

She closed her eyes, letting the warmth of his touch and the water's heat seep into her. "I just wanted to wash away the dust of the journey," she whispered.

She felt the slippery, soapy sponge caressing the hollow at the base of her neck. It slid lower and lower, slowly circling toward the valley between her breasts. A tension, an expectation, began building in her unruly body. Wantonly she arched her back, straining into his touch. A plea hovered on her lips, and she struggled not to utter it.

Achille swirled the sponge around each breast, stroking

293

each soft globe as if it were an object of reverence. And still he didn't . . .

"Please," she whimpered. "You're playing with me."

"I *play* you, my beautiful Eleonora," he said, his voice low and vibrant. "I want you to feel the most exquisite music of pleasure." She could feel his words as she felt his touch, and she drew them down deep inside her.

The silky swirls of the sponge glided lower, under the water, to her stomach, her sides. Adagio adagio he played her, rubbing, stroking, caressing. He extended her legs, slowly drawing off her stockings, teasing the soft flesh behind her knees, and then, as if sketching the first movement of a sonata with the long strokes of a composer's pen, he sponged her thighs.

She felt each note of the slick soap, reaching higher and higher, to the apex of her thighs, yet never closer. The heat of the water became as nothing. A primal yearning began its insistent chant under her skin. The tyranny of his skilled hands controlled her, enslaved her . . .

"Achille," she pleaded, wanting more, wanting him to take her to the gates of paradise. "I want . . ."

"You want what, my El?" he asked, the music of laughter in his voice. "Tell me, my beautiful Magyar, tell me. Do you want this?"

He released the sponge and slid his hands up the back of her thighs, lifting her, cupping the soft globes of her behind.

"Yes," she cried. He slid higher still, to explore the sensitive flesh of her back, his thumbs teasing the sides of her breasts. "Please, yes, more . . ."

"More?" He leaned over the edge of the bath, his magnificent torso lit by the firelight. His tongue traced the dark rose of her breast. He licked closer to the center bud.

Her head thrown back, her body strained upward, yet still he didn't . . . Her hand rose dripping from the water, and she buried her fingers in his hair to urge him. "You make me a wanton," she sobbed. "Oh, please."

She heard a deep, masculine sound of satisfaction. "Not

a wanton. A woman." He kissed her nipple, then drew its peak between his lips.

It was as if lightning struck her. A cry broke from her. No longer would she fear the storm, but crave it. Crave the lightning from the devil's hands. Her back arched higher, toward the creator of tempests.

He suckled her breast, licking it, teasing it, plucking it with his lips. Lost in a delirium of pleasure, she heard a delicious moan from far off, as if the glory inside her had been given voice.

Achille's hand slipped under the water, and his fingers began stroking the soft, wet down that harbored her womanhood. He caressed the inside of her thighs, the tips of his fingers brushing against the secret recesses of her. Her hips rose to meet his touch.

"Oh, devil, do you make me beg?"

"Shh, sweet Eleonora. Just feel the pleasure." A finger slipped in. A cry of delight trilled from her. He explored the intimate parts of her, swollen with passion. "You are so lovely," he whispered, his voice breaking.

He touched the bud of her desire. "Ahh," she cried, her eyes squeezing closed. The music of the storm was all inside her now. No rain, just clouds swelling full, hot, honeyed tension blowing, searing, arpeggios of promises playing faster and faster ...

Tension coiled tighter and tighter. She strained ever closer. Her body, her soul, began where he touched, ended where he touched.

No mind, no self, nothing but his touch, his swirling touch, the touch of a god of fire, and she his forge. He was creating her, forming her, bringing her forth.

And the music, forever the music, the song of her body, the singing of her nerves, her veins, her muscles, her blood, all the animate parts pulsing in a melody that had first been sung by the spheres of heaven.

Her moans became the sounds of his name, "Achille, Achille," a plea, a liturgy, a benediction ...

The storm of music crested. Her cry rose into the air. Her body spasmed. Ecstasy flared again and again, and the music and the light and the touch of a dark angel carried her into the oblivion of heaven.

A strand of coherent thought drifted through Eleonora's mind. *Velvet,* she thought, *the water's turned to velvet.* She stretched. So warm and dry and ... Her eyelids fluttered open.

Achille lay beside her on the great imperial bed, watching her with a smile. They were both completely nude. "You are a dream come to life," he said.

She smiled, but there was sadness and regret inside her too. *"My* dream. Or perhaps I died at the river and you are heaven's reward—"

He drew a finger over her lips. "Don't speak of the river," he admonished. "I do not want to relive that terror."

"There are so many terrors, Achille." She raised herself up on her elbow to face him. "Don't go to Vienna. Return to France, to your life the way it was before a foolish woman—"

He stopped her words with a kiss. "I cannot, Eleonora. That man no longer exists."

"But he *can,"* she cried, rising to her knees. "Constantin acknowledged you as his son! Surely nothing so paltry as an old drawing can alter that?"

"The truth of that drawing is not paltry," he said. "But for all that I can no longer claim the blood of the d'Agenaises, I am still a soldier. The war makes those skills valuable, and there are many who will pay for them with little regard to pedigree.

"I could convince myself of a thousand reasons why that drawing had nothing to do with me. Coincidence. Fraud. It would be easy to take my likeness and alter it slightly. It is not beyond the conscience of my enemies to do that, though it is beyond their imagination.

"In fact, that's what I believed had happened. That your brothers were cleverer than most. I had even convinced myself that, intelligent as you are, you had somehow become a dupe in their scheme. Until ..."

"Your mother."

"My mother." He traced the delicate softness under her eye. "I had never seen love on my mother's face before."

Eleonora embraced him, wanting to absorb into herself all the hurt, all the pain she had caused him. "Can you not find some recompense in that love? That your mother felt as she did about the man whose son she bore?"

"Is love recompense? Or is it *you* who are my recompense?" He kissed her neck, his warm, moist lips rousing her once more. "You, who are my salvation," he whispered against her flesh. "You, who are my sanity."

She stroked the sculpted muscles of his chest, reveling in their hardness. "And you who are my insanity," she said, giving in to the hunger to taste him. She trailed licking kisses along his body.

The evidence of his desire was hot and undeniable against her thigh. She reached down to touch him. She encircled him with her fingers.

He groaned. "Sweet Eleonora," he breathed. She tightened her hold and began drawing her fingers up and down. His eyes closed and his head seemed suddenly too heavy for his neck. "Yes, God, yes."

She had never touched a man that way before, never felt the solid, *alive* masculinity of him. Her breathing quickened. She wanted to feel . . . to taste . . . She nipped his side. A sensual growl came from his throat.

She kissed his hip, the furrow that led to his loins, the edge of the dark, silky curls, the—

He grabbed her shoulders and pulled her up to him, covering her mouth with his. He rolled her onto her back. He rose above her, a magnificent dark dream, then lowered himself into her.

She was lost. So splendidly lost. She wrapped her legs around his waist, and he took her to glory.

Twice more that night, they found the oblivion of ecstasy in each other's arms, and with each merging they came closer and closer to that final completion that would set their souls free.

* * *

Light streamed through the bed curtains and woke Eleonora from a delicious dream of Achille. She squirmed and mewed a protest. No, no, not yet . . .

She rolled over, wanting to twine her legs with his, to touch him, to find her anchor in him, but his side of the bed was empty. She pushed herself up on her hands.

"Achille?" she called sleepily. The bed curtains were thrown back.

"*Mein herr* is not here, *mein herrin*," the ginger-haired maid said in her cold, crisp German.

"Then where—?" Eleonora asked, her mind still groggy.

"I cannot say, *mein herrin*. The water is ready, if you wish to attend to your ablutions."

"No, I do *not* wish. Where is Monsieur d'Agenais?" Eleonora threw back the bedcovers, and the maid gasped at her nakedness. Eleonora hissed and yanked the sheet off the bed, then wrapped herself in it.

Only one marble table stood at the side of the bed. She looked frantically around her. "*Where* is Monsieur d'Agenais?" she demanded. "He has not gone. His sword is still here, his books. He would never— Did Father Eduard come for him? *Answer me!*"

The maid stood stiff with disapproval. "I cannot say, *mein herrin.*"

"Cannot—or will not!" Eleonora kicked the sheet out of the way. She glared at the maid, her breath rasping in the morning silence. This was no playacting to make her seem the demanding aristocrat.

She strode to the door and flung it open. Four Swiss guards, pikes at the ready, bowed to her, then returned to their positions, standing at attention. She spun and faced the maid.

"Get out," she spit.

The maid bowed and left. But the woman's disapproval niggled at Eleonora. Had they discovered she and Achille were not husband and wife? Was that their crime? Perhaps Achille had only been moved to another room. If so, the rest of his things would be sent for at any moment. And maybe, just maybe, she prayed, he would return.

She picked up the Voltaire he had been reading the night before. She curled up in the chair he had sat in, hugged the book to her chest, and waited.

And kept waiting. Hours passed. Eventually she washed, and dressed in a simple gown. At around three in the afternoon, Brother Koln accompanied the footmen who brought dinner, but he might have taken a vow of silence along with his other vows for all the information he gave her.

She slept alone that night, and discovered the utter loneliness of sleeping in a bed that had once held two.

Over the next week, she harassed, cajoled, pleaded with the ginger-haired maid, Brother Koln, the footmen, anyone who entered the room. They told her nothing.

While playing the game they expected, she also spent long hours apparently sulking out on the narrow balcony but, in fact, studying how she might escape. If she could get to Hervé, he would help her.

If Hervé is still here, the demon voices taunted in her head. *If he hasn't simply driven his master away. Accept it. He's left you. You sated him and he went on.*

But his sword was still here, she argued with the silent voices, and he cherished it. And his books. He might indeed leave her, but never without his books.

"Maybe Hervé has gone—and Achille with him," she whispered, standing on the balcony in the chill of the approaching dusk and holding his sword by the hilt, her hand where his must have been a thousand times. "But I have to know."

The door to the room opened, but Eleonora did not turn to see which of the servants it was. They had all become a blur to her.

Someone came up behind her. "His uncle Becket sent him that sword when he was born," said the Prioress of Saint Valeria. "A singularly poor choice of a birth present, considering that Becket used that sword in the fight in which El Müzir died."

Eleonora froze. *Achille's mother.*

"The look on Becket's face was priceless when he finally met his nephew," Madame d'Agenais went on. "He knew in a moment whose son Achille really was—and knew what he'd done by giving him that sword. But he could hardly ask for it back, could he?"

"If you are looking for your son," Eleonora said, "he is not here."

"I know."

A thought stabbed Eleonora, and she paled. "You didn't come for his things because he's—"

"Dead?" Madame d'Agenais finished for her. "No, he's not dead, though that would certainly ease the difficulty, wouldn't it?"

Eleonora turned to face the older woman. "No, madame, it would not, because *I* would not let it."

"Admirable. Foolish, but admirable." The woman plucked at her habit. "Before this, my name was Lece, Madame Batthyány."

Eleonora was taken aback, and Lece smiled. "Does it surprise you to learn that I had a name?"

"No, of course not. I am ... curious as to why you choose to tell it to me."

Lece took Eleonora by the chin and turned her face toward the last rays of the day. "You are beautiful. Though others have also been beautiful. Your eyes are definitely unique." She dropped her hand. "All of which has little to do with why Achille has formed a liaison with you."

"Madame—"

"You and my son are lovers, aren't you?"

Eleonora flushed.

"I thought so. I should hate you, I suppose," Lece mused. "Isn't that one of the duties of being a mother? To scowl and frown at her son's liaisons? Well, Madame Batthyány, such duties bore me. Your name is Eleonora, is it not? A beautiful name. In fact, Eleonora, I came here today full of admiration. You are the first, you know."

"The first what?" Eleonora asked incredulously. "Certainly not the first liaison! That I would never believe."

"And I would never ask you to believe it. My son is a man, and while a woman is supposed to burn, a man may cool his heat in any available female. You are not his first physical liaison, Madame Batthyány. You are, however, his first *emotional* one."

"You mistake the matter," Eleonora said, pushing past Lece and returning to the room. She went to stand in front of the fireplace where the swan bath had been, the sword in her hands and her shoulders straight.

She heard Achille's mother come up behind her. "No, I don't think I mistake the matter. It is your name he calls out—when he's not rambling on about his damned troubadours."

Eleonora spun to face her. *"Calls my name?"* she repeated in disbelief. "You know where he is!"

"Of course. Unless the zealous Father Eduard has mistaken his instructions. Which is doubtful."

"Instructions? What have you done?"

"I told Achille I would not tolerate his interference. I hear he nearly destroyed château d'Agenais before he rode here."

"What have you done?"

A self-satisfied smile curved Lece's mouth. "Father Eduard is, shall we say, a meddler in politics to a rather distressing degree. It seems he is aware that Charles Albert of Bavaria is slavering at the border of Passau, wanting to invade on his way to Austria. And here is a Frenchman—a comte, no less—with no baggage, other than his mistress, traveling to Passau. It took little to convince the good father that Achille was here to prepare the way for Passau's Bavarian enemies."

Eleonora gripped the sword hilt and threw off the scabbard. It slid across the floor with a metallic hiss. "You did this to your own son?" She took up a fencer's stance, pointing the blade at the paling Madame d'Agenais. "Where is he?"

"Where his babble of Tristan will do him little good."

The sword point pressed into the crisp black of the nun's habit. "And where is that?"

"You wouldn't kill a nun!"

"No," Eleonora assured her, "I would stop short of that."

"You think me an unnatural mother, do you? All I want is to find peace!"

Eleonora flicked the rosary with the sword blade. "You have, madame prioress. Now it is your son's turn. Where have you had him taken?"

"There is an abbey near here, up in the mountains. The brothers are followers of the late abbot de Rancé."

Horror washed over Eleonora, clenching her stomach and tightening her flesh until it seemed shrunk to her bones. "Rancé? You sent Achille to an abbey of Rancé's?"

She lowered the sword, not trusting herself to keep from running the woman through. "You are indeed fortunate that the Lord will forgive your sins," she said, her voice shaking with passion. "Because you, madame, have a great many sins to be forgiven. And *I* would not absolve you. Now, get out."

Eleonora wanted to see the woman scurry like a cowering dog, but Achille's mother walked to the door with dignity. "Think to your own sins, Madame Batthyány," the prioress of Saint Valeria told her as she paused at the door. "And I do not refer to those committed in my son's bed."

"Get out."

Chapter 21

The door slammed behind Lece d'Agenais, but Eleonora did not hear it. *Rancé!* God in heaven, how could any mother do that to her son? Even her own mother had only *threatened* to send her brother Gabriel to the Rancés. He had told her what they do, what they are.

They drank no wine. Ate no flesh. The polite called them austere. They rose at two, retired at seven—and spent their afternoons digging their own graves. The only words they were allowed to speak were *"Memento mori."* Remember that you die.

They were allowed no books. And the penance for one of their own followers was fourteen days with no bread, only a few drops of water, and the constant taste of a whip.

The sword slipped from her hand and clattered to the floor. The sound jarred her out of her horrified trance. Saint Stephen knew what they would do to a man like Achille.

She had to get him out. But how? How could she escape from here with Swiss pikemen at the door? Where was the monastery? Where would she even find out?

The questions tumbled until she brought herself up sharply. "That's right, panic! Be a jabbering, worthless fool. That will certainly get Achille out of that wretched place," she scolded herself. She forced herself to snatch up the sword. "Swoon later. Think of a man like Achille with the monks of Rancé. You must help him *now.*"

Hiding the sword behind her back, she opened the door a crack and peeked out. The Swiss guards were still there. They watched her with flat eyes, no smiles, no polite nods. She shut the door.

The balcony was the only way. She ran to the bed and began pulling off the bed curtains for their long gold cords. In minutes she'd tucked up her skirts, retrieved Achille's copy of Voltaire, and carefully replaced it in the bag with his other books, then put the sword back in its scabbard.

She looped one end of the gold rope over the iron balustrade, then ... stopped. She leaned over. Two floors up—and a long way down. The wall of the building was flat, hers the only balcony on this side. To the right, there was a roof of a one-story building—a storeroom of some sort, she guessed. Unfortunately, though its daytime red-orange color had changed to gray in the moonlight, the roof's steepness hadn't changed one whit.

Panic started to cloud her mind, and she took deep gulps of the chill night air to clear her head. Achille had no one else but her. Strategy, she told herself, she needed a soldier's strategy. She went back into the room, trailing the gold cord and absently closing the tall French window while she concentrated on her available options.

If only she and Achille had talked more. Think of what she could have learned from him! How she envied him his cool levelheadedness, his instinctive understanding of others' expectations—and the brilliant way he played with those expectations.

Was that the way out? Expectations? Not hers, but ... She quietly made her way to the servants' door. Her hand pressed down on the latch. It was locked, from the outside.

Still, it didn't have to remain that way. *Strategy, strategy* ... On the battlefield, the objective of a soldier's strategy was what? To win. To stay alive. To keep whole.

And time. She needed time to accomplish her objectives. How to get it? If she waited till after supper, no one would discover she had gone until morning. Excellent, excellent, she thought, and sat down to make her plans.

Supper arrived as usual, and she managed to whine and complain throughout the meal, appearing to pick at her food while actually consuming a great deal. She was in for a long, hard ride that night and couldn't risk weakening from hunger.

The maid appeared after the supper dishes had been cleared away. She gaped at the shambles Eleonora had made of the bed curtains and opened her mouth to scold, but Eleonora forestalled her. "Vulgar," she said with all the disdain she could conjure, then paid back the prissy, stiff-necked woman in full with a grand performance.

Since the things she'd need were already bundled under the bed, she indulged all her anger and frustration, throwing open the chests and strewing gowns and petticoats and stockings all over the room.

"Clothes!" she screamed. "I told Father Eduard I needed clothes! How am I expected to continue with these *rags*?" she demanded, brandishing a gold-embroidered gown that had cost more than the maid would likely see in a score of years. "What is Brother Koln to think when he sees me in the *same* dress? Here, take them! Take them all; they're yours."

Eleonora began piling them in the maid's arms, heaping them high till the woman had to crane her head to see over the top.

"Mein herrin, I cannot . . ."￼ the maid began, though the words belied the covetousness in her ginger-colored eyes.

"Take them away!" Eleonora said, propelling the less-than-reluctant woman toward the servants' door. "Out of my sight. Out, out, out." The staggering maid trundled down the narrow servants' corridor at the back of the building, then began inching her way down the steep stairs.

Eleonora stood in the open doorway, her hand shaking as it rested on the edge of the door, until the thump of the maid's wooden shoes on the stone stairs faded. Seconds turned into minutes as she stood there, heart pounding, praying to every saint she had ever heard of—including Saint Valeria.

Then there was silence. She quietly closed the door but did not latch it, then went to the bed and dragged out the heavy bag of Achille's books, his sword, her riding habit, boots, and gloves. She stripped and donned the riding habit, never realizing until then how impossible her clothes were to put on without a maid. Somehow she managed, then stamped her feet into her riding boots and pulled on her gloves.

She let her gaze circle the Roman room one last time, recalling the pleasure Achille had given her there, the *life* she had found with him, and then the ache of his absence. There was no way she could give him back what she had taken from him, but she could try to restore what others had taken—his freedom.

She looped the belt of the sword's scabbard over her head, settling it diagonally across her chest, then picked up the bag. Her muscles would soon strain from its weight, but she was determined he should have his books. They were a part of him, like his raven hair and the dark eyes that would haunt her for the rest of her days.

After a last glance at the closed main door with its Swiss pikemen on the other side, Eleonora slipped through the servants' door and began making her way down the corridor. She took the stairs one slow step at a time. An instant's panic gripped her when the scabbard scraped against the stone wall. She froze, listening, then continued descending.

As she neared the kitchen, she heard sounds of the servants eating their last meal of the day, and shrill women's voices squabbling. She grinned. Her maid must not have been able to get to her room unseen. Eleonora took a deep breath for courage, slipped past them, and made for a side door.

Outside in the quiet night, she released the breath she hadn't realized she'd been holding, and thanked the saints for her close escape. She took a moment to set the bag down and shake out her strained arm.

From her left came sounds of horses and carousing

grooms. The stables. She picked the bag up and headed there.

She went to the end opposite the noise. She peeked into the shadows and saw stall after stall of sumptuous carriages lit by dim lanterns set on posts. She crept along the straw-covered floor, her ears alert for sounds of an approaching groom, while her eyes strained into the murky light, searching for Achille's coach.

She passed gilded conveyances, one after another, none of them Achille's. Surely they hadn't taken him to his prison in his own coach! Doubt began to creep in. Had his mother only played a game with her?

There. She lifted a lantern off its peg and peered into a stall. A lanner falcon on the crest flickered in the uneven light, seeming to fly. Her breath slipped out in a sigh. Now she had to find Hervé.

A snore interrupted her. She gave a start, then frantically looked around her. Another snore sawed in the night quiet, this time clearly coming from inside the coach. She set the bag down.

She carefully lifted the coach door latch and opened the door. Hervé lay sprawled in one of the seats—dead drunk. She spit out a pithy Magyar curse.

Ten minutes later, a doused and sputtering Hervé was sitting in the open coach doorway, cursing. "What ya do that for?" he complained, glaring at the empty bucket dangling in her hand. He shook his wet head like a dog. "You're gonna make me *sober.*"

"That's the idea," she told him in a stage whisper. "And keep your voice down."

"Why?" he asked belligerently. "You runnin' out on M'sieur or somethin'? I thought you was better'n that. I was startin' to *like* you, 'n that ain't never happened before. Well, if you're runnin', don't expect my help. M'sieur's worth ten o' you."

"I agree, Hervé," she said softly. "But I am running *to* him. He's been taken away, and there are four Swiss guards at my door to make sure I don't follow him." He gave her a skeptical squint. She grinned and preened a little, saying, "Servants' door."

He gave a snort of a laugh. "Maybe I still like you." he saw the bag at her feet and frowned. "Where'd they take M'sieur?" he asked suspiciously, jerking his jaw toward the bag. "Only other time he's left that was when he sent you away at Valeria."

"They've taken him to—" she began, but her throat seized at the thought of Achille in that place. She gulped in a breath. "They've taken him to a Rancé monastery. I don't know where it is, but it can't be far from Passau. We must find it and get him out."

Hervé looked at her askance. "Knowing M'sieur, he's drinkin' their wine while tellin' 'em how to get a better vintage."

"Not these monks, Hervé," she said, her voice nearly breaking. She told him quickly of the horrors Achille faced, and ended with a plea, "Help me find where this monastery is and get him out."

The coachman leapt to his feet. He grabbed the bucket from her hand and went to the horse trough at the far end of the coach-lined aisle, where he poured another bucketful of water over his head. He shook his head with a snap, then walked back to her, still dripping water from his long buff coat. "I know how to find out," he said.

He disappeared into the room with the carousing grooms, and reappeared moments later. "Above a village called Braunau. An hour's ride. Two by coach."

"We ride," she said, and he nodded his agreement. "Saddle Chiron and two other horses. Steal them if you have to. Fast ones, that can go into the mountains off the roads. And muffle their hooves with straw. We don't need to announce our exit to the bishop's guards."

With a precision that belied his recent drunkenness, Hervé stowed Achille's books in the boot of the coach, then turned and led her into the stables. In minutes they were on their way into the mountains.

* * *

"There it is," the coachman whispered, holding a low-hanging branch out of the way. Eleonora looked down from the promotory they had gained only a moment before. In the moonlight the long stone building snaked up the slope of the mountain, snug behind its high walls. No sound, no light, came from its tiny windows.

Achille was in there somewhere. Her breath caught at the image of that sensual man in such deprivation. She remembered the rose-laden bower where he'd given her her first taste of her own sensuality.

"As silent as the grave," she said, her voice barely audible. She guessed it was nearing eleven; patrolling guards had slowed their travel. The good brothers should have been asleep for almost four hours. "How can they immure themselves from life and claim it exalts God?" she asked.

"Lord's name been used to claim worse things in this world," Hervé answered.

She shuddered and motioned Hervé to lower the branch. "Well, only one small cell of this world is my concern tonight. Let's go closer."

The moon had moved slightly higher in the sky by the time they reached the edge of the trees twenty yards from the high, smooth walls of the monastery. Eleonora pulled her horse to a halt, and the coachman did the same, though with much less grace. She silently dismounted.

Three rough woven blankets lay across Chiron's saddle, and a shuttered lantern hung from the pommel. She pulled off the blankets, handing one to Hervé, draping one over her head, and holding tight to the third. She took the thin wire of the lantern's handle, lifted it from the saddle, and stood back.

The coachman, hooded with the blanket, took the reins of Chiron and her horse, and drew off farther into the cover of trees. Eleonora faced the monastery alone, with only Achille's sword at her side.

She pulled a small knife from a pocket in her skirts, knelt down, then cut two squares from the blanket she wore. In seconds she had tied the squares over the soles of her boots to muffle the sound, as the straw had obscured the sound of the horses' hooves in town.

She kept the lantern shuttered and let the moonlight guide her toward the shadow of a doorway. Wary of snares, she opened one shutter little more than a hairbreadth. There, in a sliver of light inches from her hand, was a rusted iron bell, which the merest touch would have set to clanging.

Heart pounding from what she'd almost done, she lifted the lantern in a circle and used the faint glow to study the rest of the door. Wooden planks and leather hinges. She let out a silent breath of relief. Leather hinges made no sound—and they could be cut if the latch was locked. She closed the lantern.

She prayed once more to the saints, hoping she missed the ones the Rancé monks claimed, and lifted the simple latch. The door swung noiselessly open.

Once inside the walls, she could clearly see the dark shape of the chapel's bell tower outlined against the night sky at one end of the compound, while at the other end were the rows of tiny windows that she guessed indicated the monks' dormitories.

That left somewhere in between for her to search for Achille. A shadowed arch straight ahead marked a doorway into the building, and she stared at it for a long while, her breath coming quick and shallow. She left off the saints and rallied her Magyar forebears, calling on a thousand years of fortitude, boldness, and valor.

The moonlight guided her to the door, and she entered as quietly as before, the sword in its scabbard held tightly to her side. She stepped into a darkness that smelled of grain dust. She risked a tiny sliver of light and discovered herself in a meager kitchen. From there it was relatively easy to slip along a corridor, raising the lantern to check the storerooms as she passed.

Were the monks accustomed to housing prisoners? She came upon a corridor of tiny cells, each with a small window in the door for passing food through. At the window of each one, she listened for the sound of regular breathing coming from inside, then held the lantern high to see through the opening. Each monk, inadequately covered by a robe, looked the same. And then she realized—these cells didn't house the monks' prisoners, but their penitents.

She felt a moment of panic, then froze as a whisper of sound drifted to her from the cell next to the one she stood before. A monotone voice saying word after word, as if the man had recited them over and over until they had become meaningless sound. A sleepless monk at his prayers?

She considered retreating back the way she'd come. Perhaps there were other places where a man like Achille might be— A stray word caught her ear. It was in French, archaic French.

She strained every nerve toward that sound. The man's voice was parched and bitter. "Now hearken an ye may to the Deeds of a—"

"A valiant man," she finished soundlessly, tears falling unheeded.

Achille.

Hand shaking, she opened the door and entered, quickly closing it behind her. She turned. And swallowed a scream.

On the far wall, Achille hung facing the stones, his wrists tied to iron rings by thick ropes. The rough robe he wore had been torn from his back. Stripes of dried blood lay where he'd been whipped. His wrists were bloody and bruised from his struggle to free himself. A pile of stone dust had formed on the floor beneath each iron ring.

She rushed to him. "Achille," she mouthed against his ear, then kissed his temple and stroked his long hair. "My valiant—"

"Eleonora?" His voice was vague, as it had been when he'd been reciting "Tristan." He frowned and shook his head. "No," he rasped, his voice stronger. "No, I don't want to dream of you again." He rested his forehead against the wall and let his gaze bask on her face. "But I do, I do . . ."

" 'Oh, good and desirable love,' " he began reciting

from another troubadours' song, " 'body well formed, slender and smooth, fresh and fine—' "

"Achille, you do not dream. I am here."

His eyes focused on her. "Eleonora?" he asked again, his voice a bit clearer though it still held a faint rasp. "Eleonora, you have come for me. The knight's lady. Papa . . . Papa knew I'd find you one day. He believed in me, and in love. He told me I'd find you. Only . . . only he forgot to tell me that when I found you, you couldn't be my lady because I would no longer be a knight."

His rambling talk frightened her. "Sh-h-h, my love. I have horses to take us away from here. Can you stand?"

He shook his head as if to clear it. "Yes. Yes, I can stand." He straightened, putting his weight on his feet, a flash of pain paling his features.

With the knife she had brought, she cut the ropes that held him. He took her face in his hands and kissed her tears away, though she knew the salt must be stinging his parched lips.

His gaze caressed her face. " 'I have always desired you, for no other pleases me. I want no other love at all.' "

The troubadours' words warmed her, protected her from the sharp bite of her fear. "Are you able to walk?" she asked, careful not to disturb the ragged hair cloth that his dried blood had bonded to his back. "I can support you a little. We must go."

"First let me drink from your lips." He kissed her, softly, gently, then more thoroughly. "So many dreams of you," he murmured. Keeping his eyes on her, he shook out his arms and bent, then stretched his legs. He staggered a bit, and she reached out to bolster him, but he recovered and draped the blanket she had brought over his shoulders. She paled at the thought of the pain that caused him.

"Lead me out of here, my Isolde."

Every step seemed to take a lifetime. They'd just silently closed the door on Achille's cell when the monk in the cell next to his snuffled as if the absence of Achille's reciting voice had disturbed his sleep.

Eleonora and Achille stood motionless, hands clasped, their only link to sanity and hope, and waited for the monk's breathing to become regular once more. When it did, Achille squeezed her fingers and they continued making their way through the dark corridors to the kitchen, and then outside.

Achille's strides lengthened at once, and soon it was he who was leading her to the door in the wall—and to freedom. She could hear him sucking in great lungfuls of fresh air, and her heart ached at the pain she knew tore through him with each breath.

They reached the door and he shook his head again, then closed an unsteady hand over the latch, rattling it slightly. It sounded like thunder to her ears, but he seemed not to notice. He pulled the door open, stepped through, and—

—his shoulder hit the rusted bell. The entire heavens *clanged* in protest.

Achille cursed and started running, tugging her along with him. The noise of horses came from the trees as Hervé and their mounts trotted to meet them.

Hervé cackled and held the horses steady. With one hand, Achille braced himself against Chiron; the other kept its tight hold on Eleonora's. He squeezed his eyes shut.

"I forgot about the bell," Eleonora said. "I should have warned you."

Achille gave a huff of laughter. "Remind me to put you on report, Lieutenant Batthyány." He tugged her into the lee of his hold and gave her a quick kiss. "Right after I thoroughly thank you."

Hervé *harrumph*ed. "I see lights, m'sieur. Disturbed their dreams of chocolate and sweetmeats, you did."

Achille released Eleonora, and she saw him clench his jaw to mount. He swayed, steadied, then pulled himself into the saddle.

Eleonora's stomach clutched in alarm. "Achille?"

"It's nothing. Let's get moving," he told her, though even in the moonlight his eyes reflected pain.

The bells of the chapel pealed out their alarm. Eleonora scrambled into her saddle. "He needs food and water," she called to Hervé, and led her horse out toward Braunau. *And a surgeon to tend his wounds,* she added to herself, *and a fortnight of solid rest, and . . .*

. . . and the father he knew restored to him, and his name unclouded . . .

The thoughts stung like nettles. She leaned over the horse's neck and let the buffeting wind carry them away. She rode as she had as a child, her mind sinking into a pool of sensation, the pounding of the horse's hooves driving through her body, the horse and rider one single being of flesh and spirit.

She heard the sound of the other horses' hooves lengths behind her and she slowed her ride. They passed several farmhouses outside Braunau, not stopping until they came upon one with an isolated barn and a nearby well.

Hervé slid clumsily off his horse and sneaked inside the square stone building, then emerged to wave them inside. As Eleonora rode past the coachman into the barn, he grinned and said, "Madame sure knows how to keep a man from dwellin' on his troubles." She jumped off her horse and grinned back.

She watched Achille dismount, his face pinched with pain and exertion, and cursed herself soundly. "What a thoughtless, selfish wretch I am!" she said, rushing to him. "I should have kept to a slower pace for you."

He gave her a one-sided smile and briefly cupped her face with one hand while holding on to the saddle with the other. "If angels could ride like that, they would have no need of wings."

She blushed, pleased at the compliment, and he leaned closer to whisper in her ear, "I do not enjoy being coddled, but I do enjoy the sight of a beautiful horsewoman riding in the moonlight. Especially one who in my fevered imagination is riding naked with her hair streaming behind her."

"Achille!" A blush suffused her face.

Hervé sidled past them like an escaping lobster. "I'll go get some water," he mumbled, and disappeared out the door.

"Look at you!" she said to Achille in a fierce undertone. "You've been tied, whipped, and God knows what else. How can you think of an unclothed woman on horseback?"

Achille laughed out loud, then winced, though his smile did not fade. "An unclothed *Eleonora* on horseback," he corrected. "And how do you think I survived being bound and whipped? A fevered imagination is a wonderful boon to a man who has been imprisoned."

She helped him to an empty stall and overturned a bucket for him to sit on, but he shook his head and leaned against the half wall.

Hervé returned with water and a strip of smoked meat he'd stolen from the farm's smokehouse, muttering warnings that one of those cursed monks might have a fast mule. He seemed nervous, and Eleonora glanced at him as she used her dampened cambric handkerchief to gently dab at Achille's back.

"Is something wrong, Hervé?" she asked, keeping her voice low.

The coachman darted a look out the barn doors, then shrugged. "I don't like it," he answered. "The farmhouse is deserted, but there's fresh-drawn water in the kitchen, and the coals in the fireplace ain't cold. Might be market day tomorrow, and they jus' left early is all." He studied the darkness outside with narrowed eyes and muttered, "Damn early," then waved away his concern. "S'prob'ly nothing. Jus' jumpy from all them bishop's guards wandering near Braunau we passed goin' up."

"Guards who might be waiting for us on the way down," Achille said as he unsteadily supported himself against an empty horse stall. He sucked in a breath when Eleonora tried to remove the rough robe from his back. He looked over his shoulder at Eleonora. "That can wait. We have to leave."

"*Damn it,* Achille," she spit out. "You need to rest."

"I agree," he said, straightening. "But I don't want to rest in a monk's cell." He staggered, then shook his head. "And I don't want you harmed. Those guards have been told I'm a man who would lead invading Bavarian troops into their city. They——" He swayed, then caught himself. "They won't be too worried . . . about having nervous fingers on the triggers of their—of their——" He abruptly sat down on the overturned bucket.

"Achille!" Eleonora cried, kneeling beside him. In a heartbeat she rose and hastily cut a ragged hand-sized square from her petticoat, then soaked the fraying piece in water. "Here," she said, returning to kneel beside him. She dabbed it against his lips. "Take this into your mouth and let the moisture seep down your throat." He nodded and did so, and she brushed her fingers down his neck. "Think of it as sweet juice from a Portugal orange," she added in a whisper.

The look they exchanged was long and silent and full of words neither one could say.

Hervé's hiss from the doorway interrupted them. "Trouble," he called in a hoarse whisper. Eleonora rushed to him and peered out into the night through the crack in the doors. "One horse," Hervé said all but inaudibly, "maybe two." He turned to meet her gaze, his usually gleeful eyes deadly serious. "An' I think I heard a coach comin' up the dirt track in front o' the house."

"A coach?" Eleonora asked. "Not a cart?"

"Coach," Hervé said with all the finality of a professional who knows his craft.

Eleonora thought for a minute, a snap of a twig in the distance giving her a start. "Clumsy fools," she hissed. "They have all the finesse of marauding bears."

"Bears with flintlocks," Hervé reminded her.

She nodded, thought for a moment longer, then put her hand on his arm. "Maybe we can bolt out of here, startle them into making a mistake," she told him. "Get the

horses ready. Don't move the door; leave it the way it is."
She glanced at the lantern, its weak glow barely illuminating the interior of the barn. "And don't come between the lantern and the door. We don't want them to see any moving shadows that could alert them."

Hervé's bushy eyebrows wiggled and he chuckled, a tinge of madness coming back into the sound. "Oh, you's a good one, al'right. A right good one."

Eleonora gave him an encouraging smile and rushed back to tell Achille of their plan, while Hervé, as silently as he could, turned the horses to face the doorway.

Achille looked less ashen when he nodded his approval, and she reached to help him rise when a feral growl from the coachman made her freeze.

Her head snapped to the door. A guard stood there, his flintlock snug against his shoulder, its barrel pointed directly at Achille. For an instant, cold fingers seemed to be squeezing her heart, until she rose slowly and put herself between the guard and the man she loved.

"Lower the gun, you fool," Eleonora ordered with all the haughty command she could bring to bear. The barrel wavered slightly. She took a step forward, hiding a hand signal to Hervé with her skirts. The coachman bowed his head in acknowledgment as if he were settling the horse whose reins he held. He held Chiron.

"Lower the gun. Do we look dangerous to you?" she asked with sneering contempt. "A woman, a madman, and a man who's been beaten nearly to death?" The guard relaxed ever so slightly. She glanced down at the scabbard belt across her chest as if just remembering it. "Is this what's bothering you? I'll take it off; how's that?"

He nodded, and she made exaggeratedly clumsy movements pulling it over her head. "Curse this thing!" The sword clattered in its scabbard, and she grappled with it until it slipped out of her hold. It landed at her feet, the sword half-exposed. "Confound it!" she snapped, and reached for the sword hilt.

Behind her, she heard Achille spit out a rude oath under

his breath, followed by the sound of someone clapping from the doorway.

"Nicely played, my dear," Madame d'Agenais said cheerfully from the doorway. "But don't reach any further. This fool here may not think a frail woman such as yourself can use that thing, but I know better." Eleonora met the woman's humorless gaze. "Don't I?"

Chapter 22

"I should have known it would be you who would find us," Achille said.

"Of course," his mother answered. "The others are fools. They think you're still bumbling about in the trees outside the monastery. But I had met your Eleonora, you see. It wasn't hard to guess you'd manage to get a lot closer to your destination than those idiots imagined."

She jerked her chin toward the sword. "Get that," she ordered the guard.

"No," Eleonora and Achille said in unison. Eleonora stepped over the scabbard, and she felt Achille close behind her.

The guard took two steps forward, then faltered. Eleonora gave another hand signal to Hervé.

Chiron reared. The horse's hooves arced in the air toward the guard. The man screamed and dropped his gun. Hervé was on him in an instant, knocking him out with one blow.

In another instant, Eleonora faced Lece d'Agenais with Achille's sword pointed at her.

Lece put her hands on her hips and lifted an eyebrow at Eleonora in a gesture that was disturbingly similar to Achille's. "There are more guards outside, you know. One on horseback, two more with my coach."

"But could they get here in time?" Eleonora asked her.

Lece came forward, pulling the door shut behind her. "We'll have to wait and see, won't we?" She came closer, stepping over the unconscious guard without a glance. Her eyes dared Eleonora to attack, yet the older woman was careful to keep out of range of the deadly blade.

The mother made her way to her son. "Don't stand on my account," Lece told him, and Eleonora saw a look pass between the adversaries, who knew each other well and had met in battle before.

"I will not have her harmed," Achille stated, meeting his mother's steady gaze.

"Why?" Lece asked. "Do you love her?"

Eleonora gasped in surprise and began to tremble, and Lece turned to face her. Achille stood very still and said nothing.

"And you, Eleonora, do you love my son?" Eleonora put shaking fingers to her lips.

"I asked you, Eleonora, do you love my son?"

"God help me . . . yes," Eleonora said on a thread of sound.

"El—" Achille began, and she turned to face him.

"But it is not enough."

"Not enough to save him from me?" his mother asked. "No, it isn't." Lece's face closed up and she looked away. "It is never enough," she said bitterly. "I should pity you. In the end, love is a barbed spear that, once it pierces your flesh, tears you if it stays, and tears you if it is pulled out."

"Does it never bring joy?" Eleonora asked, her eyes on Achille's still face. "The poets—"

Lece snorted, wrapping her arms around herself. "Poets are fools who know little of words and less of passion, and nothing at all of love. My sister, however, would have me believe that love does bring joy—and contentment and happiness and all those words the poets are so careless with."

Achille looked at his mother. "Why bring Aunt Kaatje into this? She and Uncle Becket have nothing to do—"

"You didn't tell him, did you?" Lece asked Eleonora, who remained silent.

"Tell me what?" Achille demanded.

His mother turned back to him. "That your uncle, the

infamous Colonel Becket Thorne, Lord Thornewood, is the man who murdered your father."

Eleonora gasped at the bald cruelty of the words. Shock went through Achille's eyes, and then, oblivious of the pain in his back, he grabbed his sword from Eleonora's hand and held the blade in front of his mother. "Tell me more, dear Mother."

Lece paled, but held herself straight. "About love or your uncle Becket?"

Black rage leapt into Achille's eyes. "You made your Infidel lover sound invincible. And here you tell me El Müzir was bested by Becket," he taunted.

"Bested?" Lece cried. "Never, never! But Becket was more than willing to take advantage of a fortuitous accident." She hissed a curse. "Love, again." She glared at her son. "You want the truth? To this day, I blame my sister for El Müzir's death. Becket had been El Müzir's prisoner, and sought out Kaatje to use her to find his old enemy. In the process Becket fell in love with her." Lece's bitter glance slid over Eleonora. "Love changes a man, Madame Batthyány. It lessens a woman, but it enhances a man. And because of that, Becket became a man El Müzir could not defeat."

She looked back at Achille. "I once thought your dear aunt's life the most wretched possible. Until Becket. Until that damned Englishman. She had been married before, bore a son—your cousin Pierre."

"His name is Pietr," Achille corrected.

"My sister and her Flemish names! That I'm Flemish and not French is something I've always wanted to forget," she said, adding to Eleonora, "Pierre—*Pietr* is seven years older than Achille. He serves that archduchess of yours as the Chevalier de St. Benoit—"

"*The* de St. Benoit? The one who served under Prince Eugene of Savoy? Hero of Parma and Bitonto? My brothers have often talked of him."

Lece gave her a sidelong glance. "The French do not consider him such a hero, you know." A note of pride came into Lece's voice. "Such valor is in both his and

Achille's blood. Their grandfather was one of the first hussars." She made a moue of disgust. "And that blood runs through the rest of my sister's brood. Such a brood! All seven of her children have survived childhood, and survived it *robustly*—to be polite. I would say that *that* is the price of love, but no doubt my dear sister and brother-in-law would laugh and heartily agree with me. They dote. They actually dote on all their precious wretches."

Eleonora looked away, bleak with the thought that she would never have the chance to dote on a child of Achille's. "But you did not dote on your son, did you?"

"I loved his father." Lece turned away from Achille as if she had forgotten he was there. "I loved El Müzir," she told Eleonora, though her eyes were unfocused. "From the moment I saw him. It was as if my soul took wing and left my body to go nestle in his hand. I have not been with a man since El Müzir. None. Who could compare? The *power* he had. In his eyes, his voice, God save me, his touch.

"I loved him more than *life*. I loved him more than myself. I loved him more than my sister, though that was not hard. How I hated her—and her *Englishman*. I still pay penance for that."

Eleonora took the woman's hand. To her surprise, Achille's mother gripped her tightly, almost painfully, and her dark eyes bore into Eleonora's. "Have you ever *tasted* a man? Have you? Tasted him where he *is* a man? Pleasured him with your lips and tongue—"

"Madame, please! You embarrass me. You're a—"

"Nun? But I was once a woman, Eleonora, and I took no vows to forget the past. Answer me! Have you?"

"Your pardon," Eleonora said, her face flaming, "but that is not yours to—"

"*Have you?*"

"*No!* No, damn you, I have not. But I wanted to, God help me, I wanted to," Eleonora cried, her face hot with shame. "Why are you doing this?"

"Because El Müzir knew me carnally in every way that a man may know a woman. He taught me things the priests can't even imagine to make them into sins. A man can make everything into a pleasuring. His glance, his anger, even his hate, makes your body flood with arousal. A man can make it so nothing is your own, not even your soul. You doubt. You betray. And you can have no other. Think of *that* when you are in my son's bed."

"Achille is not El Müzir!" Eleonora exclaimed, her heart pounding. "Do not confuse the father with the son."

Lece turned on her, eyes blazing. "Indeed, Madame Batthyány? Haven't you confused them? Why else would you carry a picture of the father while you bed the son?"

"No," Eleonora denied, aghast at the cold and sharp truth of it. "No, that isn't—"

"Isn't it?"

Eleonora stood mute. The darkness she had accused of being in Achille was in reality in *her*, in the wrong her family wanted to do to him.

An interrupting cough came from near the door. Hervé looked apologetic, then jerked his head toward the door. "T'other guard's comin'."

"It is time to leave," Achille said, pushing past his mother to lead Eleonora to her horse. Hervé rushed to help her mount.

"No!" Lece shouted, but a sword point at her throat discouraged her from making any further sounds.

"Hervé," Achille said, "I want you on the left. Me on the right. El in the middle. We wait until the guard is just on the other side of the door and then we burst out of here like the last horsemen of the Apocalypse."

"Here," Eleonora said, backing her horse to be level with Lece and holding out her hand toward the sword.

Achille grinned and slipped her the hilt, then let Hervé give him a leg up onto the horse. He grunted at the pain. He straightened in the saddle and turned to look at the woman standing stiffly in her nun's habit. "Remind me, Mother, to one day damn you to hell for this. But for now—I offer a compromise."

"I accept none," Lece told him.

He went on as if she hadn't spoken. "I can no longer,

in honor, claim the d'Agenais lands, but there are no other
heirs. However, if you cease this pursuit and let me escort
Madame Batthyány to Vienna, I shall not publicly re-
nounce my rights. I shall sign all the lands and income
over to the Sisters of Saint Valeria. That way the king
cannot give the lands to someone else—Rachand, for instance—and there is always the hope that the next prioress
will actually deserve them."

Greed flared in his mother's eyes for a moment, but
then she shook her head. "No compromise. There would
always be a question of why you left."

Hervé hissed from his position by the door, his horse
stamping an impatient foot at the sudden jerk on the reins.

"Think on it, Mother," Achille said as all three horses
took up their positions. "Surely the lover of the magnificent and brilliant onetime sultan of Temesvár can produce
a reason that satisfies."

"No!"

He reached out and grasped Eleonora's hand in a quick
squeeze. Hervé, peering through a crack in the door, gave
a sharp nod.

They kicked the doors open and heard a grunt.

"Now."

In the shadows outside a common inn, Achille braced
himself away from the wall and glared at Hervé. "This
place is not fit for Madame Batthyány," he growled at his
coachman. "Find another or we continue downriver."

"Achille," Eleonora said gently, brushing his hair from
his face and trying to keep him from seeing her anxiety,
"you are in no condition to travel further. This place will
do fine. Hervé says it's clean."

The coachman shuffled his feet. " 'Tis that, m'sieur. The
widow lady what runs it is neat and tidy. Not a bad cook,
either, to my way of thinkin'. And it'll be quiet. Market
day was yesterday here near the wharves, so you'll get six
days w'out all that ruckus. But Madame will have to talk
to her in German. The widow Traben don't get on with
French."

"You seem to have managed," Achille said sarcastically.

"Yes, he has," Eleonora told him, "and thank God for it or he couldn't have led us here, and those last guards would have caught us."

Her voice took on a note of exasperated pleading. "We're not standing in the shadows of a riverfront inn at two in the morning because we're out on a lark! You're hurt, damn it. You need rest and tending. We *have* to stay here. No one else will have us. There's a power-mad Jesuit after us who thinks you're in league with the Bavarians, and, you may recall, a certain determined prioress who might, just *might,* be a little miffed at you for so rudely disrupting her plans. Not to mention a whole monastery full of deranged scourging monks searching for their latest convert."

Eleonora put a hand on his bracing arm, the steel-hard muscles bunched in his control against the pain. "You need to rest. Let Hervé tell the widow Traben that we'll take the room. After all, how much less respectable can it be than the residence of a late bishop's nephew's mistress?"

"Agreed," Achille said, his voice more weary than she'd ever heard it. "Though I will miss the swan."

The heat of a blush rose up Eleonora's neck and stayed with her as Hervé led them in to meet the pretty plump woman who was the widow of the innkeeper. While casting sly smiles at the coachman, she sleepily led them upstairs and opened the door to a sparsely furnished but clean-scrubbed room.

" 'Tis bright and airy in the sunshine," she assured them in solid German. She lit an oil lamp on a dressing table that also held a looking glass and an exotic ivory comb, evidence of the traders who had stayed there in the past.

The widow went to the large plain oak bed and patted the simple linen counterpane, adding, "And the bed is nice and soft." She smiled toward Hervé.

Nearing exhaustion and knowing Achille was in greater straits than she, Eleonora put on her most gracious smile. "It's a lovely room, Frau Traben," she said, knowingly giving the woman a higher rank than she was entitled to. The woman dimpled with another smile but did not correct her.

"But my hus . . . that is, *mein herr* is quite weary from our long . . . journey. Would you have some water brought, and wine, and perhaps a light supper? And if you have any fresh clean linens that you could part with . . ."

The widow curtsied. "Whatever Madame wishes," she said, with a canny sidelong glance at the silent Achille, still dressed in the long monk's robe and rough blanket. "And don't you worry none. Long as I'm paid, I don't ask what's none of my business."

She flipped the generous gulden Hervé had given her and tucked it back in her pocket. "An' you've paid for a lot of not askin'." The woman paused. "I'll send a boy up to start a fire to take the chill off the room." She left, but not without poking the coachman in the ribs as she passed.

After she had left, Hervé bowed to Achille. "If M'sieur no longer needs me, I need to settle our business with the boat down at the pottery wharves."

"A boat!" Eleonora said, her eyes going to Achille. "You can't mean to continue on in that condition?"

"We must leave as soon as transportation is available. I won't have you put in danger by my mother's ambition," Achille said as he sat gingerly on the side of the bed. He turned to Hervé. "Don't forget my mother knows you're with us now. Be careful."

"And you, monsieur! Guards and pikemen are trottin' all over the place. But since M'sieur's a gentleman, they'll be lookin' where a gentleman might be, and house by house, it'll take 'em three, maybe four days to get here. I'll return as soon as all is arranged."

"Pray Fortune smiles," Achille told him.

Hervé laughed. "Always has, m'sieur. Always has."

The coachman bowed to Achille, then to Eleonora, and scampered out with unseemly haste. Seconds later, a half-hearted scratching on the door announced a groggy boy who trundled in with eyes half-closed, went to the hearth and laid the fire, yawned so wide that Eleonora thought the top half of his head would fall back like a box lid, then trundled back out again, still half-asleep.

With a groan Achille stretched out on his stomach across the plain linen counterpane, one bare arm and one bare leg dangling off the side. He opened one eye and stared at the white linen for a moment, then closed it again. "Thank God I don't have to stare at imperial purple."

Eleonora stood at the foot of the bed, one hand on the bedstead, and let her eyes roam over his beloved body. His wrists had rope burns, while his back ... Surely those wounds would keep him from trying to go to Vienna? She swallowed to clear a suddenly tight throat when she thought of his pain.

As before, she felt a rush of guilt—but no regret. She had been intensely attracted to the man he had been, but, she realized, it was the man he had become whom she'd fallen even more deeply in love with. In her confusion, she strangled a gasp, making it come out like a chuckle.

"I am pleased to see that Madame is amused."

"I'm sorry. I'm not at all the proper nursemaid. I—I was just thinking what that gossip Vigny would have to say if he could see you now. The oh-so-elegant comte d'Agenais."

Achille rose on one elbow and twisted to look at her, then winced and plopped back down. "Or what he would have to say if he could see *us* right now."

Eleonora laughed and went to his side. "I doubt either one of our reputations would be enhanced," she said, lifting a corner of the rough blanket across his shoulders, then letting it fall back into place. The blood had soaked into the blanket and dried, bonding it to his back.

"That doesn't concern you?"

She knelt beside him. "It should, shouldn't it? But they are all so very far away, and you're here, exhausted, hurting ... I have to get that blanket off, and I don't know how to do it without hurting you more. Your wrists need to be cleaned and bandaged. And I've never tended anyone before—we have families on our estates whose task that is. You've suffered so much, I don't want you to suffer more at my hands. Those are the things that concern me."

"Ah, Magyar, you have disappointed me. I finally discover something you don't know how to do with your usual breathless aplomb—and you instinctively do it right anyway."

"What do you mean?" she asked, gesturing vaguely at his back. "I should be—"

"Doing exactly what you're doing. Nothing. The last thing I want right now is for some fluttering female to be squawking all over me, swooning and calling for every bleeder and cupper within ten leagues."

"I have never *squawked,*" Eleonora said with mock hauteur, then relaxed and added, "though I did promise myself a good swoon. It can be postponed awhile longer, but surely there's something I can do for you. I need to remove that hideous blanket. Your back . . ."

"My back hurts like hell. Which was the point, no doubt. I would prefer you wait, however, till after Frau Traben returns—then you can teach me some Magyar curses to bellow when you pull that wretched thing off. It feels like it was woven from nettles and soaked in gall."

"I'm sorry. I had to decide in a hurry which blankets to take," she said. "I chose a new one, but I guess I should have chosen an older, softer one."

"No," he said, his eyes closed, "no, you shouldn't have."

There was a scratching on the door, and Eleonora quickly opened it. The widow stood there, a huge round tray in her hands. She bustled in and set it down on the dressing table. "Tokay," she said, picking up an onion-shaped wine bottle made of brown glass. She set it down again next to two pewter cups, then gestured toward what was on the rest of the tray. "Some nice bread—full weight, mind!—and a goodly round o' Gouda all the way from Flanders. Be right back with your linens and water." She had kept her gaze steady on Eleonora, but now darted a glance at the prone Achille, then returned to look at

Eleonora. "I set it to warmin' for you. Thought you might want it that way."

"Thank you, Frau Traben, that was most kind," Eleonora said, then closed the door on the departing widow. Eleonora went to the tray and picked up the bottle of the Hungarian Tokay. "A taste of home!" She quickly broke the seal and poured the topaz-colored wine into the two pewter cups.

She took a sip and closed her eyes, savoring the familiar sweet taste. A theatrically pathetic cough came from behind her and she laughed, nearly choking on the wine. "Patience, *mein sieur,*" she scolded in an imitation of the ginger-haired valet. She set the cups on the tray, then picked it up and staggered over to the bedside."I'm not so adept at this as La Traben."

She put the tray on the floor next to where he lay, then sat cross-legged beside it, only to have to rise again when the innkeeper's widow returned with the heated water, linens, and plain crockery basin. The woman bid them good night and retired.

"What she must think of us," Eleonora said, setting the water pitcher next to the fire to keep it warm. She went back to sit on the floor next to him.

Achille touched her chin and turned her face to his. "She thinks of her gulden, nothing more."

Her face was inches from his. He pulled her to him, and kissed her gently. "Don't you want to taste Hungarian wine?" she asked with a smile.

"I am," he answered, and kissed her again.

She reluctantly pulled away and sat back on her heels. "No, really, you must drink something. And then you must tell me whether you wish to eat first or have your back tended to."

"In other words," he said, taking a sip of wine, then handing the cup back to her, "choose between pleasure or pain." He looked stricken for a moment, then buried his face in the counterpane. *"Sweet Jesus,"* came the muffled words.

"Achille?" she asked, frowning with concern. "Are you

all right? Are your injuries greater than they appear? What can I—"

"It's nothing. A stray thought. A halberd battle-ax of a stray thought. *Sweet Jesus,* El, what you have done to me. Two months ago, I was lost. There was no choice between pleasure and pain . . . They had blurred together into one long, dark miasma of sensation. Anything to let me know I was still alive." He rubbed his eyes with the heels of his palms, then stared at his splayed fingers. "I thought my only salvation was on the battlefield. Then you walked down that corridor at the château du Peyre. I can count the days we've been together on my *hands,* El. You've torn away everything I thought I was. And yet—

"And yet, you give me a choice between pleasure and pain—and it *is* a choice." He laid his head back down on the counterpane and gave her a mock glare. "I rave from hunger. Feed me, woman."

She slid the tray closer and broke up some of the bread and cheese with hands that shook. *The days we've been together* . . . "You rave, all right, but I'd say it's too much Voltaire rather than too little food. Now, eat."

He chuckled. "I think it was that groveling, ingratiating way you have about you that I missed the most." She stuffed a piece of bread in his mouth.

He nipped at her fingers. "Second most," he amended. "I think the good brothers would have walled me into a tomb if they'd known how pagan my thoughts were."

"You must have been in an absolute fury when they took you there."

"Of course I was in a fury—think of who I had left behind me in bed." She blushed and he added, "Actually, the abbot thought I was possessed."

"I can believe it," she said, remembering his previous rages. She fed him a piece of cheese, and he stopped her hand and swirled his tongue around her fingertips as if to lick them off. "How—" She pulled her hand away, fighting the urge to put those fingertips to her lips. "How did they get you out of the room without waking me? No one would tell me where you'd gone . . . if you'd come back . . ."

"I was watching you sleep when they came. You looked like a goddess sleeping there, your creamy skin and glorious auburn hair against the purple velvet.

"A polite request from Father Eduard for a visit—about clothes for you, Koln said—became, by the time I reached the bottom of the stairs, a command reinforced by half a dozen Swiss pikemen. And needless to say, there were no new clothes." He paused to pluck at the remnants of the monk's robe he'd been given. "Not for you, anyway."

He waved away more bread and cheese, and finished the Tokay in one swallow, watching her over the edge of the pewter. "Thank you for the pleasure of your company at supper," he said formally.

She took the cup from him, then quickly grasped his hand and held it in front of her to study the rope burns around his wrist. His fingers curled around hers.

"Hervé said you once dragged a *maréchal*'s surgeon from his cognac to tend to your men who'd been wounded in battle," she said. "I wish I could do that now. I don't know what to do other than to clean this with water, then daub it with a little of the wine. Will that work, do you think?"

"It will work fine, Eleonora," he told her, his eyes on her.

She gently lowered his arm, then pushed the tray to one side and stood. She retrieved the water, basin, and linens, and settled back down next to the bed. The water was steaming warm when she poured it into the basin and dipped a piece of linen into it.

"This is going to sting a bit," she said, carefully raising his arm. She bit her lip ruefully. "I don't know why I said that. I haven't any idea if it is going to hurt or not, though it always did me when my scrapes were tended by my nursemaid. Not that these are mere scrapes. Not that I'm your nursemaid."

He drew her to him and kissed her. His mouth tasted of the sweet wine, the wine of home, and when his tongue thrust into her mouth, to taunt and swirl, flick and tease, it was a kind of homecoming, warming her, welcoming her, thawing the chill that had seeped into her from the outside world. A tiny moan escaped her, and he took it into himself, absorbing the sound as he absorbed her fear whenever she was with him.

The kiss melted away to a memory, and he touched his forehead to hers. "No, you are not my nursemaid," he said, his voice rough.

He released her and held out his arm to her, inner wrist facing up. It was as close to a surrender as a man such as he would ever come. And he had made it to her.

She set about dressing the rope burns, wishing for some of the magic unguents and potions from the East she had heard whispered of, but never seen. She knew the burns stung badly, but he said nothing as she went about her work.

When she had finished both wrists, she sat back on her heels, crossed her arms under her breasts, and frowned in concentration as she stared at the blanket stuck to his back. "I think I should soak it first," she said, "and then try to lift it off. I wish I'd never taken the benighted thing."

He chuckled. "I would have been a handsome sight riding half-naked through the streets of Passau if you hadn't."

"Handsome indeed! I would have followed you instead of led," she said with a giggle.

"Forward baggage," he said, but with such affection that she faltered for a moment.

Recovering, she gave him a quick kiss on the top of his head. "Forward, maybe," she said, "but in a minute, you're going to be calling me much worse things than 'baggage.'"

She tucked linen cloths under his torso, keeping her movements smooth and unhurried, then saturated a cloth with water and began dabbing it on the blanket. Slowly the water soaked in, darkening the drab brown to the color of wet bark.

He sucked in a breath, then clenched his jaw. Even through the layers of wool and linen, she could feel the muscles of his back move under her touch. His breaths rasped with a rigorously controlled evenness. His right hand slowly dug into the counterpane.

"Talk to me, El."

"About what?"

"Anything. Anything at all. I just want to hear your voice."

She curled beside him on the bed, carefully drenching the blanket while trying not to have too much water drip down the sides and soak into the bed. He listened to her stories of her childhood, of brothers and grandfathers who fought with every rebel that Hungary had produced in the last three score and five years. And Hungary had produced a lot.

Achille smiled at that. "I would like your Hungarians, I think."

Her smile was bittersweet, but she knew he couldn't see it. "Yes, I think you would."

The water soaked through the blanket, dissolving the dried blood underneath, and she slowly began to lift the wool from his back. His muscles tightened even more, and she wanted to weep for the pain she was causing him.

"What your mother said about your uncle . . ." she began quietly, then stopped.

"Paris returns to haunt me, it seems," Achille said, then was silent for a long while. "I killed in Paris because one of those men killed Constantin," he finally whispered, his words full of sadness, "a man I thought was my father. Am I now to challenge Uncle Becket for killing the man who *was* my father? A man, the very thought of whom I have to purge from my mind or go mad? When I think of the evil El Müzir did to your family . . . And that evil is in me."

"No." She kissed his shoulder where she had pulled away the cloth. "You are not evil. There is so much good in you."

"Is there? And how much good is there in what I've done? I've killed men in duels, some over Constantin, but others . . . Remember Madame de Tauves? Her brother challenged me over an absurdity—God help me, I don't even remember what. I met him on the field the next morning—and ran him through.

"And do you know what I felt?" His hand fisted in the simple counterpane. "I felt *power*. The blade seemed to sing with his escaping life."

"Don't talk that way. You are not like El Müzir! There was nothing good in him, but there is in you. So much good."

"From where do I get this 'good'? My mother?"

"It doesn't matter where it comes from. What matters is that it's there."

His smile was rueful as he glanced at her over his shoulder. "Don't you see? It comes from you, Eleonora." She shook her head in denial. "Yes," he said, "because without you . . . In Paris, the marquis de Rachand—uncle of the one you met—let slip one drunk night about how Constantin had died. He knew more than he should.

"When I was nine, Mother, Constantin, and I went to visit her sister in England. Father left early, a matter in Paris to tend to, he said. When mother and I arrived back in France, he was dead. He'd been attacked by thugs and had survived the beating only till the next morning.

"He was an old man, El!" Achille's hand tightened in its fist till the knuckles showed white. "In those days it was common practice to hire thugs to exact revenge on those of lower rank—and a chevalier was beneath a marquis. On that drunk night in Paris, I discovered which marquis it had been and why.

"That marquis de Rachand had . . . been with . . . my mother a number of years before I was born. He'd evidently tried to form the attachment again, and she had rebuffed him. In his pique, he made my father the butt of jokes that naturally questioned the paternity of the heir of all that was d'Agenais. Constantin challenged him. The marquis refused to meet him, sent his thugs instead."

Eleonora lightly stroked Achille's shoulders and arms to gentle him. He seemed to need her, to need the contact with her.

"But the king had raised me to comte. When I learned the truth, I challenged de Rachand. Still he refused to meet with the scion of the house of d'Agenais. So I met him. In the *hôtel* de Rachand."

"In his house?" Eleonora asked, taken aback. "You dueled in his house?"

"He seemed surprised, too. But not for long. I was in a rage. We fought. I killed him. His two sons fought me. And I killed them. First Pascal. Then . . . then Thierry.

"We were friends, you see, Thierry and I. And I killed him." Achille looked at her with haunted eyes. "I ran him through, just like all the others. And it felt like justice."

Eleonora let her forehead drop to his shoulder. "But you are still not like El Müzir. You were fighting for your father, as your friend was fighting for his. Neither one of you could do anything other than what you did. De Rachand had done Constantin a great wrong, and you killed him for it. El Müzir . . . needed no reason to kill. No challenges to accept, no justice to mete out."

"But if I could have done nothing but what I did, what of Uncle Becket? Shall I challenge him? Are the Jansenists right, then? Is everything fixed? So many people are dead because I defended the honor of the man I thought was my father. Is that slaughter now to start anew? Becket and Kaatje are dear to me, El. I saw true happiness in their house. Laughter, and though I tried to tell myself it doesn't exist, I saw love there, too. Am I to destroy that? And then what of my cousins? Pietr, and all the rest.

"I am done with vengeance. The past can find peace with the dead."

"I wish to God my family could say those words."

He rolled onto his side for a moment, grimacing as he did so. "El," he said, taking her hand, "perhaps I can help them to say them."

"It is too late," she whispered. "That is something one can only realize for one's self, something we should have realized a long time ago but did not."

"I would not have realized it without you," he told her.

He rolled back onto his stomach, and she resumed her work.

"Tell me of Vienna," Achille said, his voice strained.

"Vienna?" she echoed, her hands going still.

"Your life there. Before you went to château du Peyre. The life of a hired soldier is a lonely one, El, and I want to have as many memories of you as I can."

"My life before . . ." *Before I fell with the devil's son. Before I fell—in love.* Her hands shook as she separated the wool from his wounded back inch by slow inch.

"Hungary," she said, hesitated, then started again, "Hungary and Austria have been intertwined for centuries, the liaison comfortable at some times and not so comfortable at others."

"Ah" was all he said.

"Vienna to Hungarians is like Paris to the French, or London to the English. My family has a house there," she began, and told him of her life in the city and in the court of the archduchess.

She kept her voice soft and soothing, the pain of their earlier words lessened for having been shared, and soon the warm fire, the quiet night, and the vital man so quiescent under her hands made the simple room and plain bed into a haven that no grove or grotto or Roman excess could equal. The walls inside her wavered and fell away, unnoticed, unneeded.

Chapter 23

In the early evening of the following day, Achille woke to a hushed murmur of voices and a throbbing lake of fire that had pooled on his back. He let the surprisingly silky sounds of Eleonora's German seep into his awareness to block out the burn.

She was thanking the innkeeper's widow for supper and something else . . . new clothes? It didn't matter. She could be thanking the woman for a coach and four for all he cared. It was Eleonora's voice he wanted to hear.

The door closed, and he heard the soft rustle of the skirts of her riding habit as she moved about the room. He remembered how he'd once lain between silk sheets in an opulent bed at the château du Peyre and had roused himself merely by thinking of her.

He felt a familiar tightness in his loins and smiled. Obviously pain wasn't an impediment to desire. And obviously silk sheets and opulent beds were not required. Only Eleonora.

The rustle came closer. "Achille," she said softly.

He opened his eyes and discovered her kneeling beside the bed, her face illuminated by the steady glow of the oil lamp. *Ah, even better,* he thought, *to hear and see her.* He pressed his wool-wrapped hips into the counterpane, knowing he needed but to touch her to merge his memories and his dreams.

"Hervé came by with your books earlier, and Frau

Traben brought a lotion which a merchant from the Levant gave her," she told him. "It might soothe your back."

He nodded, and she knelt beside him on the bed, daubing something cool across his shoulders. Some of the tension in him eased, but it was from her touch alone, her being near him. He could hear her breathing, and how it would quicken when she neared one of the worst of the strap marks.

He closed his eyes and reveled in the intimate companionship. It was new to him, as watching her at her ablutions had been, and he found himself wishing that the rest of his life could be made of moments like these, strung together one after the other, anticipating the one to come, delighting in the one that was, and being comforted by memories of the ones that had been.

His thoughts turned bittersweet. But his life was not to be made up of such moments. How ironic of Fate to let one woman become the instrument of both his destruction and of his salvation.

He let the thought slip away. There would be countless hours to contemplate Fate, but so few, so very few precious hours to be with Eleonora.

"I hope this is helping," she said. "I'm so awkward. There were always servants to do this at home."

"I am glad there are not servants here now," he said, and felt her pause.

She resumed her work, moving toward the small of his back. "Most of the marks will heal quickly," she said, her voice subdued, "but there are some—too many—that have cut deeper . . ."

"At first they used an ordinary whip of leather straps," he said matter-of-factly, "but as I was . . . unpenitent . . . they chose to use a whip of knotted cords."

"How they hurt you! What kind of men call this piety?"

"They call it penance, Eleonora. And perhaps it was not so undeserved."

"No! You've done nothing to deserve it."

"Have I not?" He let the words hang heavy in the air. "You know little of my sins."

"Nor you of mine," she said in a small voice.

She silently stroked the lotion along the edge of the robe wrapped low on his waist, then stopped. He wanted her to go on, to leave off the cloth and the lotion, and use the soothing balm of her touch. Her exquisite touch . . . How many times, hanging from the rings, had he conjured the memory of her touch? Of her sweet explorations of his body, of her . . . A groan escaped him.

"Would you be more comfortable on your side?" she asked.

"Perhaps later," he answered.

She rose and returned with the tray the innkeeper's widow had brought for their supper. Eleonora sat next to him on the floor as she had the night before, and they shared the bread and the cheese and the sweet Tokay wine. At times she seemed lost in thought, her eyes traveling over his body. Did he see longing in those green depths, or was his own desire making him see what he wished to see?

When they finished, she removed the tray and asked, "Is there anything else you need?"

"Yes," he said, and paused before adding, "read to me."

"I would like that." She picked up the bag of books and carried it to him, setting it on the floor within his reach. He quickly undid the buckles. "Pick the one you want," she said. "Anything but de Saxe. He gives me a headache every time I read— No! No, I'll—"

He'd dug in his hand, expecting hard leather spines, but his fingers had closed on something exquisitely soft. He pulled it out. The robe. The one he'd given her. All transparent rose silk and fluttering ribbons.

She blushed and stammered. "I—I—"

"Yes?" He brought it to his face and inhaled. "It has your scent," he told her, then held it out to her. "The room is warm, Eleonora."

"Achille, you are hurt. You can't . . ."

"It was the sight of you dressed in this that kept me sane," he told her. "The memories of you. Of your passion. I am a selfish man, Eleonora. And soon, memories will be all I have."

For a long moment, she stood unmoving, her eyes taking in the whole of him, then she accepted the robe from his hand. She bent over him and whispered, "And I am a selfish woman, Achille. And I, too, have memories, want memories."

She kissed him, her lips tasting him, her tongue slipping into his mouth. He put his hand behind her head and drove his tongue into the wine-sweetened mystery of her. He wanted her. Her wanted all of her, her deep, deep passion, her exploring touch, her laughter, her truth.

He kissed her long, twining her tongue with his, and with each stroke, each parry, she fed his hunger, fed the quickening heat in his blood. As bread nourished his body, Eleonora—through his body and his heart—nourished his soul.

The insistent ache in his loins grew intense, demanding. He eased the kiss, turning it gentle, tender, before releasing her. His breaths were ragged. "You are a gift to me, Eleonora."

She smiled, her eyes sparkling with more than a hint of wicked anticipation. "A gift, am I?" she said, her voice sultry. "Then I shall unwrap it for you."

She held his gaze and untied the stock at her neck and let the long bands hang down. Then she began unbuttoning her riding jacket, slowly, slowly, one button at a time, releasing its snug fit on her body. She pulled it open as she did so, revealing the thin cambric of her chemise stretched transparently over her breasts.

His breaths grew shallow. He swallowed. "El . . ." he whispered. She answered by letting the jacket slip from her shoulders and fall to the floor. Her fingers, her nimble, talented fingers that had once encircled— He broke off the thought with a groan, watching her undo the waistband of her skirts. They dropped to the floor.

She came closer to him, dressed in her chemise and stockings. He rolled onto his side to see her, supporting himself on an elbow, not caring that he revealed the evidence of his hardened desire.

Her gaze caressed his loins, and her own breathing seemed to quicken. She lifted one booted foot to the edge of the bed, near his waist, and slipped the boot off, then the other followed. He could see her smooth, creamy thighs banded by the tops of her gartered stockings.

Sweet God, sweet God. He clenched his teeth together, his breath rasping harsh through his nostrils. His blood pounded, in his head, in his loins. She pulled the stockings snug with long, sensuous strokes of her fingers. With a shrug, the chemise was gone.

She fluttered the silk robe in front of her, obscuring his sight of her round, firm breasts and her luscious dark rose nipples that begged to be kissed. He growled a protest.

The robe skimmed over her arms, and she closed her eyes as if to savor the sensation. She started to tie it closed.

"No," he said in a hoarse whisper. She left it untied.

Her hands went to her hair. Pins came free, and slowly the rich, thick strands of her hair fell unbound. Inside him, coherent thought had ceased to be, and like a painting in a gilded frame, each moment with her was frozen in his memory, gilded by the raging, demanding hunger that made his vision shimmer, made him see only *her.*

She knelt on the floor beside him. He buried his fingers in her hair. "You are so . . ." he began, his voice unsteady. *"Sweet God,* there are no words. My glorious Magyar countess, there are no words."

She pulled his hand from her hair and kissed the palm. "Then let us not use words," she murmured. She pressed her lips to the pads of his fingers, one by one, then lightly flicked her tongue between them.

He growled. "There were no wounds in the world that will restrain—"

"Do you want to ravish me, Achille?" she asked, her voice silky, suggestive. She nipped along his arm, her lips, her tongue exploring the contour of his muscles. "Do you want to push me to the floor? Do you want me to open myself to you? Do you want to fill me in one swift—"

"*Sweet Jesus, you torment me.*"

"Do I?" She trailed kisses on his chest. "Any other man would have already thrown himself on me. Spilled himself in his impatience. But you are not any man, are you, Achille? For you, there is pleasure in the anticipation. The whetting of your appetite can be as satisfying as the sating of it." She laughed, low and voluptuous, and he felt the vibration of it against his stomach. "Or almost as satisfying."

With her mouth, she explored lowered. His eyes closed without his wanting them to. He wanted to take in the sight of her, but her lips were so warm, her tongue so . . .

He felt the wool around his waist loosen, then fall away. His breath caught, suspended in anticipation. The sweetest hot agony of anticipation. How well she knew him. How well she . . .

She kissed him on his hip, then traveled inward, to the edge of the private darkness that grew there. "*El,*" he rasped.

"This is a gift," she whispered, her mouth so close to him that he could feel her breath puffing against his blazing flesh. "A gift of memory . . . and pleasure."

A soft kiss. "*Ahhh.*" Another kiss, moist, bold. "*Sweet God.*" The tip of her tongue traced liquid fire along the length of him. A gasp burst from him, and the muscles of his stomach tightened.

Her lips encircled him. "*Oh, Jesus, oh, Jesus.*" He was engulfed in a humid heat, released, then engulfed again. Sound beat unheeded on his ears, a groan, a benediction . . . "*Eleonora,*" he said, the word an exhalation and a prayer.

There was no heaven, no world, no mountains or rivers, only *her,* only her. Whatever had been solid inside his body was solid no longer. Like melted stone straining to burst forth from the earth, it sluiced through his veins, burning everything in its path.

"El, El, I am but a man. Sweet God, forgive m—" The

sound undulated into a long, broken groan. *Pressure, pressure . . . fingers of fire ripping it away . . . release, release, sharp reckless honeyed . . . bliss.*

Achille collapsed onto his stomach, and he lay there unmoving except for his breaths coming in huge gulps, and his tears making his cheeks wet. Peace suffused him. His body. His heart. His soul. *Eleonora's gift . . .*

He felt her climb into the bed on the other side of him, then felt the softest of touches brush his hair from his face. He turned to face her and blinked open his eyes. "Would you like some wine?" she asked, her voice a gentle murmur.

She was sitting on the counterpane, her feet tucked under her, extending a pewter cup. " 'I have always desired you, for no other pleases me,' " he quoted. " 'I want no other love at all.' "

She blushed and smiled, and he drew her to him and kissed her tenderly. Her lips tasted of the Tokay, but her eyes spoke of love. Not a poet's love, or a troubadour's, but the love of Eleonora. A much more precious thing.

He took the cup of wine and drank deeply to clear a sudden tightness in his throat. His hand trembled as he gave the cup back to her. "I never thought to see you looking at me that way. There are no walls in you. You humble me. And twice you've given me pleasure with none for yourself."

"None?" she said with a soft laugh. "I seem to vaguely recall something about a rather memorable bath in a swan."

He propped himself onto his elbow and tugged at a loose ribbon on the silk robe she wore. "Vaguely? Then I shall have to . . . What's wrong, El? Your eyes grow clouded."

"We're saying good-bye, aren't we?" She wiped at a stray tear. "I mean, I know we'll be here another day, and then two on the boat to V-Vienna. But this is still good-bye."

He wanted to banish the shadows from her eyes. It was

a new feeling, a sort of constriction around his ribs, that made him want to take away the burden of her sadness. "I want to lie to you, Eleonora. I want to say the comte d'Agenais will be going on with his life as he has, that instead of the women who capered at the periphery of his days, there would be one woman, and one woman only, at the center of his life.

"But I cannot say those things. Because no matter that the comte d'Agenais still exists in law, he does not exist *in here*," he said, tapping his forehead. "I don't know who I am now. I may never know. I cannot ask you to leave your life when I have nothing to offer in its stead. I am a man alone, Eleonora."

She blinked, and a tear spilled down her cheek. She pressed a hand to his naked chest, over his heart. "Never completely alone, Achille, never that."

He lifted her hand from his chest and kissed it. "Never that," he echoed.

Her eyes met his, then darted away. She bit her lip. She pulled her hand from his hold and impatiently shook back her hair. Her face seemed to crumple, a sob escaping.

"El, I'm sorry. I don't want to make you so sad."

Another sob. She hid her face in her hands. "I'm so ashamed."

He pulled her hands from her face. "For what you did—"

"No!" A watery, self-deprecating laugh escaped her. "No, it's the opposite of that. I thought I wouldn't like . . . I mean I didn't think I would feel anything . . . I am being torn asunder, and still my body craves you." She crossed her arms under her breasts and rubbed her arms in agitation.

A houri she looked, Achille thought, a delicious embodiment of all that was possible for a man to enjoy in this mortal life. No pasha could pray for a more sensual woman.

That thought stung him, for wasn't the man whose seed had spawned him a Turk? Then somewhere, deep inside, like a coil of incense scenting a room, came the realization

that that blood was indeed in him. He could dream of hou-
ris, and the dream would be his by right of blood. But his
dream, his harem, would be filled with only one woman,
one highborn Magyar countess.

He drew a fingertip along the swelling of her breasts.
She looked into his face, her lips moist and parted.

"I want to ravish you, Eleonora," he told her, stretching
out beside her, settling himself to be near her.

"Your back—"

He cupped her breast and let the pad of his thumb play
with her nipple. She moaned, and her eyelids fluttered.

"I want to push you to the bed," he said, gently pressing
her down. Soon she lay on her back in front of him, her
hip against his, every part of her body within reach of his
hand, his lips. His voice was low and seductive. "I want
you to open yourself to me. And I want to fill you—"

"Yes," she whimpered. "Oh, yes."

"But slowly, Eleonora. Slowly. We have all night."

In the early morning, a tapping on the door woke
Achille from a dream of Eleonora. The tapping sounded
again.

He slowly pushed himself out of bed. The fire on his
back had eased considerably, but as he glanced at the still-
sleeping object of his dream, he thought that the lotion
from the Levant had had very little to do with that easing.

He opened the door and revealed the tiny fellow who
usually laid their fire. The boy held a heavy sack out to
Achille, blinked sleepily at him, and said, *"Für mein
herr."*

Achille took the bag with a nod, and the boy yawned,
then ambled away.

"Mmmm," Eleonora murmured from behind him. He
smiled, then his smile widened when she stretched luxuri-
ously. She opened her eyes, and when she saw him, her
face lit up with so much love and trust. *Such a gift*, he
thought, his chest tightening.

"Is the sun shining?" she asked, caressing him with her
gaze. He thought he could hear her purring from where he

stood by the door. "Even if it isn't, it *is.*" She grinned and stretched again. "I feel so *good.*"

He laughed, a full, heart-filling laugh. A tapping came on the door again. "Cover yourself," he told her with a chuckle. "Brother Koln has an apprentice in training here." She squirmed under the counterpane and pulled it up to her chin, her great green eyes peeping out over the top at him. Love welled up inside of him at the sight. It was a feeling he shouldn't feel, couldn't let himself feel, yet just for a moment . . .

He opened the door. "Little man," he began with an indulgent smile, the fruit of his laughter and love, but when he saw who was standing there, the smile disappeared behind his usual mask.

"Mother," he said, bowing as gracefully as he could with a monk's robe wrapped around his waist.

It took a moment for Madame d'Agenais to respond. She stood as she usually did, tall and haughty, yet now there was a look of surprise on her face, of confusion and shock.

She pushed past him into the room. He closed the door and threw the bag he still held onto the floor. "You look shaken," he told her, going to stand by Eleonora's side of the bed. "I would expect more triumph at your having found us."

His mother stared at Eleonora, who had been able to push herself into a partial sitting position, covered to her shoulders with the counterpane.

"You are beautiful," Lece said. "No wonder my son lov—"

"Mother," Achille broke in, putting his hand on Eleonora's shoulder, wanting to comfort her but also wanting to touch her, to feel connected to her. Eleonora reached up and covered his hand with hers.

Lece raised her eyes to her son. Achille frowned, not trusting the look of vulnerability on his mother's face. "Do you know, I never saw your father laugh. Not like that, not with so much joy and happiness and peace. *She* has given you that, hasn't she?" Her gaze went back to Eleonora.

"You gave him what I could never give El Müzir. I should hate you for that, shouldn't I? Isn't that the duty of a jealous woman?"

Madame d'Agenais regained her composure and unabashedly went to sit on the foot of the bed. "But such duties bore me." She leaned back, supporting herself on her elbow, and gazed at her son.

"Most of your duties as a mother seemed to bore you," Achille said. "Such as telling me who my real father was."

Lece looked surprised. "What good would that have done?"

"The truth is always—"

A shout of laughter burst from her. "Sir Tristan, to the life! You were such a bright, intense little boy—I would actually feel a niggle of pride for you, now and again—and then you discovered those troubadour songs of yours. Such passion you had for them. I was quite sure El Müzir would not have been pleased at discovering he'd sired a Tristan."

She studied the two of them for a long moment, her gaze going from one to the other. Her eyes rested on where their hands met, then she looked up at Achille.

One foot moved in agitation. "I may not have been the . . . *best* mother to you," she grudgingly admitted. "How Constantin loved you! When he called you son—and believed it—I thought him an old fool. When you were growing up, all I could see was El Müzir in your face. It wasn't until after I'd seen that likeness of him after so many years that I realized that there is much in you that is not El Müzir.

"Perhaps Constantin was more your father than I realized."

Achille was silent. There were few things he could sense in that moment: the warmth of Eleonora's fingers on his hand, the rustle of the counterpane over her naked body. The man he had been would have sneered at his mother, cut her with words for her sentimentality, because he would not have trusted her. But Eleonora had shown

him that trust was something required of both those involved.

He heard Constantin's—his father's—laughter in his
head. *Well, Sir Tristan, one day a lady will touch your
heart* . . . Achille squeezed Eleonora's shoulder and looked
at the prioress lounging at the end of the bed. "Thank you,
Mother."

Lece stood up with resolution, shrugging off her emotion like an unneeded cloak. "Now, to business. I have decided to take you up on your compromise," she told him.
Her fingers began to absently work through the beads of
her rosary. "I call off Father Eduard, and you sign over
d'Agenais lands to Saint Valeria. And if you ever choose
to claim El Müzir as your father, you will no longer be my
son. The son of Lece d'Agenais will be dead."

"A harsh punishment indeed," Achille said ironically.
"Agre—"

Lece held up her hand to stop him. "Some of your annoying honor must be rubbing off on me, for I feel obliged
to tell you that Father Eduard is proving to be a pest. I
find I am unable to call off this search. I can get you only
an hour, perhaps two. Once you're out of Passau, you'll be
safe.

"Hervé has already arranged for your passage on a boat
mastered by some fellow named Michel Corde off the pottery wharves—"

"You captured Hervé?" Eleonora asked her in dismay.

"Of course. How do you think I found this place? Yes,
yes, he is quite unharmed. I gave him a choice of visiting
the monks of Rancé or driving back to d'Agenais at great
speed. He seemed to rather prefer the latter. By the by,
Beaulieu is stuck in Regensburg with a broken wheel and
a smitten son, neither of which please him, I imagine. I
sent word he was to return to d'Agenais until you sent for
him.

"There are clothes in the bag. Dress quickly and go to
the docks at the end of the pottery wharves. A boat downriver is your only hope."

She went to her son and, to his startled amazement,

pulled his head down to kiss his cheek. "I have found peace, my son," she said, lifting her rosary. "I hope you can find yours."

Lece bent her head and kissed Eleonora on the forehead. "Thank you for what you have given my son." She let her gaze travel down the outline of Eleonora's curves under the counterpane, then gave her a roguish grin. "I refer, of course, to *emotional* sustenance."

She went to the door and pressed on the latch to open it. "That pestilential Jesuit is going to discover what it means to cross a prioress of one of the most influential convents in Christendom! If I didn't already have much to ask forgiveness for, I would sell the wretch to the Turks!

"Farewell, my son." The door snapped closed behind her.

Chapter 24

❧❧❧❧

The man on the docks crossed his stocky arms with a show of bravado and glowered at Achille. "Been told not to ask questions," the man said. "But not asking questions costs money." His glance took in Eleonora. She translated for Achille, though she was sure the man had already made up his mind not to take them.

"We've already noted that peculiar custom, and it is getting tiresome," Achille said, looking quite at his leisure, even a trifle bored. How she envied him his insouciance.

Eleonora shot him a reproof just the same, and translated, "A gulden." She herself had to force to keep her smile in place and not to look around her, though to her anxious mind, every footfall amongst the shops behind her belonged to a Swiss pikeman.

The man whistled through his teeth. "That's a lot o' not askin'." He studied Achille with narrowed eyes. "You kill anybody?"

Achille raised an eyebrow and stared levelly at the man after Eleonora had repeated the question. "Not in the last day or two."

"He's not going to let us—" she began in an undertone.

"Tell him," Achille said.

The man chuckled when Eleonora repeated what Achille had said. He pursed his lips for a thoughtful moment, uncrossed his arms, and nodded. He jerked his head toward the wide, flat-bottomed boat behind him. A simple houselike structure sat in the middle of the deck, with just enough room between the house walls and the boat's side to walk from one end of the boat to the other. A ragged pennant flapped desultorily in the early morning breeze.

Six brawny oarsmen, four for the bow, two for the stern, watched with curious eyes as Achille helped Eleonora across the unsteady plank to board. He followed, carrying his books and his sword.

"You can use the room t' the back," the stocky owner said. "An' y' might wanta consider stayin' in there, leastways till we're past the city walls. River runs fast in spring. We'll be in Vienna tomorrow."

Eleonora gently pulled the shirt from Achille's back as he sat crossways on the single wooden bench in the rough-finished room. She was grateful the boat's ride was mostly smooth, with only occasional dips and sways, nothing at all like the emotions crashing inside her.

She had wanted to move the bench closer to the window that had been covered in oiled paper, but all the furniture in the room had been attached to the deck: the bench, the narrow bed that dominated the small space, and a table under the window.

She could just hear the faint talk of the two oarsmen outside in the stern; they had briefly discussed their curious passengers, but due to lack of any information, they had quickly exhausted the topic and had moved on to sweethearts and wives.

"You should have rested last night," she told Achille, keeping her voice low.

He glanced over his shoulder at her. "Should I have?" he asked, the faintest hint of a chuckle in his voice.

"Yes," she said, then kissed him on the shoulder and added in a whisper, "but I'm glad you didn't."

He sent her a smile that made her hands tremble at the task of dabbing Levant lotion on the last of his wounds. She went to the narrow bed and shakily began wrapping the bottle in linen cloths. Achille came up behind her and caressed her arms. She leaned back against his chest and closed her eyes.

"I feel much better now," he murmured against her hair. "Thank you, Eleonora Sophia Juliana, the countess Batthyány," he said, the words unsteady. "My beautiful, proud Magyar."

"I don't feel very proud." A sob came from her throat. "My life before I knew you seems so long ago. What I have done to you."

"Indeed, Madame Batthyány, what you have done *for* me." He kissed her on the nape of her neck, and a delicious shiver went through her. "Are you heated, madame? I regret I have no vin du champagne to cool you."

"Achille," she whispered, and broke from his hold. "Don't go to Vienna. Have the boat stop at Duernstein, Grein—"

"No, Eleonora. I vowed to see you safely to Vienna, and I shall. It is—it is almost the last service I will do for you."

"Almost?" she asked in a whisper, a hated curl of fear rising inside her.

He held her close, his arms wrapped around her. "My last service will be harder than any battle I have ever faced, any swordsman I have ever fought. But I must do it, Eleonora. For you."

Achille rubbed his face against her hair. "How I would love to spend the rest of my days with you. I have indeed found salvation in a woman's arms. Your arms. But in finding you, I have also lost you. But remember always, my Eleonora, that I love you."

She stroked the arms that held her so tightly. "Achille . . . you have not lost me! I am here. I want always to be here, in the arms of my beloved. Passion is a glorious thing, my Tristan, but now I know it is not what your poets sing about."

She turned in his arms and gazed into his face. "Tell me what you see," she whispered, her voice breaking. "Tell me what you see in my eyes."

A look of love and infinite sadness washed over him, and he drew a finger along the soft flesh under her eye. "I see no walls. And I see what I have always wanted to see, what I did not believe existed. I see love."

He embraced her fiercely. She felt him shake his head, the movement stroking her hair. "But that is all that we will ever have," he told her. "Our love and our memories. You are a highborn lady. I am the bastard son of a daughter of a minor Flemish house who married an old French chevalier, and a Turk. An evil man, with no honor, no nobility, no matter that he was one time a sultan of Temesvár. I am a man with nothing other than my soldier's skills to peddle. Nothing to offer the woman I would have as my lady. I cannot ask for so much as a token, for I have nothing to give in return.

"Do you see, Eleonora? That's why my last service to you, my lady, will be to leave you."

"Achille . . ." She pulled back, though still held in his arms. "I care nothing for your rank, your wealth. Only you. We can get off at Grein and never see Vienna again."

"There would be no honor in dragging you down with me as I fall, in taking you from your family. They mean everything to you. Most will think me ruined, and I would not have that stain upon you."

"There is no hope . . . ?"

"No, my Eleonora. Only memories. And not even Fate herself can alter that."

They did not sleep that night. Outside, the Danube flowed its convoluted course, while inside on the bed, Eleonora lay wrapped in Achille's arms. They had not made love, just held each other, murmuring softly the sweet words of lovers. But Eleonora gently pulled free and sat up, wrapping her arms around her knees.

"Grein is not far," she said. "Tell the captain to stop there. I—I can go on later to Vienna."

He stroked her back, as if the contact fed him. "I can feel you trembling," he said, and rose to sit beside her, his arm around her. "There is such sadness in parting from you, my sweet Eleonora. But, oh, how much sadder I would be without ever having known you. You are a precious gift."

A sob broke from her, and she buried her face against her knees. "I am not worth your love. You *must* get off at Grein. You must! *You can't go on to Vienna.* I am a selfish coward not to have parted from you sooner."

"Sh-h-h, El," he murmured, his hand caressing her shoulder. "Come back to my arms. We have the rest of the night together."

How his touch clouded her mind! But she needed resolve. She could not falter now. There was no time, no time. She broke out of his hold and clambered off the bed. "You can't go to Vienna! *You can't.* I have kept something from you—out of shame, out of guilt, out of unending selfishness. Out of *fear* that you would feel nothing but contempt for me."

"Contempt? For my Isolde?"

"Yes! For your *Isolde.* I told you part of it. I was to lure you to Vienna. My brothers keep spies on the docks, night and day, to watch for my arrival with the son of the devil to—"

"To have me answer for El Müzir's sins," he finished for her. "Do you think your Tristan so weak that he cannot elude a few spies?"

"The spies are not there to attack you, Achille. They are there to send word to my brothers when we arrive. It is my brothers you are to meet." She turned to face him, supporting herself against the bed with her hands. *"My brothers.* Soldiers, Achille. Soldiers who are to capture you, chain you, convict you—and then punish you for your father's sins against my family."

She pushed off the bed and began pacing, her arms wrapped around herself. "A son destroyed for a son destroyed. We—*we,* Achille, all of us, including me—we are to sell you to the Turks. As a slave. Saint Stephen forgive me, *as a slave.* Don't you see? We have been *bred* to hate. El Müzir's sins have become our own. Get off at Grein! Not for my sake, Achille, not for the sake of the wretched coward who stands here, but for the sake of the woman you believed me to be. For her sake, get off at Grein."

For a long moment, he sat as if listening to some inner voice. "Perhaps this is my Fate, Eleonora," he told her, his words soft, but the light in his eyes grew more and more intense as she watched. "For the sake of the woman I love, for the sake of the woman I know you to be, I will not run. There may be one more service I can do for my lady."

"Please do not," she pleaded, her heart in her eyes. But already she knew he would not heed her. The lessons of Constantin—the lessons of his father—ran too deep in him. As her own Magyar blood ran deep in her. She spent their last hours together, not in honeyed passion, but in pleading, cajoling, demanding, that her lover not go to his destruction at her family's hands.

A shout interrupted a passionate plea. She listened closely, having been oblivious to everyone, everything, but Achille for the last hours. She heard the ship's owner begin shouting orders to the oarsmen, and she tensed. *Vienna.*

She heard the usual coarse shouts of welcome from one boatman to another, but interspersed among them were casual—too casual—inquiries as to passengers. No doubt word of their arrival was already on its way to her brothers.

Long minutes later, they docked. *Not so soon.* Her knees shook, her stomach knotted, and her heart shattered.

Achille stood and belted on his sword. He confronted her as he must have confronted his enemies on the dueling field, potent, powerful, forceful. His hands gripped her shoulders, and he kissed her—deep and full of demand.

"D-don't go—" she stammered when he broke off the mind-spinning kiss.

He picked her up in his arms. "Fate grows impatient, my Isolde," he said, and kicked open the door and carried her onto the deck.

The confusing din of the wharves swirled around her, including the boatman's laughter when he saw her struggling in Achille's arms. "I see how it is now. 'Tain't murder. 'Tis kidnappin'!" he said, all smiles, and threw down the plank for them to cross.

Achille strode onto the dock. Gunfire cracked overhead. Eleonora screamed, "Leave! Please God, leave *now.*" The sound of horses' hooves advanced at an urgent clop. Everywhere, boatmen began bellowing orders. "Cast off, cast off!"

Achille let Eleonora's feet drop, then pushed her behind a haphazardly piled stack of huge chests.

"I want to fight with you," she cried.

"Stay there," he commanded, and she found herself obeying.

Three men on horseback charged out from the narrow alley between warehouses. Her brothers. "Stop!" she screamed, but her voice was lost in the clamor.

Achille drew his sword. The horses approached. At the last moment, he leaped onto the chests as if they were giant stair steps and threw himself onto the nearest horseman. They hit the ground rolling.

In seconds the two bounded to their feet and faced each other. "Well met, devil," her brother Gabriel snarled, eye to eye with Achille as they circled.

"Well met, bear," Achille answered back.

The bear lunged. They fought, both quick but Achille quicker, both tall and muscular but Achille more lithe than her stockier brother.

Eleonora watched, her hand clamped to her mouth to muffle her screams. But they were not matched in skill. Her gaze was riveted on Achille, on the duelist who had never lost. Cold, controlled fury was in his eyes. Rage that sharpened his sight, honed his reflexes, and smothered mercy.

He's going to kill Gabriel.

The docks had fallen still, but for the sound of blade meeting blade. She could hear her brother's harsh, ragged breathing. Achille was unruffled. Her brother stepped back. His heel caught on a coil of rope. He slipped, his head skimming a mammoth anchor chain. He rolled, eyes clenched, and shook his head, dazed. Achille readied for the thrust.

Cursing the devil, her younger brother leaped off his horse and charged Achille, sword extended. Achille spun, swiped at the blade, and sent it tumbling from Christophe's hand. Momentum carried her brother toward Achille, whose blade was ready.

Her brother's green eyes widened in surprise as he saw death approaching so unexpectedly.

"*No!*" she shrieked.

Achille sidestepped the rushing Christophe, then grabbed him by the nape of his jacket. For a long moment he held her youngest brother suspended like a cat, and pointed his blade at the recovering Gabriel. Achille's breaths were deeper now, but still controlled.

He snapped the sword point away from Gabriel and released Christophe. "This does no honor to Constantin," he said, and threw his sword aside. It clattered to a halt at Eleonora's feet. His eyes met hers and held. "I am done with hate."

Endres, the eldest of them since Imri had died, led Achille away in chains.

"We can't continue," Eleonora said urgently as she sat in a window seat in the library of her family's home and looked outside. It was nearing midnight. She, her brothers, and her old grandfather had been there since they'd sat down to a supper no one had eaten. No one except her mother, who had refused to witness Achille being taken to the cellars in chains, refused to even look at him. *She* had managed to find a hearty appetite, and then had gone to bed.

Eleonora's throat was raw from screaming, her body exhausted from shaking. She had to stop this insanity. She had to convince her brothers. It was the only way to save Achille from the Turks who were waiting impatiently below, in another room. Mother was beyond listening.

No one had answered Eleonora. The only other sounds in the room came from the singers in the streets outside indulging in the latest fashion of serenading their sweethearts.

"We can't continue with our original plan as if nothing has changed," she went on, moving her gaze from brother to brother to brother. "We can't do this to an innocent man!"

Christophe sat on the edge of the sofa, elbows on his knees, tapping his heels against the carpet. He flushed and glanced at their middle brother, Gabriel, pacing by the fire.

Gabriel, in turn, broke his sister's gaze and squinted to peer out into the night. "Damned caterwauling. Every damn night. Why is it no one who can sing ever falls in love in Vienna?" His cuts had been bandaged, but his pride was still raw.

Endres, twelve years older than Eleonora, stood quietly next to their grandfather's chair. He did not look away from her gaze. "Monsieur d'Agenais does not appear to be an innocent man. And what happened on the docks proves that he is a dangerous one." He pulled a key from his waistcoat pocket and held it out to her. It was the key to the shackles binding Achille. "We have to do it, El. You know we do."

Her grandfather, smoking his pipe as he sat by the fire, said nothing.

"I know nothing of the sort!" she cried. "He could have killed both Gabriel and Christophe—and he did not. He is not the devil who wronged us! Look at us! We have invited Turks, *Turks,* into our house to act as agents for our retribution. They await below with their gold, pacing, pacing, anxious to take away their slave. We are no better than that wretch El Müzir we have been taught to hate!"

"Not so loud," Christophe said in a stage whisper. "You'll wake Mother."

Gabriel snorted. "She's two floors and half a wing away. Not that it matters. She's always with us, isn't she? At least in this."

"*This,*" Eleonora spit out. "We are about to destroy a man, and all you can call it is 'this'?"

Christophe tugged on his uniform sleeves. "You don't have to talk like we're going to kill him."

"Aren't we?"

"He'll still be alive, El," Endres said to soothe her.

She closed her eyes and sat back against the window shutter, quailing inside. "Will he, Endres?" she said, her voice wavering. "Would you call being a slave to those grinning beasts downstairs being *alive?*"

"We have to do it," he answered.

"Don't you see what that makes us?" She wrapped her arms around her stomach. "It is evil. It makes *us* the beasts."

Endres looked sad, rubbing the key with his thumb. "Perhaps, Eleonora. But think of your niece, little Sophia. And we have another one on the way. They, at least, will be free if we end it, and end it now. Otherwise, it will never be over. Gabriel may never marry, since marriage to a professional soldier is well nigh no marriage at all, but Chris probably will. What of his children? And you. You'll remarry someday and want a family. Do you want your sons and daughters waking in the night screaming of devils?"

She gasped at the unexpected stab. "*My* sons and daughters! How dare you say that to justify the horror we plan! You know I couldn't give Miklos a child."

Gabriel paused in his pacing and looked at her. "*You* couldn't give— What did you have to do with it? After that Janizary at Nish, I'm surprised Miklos could *be* a husband, never mind father any children."

Endres frowned at him. "You shouldn't talk of such—"

"What Janizary?" Eleonora demanded, ignoring her eldest brother's words. "What are you talking about?" She'd gone numb inside.

Gabriel resumed his pacing. "It doesn't ma—"

"*What are you talking about?*"

Her middle brother shrugged. "Miklos was wounded by a Janizary in . . . a place a man don't much like being wounded in, if you get what I mean. Coulda knocked me down when I heard he'd asked you to marry him. And I *fell* down when you accepted him."

The world as she had known it seemed to yawn open before her. A child! She could have— "Why didn't you tell me? How could you keep something like that from me!"

Gabriel's face turned ruddy. "Why are you so upset? Miklos gave you the wealth and position of a count's wife. What more did you need? So there are a few less brats in the world. Why should that matter? And Miklos's *abilities* were hardly any concern of ours. We had more important matters on our minds."

"More important? *More important?*" Rage made her sight shimmer at the edges. "I am a *woman. Giving* life is more important to me than taking it!"

Gabriel looked uncomfortable at his sister's passionate words. He shrugged defensively. "Well, it ain't exactly the sort of thing a man talks to his sister about."

Endres cleared his throat. "Then why are you talking about it now? We have other— El, are you all right?"

Children. She could have . . . Wonder and giddy delight blew through her, dissipating her rage. Tears were falling from her eyes as laughter bubbled up in her. She could have children! She could have Achille's . . . Her arms tightened around her. *Oh, dear,* she thought. She put her hand over her mouth and giggled. *Oh, dear.*

"El! Are you all right?"

"Oh, yes, Endres," she said with a watery laugh. "Oh, yes, oh yes."

"You're crying," Christophe said.

"You're laughing," Gabriel said.

Endres looked at her in disapproval. "You're crying *and* laughing. What is it?"

"Nothing," she said, smiling and biting her lip. "It's nothing. It's just that I haven't been as . . . careful . . . as perhaps I should have been."

"What do you mean?" Christophe asked.

Gabriel stomped over to his younger brother and cuffed him on the ear. "You *know* what she means, bear-brain."

"I know, I know," Christophe said, rubbing his ear. "I meant *who*. I didn't think she'd been with anyone but . . ." His voice trailed off into shocked silence, and the color slowly drained from his face. *"God in heaven."*

Gabriel's sword hissed from its scabbard. "I'll kill him." He started for the door.

"No!" Eleonora screamed, and ran in front of him. She threw her back against the door. "No, I won't let you."

He stopped two paces in front of her. "Get out of my way. Any man who rapes my sister is *dead.*"

"He didn't rape me."

Gabriel narrowed his eyes. "What are you saying?"

Christophe sneered at him from the sofa. "You *know* what she's saying, bear-brain."

"Are you carrying his child?" Endres asked softly.

Eleonora tried to steady her breathing. "No," she answered, then amended, "that is, I don't think so. I'm not sure."

"But you could be," he stated in that same soft voice.

Her eyes went from brother to brother to brother. Christophe, Gabriel, Endres, and then to her old grandfather, who sat quietly watching his grandchildren.

"But you *could* be," Endres said again.

"Yes."

Gabriel lowered his sword and gave her a look of disgust. "How could you do such a thing?"

She heard a chuckle from the chair by the fire. "He's a mighty handsome fellow, Gabriel," her grandfather said.

"He's a *Turk.*"

Eleonora straightened and tugged at her bodice. *"Half-*Turk."

"Quarter."

The four of them turned toward their grandfather. He released a gray puff of smoke from the corner of his mouth.

"What did you say, Grandfather?" Eleonora asked.

Another cloud puffed. "I said, 'quarter,' my dear." He clenched the pipe stem between his teeth, then shifted in the chair to get more comfortable. They didn't leave off staring at him, and he sighed.

"That handsome fellow you have in chains is one-quarter Turk. I can't speak for his mother's family, of course—"

"She's Flemish, though she lives in France," Eleonora said.

Christophe, who had buried his head in his hands, raised it at that. He looked taken aback. "I—I never thought about him having a mother. He's just always been the devil's son."

Gabriel rolled his eyes. "And how do you think sons get into this world?"

The old man by the fire gave his four grandchildren a sardonic look. "On his *father's* side," he began, then paused for a moment, remembered sorrow washing over his face, "the man you know as El Müzir was half-Turk. His father was, no doubt, a Turk. His mother was Hungarian." He leveled his gaze at Eleonora. "Magyar, in fact."

"*Magyar,*" she gasped. "Achille's grandmother was Magyar?" Her grandfather took a long, thoughtful draw from his pipe, then used it to indicate a box high on a shelf. "It's all in there."

Eleonora snatched up a stool and rushed to the shelf. With shaking hands she took the plain, polished wood box from its resting place. "Who was she?" Eleonora asked. "Where did she live? How did it—"

Her grandfather shook his head sadly, and her words faded into the silence. "Her name was Helen," he said softly, "and as beautiful as the legendary woman she had been named for. She was of the House of Vasvár. Pasha Mehmed Ápafi saw her—I don't know where—and coveted such a prize. He killed her family and abducted her when she was fourteen. At fifteen she bore him a son—the one called El Müzir. She escaped during the siege of Vienna. She and I had once thought that we might . . ." Her grandfather fell silent for a moment, then cleared his throat and went on. "When she returned, I had long since been married, and she . . . she returned home only to die alone. That box was her death gift to me."

Eleonora sat on the floor beside him and lifted the

smooth lid. The papers inside had been neatly folded, as if carefully read and put away. Some of the papers were letters, but others carried official seals of office. El Müzir had been the only heir to the House of Vasvár. It was documented. It was provable. Hope started to blossom inside her. And now Achille was the only heir to the great estate of Vasvár.

She rose and gave the box to her grandfather. "It's true. Achille has Magyar blood in him!" She spun to face her brothers. "Send the Turks away! Surely you cannot—"

"He's still the son of El Müzir," Endres said with the infuriating logic that years of hate had given him.

"No! He is the son of the House of Vasvá—"

Distant shouts interrupted her. Maids screaming, footmen cursing . . . Gabriel ran to the door and flung it open. A panting footman stood there, hand raised to knock, eyes wild with fear and excitement.

"*Turks!*" he cried, flailing his arms about. "The Turks, my lord! They rushed us—they headed for the cellars!"

"*Achille!*" Eleonora cried. Without conscious thought, she grabbed her skirts, tore the key from her brother's hand, shoved the servant aside, and flew down the hall. She jammed the key in her pocket and started down the staircase, taking the steps two at a time. Hers was an old house, tall and narrow, built when Vienna's inhabitants still sought protection behind city walls, walls besieged by Turks. Servants ran past her going up, making the long ribbons on her gown flutter in the breeze; others rushed ahead of her, already on their way down to the cellars, down to the Infidels eager to claim their human possession.

Achille. She jumped the last three steps and landed on the ground floor at a run. Servants milled about excitedly, mostly footmen this close to the cellars; she pushed past them. One clutched an ancient flintlock.

"Why are you standing around?" she screamed. "Get down there—" She skidded to a stop in front of the entrance to the narrow enclosed stairs that led to the labyrinth of cellars honeycombed under the house. A Turk stood there, balanced on the balls of his feet, arms crossed, a scimitar in one hand. His eyes scanned the crowd of footmen who stood just out of blade reach. His cold black gaze stopped on her for a fraction of a heartbeat, then went on.

She spit out a curse, turned, and elbowed her way back through the servants until she reached the one with the flintlock. She yanked it out of his grasp. She spun back around and discovered a path miraculously open for her.

Eleonora stared with narrowed eyes at the Turk. Without breaking their locked gazes, she tightened the screw holding the flint in place, pushed it back with her thumb to cock it, then held the gun up to her shoulder. Her line of sight down the barrel was aimed directly at the Turk's head.

"Move" was all she said. It didn't matter if he didn't speak her language. He knew what she'd said. She could see it in his eyes. He swallowed.

And threw the deadly curved blade to the floor.

Footmen swarmed over him, but for Eleonora, the man had ceased to exist the moment he no longer blocked her way. She picked up the discarded scimitar and headed down the stairs.

"Madame!" a footman cried. "You can't go down there! There are more of them. Madame, they're armed!"

Eleonora ignored him, and descended.

Carrying both the Turk's curved sword and the flintlock made her awkward, and her shoulder scraped against the rough stone wall, nearly tearing one of the ribbons from her gown. Built during the siege sixty years earlier, the rabbit warren of tunnels and rooms had long since been unused—until her mother had decided it was the perfect place to chain the devil's son. Tears threatened to blur Eleonora's vision, making it difficult for her to see the narrow steps in the wavering light of the torches, and she impatiently blinked her tears away.

She heard the footmen's shouts of surprise and confusion, then fighting curses coming from the doorway above her. More Turks! The door slammed shut.

She swallowed her fear and continued on. Achille. She had to help Achille. From up ahead, just out of sight, she heard loud, demanding voices, punctuated by the rattle of chains. Achille's chains. Her foot landed on the soft dirt of the cellar, making no sound. To her right, a scene from one of her nightmares seemed to be playing itself out.

Two massive Turks held a struggling Achille against the rough stone wall, his wrists still in shackles. A third Turk chuckled nearby, studying his soon-to-be-acquired prize, his scimitar swinging idly back and forth in front of him. Two more men stood impassively in the background, waiting. A hired guard lay dead a few feet from the cell where Achille had been imprisoned.

A bag bulging with coins lay on the ground at the grinning Turk's feet. *Gold to pay for their slave.* She crushed the stab of mind-clouding guilt; Achille needed her clear-headed. She moved into the shadows just beyond a flickering torch that had been stuck in an iron sconce. She propped the sword she carried against the wall and lifted the flintlock to her shoulder.

Achille caught sight of her, his face paling. His struggles increased.

"Release him!" she called out, the barrel aimed at the grinning Turk who was studying Achille. The Turk laughed. She pulled the trigger. The Turk dodged at the last moment, leaping toward her, his sword swinging out. The blade smashed the flintlock from her hold, the force of the blow knocking the sword from his hand. She jumped out of his path. He went tumbling against the wall, reaching out for the sword she'd propped there. It was just beyond his grasp.

"No!" roared Achille. His feet kicked out. He pulled free, clamped his hands together, and swung his shackled wrists into the face of his captor on the left. There was a sickening crack, and the man started sliding down the wall.

Eleonora pulled the torch from its sconce, sending the feeble orange light careening along the walls. She swung it at the Turk who'd leaped at her, and he danced back.

She swung it again and again, the whoosh of the flame echoing off the stones.

She glanced behind her. Achille elbowed his other captor in the stomach, then used his shackled arms like a club and knocked the Turk into the two other guards closing on him.

He ran to her, bending down to snatch up the sword the Turk had swung at the flintlock. The unarmed Turk leaped aside. "Run!" Achille shouted, grabbing her arm and pulling her along with him as he headed down one of the tunnels. Their feet pounded against the dirt, side by side. He turned right, then right again, then left. Another left, and they found themselves in a dead end.

In the distance behind them, Eleonora could hear the bellowed orders of the Turks trying to find them. Winding back and forth through the tunnels could prove to be a long, deadly cat-and-mouse game. She threw the torch on the ground and, bending over to suck in breath, leaned against the back wall which had been hollowed out from the dirt itself.

Achille dropped the scimitar at his feet. "If this keeps up, madame la comtesse," he said, his breath steadier than hers, "I shall have to start calling *you* Sir Tristan."

Her laughter came in ragged huffs as she dug into her pocket and held out the key to his shackles. "Here," she said, "Sir Tristan has a wonderful surprise in his skirts."

Achille looped his bound arms over her head and lowered his head to hers. "And an even more wonderful surprise under them," he murmured against her lips. He kissed her tenderly.

She reluctantly pulled her mouth from his. "We don't have time," she said, and paused, expecting him to raise his arms. He grinned and did not, and laughing, she called him a *wretch* and turned in his hold to unlock the iron bands around his wrists.

He threw them aside and ran his hands up her arms. "I never thought to touch you again," he said, almost to himself. "It is you who are my salvation, Eleonora. Constantin was right. What he believed was true. It is only love that is worth fighting for. Fighting for anything else is mere brutality. There is not much time left to me."

"Don't say that," she whispered, and he traced her lips with his finger.

"I go to fight. The odds are against me. But I want you to know my love for you is everlasting. Say you will be my lady wife. Let me hear the words, though I know I will not survive to enjoy the heaven that life with you would be for me. Say *yes*, Eleonora, so that I may go to fight for my lady."

"Achille," she said, the single word a melody of happiness and sorrow. Unable to speak, she nodded, then manage a "Yes" on a thread of sound. "Yes," she said again, her voice stronger. "I love you."

He cradled her face in his hands as if holding the most precious thing in the world. "So many gifts you have given me, my beautiful Eleonora." He touched his lips to hers as if to seal their oath. "May I ask for one more? A token . . ."

"You have my heart," she answered, and pulled a long ribbon from her gown.

He took it, kissed it, then slid it under his shirt. "I must leave you now, my lady." He picked up the sword. He went to the entrance, turned, and gave her a courtier's bow. And then he was gone.

"You will forever be my lord, Achille," she said into the emptiness.

A long moment passed, then another. She grew restless. She should be with him, not cowering in the darkness. She picked up the torch and started back the way they had come.

She neared the end of the tunnel that opened up near the cell where Achille had been kept. Grunts and curses reached her ears. She trotted to the corner, then peered around. Achille was fighting two of the massive Turks. He was fierce, unrelenting, but she could see that his wounds and his previous fight were sapping his strength. Behind him, two of the invaders lay dead, while another fought her brother Gabriel on the stairs.

Finally, she thought with disgust. It had taken her precious brothers long enough to get there.

Achille faltered. One of the Turks' blades swept close, slicing into his sleeve. The other lunged. Achille retreated, barely eluding the deadly point.

A growl came from her throat. She gauged the distance, took two leaps, and threw the flaming torch into the face of one of Achille's attackers.

He screamed and jumped back. Achille leapt into the opening, his blade arcing into the man's neck. He spun to face the other, ducked a sweeping cut meant to send the head from his neck, and plunged his sword home.

Realizing he was suddenly alone, the last Turk scampered back from Gabriel's sword and threw his own to the ground in surrender.

Gabriel came to stand beside Eleonora and Achille, Endres and Christophe behind him. Endres kicked the bag of gold still lying where the Turk had left it. "Here," he spat at the lone Infidel. "Take this and get out." The Turk darted a look at Achille, and Endres snarled. "The deal is off. *Off,* do you hear? It should never have been made. Take your heathen gold and get out. *Now.*" The man took the bag with a flourish and headed for the stairs. "Let him pass," Endres called out.

In the ensuing silence, a weary Christophe leaned against the wall and slid down it to sit on the ground. "Damn me," he muttered.

Endres bowed to Achille, who was partially obscured in shadow. "We owe you many and deep apologies," he said. "And our gratitude for saving our sister's life."

Achille slid a glance over Eleonora and grinned. "We're almost even on that score," he answered.

There was a scuffling at the bottom of the stairs. "Why is he not bound?" a woman's voice screeched. "Bind him at once!"

The three brothers looked at one another, but did not move.

Eleonora's mother came to them. There was gray in the deep fire of her mother's auburn hair, and her eyes were more gold than green, but the resemblance between mother and daughter was striking all the same. *Except for the madness,* Eleonora said silently. *Pray God, except for the madness.*

"Why do you all do nothing?" her mother demanded. "Bind him!"

Achille bent to pick up the torch Eleonora had thrown, then jabbed it into the empty sconce, his face suddenly illuminated. "I think not, madame," he said.

Her mother gasped and stood as if turned to stone. Then, as if in a trance, she slowly went to him, hand outstretched. She put trembling fingers to his cheek. "I did not know. You are ... you are so like him."

Achille was silent for a long moment, his dark gaze studying her mother's face. "I have seen that look before, madame," he told her. "On my own mother's face. When she saw someone she once ... loved."

"Love," Eleonora's mother spit out. "Devil! How dare you say such a thing!" Her arm went back to slap him, but Endres caught it.

"Release me!" The woman struggled to free herself from her son's hold. "He must pay! He must pay. Don't you see? He killed Imri. He must pay for that! He left the boy to die. He left him to die. He left *me.*" She sobbed. Tears fell from her eyes. She stared blindly at Achille. "How could he do that? How could he leave me? Don't you see? He left me. He must pay."

There was a long, painful silence until Christophe quietly said, "It all makes sense now, doesn't it?"

Endres gently wiped his mother's tears away. "The devil is dead, Mother. It is over. There will be no more talk of vengeance, and no more nightmares for little Sophia."

Their mother babbled, but Eleonora went to her and embraced her. "No, Mother," she said softly. "We are through with hate. We are free of it now. It is love that will heal our wounds, that will honor Imri." The older woman calmed and slowly nodded as Endres carefully led her back up the stairs.

Eleonora watched her go, sad but also feeling free of

her mother's obsession for the first time, feeling hope that her family would indeed be healed.

Achille pulled Eleonora's ribbon from under his shirt and kissed it, then held it out to her. She did not take it.

"My lord," she said with a curtsy, "it seems in all our obsessions with a devil's son, we didn't take time to consider that the devil himself had once been a son. Grandfather has papers that tell of El Müzir's parents, Achille. He was the son of a pasha, and of a Hungarian woman he'd kidnapped. A Magyar, Achille. There is Magyar blood in you. And you are the only heir to the great House of Vasvár." She lowered her eyes and held out her hand, palm upward. "If you choose to accept the challenge. Being a Magyar lord is not for the spoiled, indolent—"

In one smooth motion, he wrapped the ribbon around her wrist and pulled her to him. He kissed her pulse at the base of her hand. "I can feel your pulse against my lips," he murmured, then took her mouth with a fierce, sweeping kiss.

Gabriel *harrumph*ed beside them. "I don't think I like your kissing my sister like that."

Without warning, Achille raised the sword he still held to Gabriel's throat, though he kept on kissing Eleonora. Christophe rose and boxed his older brother's ears. "Bearbrain," he said. "*She*'s liking it just fine. *He*'s liking it just fine. What you like doesn't matter at all." He gave his brother a push and they both headed up the stairs, leaving Achille and Eleonora alone.

He dropped the sword and wrapped his arms around her, kissing her for a long, long time. When he lifted his mouth from hers, he caressed her face with the backs of his fingers, then held out his hand to her. "My lady wife."

She twined her fingers with his. "My lord Magyar," she answered.

He kissed the fingers he held, one by one, then slowly slid his lips over hers and kissed her again.

"Mmmm," she said, pulling away slightly. She traced the line of his lower lip with her finger. "There is something else, monsieur Magyar. A rather important something if we are to reestablish the House of Vasvár." A laugh of utter happiness burst from her. "I can have children, Achille. I can have your children. The fault, I learned, was ... elsewhere. It seems the House of Vasvár can truly be reborn."

He laughed and hugged her tightly. "Ah, my sweet, sweet Eleonora. Fate has indeed been kind."

He kissed her again, then bowed to her and offered his arm to his lady. She curtsied and laid her fingers on his sleeve. They made their way up the stairs, walking up out of the darkness together.

Avon Romances—
the best in exceptional authors and unforgettable novels!

WARRIOR DREAMS Kathleen Harrington
76581-0/$4.50 US/$5.50 Can

MY CHERISHED ENEMY Samantha James
76692-2/$4.50 US/$5.50 Can

CHEROKEE SUNDOWN Genell Dellin
76716-3/$4.50 US/$5.50 Can

DESERT ROGUE Suzanne Simmons
76578-0/$4.50 US/$5.50 Can

DEVIL'S DELIGHT DeLoras Scott
76343-5/$4.50 US/$5.50 Can

RENEGADE LADY Sonya Birmingham
76765-1/$4.50 US/$5.50 Can

LORD OF MY HEART Jo Beverley
76784-8/$4.50 US/$5.50 Can

BLUE MOON BAYOU Katherine Compton
76412-1/$4.50 US/$5.50 Can

Coming Soon

SILVER FLAME Hannah Howell
76504-7/$4.50 US/$5.50 Can

TAMING KATE Eugenia Riley
76475-X/$4.50 US/$5.50 Can

1 Out Of 5 Women Can't Read.

1 Out Of 5 Women Can't Read.

1 Out Of 5 Women Can't Read.

1 Xvz Xv 5 Xwywv Xvy'z Xvyz.

1 Out Of 5 Women Can't Read.

*As painful as it is to believe, it's true. And it's
time we all did something to help. Coors has committed $40
million to fight illiteracy in America. We hope
you'll join our efforts by volunteering your time. Giving just a
few hours a week to your local literacy center can
help teach a woman to read. For more information on literacy
volunteering, call **1-800-626-4601**.*

LITERACY. PASS IT ON.